Jephte's Daughter

by the Author

Jephte's Daughter, 1989
Sotah, 1992
The Sacrifice of Tamar, 1994
The Ghost of Hannah Mendes, 1998
Chains Around the Grass, 2002

Naomi Ragen

JEPHTE'S DAUGHTER

The Toby Press

First published 1989
The Toby Press Readers Guide Edition, 2002

The Toby Press *LLC*
www.tobypress.com

ISBN 1 902881 50 8

A CIP catalogue record for this title is available from the British Library

Designed by Breton Jones, London

Original cover photography by Robert Wheeler for The Toby Press

Typeset in Garamond by
Rowland Phototypesetting Ltd., Bury St Edmunds, Suffolk, England

Printed and bound in the United States by
Thomson-Shore, Inc., Michigan

Dedicated in gratitude
To my mother, Ada Terlinsky,
And to my husband, Alex,
For their love, inspiration and support

Author's Foreword to the Reader's Guide Edition

There is something indefinably moving in the relationship an author has with her first book to see print. Perhaps because it finally provides the incontrovertible evidence needed to convince skeptical friends, relatives and acquaintances that your claim of vocation is no idle boast. Or perhaps it is the aura that hangs over all dreams made flesh . . .

Jephte's Daughter was my first published novel. I wrote it in a rush over a year's time, little realizing in the innocence and passion of bringing to life the tragedy of a local ultra-Orthodox girl, what a storm of controversy would greet it's birth. In bringing to the attention of the public the whole subject of domestic abuse in Chassidic circles, as well as the rich inner life of ultra-Orthodox women—a subject hardly touched in American Jewish literature of the time—many felt was an unwelcome intrusion into that very private community.

While I appreciated those feelings, I could not agree with them. Literature is the way mankind speaks to each other and to itself. To put any society off-limits to literary exploration, is to deny not only the society's worth as a source of powerful truths to others, but also to surrender to a self-serving censorship which denies society members the ability to view themselves honestly, and with a clearer perspective towards improvement.

While the decision to explore a world I admire, and love

and know so well was not without its pangs of conscience and pitfalls, I am happy to say that today, twelve years later with the re-publication of *Jephte's Daughter*, the Jewish world has grown to accommodate its reality. The growth of shelters for battered Orthodox Jewish women, guidelines for Orthodox Rabbis in handling domestic abuse, and outspoken Orthodox women's organizations are proof to me that words are tools for the betterment of the human condition. The writer not only has the right, but the obligation to shine the light of inquiry on that world they know best, whatever the personal price.

Naomi Ragen
Jerusalem, 2001

And Jephte vowed a vow unto God, and he said: "If You will give the Ammonites completely into my hands then whatever comes forth from the door when I return in peace I shall sacrifice to God."

. . . And when Jephte neared home, behold his daughter, his only child, for he had no other son nor daughter, came out to greet him with dancing and with drums. And when he saw her, he ripped his clothes and said: "Alas, my daughter, you've undone me and now you are undone. For I have opened my mouth unto the Lord and cannot take it back."

—Judges, 11: 31–35

Dear children, do not be afraid of life. How good is life once you have done something good, once you have been true to the truth within you.

—Aliosha,
The Brothers Karamazov
FEODOR MIKHAILOVICH DOSTOYEVSKY

Prologue

"But where are the women?" the correspondent of the *Australian Daily Star*, newly arrived in Jerusalem to cover the war in Lebanon, asked plaintively. He was a big, nervous man with close-cropped hair and a red face that the burning, late June heat in Ben Gurion Airport bathed in sweat, giving him the look of sautéing meat.

An Israeli reporter in the press section, which had been thoughtfully roped off from the restless, vaguely threatening ocean of milling Hassidim in long beards and sidecurls, looked at his colleague in amusement and pity. He, too, had no idea why no women were there. In fact, he knew less about the mysterious, sequestered lives of the wives and daughters of these men than the Australian did about aborigines. What was the point? They were dull, pale creatures, covered up from head to toe winter and summer, zealously successful in ridding themselves of any taint of womanly allure or feminine promise. He would never have guessed the real answer, which lay in thousands of years of Jewish law, custom, and history as well as in the prejudices of insular little villages in Poland and Lithuania, things of which the Israeli, being a secular Jew, was totally ignorant.

So he answered with dishonest bravado: "Home with the babies, of course."

Puzzled by the cliché, the questioner nevertheless latched on to his colleague gratefully, with a renewed vigor of interrogation that was essential if he was to make acceptable feature material for Australian readers—tired of the blood and gore of recent war stories—from the arrival of one incredibly wealthy Abraham Ha-Levi from California.

"Are these guys your pope and College of Cardinals, then?" he pressed on. The Israeli laughed too loudly and slapped the Australian on the back. He turned and repeated the remark in Hebrew to some other local reporters, and the laughter exploded from the sweating, bored men in welcome relief. The Hassidim glanced at the group, their eyes narrowing in resentment and contempt at the total ignorance such levity revealed. For most of them, this day and hour was one they would remember all their lives. They would savor each detail and it would become the stuff of lore, passed down from generation to generation in loving, cherished wholeness, embellished finally into myth and allegory.

One of the Israelis put a comradely arm around the Australian, taking pity on him: "Habibi, let me explain it to you. We've got Reform Jews, who eat pig and see nothing wrong with it. Conservative Jews, who eat pig and feel guilty about it. Orthodox Jews, who don't eat pig. And these fellows, who won't drive ten miles near a pig farm. Do you think we could decide on a pope?"

Ironically, the foreign reporter had really not been that far off the mark. For the somber, expectant men around him really were an elite, the golden diadem of rabbinical scholars and judges, heads of the most prestigious Talmudical academies of Jerusalem.

They stood in their heavy black overcoats and wide-brimmed hats—in pious disdain of the unbearable heat—as if waiting in a synagogue on Yom Kippur for the holiest of holy prayers, Kol Nidre, to begin. They waited impatiently, whispering rumors, trying not to look at the tourists, especially the women. They regarded a TV camera crew, jockeying for a position, with outright hostility. Their women and hundreds, even thousands, of Hassidim throughout the world waited at home for a personal word that the miracle, the resurrection, had indeed taken place.

Until just recently, most of them had believed that the Ha-Levi dynasty, founded in 1780 by the saintly Israel Ben Dov Ha-Levi, had perished under Hitler's murderers and lunatics. And then, two months before, the electrifying news had begun to circulate in the narrow alleyways of Jerusalem and Brooklyn that Abraham Ha-Levi, the youngest of Rabbi Yerachmiel's four sons, was alive and well in America.

"But tell me, mate, what's the story here? Who is the guy? Why's he come? What's going to happen now?" the Australian pressed, getting a little desperate.

The Israeli, in the briefest of summer shorts and a shirt open to mid-chest, scratched his bare head. He had been sent to cover the spectacle but was as much a puzzled outsider to its meaning as was his questioner, something no Israeli would ever admit. He was rescued from his embarrassment by a sudden, startling change in the crowd, which surged, wave-like, pressing closer to the gates leading out of the air terminal.

Abraham Ha-Levi stepped out of the door leading to the long walkway, hardly aware of the well-wishers and the curious who stared at him from all sides. He walked with a proud straight back, a princely lift of his elegant, graying head, accepting the obeisance like an exiled king. No smile crossed his lined, aristocratic face as he looked over the welcomers, but he nodded slowly, pensively, accepting their possession of him. He took out a monogrammed linen handkerchief and wiped the rivulets of sweat that ran with surprising suddenness down his forehead.

A sea of black-coated men encircled him, bursting out in tears, dance, and song. A few came up close and kissed the corner of his black coat. They shouted blessings and wept. "Praise be to God!" went up, drowning out the noise of the taxis. Tourists reached for their cameras, thrilled at their luck. The reporters smiled, contented. What the hell, with a few good photos, it would fill up space, like pictures of monkeys in refrigerators, or endless expanses of thighs.

One of the faithful motioned toward a taxi, but the last surviving son of Yerachmiel Ha-Levi, sole heir to a two-hundred-year-old Hassidic dynasty long mourned, lifted his hand in a small gesture of disdain and suddenly there was a moment of awed silence as a silver Rolls-Royce pulled up at the curb. As he entered the vehicle, a young boy began to sing psalms in a voice of heart-piercing sweetness and clarity that rose like smoky incense above the heads of the crowd, bringing a moment of silence. Then a shout of joy went up, reverberating into the nearby orange groves. The princely carriage was the final proof that this indeed was a true Ha-Levi. As it pulled away from the curb, the crowd watched, somehow dissatisfied, and began to quietly disperse.

"Christ! Now what the bloody hell was that all about?" the Australian wailed, looking around him frantically for answers.

Part One

Chapter one

Founded in 1780 by Israel Ha-Levi, the most distinguished student of the Baal Shem-Tov himself, the Ha-Levis lived lives of incredible luxury and opulence in Hassidic courts that mirrored those of real royalty. Until that time, such ease had been considered scandalous, tantamount to apostasy. Jews who wished to reach spiritual heights felt they needed to punish themselves into spiritual fitness by denying the needs of their bodies altogether. The more one tortures the body, they reasoned, the higher the soul soars.

And so they slept on hard benches and rested their heads upon rocks. They put stones in their shoes, disrobed and rolled in the snow, then immersed themselves in ice-cold ritual baths. For some, even this was too soft—they knocked a hole in the ice of a lake. Some fasted all week and ate only on the Sabbath. The body was the lowly, fleshly casement of the soul that was to be given no quarter.

But Israel Ha-Levi, an intense and sensitive young boy, heard a different message. If man is made in the image of God, he reasoned, one must honor that image by exalting every aspect of existence, living each moment as befits the servant of the King of Kings. And he had blazed the way, being the first and only Hassid to live in splendor. Supported by his faithful, he had traveled in a silver carriage and had sat on a gold throne as he dispensed advice to the thousands who flocked to his rabbinic court. When rival Hassidic groups complained that he had given in to his Evil Inclination, his reply was cryptic and unrepentant: "Satan is in everything the Hassidim do," he admonished, "but he does not know that beneath this opulence lies a holy kernel." From then on, despite their own bitter poverty, his disciples had seen to it that their rebbes, all direct male descendants of Israel Ha-Levi, had lived in unmatched riches as a way of serving God.

The Rolls, large and ostentatious, was almost impossible to navigate through the narrow streets of Meah Shearim, where even people walked single file. The chauffeur/bodyguard (for the Ha-Levis still had their violent detractors among rival Hassidic groups) cursed the traffic and the unwieldy vehicle, and wondered at the insanity of shipping such a thing halfway around the world for only a week's use.

But looking slyly in the mirror at his employer, he could not help being filled with a grudging respect and envy for the man, who exuded elegance and wealth. He studied the man's large, inscrutable eyes, the craftiness of his thin, hard lips. Yet his forehead was high and intelligent, almost brooding, giving him a look of sadness. This, of course, did not interest the driver, who feasted his eyes on the beautiful dark cloth of Ha-Levi's immaculately cut suit. But it was beyond his narrow experience to have guessed that the garment was made from wool grown on Ha-Levi's own large sheep farms in California, flown to London for processing, and finally custom cut on Savile Row by a tailor whose full-time job was to do nothing else but create dark, perfect suits for Abraham Ha-Levi.

Suddenly, he caught the slight, authoritative movement of his employer's hand motioning him to pull over, although they were nowhere near their destination. Understanding instinctively that this was not a man one questioned, he did so, despite the cars behind him that honked frantically, their way completely blocked.

Unhurried, Ha-Levi got out of the car and walked through the doors of a large, noisy yeshivah. He closed his eyes for a moment, breathing in the dust and worn paper of the massive Talmudical texts and listened to the singsong of young voices filled with the excited sense of discovery as they delved into the meaning of the text, source of all Jewish learning.

For a frightening half second he thought he was going to cry.

The face of his dead father, the voices of his dead brothers, flashed through his mind. He knew, and had always known, that the genes of genius that had made the halls of the yeshivah their victorious battleground had skipped him. Instead, he was heir to a perverse talent for something his family would not only have deemed unnecessary, but scorned: a talent for making money.

Of all the Ha-Levis that had ever lived, he was the only one who had financed his opulent life-style through the honest work of his own hands. In a way it was a cruel irony. God had blessed him with riches, cursing him. Because of his success, the scholarship of his family would be forgotten forever. Only the memory of the money would remain. Surely the fact that only he, the least scholarly and most rebellious of all, had been the only Ha-Levi to survive, was a divine message that the faithful service of the Ha-Levi family was no longer pleasing to Him.

He had never wanted his part in that service. He did not want people flocking to him for decisions about how to find God, how to heal the sick, who to marry or divorce. He was not the type, as his father and brothers had been, to get involved in people's lives. He sighed, thinking sadly what little difference it made what he wanted.

He returned to his car and was driven without further detours to his final destination, the greatest yeshivah in Jerusalem: Ohel Moshe, the Tent of Moses. On the wide steps hundreds of Hassidim waited to see him, to touch the corner of his garment. Pushing through the crowds, he was shown into the study hall and then taken up the stairs to a small office. Behind the desk sat a small, wrinkled man, almost shrunken looking, with a dark suit and a white beard and sidecurls. He was the great scholar and recognized leader of Jerusalem's great rabbinic council, chief judge of the rabbinic *beit din*. He was a man who at the age of three had already memorized long tracts of the Talmud, and by the age of five had posed questions of such breathtaking precision and insight to the chief rabbi of the community that the sage had stood up before him and proclaimed him a "Light of the Generation." Rabbi Magnes was silent, barely looking up from the large, open volume of Talmud on his desk. He waved his hand slightly, indicating he was waiting for Ha-Levi to begin speaking.

"*Kavod harav*," Ha-Levi began, so unnerved by the offhand reception he rushed headlong into the reason for his visit, with no softening words of introduction. "I am looking for a son-in-law. A man who will be the greatest scholar of the next generation, who can receive the mantle of the Ha-Levi dynasty. I am a man of wealth and influence. I can offer a life of every material convenience. And, of course, no amount of charity would be too much for me to give in my gratitude for your help. Perhaps a new study hall?" He hesitated. The old man had not reacted. What could he say to impress the quiet, penetrating eyes that peered out at him beneath those heavy brows of white hair?

The rabbi looked up with an ironic smile and slowly, painfully, pulled himself up from his chair and walked to the window. Ha-Levi cracked his knuckles impatiently, unaccustomed to the slow pace of men who live for the next world. He saw the rabbi staring at the huge car that had attracted the attention of dozens of yeshivah students in the street below. Finally, Rabbi Magnes turned to him sharply: "You have come to the wrong place, your car has made a wrong turn." He sat down again and dismissed him with a wave. "The *shuk* is down the street. Go there if you want to make a purchase."

Ha-Levi's face went white with the insult, but his business sense soon asserted itself; anger had no place in negotiations. "If *kavod harav* can find me such a one," he repeated patiently, respectful but just a tiny bit patronizing, the way one spoke to an aging parent bordering on senility, "one in whom he sees the seeds of greatness, an *illui* who will light the world with his understanding and his scholarship, I promise he will have every material need satisfied so that he may spend all of his life concentrating on his studies with no thought to a livelihood. He will have a wife whose piety and brilliance will match his own. And," he added, most delicately, "my daughter, Batsheva, is a girl of great beauty. California is such a dangerous place for such a girl. She must marry now, so that she may leave America forever before she is tainted by it. There is only so much I can do to protect her."

"You speak only of what you want," Rabbi Magnes said probingly, his dark eyes—piercing in their clarity and vision—examining the man before him. "You know that the Torah forbids one to force a child to marry against her will. The choice must be hers."

Abraham Ha-Levi took the rebuff with unaccustomed humility, noting with satisfaction that at least Rabbi Magnes had sat down again. Good. This was the right approach then. "She is a dutiful child who understands her responsibilities."

"Her responsibilities? Ah," the sage said with deceptive mildness, cocking his head to one side with a look of studied confusion. And then with stunning suddenness, he brought his fist crashing down upon his desk. "And what of your responsibilities? Where have *you* been for the last forty years?"

Ha-Levi went limp, crumpling in his chair like a puppet suddenly gone loose and ragged, bereft of the solid, guiding hand inside it. He fumbled, searching for his handkerchief, and wiped the heavy sweat from his brow. It was not only the day's journey that had finally caught up with him, he realized, draining him of all strength, all pretense. It was life itself. Today was a day of judgment and the prosecutor sat before him much as his father had so many years ago. He felt again like that frightened, guilty child. "Please, please. Forgive me," he said in a hoarse whisper, unable to meet the stern, judging eyes. "I am a tormented soul who has come to you for kindness. They are all gone, you see. Every one of worth—my father and brothers, brilliant scholars, all dead, murdered. I am the only one left."

He lifted haunted, tortured eyes and faced the man before him. "The most ignorant and least worthy of them all. How could I stand in their place? So I hid, I ran away, hoping no one would find me." He straightened his shoulders. "But even a criminal may repent. I have come then, to fulfill my responsibilities. My daughter, my Batsheva, I have watched over her so carefully. She is so innocent and good. Please, try to understand. My father's sainted name must be rebuilt through her. She is the only one who can bring from the ashes a new generation of worthy namesakes." For the first time he saw a gleam of pity and understanding in the stern eyes that bored into him so deeply.

"Does your daughter wish to leave America, her family? Has she ever been to Jerusalem?"

Ha-Levi flushed. The truth was she didn't know anything about this at all. But what did it matter, he thought impatiently. She will do her duty as I must do mine. She will rejoice in her responsibilities because she is the remnant, she is the Ha-Levis' new beginning, the repository of genes of generations of scholars and *tzaddikim* and she knows it. To the rabbi he answered: "She understands the Fifth Commandment well. But of course the boy must be an unquestioned genius and very pious. He must be worthy of her and of my name."

"Genius. *Oy!*" The sage slapped his desk with an impatient hand. "And what other qualities do you seek?" he asked evenly. Was there a spark of amusement in those razor-sharp eyes?

"I seek strict adherence to the Law, a trembling fear of God, and extreme diligence in studies."

"That is all?" the rabbi asked, raising his brows slightly. Ha-Levi shrank. What had he left out? "Ah, yes of course. Kindness, gentleness."

Rabbi Magnes nodded, his heavy brows contracted as if in pain. "I can do no more for you than Eliezer, Abraham's servant, did for him in seeking a bride for Isaac. I will seek a bridegroom, but God must provide him." Then the great sage sighed and looked toward heaven. The Fifth Commandment was honor thy father and mother.

Chapter two

"Let's talk a little bit about *midos*," Rabbi Silverman said mildly, stroking his white beard. A collective groan went up around the room, rising deep from the throats of all twenty girls.

"Not *midos!*"

"It's too hot to improve our characters!"

"It's too late, we'll be graduating next week!"

"Anything but that!"

Rabbi Silverman looked with dismay at the listless group of young women fidgeting behind outgrown wooden desks. The future hope of the Jewish people. He shook his head. It was hot and through the open windows the muted sounds of bustling traffic, children's laughter, and the collective footsteps of busy, working people on the dry, dusty pavement invaded the classroom. They would soon be, if they had not already been, taken in hand by maiden aunts or professional matchmakers. Their minds were already out of the classroom, out of Brooklyn, far away into the summer of their eighteenth year.

Yet there was still so much to teach them, so much they needed to know.

Only a few would continue their studies to become teachers, while a few others might learn shorthand and typing and work for a religious businessman until the right man came along. They were being trained mostly to be good Jewish women, wives and mothers. Obedient, chaste, charitable, and pious. Only once in a while did he come across one that made it worthwhile to be a teacher; someone bright and curious, who had not yet been browbeaten into total unquestioning acceptance. He sought her in the back of the classroom, but she was one of the dreamers, looking out of the window.

"We will start with humility and pride," he said with determination. "According to *Mesillat Yesharim*, why can't a person regard himself as superior to others?"

The girls who had no idea slumped low in their seats while those with no interest continued to look at their long hair, pulling off the split ends. They were all from strict Hassidic or Orthodox homes, yet they were not a homogeneous group. Some were the plump, dark daughters of butchers and rabbis, dressed in homemade blouses with wrist-length sleeves in dull, opaque colors and mid-calf skirts with sensible low-heeled shoes. Then there were the daughters of accountants and doctors, with lipstick and cheeks redder than God-given, dressed in the latest colorful styles Abraham & Straus department store could supply, their sleeves barely touching their elbows, their skirts barely covering their knees. Even the strictest girls had pushed their sleeves up to their elbows and fanned their faces with their notebooks.

A few hands were raised dutifully. There were always some whose virtue remained intact, no matter the temptation.

"Chava?"

"A person shouldn't pride himself on his natural qualities because they are all God-given. Should a bird pride itself on flying?" she said in a prissy singsong, her round, smug face flushed with pleasure.

"Correct, correct. If only you didn't take so much pride in giving the right answer," he said dryly. The class sat up and laughed. Better.

"Chaika."

"If a person considers himself in relation to others, then he might feel superior. He has to look at himself subjectively, in terms of how much more he has to accomplish."

"Very true. When the great sage Yochanon Ben Zakkai was dying, he quaked with fear. 'There are two paths before me,' he told his students, 'one to heaven and one to hell, and I don't know which one I'll travel on.' Now, why did he feel this way, this great man? He felt that perhaps he had not made the most of his God-given potential. God created this world as a test so that we might enjoy His goodness in the World to Come—" A hand raised urgently, waving, insistent. He nodded, pleased to have drawn her attention away from the window. He wiped beads of sweat from his forehead. "Go on, Batsheva." She never let anything pass without a fight. She was a hard student, but a rewarding one, unlike any girl he had ever taught. If there was a heirarchy in the class, she was certainly on top.

Luminously beautiful (he was not blind after all!), incredibly wealthy, bright. Her problem was that she knew this gave her a certain invulnerability toward criticism. Even her clothes. Such bright colors, such different cuts. Always modest, technically. But they made her stand out, which her unusual height did anyway. She was five-foot-eight in a class where the tallest girl was five-foot-four. Girls were not supposed to stand out, but to fade away with maidenly modesty into the background.

"Go ahead, ask, Batsheva." He nodded encouragingly when she hesitated.

"Then why does Beit Hillel teach that it would have been better if the world had never been created at all?"

"Well, we have the possibility in this world of overcoming tests and rising to the highest heights, way above the angels. But we also have the ability to fall to the depths of *Gehennom.*"

"Adam ate the apple. Wouldn't it have been better for him not to have been created than to fail the test and fall to hell?" she persisted. She had a passionate voice, an urgency and sincerity in everything she did.

"It's probably true that for most people it would have been better for them not to have been born at all and confronted with evil. But the test does give the possibility of wonderful achievements. What other creature has this choice and can rise so high? Animals do what their bodies tell them. Angels are pure spirit. Only man has that terrible struggle between flesh and spirit, that wonderful ability to rise so high—" That sounded rather good, he congratulated himself. He watched her knit her brows a little in thought and his heart sank. "Still not satisfied?"

"But how could God create a world when He knows most people will still fail?"

The atmosphere in the class suddenly changed, becoming charged with the rare oxygen of challenge. Girls were not taught to challenge. They were taught that most things were beyond their understanding and that they should blindly follow tradition. They were taught that the authors of scholarly books were not mere men, as we know them, but that their scholarship and piety put them on a level of unquestioning infallibility, which was filtered down into the male rabbi/teacher of the moment. The girls watched Batsheva with a mixture of horror and awe, the way they would have watched an aerialist in a circus performing without a net.

Rabbi Silverman, patient man, teacher of girls, was not used to vigorous questions, to challenges where his ready answers were not accepted. "It is such a great blessing to be able to reach spiritual heights, that it was worth it," he repeated somewhat lamely. "Now let's go on to something else."

"But," Batsheva persisted, "what was the point—?"

"Batsheva," he said, a little more loudly than necessary, "we need to go on."

She slumped forward in her seat, tapping a sharp pencil in rhythm on the desk. The question of existence was occupying her lately, along with her need for a new spring wardrobe and a haircut. She was at the age when her mind pondered everything—from the meaning of the universe to the cause for certain pimples—with equal interest and urgency. Partly she was interested in Rabbi Silverman's explanation, and partly she enjoyed exercising her privilege of baiting him. The other girls, most of whom lived within a few blocks of the school, had parents who were called in regularly if a girl acted up. Being a boarding student allowed her to do pretty much as she pleased, even though on occasion (like the time Rabbi Fuchs found the copy of *Women in Love* hidden in the Hebrew grammar text during class) they resorted to long-distance phone calls. But her father usually backed her up anyway.

He was in favor of scholarship and when she had explained *Women in Love* was a classic, even though it was written by D. H. Lawrence, who had also written *Lady Chatterley's Lover*, he had told the school that his daughter was getting special tutoring in English and not to worry.

School was ending. The air was thick with the heat of promise. She slipped her hand discreetly inside her collar and caressed a downy shoulder. She was a woman. She had carried that secret around with her quietly for some months, almost bursting with it, not knowing what would happen, but positive it was a bomb, or fireworks, ready to go off. She looked at the girls around her with affection, and a little contempt. Most of them would be married by this time next year, to short local boys who wore black-rimmed glasses and black felt hats. They would work to support their husbands, allowing them to study all day in the yeshivah until the children came. Then their husbands would find work as rebbes in Brooklyn yeshivahs, or join the family business. They would never leave Brooklyn, except, perhaps, for the Bronx or Queens. She felt her eyes moisten with sadness. They would never see California.

She, too, would marry. But not so soon. She had so much to do, to learn. And the man she married would be . . . she shivered. She could not imagine. But special, so special.

Batsheva Ha-Levi. She was the one exception to the rule. Her intelligence, her beauty, her sweetness of character (her father's money) would save her from their fate.

There had never been a time in her life when Batsheva Ha-Levi hadn't felt herself special—not necessarily better—but simply irreconcilably different from everyone else, even those who shared her religion and friendship. It was a feeling that grew strong within her long before she understood anything about wealth or beauty or any of those things that set one human being apart from others as an object of envy or admiration in any society. Perhaps it stemmed from her mother's unconditional, solicitous love; her father's assumption that she was not like other daughters, other girls. Or perhaps it was simply a condition unavoidable to any American-born, Orthodox Jewish girl living within and yet totally outside of the culture and norms of the country of her birth.

In the bustling New York neighborhood where she had spent the greater part of her childhood, Orthodox Jews were a significant minority. There were synagogues and *shteibels* on every street; Orthodox day schools and yeshivoth; strictly kosher bakeries, pizza shops, and butchers whose storefronts boasted signs in Hebrew. There, she and her friends felt at home building little wooden booths on Succoth, dancing with the Torah through the streets on Simchat Torah. As for those who passed by and looked at them queerly, who were they but foreigners?

But the older she got, the more she realized how artificial her world was. She was on an island, in a little golden ghetto. The great floodwaters of the outside world, which her parents and teachers fought so vigilantly to keep at bay by forbidding television, allowing only Disney movies, and carefully monitoring her every waking hour, trickled in anyway through a thousand tiny cracks.

As young as three or four, Batsheva saw Santa Claus on every street corner and begged passionately to be allowed to sit on his knee. She saw shop windows filled with delicious chocolate Easter eggs and yellow marshmallow bunnies and cried miserably to have a taste. She saw little girls in their white communion dresses, with perfect little hats and gloves, and pleaded in frustrated longing to be just like them.

But the way a child gets used to his mother's cooking, no matter how bland or incredibly spicy it might be, so that nothing else can quite satisfy his hunger and give him the same feeling of well-being, so Batsheva accepted the life of her parents as the norm against which all things must be measured. By the age of five, used to her parents' steadfast denials, she learned to look at all these things the way a tourist might look at the wares of an exotic and alien race somewhere far away from home: with curiosity and admiration, but with a lack of desire to actually take anything home.

Thus, while Santa Claus remained appealing, along with the beautifully decorated trees and the sparkling heap of presents, the idea of such things suddenly appearing in her living room next to her father's bookcase of Talmuds and her mother's silver candlesticks seemed as ludicrous and frightening as Santa Claus suddenly putting on a yarmulke and talking Yiddish.

By age six, she had learned to pass judgment on everything, tagging it as something that belonged either to "our way" or to "their way," a process of selection that became as natural and automatic to her as breathing. "Their way" was Friday-night car rides and drive-in movies; "our way" was the hushed, candlelit quiet of a contemplative and joyous Sabbath dinner. "Their way" was Saturday-morning cartoons, washing the car, going to the beach; "our way" was putting on beautiful clothes, going to the synagogue, reading and talking.

The Sabbath was in many ways a day of "don'ts": don't turn on the lights, don't turn on the radio, don't use the car, don't draw (even with your finger on a moist window), don't tear or cut, don't handle money (that meant no bus rides, no movies, no eating out); don't cook, wash, or clean; don't answer the phone . . . the list went on and on. And while many of her friends freely admitted they found the Sabbath day something of a tedious bore, Batsheva never did.

Sitting at her father's side in the men's section of the synagogue long after most girls her age had been banished behind the grillwork partition with the women, she found magic in the emotion-filled chanting of prayers, in the sudden emergence of the holy Torah scroll covered in velvet and gold braid and a silver shield. She loved watching the way the light bounced off the tinkling silver bells that decorated its wooden handles, the incredible reverence in the hands of the men as they lifted it up before the congregation. The sudden unveiling of the stiff, yellowish parchment inscribed by hand with the ancient and sacred words of God never failed to raise a field of goosebumps down her arms and to lift the little hairs at the back of her neck. And while the other women and girls had to content themselves with kissing their fingertips and pointing them in the direction of the Torah, she, lifted in her father's strong arms, was able to reach out and actually, thrillingly, touch the scrolls themselves as they passed around the men's section, cradled securely in the arms of the synagogue's most respected men.

Some of her earliest and happiest memories involved Sabbath afternoons. Sitting in her father's lap, the back of her head pressed into his shoulder, she never tired of listening to his patient retelling of the stories of the Torah, which were as beloved and familiar to her, as firmly entrenched in the life of her imagination, as Cinderella, Snow White, and the Three Pigs were for other children. Rachel and Leah, Sarah and Abraham, were as close and real to her as her parents, her friends.

Her favorite story was *Akedat Yitzchak*, the near-sacrifice of Isaac. The shivers would run down her spine imagining kind old Abraham, who had waited so long for a child, holding his cherished son's hand and leading him away to be sacrificed because God had asked him to. She imagined the old man's terrible sadness and fear and yet his brave steps forward. She imagined the boy's trusting eyes fixed upon his father, his faith never wavering even as he laid himself flat upon the rock and waited. And because she knew it would all end well because God was good and hated cruelty of any kind, and that father and child would get all the credit without actually sacrificing anything, the story always made her happy.

She loved those instances in the Bible where people took flying leaps of faith headlong into the fearsome unknown and God was always there, like a good father, His arms outstretched to catch them: the children of Israel plunging headfirst into the swollen waters of the Red Sea; Daniel in the lion's den; Moses defying Pharaoh. Not only did they all come through unscathed, but they were also showered with rewards. All you had to do was believe.

And as she listened to her father, trusting implicitly in every word he said with every ounce of her mind and heart, she sometimes forgot that these were God's words and not her father's, imagining that he and God were one, teaching her how to be wise and good, directing her steps and keeping her from all harm.

Most of all, she loved the Sabbath day because as long as she could remember, it had been her day with her father. No matter what he did all week or how much work was left still to be done, by Friday at sundown he put it all behind him, crossing some invisible border from one world into another. In the Sabbath world, there was no such thing as bank overdrafts, unsatisfied customers, lazy workmen, unscrupulous subcontractors. The phone would ring unheeded. He never, under any circumstances, spoke a harsh or saddening word on the Sabbath. For a man who hardly had time to talk to his family during the week, he suddenly had all the time in the world, and he gave it generously to her and her mother.

The Sabbath was a rare day of freedom for her mother, too. In those days of her early childhood, before the wealth had come, bringing with it a house full of servants, she had seen only her mother's back most of the time: leaning over the stove or sink, bent low to make the beds and wash the floors. But on the Sabbath her mother was even forced to leave the dishes unwashed until after sundown.

Her mother took on a special beauty as she sat wearing her girlish print dresses and little hats in the synagogue. She loved the special timbre of her mother's voice as she joined her father in singing Shabbat *zemirot*, and the way her skin glowed in the light of the Sabbath candles. She loved to watch the way her mother's eyes lit up when her father said the *kiddush* over wine and how her lips trembled as she sipped the sweet liquid from the silver cup he held for her. It was only then she saw clearly the beautiful, hidden current that flowed so strongly between her parents. It was like static electricity erupting into visible golden sparks on a cold winter's night. Those moments, and when she saw her father reach over and gently squeeze her mother's hand, were the only times that she thought of her mother as a person with a separate existence, rather than an appendage to her and her father, simply "Ima."

It was difficult not to take her mother for granted. She was always there, hovering at their elbows at mealtime lest they not take enough to eat or take too much and injure their health. She carefully doled out the portions, making sure he and Batsheva got the most succulent slices of roast beef, the tenderest morsels of chicken. And only when her father decisively put down his fork and knife and announced: "I'm not eating another bite until you sit down," did her mother finally take her place by the table, taking whatever was least desirable and leaving the rest for them as second helpings. Batsheva, looking at her father, very early adopted his attitude of helpless exasperation with her mother's rather silly self-sacrifice. It was only many years later that she understood it for what it was: the misdirected outpouring of a simple heart overflowing with boundless love.

Mrs Fruma Ha-Levi had been the baby of the family, the youngest of a second marriage. Her mother, like the woman who had mothered her older half-sister, had died young, weakened by inhaling steaming pots of boiling laundry and beating endless city dust from rose-patterned pillows, finally killed by the poisons in the rank tenement air.

One of Fruma's earliest memories was that of her sister looking down at her with contempt, finding new specks of dust where she had been entrusted with polishing, streaks of moisture on plates given her to dry. It had taken years for her to see her sister honestly; not as a bully but a frightened girl just a few years older than herself, with a household and small child thrust into her young, unready hands. Her sister had hardened simply to keep from dissolving. It had taken great courage.

But time somehow hadn't made her any kinder to herself. She remained convinced she was hopelessly incompetent, impossibly deficient. Sometimes she would admit grudgingly that she had always been a good student. Her teachers, especially the kind old rabbis who had taught her to read Hebrew and say the daily prayers, had praised her for learning so quickly. In rare moments of insight, she was even willing to admit that it was not lack of intelligence but rather lack of confidence, a timidity, that made her seem and feel simple, even stupid. She lived in constant dread that her husband and child would see her with her sister's eyes.

As a young girl she had dreamt few dreams, made few plans. Only once she had envisioned herself walking through the desert in a beautiful flowing gown like the queen of Sheba, gaining comfort from the dream's impracticality. It was so far removed from reality it gave her nothing to strive for, to fail at. Her father, a butcher, had been a grim and humorless man who had taken out his frustrations over losing two wives and being left with only daughters by hacking away at meat with unnecessary vigor. She had never been pious enough for him. Never obedient enough. Never clever enough. His eyes registered a chronic disappointment when they looked at her, saying: "Never mind. You wouldn't understand."

And so the first time she had looked up over the blood-stained counter in the butcher shop and her eyes had met those of Abraham Ha-Levi, she had felt herself the poor girl in a fairy tale face-to-face with the handsome prince who embodied her only hope. And even though he had courted her and married her—with no ulterior motive she could ever see—still, the feeling had remained that his attraction and love was undeserved good fortune capable of vanishing any moment in a puff of smoke.

Her husband was in many ways like a wonderful father. He never criticized, but always smoothed things over, accepting her shortcomings, never pushing her beyond herself. In the early days of their marriage, the house had been a shambles, the result of having promised herself, never again, as long as she lived, to dust, polish, or dry a thing when out from under her sister's thumb. And he had accepted the chaos, as he had accepted her cooking, night after night of over-cooked, if not downright burnt, meatballs and dry stew. After a hard day's work, he had patiently dusted off the shelves, washed the morning and afternoon dishes, done the laundry, until finally his love had broken her down, the way her father's and sister's criticism never could.

She had taken up her dustcloth, her mop and broom the way an artist takes up his paints and brushes, in joy and determination. She had bought every cookbook, studying them as if for a degree, practicing endlessly to perfect the most savory kugels, the lightest cakes, the most succulent gefilte fish. Her reward had been his few words of praise and the knowledge that she, for all her shortcomings, was able to take care of him and make his life easier. She never dreamt of being an equal partner to him—he was beyond her from the first, a brilliant, handsome man who had impossibly fallen in love with her. Whatever position she held in his life, as long as it enabled her to be near him, to care for him, was good enough.

When Batsheva was born, after the years of heartbreaking childlessness, she looked at her from the first as a tiny version of the man she loved, a being superior to her in every way. She left discipline and instruction completely in his hands. And when her husband and her daughter disagreed, she stepped back and watched in helplessness and wonder, the way a simple jury member might contemplate the clash of two brilliant and learned lawyers.

Because of this attitude, Fruma Ha-Levi exasperated her daughter in other ways as well. For example, for as long as Batsheva could remember, there had been Sunday-afternoon outings that her mother consistently refused to join. "You two go," her mother would urge, making a little shooing motion with her hands. "What do I understand about such things? Go, go. Enjoy yourselves."

Thus, while her friends spent their Sundays with their

parents at the Bronx Zoo or Brooklyn Botanic Gardens, she and her father would explore the Metropolitan Museum, the Museum of Modern Art, the Guggenheim and Whitney, as well as fine little uptown and SoHo galleries.

At first, Batsheva had held on to her mother's hand and tugged her, but later she came to accept her refusal as inevitable and even desirable. She had her father all to herself for a few precious hours. With him as her guide, she explored a whole world her friends knew and cared nothing about. He did not lecture her, but she learned from his silent pauses and lingering attention, his expressions of skepticism or total admiration, how to appreciate the finest in art, sculpture, and photography; what was really a masterpiece and what was merely novel and pretentious. She learned to follow his footsteps carefully.

Her friends were sensible, practical girls who admired tangible things. To them, a fine mohair sweater or a pair of calfskin gloves were beautiful. Even a pretty oil painting might capture their imagination as they envisioned it over the couch, matching the rug.

By the age of nine, Batsheva already perceived the unbridgeable gap between herself and almost everyone she knew. For all her senses were constantly honed and the world around her was a completely different place from the one her friends saw. They would never even notice the light hitting an old door, dissecting it into a symmetry of shapes, which brought the sting of wondrous tears to her eyes.

And the more she learned to admire the skilled hand, the wise eye of the artists and photographers she loved, the more she began to perceive the world as a giant canvas and God as the greatest artist of all. So that later, when she finally learned about Darwin, the idea was as absurd and incomprehensible to her as the suggestion that the Mona Lisa had come about because a few cans of paint had accidentally tipped over and dripped their colors onto a chance canvas.

And with every beautiful thing she saw for the first time, her love for Him grew—filling her with an ache of gratitude for simply being alive and bearing witness. It was a love that had nothing to do with pleasing parents and teachers, that owed nothing to periodic school brainwashings and rabbis' speeches. It was secret and independent, and it informed the core of her being.

Often she longed for a sister or a brother who would understand. Or at least a cousin. But as an only child of a mother and father whose relatives were all dead, she had no one but her parents. And really, not even both of them since only her father understood her completely. Her mother, in giving her love and approval so unconditionally, had relinquished her role as teacher. In many ways, she was her father's "creation," the product of his instruction. However, her mother's love gave her enormous confidence and independence. There was simply nothing she could ever do to lose it. She sensed early that this was not the case with her father.

She perceived, however, in the growing gap between her and her friends, that her father had actually given her the dispensation to go her own way. Once, perversely, she had written a composition describing the beauty of an altarpiece she had seen at the Metropolitan. Not surprisingly, a shocked Rebbitzen Finegold had ripped it to shreds: "Anything used for idol worship cannot be beautiful," the woman had said severely. When Batsheva related the story to her father, she forced a few tears but not enough to blur her seeing quite clearly—and with triumphant satisfaction—his dismissive wave of the hand, as if dealing with an insect too insignificant to squash. By age ten, tired of battling, he had switched her to a different elementary school: "One where they will teach you more than Bible stories and how to make challah dough," he told her dryly.

There she met an American-born crowd of American-born parents who felt traditional religious girls' schools were too heavy on morality, self-sacrifice, and modesty and too light on social studies, English, and math. They were parents who expected their daughters to learn trigonometry and pass the Regents; parents who longed for sons who would be Talmud scholars and doctors, and daughters who would go to Brooklyn College and become rabbis' wives and teachers in the public school system. The teachers were Israelis who spoke crisp modern Hebrew, saying "To-rah," not "Toy-reh"; "*galut,*" not "*gah-lus,*" in sharp distinction to the Old World, European rabbi-teachers of the school she had left.

And although she felt a palpable lessening of pressure to dress, behave, and think in certain limited ways, she still felt left out. She began to resent her father's silent insistence that she was different and begged to be taken to amusement parks and playgrounds, insisting that her mother come along as well. But then, after tramping around in the grass, a few stomach-turning hurtles down the roller-coaster, she became bored and listless and eager to return to the old pattern of her Sundays, finally accepting the irrevocable fact that, like Eve in the garden of Eden, her eyes had been opened and there was no turning back.

When she was thirteen years old, she looked through the grillwork partition in the synagogue and discovered boys. Actually, *the boy.* Despite her very sheltered life, and her ignorance about the mechanics of love, when she found him, she felt the thrills, the budding sexual joy, as deeply as any girl who ever screamed for Elvis. She sat back, glad for the first time for the partition that kept her face suffused in shadows, allowing herself to study him the same way she had noticed women like her mother studying his father, the rabbi: with serious pleasure.

The rabbi had three sons. The youngest was the best looking—with black hair and blue eyes and flashing white teeth. Looking back on it later, she could not understand why she hadn't paid more attention to him. Perhaps it was the genuine friendliness of his manner, which seemed callow, even brotherly. Ah, but it was not a brother she wanted. Although she did not attend coed synagogue youth groups, her friends who did described with despair the jolly platonic kidding with boys that was their meager substitute for romance. All the girls she knew were besieged, enfolded, asphyxiated by brotherly love.

The middle son had no looks at all. But his imperfections—the long, pale face, the rounded shoulders, the weak body, and especially, the prominent, black-framed glasses—were just those things that made men attractive to many Orthodox girls, the way leather jackets and college-letter sweaters attracted other girls. They were proof of long, relentless hours spent hunched over, studying the Talmud in sunless yeshivah halls.

For religious girls, whose final status was to be determined solely by their husbands' achievements, marrying such a scholar, who might himself rise to head a yeshivah, meant reaching the highest rung of all. And although the girls in Batsheva's world might in a pinch have considered a doctor, lawyer, or CPA who learned Talmud on evenings and weekends, they would do so only after a recognition of failure.

The way other girls trained to be nurses, Batsheva and her friends endured minor fast days, praying with parched lips to raise their spiritual level to be worthy of such men. They endured hardships to be worthy of receiving a life of even greater hardship. For they knew that if they succeeded, it would mean years of supporting a husband as he slaved through long days of explicating endless Talmudical minutiae. They imagined working at two jobs to earn a living, happily taking the burden of earning a living off his shoulders.

Their reward, as they saw it, would be to sit by him in the evening, after the six or seven little ones were in bed, to be regaled with brilliant discussions on intricate points of law. Their home would become a meeting place for the wise, and with his help and inspiration, they too would scale new spiritual heights.

However, although his clear blue eyes and deep tan were a silent reproach, Batsheva never wavered in her love for the rabbi's eldest son. For aside from his elegant tall body, his black wavy hair and confident manner, that which set him apart, lending him a glamour and renown that reached far beyond their little community, was that he sang. He had, in fact, composed several songs incorporating the words of Hebrew liturgical poetry. The tunes were slow, mournful ditties that picked up speed by the second chorus and ended on a note of rousing hysteria. A few even had echoes of Baez and Dylan.

At one point, it was rumored, he had formed his own band, a group that combined biblical verses with a bazouki beat. Some even said they had seen him and his band on a late-night talk show on a local television station. They called themselves The Singing Scholars. But the rabbi soon put an end to that: He forbade him to appear on television again and severely limited his live appearances. Batsheva understood the reasoning: Anything unrelated to Torah learning was a waste, a sin. But it made her wonder, for the first time, in her heart of hearts, if the rabbi knew what he was doing.

She wanted him to be a star. She longed for it, feeling his success would leaven her days, which were heavy with memorizing the constitutional amendments and long passages from the Book of Kings.

More and more, she felt the onus of proving her worthiness weigh on her. Would he want a college girl? Or would he shun one who had ventured so far into secular knowledge, endangering her purity? But then, would he look down upon a mere Hebrew Teachers' Seminary graduate as an unsuitable partner to his own brilliance? The ideas went around and around in her head, giving her no peace. It was, she decided finally, bright intellect he sought. A woman who could quote effortlessly from the Bible and Code of Jewish Law. Someone who could pitch a heavy conflict between Rashi and Maimonides with the best of them. And so she slaved through the short bitter winter, allowing her unfounded convictions on his beliefs, desires, and preferences to shape her future, convinced she was molding herself for him in the end.

Walking out of the synagogue when he was near, she didn't even dare to glance in his direction, her heart beating so loud she held her palms over it to lessen the sound. But when she was safely home, she kicked herself for being a coward and searched for any excuse to walk past the rabbi's house, terrified yet aching with desire to catch a glimpse of him through the windows or on the porch. She practiced for hours in front of mirrors just how to faintly turn her head, allowing just a ghost of a smile, should he actually notice her. And when she did see him, how she floated on his image, agonizing over how she had looked to him, until she began to hate her imperfections, to loathe the poor material she had to work with to form (oh, hopeless dream!) a package able to tempt him who was perfection.

Sometimes her reward was not actually seeing him, but hearing the music of his guitar drift out from the living room into the street. He had a high voice, a disappointment, although she would never admit it to herself. His face and his body demanded his father's sonorous alto, yet he had inherited his mother's rather nasal whine.

And then, one Sabbath morning, as she sat in worshipful concentration, she looked up and noticed the faces of other girls pressed into the partition, their gaze rapt, their heads turned in the same unmistakable direction as her own. Looking at them, some of them high-school girls with lipstick, and others even younger than herself, all their youthful hope and desperate longing so clearly and pathetically revealed, she began to see herself more clearly. The ache did not go away, nor did the longing. But its sharpness dulled. Soon after, her parents moved her to California.

By the time she returned to New York to enter the Bais Sarah High School, he was already engaged. The girl, she had it on the best of word, was a beautiful redhead, barely seventeen, who hadn't even graduated from high school.

Her last week in high school passed like a dream—the hugs from her friends and the people she boarded with; the giggles and promises to write reminiscent of a send-off to home from summer camp. Only when she said good-bye to her old teacher did she feel some door pitifully and joyfully clang shut. She had learned all he could teach her, but there was still that ocean out there she wanted to know. But when the plane lifted off, taking her home to California, she felt the heavy sadness, the seriousness of Brooklyn and Bais Sarah lift from her shoulders. Like a bird fleeing the winter and winging its way south, she already felt the warmth of the sun dispelling all unpleasant thoughts. I will sleep and swim in the pool, she told herself, and read and read and read . . .

Batsheva leaned back into the hot fragrant grass and wiped the tears from her eyes. "Anna, Anna," she cried. "Why?" But she knew why. Life with Karenin, his cold hands all over her body. She shuddered. And to be severed from one's child forever. But still, to throw oneself under a train? Heavy metal tearing one's flesh apart, crushing one's skull? But after death there was heaven, peace. Still, it was a mortal sin to take one's life. Perhaps Anna knew this but felt she had lived enough. What was life really, without Vronsky, without passion? Of course she only knew about passion from books: *Marjorie Morningstar, Women in Love, Lady Chatterley's Lover* (no one must ever find that book, hidden between her atlas and a heavy history text).

She slipped her hands up the long sleeves of her silk nightgown, rubbing her smooth young flesh sensuously. She knew no men other than her father and the rabbis in school who had taught her Torah, Prophets, Talmud, and Mishnah. She enjoyed studying, but for a long time she had not been able to concentrate on such things. She had persevered because she was unable to confess to her father that she was no scholar, but simply a teenage girl who needed a man's arms around her, his lips on hers. Yet she was revolted by the thought of any man touching her.

How shocked her father would be if he could look inside his neat, obedient little girl and see the bubbling turmoil of confusion. How strange it was. One day she had been playing with dolls, and the next . . . She was ashamed and stimulated by her feelings, and tired of denying them. How would it be, she wondered, to have a man's body on hers? Would it hurt? None of the books said that it did, except Marjorie Morningstar admitted, "Shock shock, then terrible humiliation." But she couldn't quite believe that could be true.

The coming together of a man and woman was a holy thing, after all. God had chosen this way of replenishing the earth. God did everything so elegantly, with such an exquisite attention to detail. She knew this from studying the flowers in the garden and watching the morning sky, all mauve and pink and orange. So beautiful. But God had looked at all this, His ideas, His wonderful sense of color and design put into action, and had said merely that it was good. Not great. Not fantastic. Just good. But when He had looked at man and woman together, He had said it was "very good." So you could just imagine.

But that was her problem—she couldn't imagine, and the Bible—source of all truth, to be relied upon where other books were not—was very vague on details. "He came in unto her." Ruth uncovered Boaz's feet on the threshing floor. Between the lines, though, hadn't Leah and Rachel fought over their time with Jacob, trading things to get an extra night? So it must be very . . . Would he crush you with his weight—ugh, fat men were awful!

Even if one shouldn't judge by outside appearances, if souls were unconnected to the appearance of the body, still, one wouldn't ever want to get into bed with a fat man. You'd have to be on a very high spiritual level to do that.

As she thought, the wind picked up strands of her black silken hair and blew them across her face. Someone standing above her looking down would have stopped breathing for a moment, she was so very young and lovely. The light dappling her head turned her hair a bluish black, like a raven's. It was her one great, evil vanity, she thought. It was down to her waist and it took her hours to comb it and to pin it up primly every morning. But now, alone in the house except for the servants, she let it hang down in a thick silken scarf, caressing her back and hips.

She was sure about her hair, but not her face. It bothered her that she did not have the picture-perfect features of a cheerleader. Her nose was nicely pointed and small. But her eyes were odd, remarkable, such a strange color—so light blue they were almost white. A magical color, Elizabeth had assured her, that people stared at and got lost in. But maybe she was just being kind. Elizabeth was awfully kind.

Elizabeth was really beautiful. Shining strawberry-blond curls, large googly green eyes. Very womanly. Sexy. Like Marilyn Monroe. She was her idol, her mentor.

She lifted her hand to her cheek and felt the heat of the California sun turning the skin a soft glowing pink. She pointed and stretched her long slim legs and toes so that her nightgown fell down around her hips, exposing her legs. They were so pretty, she thought, the slim ankles, the slightly rounded calves. Her waist was sweet too.

She sat up, hugging herself. She was so pretty, any man would surely love her. An ache began inside her, a familiar unquenchable longing. She jumped up and ran toward the grotto and the kidney-shaped pool with its Greek columns and fountains, ran as if she were being chased by demons, and jumped headfirst into the water.

When she came up, subdued and ashamed, she looked around carefully. Ima would have a fit. She would get a lecture on maidenly modesty, "*kavod bas melech penima*—the honor of a king's daughter is within." Whatever you wanted to do—that's what they told you—parents, teachers. Don't go out into the street yourself. Don't expose yourself through revealing clothes. Don't dance, don't sing, don't . . . bring attention to yourself. But she wanted everyone to look at her, didn't they understand! She was eighteen, and ravishing, and without a lover! Oh, Vronsky, Vronksy, she whispered passionately, then giggled, rushing to the pool dressing room. The wet silk clung to her like a second skin.

"A wet T-shirt contest at the holy Ha-Levis'! My dear child, you have made my day. In fact, you've made my life!"

"Elizabeth!" A blush spread to Batsheva's face and she crossed her arms to cover her breasts. Then, seeing the other girl's face break into a wide grin, she giggled. "I forgot about our lesson."

"You break my heart, dear infant." Twenty-two years of age, Elizabeth loved to play the role of wise older woman. She couldn't help it with Batsheva. Even though there was only a few years' difference between them, the girl was such an innocent she seemed like a little kid. Bubble boy, she called her privately, brought up in a golden cocoon, wrapped in cotton wool.

"I'm so glad you're here. I need to talk to you desperately."

Always melodrama, Elizabeth thought. And for a kid who wasn't allowed to watch soap operas. "Anna Karenina. Why, why did she do it?"

"Russians are given to dramatic gestures of vodka-soaked intelligence," she said mildly, leaning back the full length of the lounge chair and sliding her open notebook over her eyes to shield them from the sun. I'm even beginning to sound like him, she thought. A Graham MacLeish clone. A tan, that was what she needed. An all-over, no-suit-marks tan by 9 P.M.

"Seriously, Elizabeth," Batsheva laid an urgent, earnest hand on the older girl's relaxed arm, "don't you think she had no other choice? I mean, it was either Vronsky and no child or Karenin and his cold, old hands. But it was such a terrible, mortal sin."

Desperate. Mortal sin. Novels had not improved her vocabulary in the proper direction, Elizabeth decided. Oh well. She peered at her sideways through slit-opened eyes. Why, there were tears in her eyes, the little dope! Reluctantly, she moved herself into a less comfortable and more serious position.

"Oh, it was much worse than a sin, which can be delicious, my child. It was plain dumb. If women killed themselves over every missing link of the male gender they screwed, there would be no continuation of the human race as we know it." Oops, forgot where I was. *Screw* is not an acceptable word in the Ha-Levis' home. They had no television. Batsheva went to very select movies that Ha-Levi Elder personally screened before she was allowed to see them. She had never even been to the theater or a ballet. The school she went to was about the same as St Mary's, except it was full of rabbi-teachers, instead of nuns.

They certainly had gone far afield from the original topics of study: diagramming sentences, pluperfect subjunctives. She had begun tutoring the girl on the finer points of grammar as a way of earning food money. She had been an English literature freshman at UCLA and Batsheva a ninth grader. Without realizing it at first, the lessons had gotten off the track and they had wound up learning literature: D. H. Lawrence, E. M. Forster, Joseph Conrad, Virginia Woolf, Henry James . . . anybody the snobbish, wonderful, exquisite Professor MacLeish had pronounced worth reading. Blond Viking with the Oxford accent.

And always, the tutoring sessions had gone beyond the books and they had wound up discussing philosophy, boys, makeup, Elizabeth's latest live-in. Sometimes she felt the girl was living vicariously through her. Talk about strict parents! Compared to old man Ha-Levi, Elizabeth's old man, with his belt and his drinking and his 12 P.M. curfews, looked like Robert Young. She felt sorry for the poor kid.

To be fair though, the guy had always been nice to her, even though she knew he disapproved of her close relationship with Batsheva and the books that she gave the girl to read. Why he hadn't fired her (thank the Lord, because the money was paying for room and board: He was a generous man) was a mystery to his credit. But he gave her, rationally or irrationally, the willies. Bearded patriarch in his thousand-dollar funeral suits. Jews. She didn't understand them, didn't feel fully comfortable with them. There weren't any Jews in Cortland, California, pear center of the nation. Just good Methodists and Presbyterians. Even Episcopalians were considered strange.

She had gotten to know many at UCLA. A few times she had even been the shiksa at boys' homes, enduring their parents' fake cordiality. Don't steal my precious boy, designing Gentile! It was a role she could do without. But most of them had been nothing like the Ha-Levis. It was hard to believe they practiced the same religion. There had been ham sandwiches for dinner with a glass of milk. Golf games on Saturday mornings. One day a year in the synagogue for Yom Kippur.

It wasn't that the Ha-Levis were stricter, "orthodox." They lived a whole different life that went far beyond food and weekends. Every single minute they were awake, there was some other rule they had to keep. They had blessings to recite over everything that went into their mouth. And there was precious little that could go in: Meat had to be from a kosher butcher, even the milk had to come from cows that were specially watched. They prayed three times a day, at least the old man did. Batsheva every morning. It was as if the house itself were some kind of a tabernacle and every movement was part of a religious ceremony. Wake up, wash your fingertips in ritual water three times each. Say morning prayers. Blessings over breakfast, before and after. Kiss the prayer box hanging on the doorpost as you leave the room or enter it . . . You didn't visit God when you needed something. You carried Him around with you every moment of the day. And He was heavy.

"Don't you ever feel like you're trapped? Don't you ever feel that you'd like to run away with the chauffeur and have a Big Mac at McDonald's with French fries and a Thick Shake?" she had asked Batsheva early on in their relationship, with reckless disregard for getting the ax if the old man overheard.

"You don't understand, Elizabeth. It's not my parents who are asking me to do this. It's God. Jews have been chosen to be holy. In what they eat, how they dress, how they behave . . ."

"You really believe that, huh?"

In answer, Batsheva had brought out some photographs of a snake she had taken at the San Diego Zoo. Very nice shots. Child had a great eye.

"You see those diamonds—how perfectly they're shaped, how beautiful the pattern is? There has to be a God, don't you see?"

Faith, clear-eyed and unquestioning. Blessing or curse?

Remembering, she sat up and looked at Batsheva, narrowing her green eyes—the clear, appraising eyes of a smart country girl come to the big city.

There was something truly fine about Batsheva, Elizabeth thought with just a touch of envy. A delicacy of feeling that made her sympathize with everyone. She was the type who would have become a Mother Teresa, washing off lepers' hands. There was something really sincerely undesigning and young about her, and not just a veneer to please parents and teachers. She was clean in mind, body, and spirit like a young athlete.

She had also been young like that. Pear Princess in Cortland. Summer prom dresses. Let Bats out of her bubble and into the real world to claw after love, money, friends, and we'd see how far her innocence lasts. She admitted to herself that she loved city life with all the honest greediness of a child in a candy store. Like a tame lion thrown back into the wild, she had made some dangerous escapes and learned some hard lessons about the price of living in the jungle.

At first she had been attracted to men with chiseled features and square jaws wearing raw-silk business suits. But as soon as she got close to them her heart would slow down, her eyes narrow and clear, her nose sniffing out bullshit the way only a country girl's can. She was too smart and too sincere herself to settle for facades. Her mother's honest Methodism: "Rather a sincere insult than a false compliment." Yes, Mama.

She was looking for someone better than the rough, slow-talking boys she had grown up with, and with her instinct she realized these men were not nearly as good. They were like cardboard cutouts. Their needs were basic and predictable. They saw people as disposable, to be used up for their ideas or bodies or connections and then discarded. Oh, they made lots of noise about openness and freedom, but essentially that was it. The women were like that, too.

She had been careful not to be used, but had experimented with using. She had gotten a rich boy to help her find, furnish, and move into an apartment with hints about his sharing it and then had dumped him as soon as the work was over. Other men had helped her in math and science, or gotten her part-time jobs. Her full-breasted figure gave a misleading clue to strangers. It made her seem soft and yielding and simple when in truth she was just the opposite.

She found her meetings with Batsheva a welcome respite from all that. In a way, the girl was like her younger self, the self that still believed in people. A refreshing escape from the real world. She looked at the girl so innocent of her beauty. Voluptuous innocence. It would be so easy for her to go the same way. Thank goodness old Abraham was keeping her under lock and key. Maybe he was not so crazy after all.

"Shameless hussy! Go put some holy clothes on your holy behind so we can do some work. If Daddy sees you like this, he's sure to chalk it up to my corrupting influence and order thirty lashes."

"I wish you wouldn't talk about him like that. He's not so bad." Her voice had a stiffness in it, a formality.

Uh-oh, as usual, took it too far. Honor thy father and mother. "Sorry." She clapped two hands over her mouth. "As usual, verbal diarrhea." She was talking too much. Pure nerves. But it was done. The letter was sitting there, along with faculty announcements and late papers, awaiting his pleasure. White envelope, neat, businesslike. A formal proposal.

Dear Prof. MacLeish,
Four years ago you told me that the university frowned on student-teacher lovers. I wanted to let you know that I am graduating in two days and am therefore no longer a student.

I will wait for you tonight at nine at Fat Henry's in a corner booth. I will wait a long time.

Sincerely,
Elizabeth

"You haven't answered me. Why did she?"

Elizabeth ran exasperated fingers through her hair. "She?"

"Anna!"

"Seriously, if you want my opinion, she did the right thing. Life is just a game. When you lose too many points and back yourself into a corner, the smart thing is just to bow out gracefully.

She left with some self-respect. A life with Karenin would have frozen off anybody's tits. And Vronsky was, in the final analysis, a total ass. They were all using her. It made perfect sense and took courage for her to take control of her life again."

"By killing herself? Oh, Elizabeth, those cold heavy wheels crushing her face . . ."

"Messy, but effective."

"Would you ever do such a thing? I mean, if . . ."

Sitting in the dark, nursing a drink, fending off the losers hour after hour, watching the door open and close, but it never being him. Going home alone. A stone fell into her stomach, crushing the butterflies. "No. I . . . don't think so." Her face was serious for a moment, losing some of its gay cynicism. "Too much of a coward, I guess. Now, no more delay tactics. To work."

"All right, but I have to sneak up to get dressed. Wait for me in Aba's study."

She had been in the Ha-Levi house countless times, but it had never ceased to amaze her. Unworthy envy, bury your green head, she told herself, looking at the polished brass, the gleaming grand piano. It always reminded her that no matter how far she went, she would always be a country girl, her eyes wide with wonder at the rich people's banquet. She didn't like to be reminded.

She wasn't in a good mood when Batsheva came back. The lesson was on Wordsworth. Time and remembrance at Tintern Abbey. You had to be in the right state of mind for old Wordsworth.

"Wordsworth is turning to past experiences as a relief from present stress. For Wordsworth, nature, landscape, is a spiritual restoration," she read without much interest from her notes. She could almost hear MacLeish's deep, melodic voice. Impressive as hell. "Nature is the anchor, guard, and guide of all my moral being."

"I love the Romantics. Wordsworth, Coleridge. They'd understand my snake. They could see God in the diamonds."

"In a way you're right. The translucence of the eternal through and in the temporal. What I like about them is this idea of the continuum. Like a rainbow. They believed we are all one great chain of being, interconnected with each other, with nature, and that you have to break the boundaries of the ego and establish a connection with the universe. They believed that we choose what we shall see and hear and what we make of it. They believed that there is an organic, creative principle at work in man, in society, in nature, and God and poetry. It's a world that's constantly in flux, a world of becoming, not being."

"I'm not sure I follow you."

"Look, the minute you say, 'I am Batsheva Ha-Levi, religious girl who likes hamburgers and tall men with glasses,' you are setting limits. This is what I am and what I will always be. The Romantics believed that was the death principle, dejection. But if you say, 'I am Batsheva and each moment whatever form my life is to take is slowly unfolding within me and will continue to do so,' when you don't set any limits but work with this creative principle, you have joy."

"In other words," Batsheva said, excitedly, "God can have no world without man, because it's man's perception that allows the world to exist. There is no good or evil without man, who must define good by rejecting evil."

Elizabeth's jaw dropped. "Very nice. You think of that by yourself?"

Batsheva smiled with modest pleasure. "It's been on my mind, but you can't talk about this stuff with teachers, especially rabbi-teachers. But let's stop now," Batsheva finally begged her.

"I guess you won't be needing me any longer, now that you're off to college yourself."

The thought hadn't occurred to Batsheva that these lessons

would ever end. And it was not at all certain that that was where she was off to. She had idly browsed through college catalogues she had sent away for secretly. Paris, London. She wanted to learn photography. She wanted to learn Torah and Kabbalah, and how to be a holy person. She wanted to have beautiful babies to cuddle and fuss over. To have her own house with beautiful furniture and to be its undisputed mistress. She wanted a life filled with adventure. Her parents had not spoken to her one way or the other concerning the future, and it made her nervous. We shall see, *maideleh*, her father had said gently, stroking her head when she asked if she could continue her studies in a seminary and the university. But I must apply now, she had pleaded, but he had turned away with an odd silence. Impulsively, she hugged Elizabeth. "Don't ever let's stop seeing each other. Promise me you'll always be a friend, no matter what."

Elizabeth hesitated. She believed in words, in their power and obligation. She believed it when someone told her they would talk about love again in four years. Believed that he wouldn't forget. Sweet little dopes, the two of them. Sisters. She hugged her back. "I promise."

I honor and respect my parents like a good, religious Jewish girl, Batsheva thought. But I don't understand them. She had studied the Torah, the Mishnah. Her father had even paid for special tutors to teach her Talmud, which girls in Bais Sarah were not considered bright enough to learn. Talmud, the reserve of male scholars, rabbis, contained the basis and rationale for the Law, for all they did.

And what she had learned was that the Law advocated a life of spiritual striving, and yet her parents lived surrounded by exorbitant material wealth next to movie moguls and actresses in Beverly Hills. Yet her father was not like them. He was not a materialistic man or a show-off. He treated their possessions the way she had seen rabbis treat ritual objects—silver wine cups, menorahs—using them simply to make their inner lives more beautiful. The material exalted the spiritual, uplifted it. Still, it was an odd life-style, surrounding yourself with objects only to belittle their intrinsic value. She would have preferred a simpler life, a smaller house. Fewer things.

Her mother had not changed with the wealth. She was still a gentle, quiet *balabusta*. She woke early and puttered around the house, keeping everything running smoothly, keeping the servants in line, or appreciated, as the case might be. Her mother, overweight and cheerful, liked nice clothes and seemed to rejoice in the many lovely objects that filled the house. Yet Batsheva always sensed that her mother, too, was uncomfortable in the elaborate setting, that she could not really believe the house was hers. Even religion, Batsheva thought, is Aba's, and Ima partakes in it, like everything else in the house.

She wondered as she dried her hair and patted the soft, thick towel over her sweet naked flesh, where her father was now and what he would bring her when he came home. It was an old game she had played as a little girl when they had been poor tenants in a roach-infested walkup in the Bronx. She would hear his weary, dejected footsteps on the staircase after a day's backbreaking labor of bricklaying in the New York sunshine and run down the steps into his wide-open arms. Always, no matter how tired or heartbroken he was from the indignity of his descent into a common laborer, his poverty and his aching bones, always, his face would break into a smile of such happiness and pride. She would squirm out of his caress and slip down to his feet, thrusting her eager small fingers into his pockets, and there, always, no matter how little there was to eat or wear for her parents, there would always be a joyous surprise—chocolate, a wind-up toy, a stuffed animal . . .

Only on Yom Kippur did he catch her hand in his and

look at her with such tormented, fanatical eyes she had never forgotten it. She began to be afraid of him. But he had only kissed her fingers, one by one, and said "I am sorry, Sheva. I promise you, with God as my witness, I will never come to you empty-handed. You are my future, the last hope of the Ha-Levis." She had had no idea what he was talking about.

He seemed sometimes to have a certain demon behind him that whipped him on to more and greater efforts. And as if he had made a pact with the devil, he seemed to succeed at whatever he tried.

First he was made a bricklaying foreman, and then he quit and got his own team together. With the money he saved, he bought his first piece of property, a burned-out apartment house in a Jewish neighborhood. Miraculously he was able to borrow the money and rebuild it with his own crew.

After that, the presents in his pockets began to change. First there were expensive chocolates in beautiful little boxes, and then tiny jewelry cases with gold, turquoise, emeralds, and tiny diamonds for her ears, throat, and arms.

They moved out to an expensive Riverdale apartment house. She had been happiest then, on the crowded block full of new friends, in the packed, noisy synagogues and *shteibels* where her father would pray on the Sabbath with other Jews in long black coats, fur-trimmed hats, and silk overcoats.

But her father had known no peace. He isolated himself from the other Jews, modern Jews with three-piece suits and hats. He sometimes took her for Sabbath walks and would nod stiffly to his neighbors. Then his business had prospered and he had disappeared for days, even weeks, traveling all over the country, buying property in Texas and California. And soon he was sending her presents instead of bringing them. And finally he had uprooted them to the West Coast.

They had not believed their eyes when he had driven them

up to their new home. It was a palace, she thought. A golden palace. A long road wound up a hill and there at the top in white stucco with a red-tiled roof, overlooking the whole valley, was their house. Behind it was a pool the color of lapis, a deep pool with a grotto and a fountain that sprayed water through the mouths of naked babies and fairies.

She had felt like a princess standing there, surveying the valley. She loved to watch the mountains, never tiring of the view because it was never the same. The mountains would rise up in the clear sunlight, turn pink at dawn and golden at sunset. A deep fog would appear in the valley and she would feel as if she were an angel gazing down from heaven.

But if New York had been an island, a ghetto, California was another planet altogether. There were no neighbors they spoke to. No religious girls her own age to be friends with. And even though Pico Boulevard was full of kosher butcher shops and places to eat, it was a drive, not a stroll. There was no feeling of community, of being part of a little world. And on the Sabbath her father invited nine other men and their wives as guests, usually people her parents' age, setting up his own little synagogue right in their home. The isolation was awful but at times also beautiful and liberating. No one was looking over her shoulder either.

Since moving to California, she had spent the school year in New York, boarding with a religious family and coming home on holidays. The other girls at Bais Sarah had the same boring lives, she thought. They all thought about boys constantly, but the good girls pretended not to, pretended that they didn't care about looks at all, as long as he was a scholar and they would be able to support him. Bad girls (herself, Faygie, Chaika) bemoaned their manless existence and wondered if all men had to have hairy chests. They were divided over whether they liked it or not. Esau had a lot of hair, Faygie pointed out. And you know how he turned out.

Faygie had it even harder than she, Batsheva thought. Her father was a butcher and she was his advertisement for being strictly kosher. She had to wear sleeves down to her wrists, winter and summer, and frumpy dresses that fell below her calves. But she would always roll up the skirts at the waist when parents and teachers weren't looking and push up the sleeves. They discussed for hours ways of getting around not wearing lipstick on the Sabbath. The reason you couldn't was because it would change the shape of the tube. If, however, before the Sabbath you put some on a piece of wax paper, you would be allowed to kiss the paper and get some color on your lips. But since the "good" boys were all hidden away behind the impenetrable walls of their yeshivahs, it was really all a waste of time anyway, they sighed.

But recently Faygie's father had arranged an "introduction" for her, and they had discussed it in feverish detail.

"What is it like?" Batsheva had begged her.

"My father brought him home and my mother served tea and cake. And first they talked to him and his parents alone. Then they brought me in and I sat across the table from him and our parents kind of walked into the living room and—"

"Left you alone with him!"

"Well, the door was open, but we could talk."

"What did you talk about?"

"First I have to tell you this." At the most dramatic junctures of life, Faygie always had to tell you a joke. It was maddening, but it allowed her to keep her sanity, Batsheva supposed.

"A boy is going to meet a girl and he is terrified so he asks his rebbe: 'What should I talk about?' So the rebbe says, 'My son, talk about food, family, and philosophy.' So he meets this girl and they sit there. He sort of hems and haws. So he finally asks, 'Do you like blintzes?' She shakes her head no. So he hems and haws and says, 'Do you have a brother?' Again, she shakes her head no. Then he flounders around and remembers—philosophy.

'If you had a brother, would he like blintzes?' Seriously, it was pretty boring. He told me what he was learning in Talmud. He talked and talked . . ."

"And that's all?" Batsheva had asked in terrible disappointment. But then she had brightened. It wasn't going to happen to her that way. It was going to be like Ursula and Birkin; like Mellors and Lady Chatterley; like Anna and Vronsky . . .

A small, invisible organ at the center of her body swore this to her, and she believed it with all of her heart.

Chapter three

Abraham Ha-Levi rested his weary forehead in his palm and sat in Batsheva's darkened room studying his sleeping daughter. He had just arrived back from the grueling twenty-hour trip between Tel Aviv and California. He was exhausted in body, but eager and fully awake in spirit. Exhilarated. He had crept in just for a moment to see her, as he used to when she was a baby to check if her breathing was all right. They took such tiny breaths when they were babies and at any moment they could stop.

He studied her calm, healthy sleep, untroubled by any past and warmed by dreams of a wonderful future. And why shouldn't she have such dreams? Hadn't he spoiled her, given her everything, given in to her every whim, fought for her against her teachers, who cautioned him against her wide-ranging reading, her constant visits to art museums, concerts? Bais Sarah was a conservative school, he had thought then, meant for girls with limited intelligence and little willpower. Girls who needed firm guidance every step of the way down the right path to Jewish wifehood and motherhood.

His Sheva, he had always believed, possessed the Ha-Levi insight and their natural piety. But now, knowing what he would be asking of her in the morning, he wondered if they had been right and he wrong. That tutor, that Elizabeth, had filled her head with a great deal of modern nonsense. But Sheva was attached to her and they were after all only studying English. But if she discussedd this arranged marriage with Elizabeth, there was no telling what he would have on his hands.

What if she refused outright to consider marriage now, any marriage? He knew she wanted to go back to school, to learn photography and other such foolishness.

Yes, he chewed on his lower lip, what if she outright refused? According to the Law, you couldn't force her to marry anyone. She was a free agent. No rabbi on earth would perform the ceremony knowing she was being forced into it. He looked at her wide childish brow, her sweet lips, like a small flower. He loved her more than his own life. She was everything to him.

But inside himself, he already felt a certain iron wall going up, a steel girder that enclosed his emotions, steeling him against his tender love for her. As sometimes God ruled with infinite compassion and mercy, and sometimes with stern, unbending justice, so must he, Abraham Ha-Levi, now take hold of his father's feelings and act like his own father would have expected him to.

He, the last remnant of the Ha-Levis' glorious two-hundred-year-old name and mission, must protect that heritage. It was no cruel irony that had given him that duty—*dafka* him, the rebellious son, the son who wanted to draw, to study art and medicine, the son who ran away from home to the university only to be brought back by his heartbroken father and mother. He had always known his lineage, the part he was expected to play, and he had always sought an escape. This was a gift, a way for him to do absolute repentance and redeem, finally, his father's and brothers' name. He had no choice, no choice at all.

And then, suddenly, looking at her face, his anguish was turned to joy. It was a woman's face, a child no longer! How had he missed that! She needed a husband, a home, children. It was a gift he came to give her now, the greatest of all the gifts he had ever bestowed upon her.

To have the greatest scholar of a generation as a husband—why, it would fill her with joy! She was so bright, he could teach her so much. And being a scholar, he would understand intuitively her needs, be sensitive and kind to her whims.

A smile crossed his lips. She was a lively little thing, so full of life. A man would take pleasure in that. And he, her father, would shower her with such gifts! No bride would ever begin life more elegantly, or with greater potential for happiness. How could a *goya*, a shiksa like Elizabeth, understand any of this?

Morning broke slowly. Batsheva stretched all her young limbs like a young cat delighted with its suppleness. She closed her eyes and said her morning prayers, then jumped out of bed when something caught her eye. There on the vanity was a package wrapped in silver paper with a large pink bow. It shone and twinkled as she laughingly twirled around the room with it, holding it up to the morning light. Aba was home! It must have come from him.

With delicate fingers she pried open the wrapping paper and found a glass-covered music box. Inside, a horse-drawn sleigh carried two lovers around and around a tiny village through ever-falling snow. It played "Lara's Theme" from *Dr Zhivago*. She thought of cold snows and of Anna on her way to the train station, then shook her head at her foolishness and ran out into the hall with the box.

She found him in the sunroom having just finished his morning prayers. She waited impatiently as he folded his prayer shawl and kissed his tefillin. The vision of him in his ritual garments subdued her somewhat and instead of running to him and flinging her arms around his waist, as she wanted, she walked to him sedately, lifting her forehead up for a kiss. Only her voice betrayed the overwhelming happiness she felt in seeing him.

"Welcome home, Aba, and thank you for the box. I love it!"

"You shouldn't use that word for a box, surely. You love me, your mother, God, and one day soon, very soon, a husband."

"Oh, Aba, what would I need with a husband?" She laughed merrily and saw his face blanch. "Aba?"

"It's nothing. Come. I must talk to you." He took her hand in his, her little, girlish hand, and stroked it as they walked out into the garden. She laid her head on his shoulder in a long-abandoned gesture of childish love.

"Sheva, you know something about the Ha-Levis, yes? But now I want to tell you something you don't know. I told you that your grandfather and uncles were scholars, but I didn't tell you that they were the heads of a two-hundred-year-old dynasty with thousands of followers all over the world who looked to them for guidance. I am the last Ha-Levi." He stopped, taking out a handkerchief to wipe the sudden sweat that came pouring down his forehead. "No, *you*, Sheva, are the last. I have been to Jerusalem to find the finest scholar in the Jewish world, a light, a giant of the generation to come. When he is found he will come here to meet you and you are to consider him as a bridegroom."

Batsheva stared at him. Her merry eyes searched his for a sign of levity, but there was none; for patience and understanding, but there was none. His eyes were a dark, unreadable whirlpool. She felt lost as she stared at him, at the strangeness of his kind eyes gone stern and unseeing.

She was frightened and confused, yet excited too. It was a man they were discussing. Marriage, yes, but also a man, a lover.

She turned, walking a little away from him. The flowers were in bloom, she thought, holding their heads up in the sharp sunlight like a living palette of colors. It was such a beautiful day and the flowers were so fresh and young and fragrant. If they could only stay that way forever, never changing. She was filled with an inexplicable terror, a sense of unbearable loss.

"Come, say something."

Her eyes filled with tears and she shook her head.

"Ach. I should have let your Ima speak to you." Old man, worried father, he sat down heavily on the garden seat. "Instead, I have botched it. Come to me, child."

She walked to him slowly, then knelt in confusion, laying her head in his lap. He stroked her head gently. "My dear child, my *tireh kindeleh*. You will decide, I promise you. No one will force you. And if he is not handsome and charming and a prince of a man, you will not be *allowed* to marry him, hear? You must give this a chance, this idea. It means so very much to me."

"It's just that—I did not think of marriage yet. I wanted to travel, to learn, to go to the seminary and the university . . ."

"You will do all these things." He stroked her head gently, with a soft, subtle pressure. "Do you think marriage means the end of life? Of course you shall do all these things, but as a free woman, a married woman with her own home. Who will tell you what to do then?"

His eyes had become human again. She hugged his legs and thought: Maybe they will take months, even years, to find him. She jumped up and twirled around, shaking her finger at her father in mockery. "I will have no fat men, no one with bad breath, no short men with glasses, no tall, skinny men." She thought of Vronsky.

"You must promise me one thing, and promise it truly."

She looked at him warily.

"You must promise to meet this man with an open mind."

"Elizabeth says people with an open mind get a lot of garbage thrown in . . ."

"Elizabeth, Elizabeth. You talk to her of such things?"

"She is my dearest, wisest friend."

He looked at her craftily, his hands in conference, drumming against each other, and thought: We will have to have a little talk, Elizabeth and I.

The rest of the day was one of total chaos for her. Her feelings made her want to laugh and cry, to shout with joy and fury at the same time. But each time her anger took over she thought of her father's eyes, the eyes she had seen watch over her every need with such love ever since she could remember. He would never do anything to hurt her. Aba could never . . . But then she thought of the way his eyes had changed and clouded over like a stranger's when he said: "You are to consider him as a bridegroom."

A tiny seed of fear sprouted in her stomach. What if she did not like him? And worse, what if she did! She did not want to leave her home. But then again, it meant travel, adventure! And a lover.

She ran to her room and closed the door, looking at herself in the mirror. Slowly, she took all the pins from her hair and let it cascade down over her breasts and back. She took up her silver brush and gazed into her eyes, brushing with long, sensuous, dreamy fingers.

"Sit down, sit down, my dear."

Elizabeth dutifully smoothed her pleated dress beneath her. I look like an MBA student. Dressed for success with closed-toe shoes, little silk bow tie. She had no idea what Ha-Levi wanted, but she decided to treat the royal summons seriously. Where there was wealth, there was power, right? No need to tweak your nose at that if you were a poor country girl.

"How long has it been since you began tutoring Sheva?"

"Nearly four years, sir."

"Ah, such a long time. I hadn't realized . . ." He got up and paced, his hands behind his back, his head bent forward in concentration. "And what exactly do you tutor her in?"

"Grammar and English literature."

"What kind of literature?"

Was that a threat, a challenge? Maybe not. "Well, it's been rather eclectic, I'm afraid. Everything from Shakespeare to Forster, Conrad, and Lawrence." Oops, shouldn't have mentioned Lawrence. People only remembered Lady Chatterley when you said Lawrence, even though that was one of his worst books and not particularly interesting either. She waited a little tensely for his response.

"A little risqué, no, for a sheltered child like Sheva?"

"We didn't do the controversial books. Just the classics."

Suddenly, he sat down in a chair beside her, his eyes peering intently into her own. "You don't very much approve of the way we live, or how we treat Sheva, do you?"

She swallowed hard, then took a deep breath. "I don't understand it. I don't think it's natural for a teenager like Sheva to be so isolated and restricted."

He smiled and she relaxed her grip on the chair. "Of course you don't. How could you? We do not live as Americans. We follow the path of our ancestors. We live in the community, but are not part of it. We isolate ourselves in order to fulfill a different destiny, to preserve something very precious. You can understand that, can't you?"

"Yes, but there has to be a balance between preserving the past and living in the present. I can't see how a little fun, a few dates to the movies, could hurt your daughter."

His brows knitted together. Uh-oh. Couldn't leave well enough alone, could you, Liz? she thought. But so what. That was the truth.

"You don't understand. You play at love. You find partners

in supermarkets or classrooms, knowing nothing about their families, their beliefs, their commitments. That is all right if your own life is so vague . . ." He got up with a sudden energy that frightened her and went to look out of the window. "I was born in a small town in Poland. My father and his father and his father before him were considered saints. They had thousands of followers that came from all over Europe to eat at our table, to have a private audience with them. Their existence was not an accident, but a linked chain that went back to Sinai. Any break in the chain, and we perish for all time." He paused, searching her face kindly.

"I was like you once. I believed in Western values: freedom for the individual above all and family and heritage and custom be damned. I was in Warsaw at the university when Hitler took over. Studying art. I did not want to be a link in a chain, but only myself. The Nazis, they understood about the chain and the links. They believed in it and wanted to destroy it. The SS surrounded my father's house and marched everyone into the synagogue. They poured kerosene around the building and set it on fire. They waited outside to shoot anyone who came screaming out, anyone who tried to quench the fire by rolling on the ground. Do you know why I am alive? Because I ran away from my family. And because I ran away, God has made me the last link, you see. That is God's sense of humor. So you see, we are not free to choose our fate. There is a yoke to be borne and freedom is only an illusion. I am not free. God has put me here on earth for a reason. He has chosen Batsheva to be the next link in the chain."

Elizabeth cleared her throat, fascinated and appalled at the story. And for one of the few times in her life, speechless.

He looked over at her and smiled. "So why, the young American college girl is asking herself, why does this old man tell me such terrible stories? What does this have to do with me? I will tell you. Batsheva thinks very highly of you. She is young and impressionable and you are, she thinks, a woman of the world, a mentor."

"I hope a good one."

"That is why you are here now, listening to the rantings of an old man. You must be a good one. Everything depends upon it. I am arranging a marriage for Batsheva in Jerusalem with the kind of person needed to carry on our family. I have just told her about it and she is a little shocked. She will no doubt tell you all about it and ask your advice."

"Now, wait a minute. I just teach the child stories . . ."

"Let us not fool each other, my dear Miss Elizabeth. You have her trust, more than a parent. I am not asking you to understand and approve of how we live, just not to sabotage my efforts."

"It will be difficult for me not to express an opinion, and I cannot lie." Ah, that felt wonderful.

He nodded approvingly. "I am glad to hear that, because I need to believe that you are honest, trustworthy." He sat down behind his desk and took out a checkbook. "My daughter tells me you are planning a trip to England to continue your studies at Cambridge?"

"I am waiting to hear about a scholarship." Her eyes followed his poised pen intently.

"And when would you need to leave for this term of study?"

"As soon as possible. As soon as I hear about my grant."

"Would ten thousand dollars be enough to tide you over? No, perhaps fifteen thousand with all the extra expenses. A graduation gift, let us call it."

He wrote rapidly, a small smile lurking in the corners of his mouth. "I guess you will be able to leave soon. This week, no?"

She stood up and held her open palms against her cheeks. They felt so hot, burning with anger and embarrassment.

"You have a beautiful daughter, Mr Ha-Levi. I would not want to hurt you or her in any way."

"Of course not, my dear, of course not."

I ought to say: "Please do not cheapen this discussion by trying to bribe me." That's what they say in the movies, in books. But I may not get that scholarship. And Graham MacLeish, who had indeed shown up at Fat Henry's with a bottle of champagne and a teenager he had introduced as his visiting daughter, had made his apologies and said that wasn't it a wonderful coincidence that he would be guest lecturing at Cambridge next year, and wouldn't it be wonderful if her scholarship came through.

She cashed the check the next day and called Batsheva from the airport that same night. "If you need me, write. I'll be there for you." Liar and hypocrite.

Chapter four

Israel's major airport, Ben Gurion, is a tiny place by international standards, but one of unmatched variety. There you will find groups of Arabs with red or black kaffiyehs wrapped around their heads, sitting next to black Abyssinian priests and Hassidim in fur-trimmed hats and white stockings. There, too, are the Israelis returning from New York, Los Angeles, Rome, and Paris, outlandishly dressed and beaming from the heavy load of suitcases that bulge with mysterious and wonderful surprises, like the pockets of a small boy.

And always, as in any international airport in the world, there is the endless stream of exotic, seductively dressed women, who bring the pungent swish of nylon stockings, the heady mixture of expensive and cheap perfume, the inviting click of high heels down a long corridor.

Isaac Meyer Harshen—waiting to board the 7 P.M. TWA flight to New York and from there the connecting flight to Los Angeles—saw, heard, and smelled none of this. Nor was he conscious of the women who briefly turned their heads to smile at him, or simply to stare.

It was his height that was the initial attraction. His long legs and slim, aristocratic body that even the plain black suit (battle fatigues of the army of the faithful) could not hide, made him an exceptionally attractive man. His hair was thick and dark and curly with small *payot* over his ears. His face was narrow, but distinguished-looking, with large, serious dark eyes and lashes extravagantly thick for a man. His short beard was a dark brown and neatly trimmed to reveal full, sensitive lips. His hands, too, were elegant, with long white fingers and immaculately clean nails.

He was totally unaware of the effect he had upon women. Indeed, had Isaac Harshen had the least consciousness of those who stopped to regard him with interest, he would have looked up immediately from the Talmud he was immersed in, pursed his lips in disdain, and whispered: *prutzas*. Whores.

Isaac Meyer had never been out of Israel before. As a matter of fact, except for several trips to visit other yeshivoth in Bnei Brak, or to pray at the graves of saints in Hebron, Bethlehem, Safad, and Tiberias, he had hardly been out of Jerusalem. Ever since his father had wrapped him in a prayer shawl at the age of three and delivered him to the rebbes at the *heder*, he had followed a straight and narrow path from his home in Meah Shearim to the yeshivah and back again, with few detours.

He had never listened to radio broadcasts, even the news, because it might taint his purity of thought; and a television, which did even more to excite the imagination, was completely *treife*, full—he had heard—of lewdness and all kinds of evil temptations, as were movies, concerts, plays, museums, and all other places where men and women were allowed to mingle freely, leading to adultery and all kinds of looseness. This was the clear opinion of the men who taught him and brought him up and he had never had either the inclination or the courage to question it.

His rebellions had been brief and swiftly crushed. He had

not liked the first day in *heder*, although the rebbe had tried to ply him with sweets, to sing and dance with him. He had wanted his mother and had cried for her. But, slowly, he had given up hope and understood that he must repress his feelings and soon his mother would come back to him. But she never did really. Not completely.

From then on he was surrounded by a world of somber, bearded men: his father, uncles, grandfathers. They had taken him and shaved off all his long curls and left him only two long ones at the temples for *payot*. The stubble of his scalp had itched and itched until it grew in.

And all day, from 7 A.M. until 5 or 6 P.M., he spent bent over his books in the sunless classroom, endlessly repeating in monotonous rote the *aleph-bais*, the prayers, the words of the holy Torah. Until second grade he had rebelled in his heart and spent hours looking out of the window into the street, watching the men and the pretty women passing by.

But then a new teacher entered his life.

"You are wasting time for which you are accountable to your Creator, Isaac Meyer," the teacher told him, pinching his ear and leading him to the corner as the children around him pointed and stared. "A person who passes by a tree and looks up to say 'What a beautiful tree' is deserving of death," his teacher told him, "because he is wasting valuable time for learning Torah."

The teacher had a long stick that reached far. It smashed the nails of those whose attention wandered even for a second. It poked the ribs of those who prayed too quickly, without the proper concentration and devotion. It tore welts into the backsides of those whose speech included impure words. Even Hebrew was not allowed to be spoken, the language of the land. It was the language of the Zionists, the unholy men who had degraded the language of the Bible into a street language. They spoke in Yiddish, studied in Yiddish.

He was afraid of the stick and desperately craved approval from his teachers, his parents, the other children. And then, suddenly, quite by accident, he asked a question that the teachers did not know the answer to. They looked at him in wonder. They called in the principal, and then the principal called his parents. They called him a *gaon*, a brilliant light of the generation. He began to study day and long into the night, always searching for better questions, but sometimes coming across wonderful answers.

And then he began to learn things by heart and found it very easy. It created a picture in his mind that he could call up at any moment. He could tell on what page and what part of the page of an eight-hundred-page volume a particular passage could be located. Soon he had learned every page in all twenty volumes of the Talmud by heart, as well as those in many hundreds of books of commentaries.

His teachers treated him with awed respect and solemnly discussed what should be done with his education when he reached his Bar Mitzvah. It was decided that he be entered in the city's most difficult and exacting Talmudical academy under the direct supervision of Reb Avigdor, himself a widely revered scholar, author of many original commentaries upon the Talmud.

Under Reb Avigdor, his learning knew no bounds. He learned to use not only his memory, but also his perception and creativity, to make intuitive leaps of understanding between tractates to infer the solution to difficult points of law. Most of all, he learned to respect the letter of the law, dedicating himself to weighing the minutiae of Talmudical exegesis the way one weighs diamonds: If a man hires the donkey of another man to deliver a load of hay and he uses it instead to deliver figs and the donkey falls down and breaks its leg, destroying the load, who must pay? The donkey's owner, or the one who rented it, and how much should the damages be, and on what grounds . . . ?

At thirteen, he grew lip hair, and his voice began to change.

Inside, he felt an uncontrollable longing he didn't understand. He looked at pictures in the street of movie marquees with women in long clinging dresses in the arms of handsome men. He began to study the way the cloth clung to the bodies in the pictures, going over each detail at night in bed until the unthinkable happened. Then, full of guilt and apprehension, he would devise punishments for himself. Sometimes he would say psalms all day, and sometimes immerse himself in a cold *mikvah* in the morning, before the water was heated up for the day. It became pure torture to walk in the street, to be near women. He averted his eyes from them, as he was taught, so as not to let his *yetzer harah*, his Evil Inclination, rule him. It was as if an angel and devil struggled over his soul every minute of the day. Then, after years of repression, it became unexpectedly a little easier for him as he developed a fine sense of contempt for both his weakness and the women that aroused it. They were *prutzas*, or other men's wives, or those who would one day be other men's wives. Off limits even to look at. The dropping of his eyes, the fearful pounding of his heart, the almost hatred of himself for his longing, eventually became his habitual reaction to any woman who was not a close relative. His emotions, constantly and cruelly cut back like the shoots of living grasses, finally began to wither and to send out shoots no more. All his affection, his tenderness, he poured out into his studies and toward the old men who were his teachers and guides. Each word they uttered he wrote down like a lover, to pore over in private in order to extract the greatest joy and meaning from it. The teachers and their words—only they would give him eternal life. Everything else was chaff.

And so he had almost ceased to think of women entirely by the time he was twenty-three years old and Reb Avigdor approached him with the heady news about Abraham Ha-Levi's visit and the search for a bridegroom for Batsheva. He knew he needed a wife. The Torah commanded one to "be fruitful and multiply." He needed at least four children, two boys and two girls to fulfill this *mitzvah*. Also, vaguely, he understood that in order to keep learning, he must have some form of livelihood that either a working wife or a father-in-law would provide.

But now, actually on his way to meet his future bride (for so she would be, he had no doubt, if it was *Beshert*, if God decreed), he gave some thought to what he expected in a wife. If he had been before a congregation, or in front of a classroom, he would have phrased it thus: The only purpose in life for a true daughter of Israel was to bear Jewish children and to make it possible for her husband to learn. Whatever sacrifice a true daughter wishes and is fit to make to advance these two goals, was fitting. When a woman prayed to thank God for making her according to His will (just as a man prayed each morning, thanking God for not making him a woman), she prayed to be able to bear as many children as possible and to take every burden off her husband so that he might increase his learning. Of course this was difficult for the woman, but life was no easier for her mate. Man was made by God to be the scholar, while woman's intelligence was given only to lighten his heavy load of Torah learning by being the wage-earner, cooking, cleaning, raising the children and keeping them disciplined and quiet. He knew nothing about the inner workings of a woman's mind or heart, having only the stern example of his mother and sisters to learn from. And their narrow but not unhappy existence taught him this: that a pious daughter of Israel yearned and strove only to see her husband succeed in his studies. What other happiness was there for her aside from that and bringing children into the world? And if her joyous good fortune in life was to be the partner of a gifted *talmid chacham*, a Torah scholar, she would consider herself the most fortunate of women because in no other way could she ever have any stature in the World to Come.

He went to the bathroom and washed his hands. Being

face-to-face with the ordinary people of the twentieth century made him feel contaminated, physically soiled. He looked at himself in the mirror, wishing his beard was already flecked with the gray of age. Only then would he get the total respect he craved. Only then would all his ideas be taken with total seriousness, not questioned as they were now by teachers and colleagues. The long, pointed stick of his rebbe was internalized now and he used it more mercilessly than his teacher ever had, beating himself into submission to some impossible ideal born of constant moral lectures on man's need to improve himself. I must hurry, he thought. He was always in a hurry. The yeshivah taught one not to waste precious time. But often it became just a hurry sickness, an irrational anxiety. He hurried to escape his thoughts, to escape his worries. He hurried without reason or goal. But most of all he hurried to get away from himself, from his deepest fears, fears so terrible he could not face them. And what Isaac Meyer Harshen feared most was that he was a hypocrite and, ultimately, an unbeliever who did not think that God could search the depths of his soul, in which was hidden this fact. He understood this sin, but intransigently refused to repent. In pure fact, this was the one thing that helped him to maintain his sanity, the arrogance of his independence. On the outside, he kept every shred of law and custom. But in his heart he felt the dark, secret joy of doubt. To that part of his conscience no pointed stick had ever been able to penetrate. He washed his hands again and went out to join his rebbe.

Reb Avigdor, his teacher and mentor, was a man esteemed throughout the Jewish world as a final authority on many ritual matters. He admired Reb Avigdor with all his heart, but did not understand him always. Spending Shabbat with him, he would be startled to find the sage rising early to help his wife set the table for lunch. Other times, Reb Avigdor would say he had to leave early because he had promised his wife to help with the cleaning. The students would look at each other in amazement and search for the hidden, Kabbalistic meaning of such behavior, never dreaming that the simple truth, openly revealed, was all there was. Reb Avigdor had been asked to accompany Isaac to America. Unlike his student, he sat in the airport looking around him with a child's wonder and simple pleasure. He had never been out of the country before, never been on a plane. He looked over the different kinds of people, averting his eyes from the most obviously immodest women, but enjoying the colors and sounds, the newness of experience. He regretted that his wife was not with him, knowing that she would have much of value to say about it all. He liked to talk to her because he firmly believed she was so much wiser than he. His open, cheerful face contracted a little, thinking about their last conversation. He had discussed this match with her and she had shaken her head.

"The girl has seen too much. She is not like the girls of Meah Shearim."

"But," he had argued, "she is the daughter of Abraham Ha-Levi, Reb Yerachmiel's granddaughter."

"For all that, she is a rich American girl."

The words weighed on him somewhat, but he would have to leave that in God's hands. He was only the messenger. And truthfully, it was not the girl who worried him. Women were naturally pure souls, on so much higher a spiritual plane to begin with than men. That was why they needed fewer commandments to mold their character. They didn't need to pray three times a day, or wear tefillin. Men were made of coarser matter that needed constant prodding, constant reminders that they were the possessor of a holy soul formed in the image of God.

No. What worried him was Isaac.

What kind of man asks nothing of the physical appearance of a future bride? Who asked only if she was pious and Godfearing? Could it be that such a young man could have reached such a high spiritual level that he was beyond such petty thoughts of outer beauty? It was awesome. And yet, a small doubt crept into Reb Avigdor's heart. Awesome and completely against man's nature. He had often had misgivings about this most brilliant of his students. A mind that was a gift from heaven. Such retention and clarity! Truly, a gift from God to this generation, to make up for the scholars wiped out in the Holocaust by the most bestial of men. But his heart? Where was his heart? Other students came to him confessing their desires for love, for intimacy, for wealth and power. But Isaac confessed only one thing, asked for guidance for only one thing: I have wasted time today instead of studying Torah. How might I spend more time studying Torah, increase my concentration, my insight and understanding? He was a pure flame of consciousness that seemed to live on the oxygen of scholarship. Almost incorporeal, so little did he allow his bodily desires. He took no vacations, no side trips to sightsee or bathe in the sea, as did the other students. But he was a constant presence, a fixture in the study hall.

His parents, seventh-generation Jerusalemites, were thrilled about the match, which had everything such parents dreamed of: *yichus*—the right family, and material wealth that would take the burden of years of support off their shoulders. They had three daughters and thus three sons-in-law they needed to support with down payments for apartments and food money.

Also, they had begun to worry about Isaac's seeming lack of interest in a *shidduch*, a match. Once he had even broached the subject of being on such a high spiritual level he could not marry at all, making them both ill with worry. If he did not marry there would be no grandchildren, and no generous father-in-law.

So Reb Avigdor had kept his misgivings to himself, accepting the role of messenger from his friend and teacher, Reb Magnes. As it was written: Forty days before conception, a *bas kol* goes out from heaven that decrees, "This man is destined to marry this woman." It was not for him to decide.

Chapter five

The week before Isaac Meyer Harshen's arrival was spent in a frenzy of shopping. Batsheva and her mother took the limousine to Rodeo Drive and bought clothes, hats, and shoes. The storekeepers recognized the Ha-Levis and did not waste their time. They brought out only the most modest clothes: dresses with high necks and at least elbow-length sleeves; no pants, or, heaven forbid, jumpsuits. The clothes were all of the most exquisite materials—pure silks, wonderful cashmeres, satin moirés, angoras. They knew Mrs Ha-Levi's style, like Queen Elizabeth's, ran to frumpy belted dresses with matching hats that tended to emphasize her plumpness. But the fashionable pencil-thin saleswomen had learned to flatter her nevertheless in whatever choice she made.

If the elder Ha-Levi was the queen, they took solace that Batsheva was Lady Di. What an exquisite body! Even in stores that catered to movie starlets, producers' mistresses, and models, she glittered like some rare tropical bird. She had an unerring eye for color and style. She always chose jewel colors—ruby reds, emerald greens, lapis. She was like a piece of polished crystal that sparkled, from her shining black hair to her white, even teeth, to the sheen of her lovely, healthy skin. Often they had tried to find a color to match her eyes, but it was impossible. There was no such color.

The elegant saleswomen gave her a grudging admiration, too, for the way she handled the producers, casting agents, and directors who inevitably came up to her with propositions, decent and indecent. Grudging, because they thought she was foolish not to follow through, as they would have in a moment.

Yet there was something very fine about the girl, they thought, something very genuine. This was rare in Tinsel Town, where everything was a fake. It began with the movie lots that created fake floods and earthquakes and filtered down into the most intimate conversation between man and wife. Feigned friendship and sycophantic praise hid boredom, contempt, and real malice. Hypocrisy and falseness were the name of the game, and this girl was so real. Her modesty was real, her beauty was real, her sensitivity and kindness were real, for often she would buy something she didn't really want to compensate a saleswoman for a long, unsuccessful session of try-ons.

Batsheva looked long and hard into the mirror, but always discarded the dresses. They were not right. The dress he must see her in for the first time must be perfect, perfect. It must say all she wanted but dared not, there in front of his rebbe and her parents. It must speak of her youth and innocence and beauty and hint of her terrible longing for him. It must fill her with power to choose him if she wished. The choice must be fully in her hands. He must be rendered almost helpless. She must be able to make him love her, if she wished. In the month that had passed since her conversation with her father in the garden, she had begun to get used to the idea of a husband. It was just a lover really. It was a man you would be wholly connected to, whose body, mind, heart, and soul would intertwine with your own in a beautiful, irrevocable intimacy.

"Try one more," the saleswoman suggested wearily.

Batsheva undressed slowly. She would have freedom as a married woman from her parents, her teachers. She would read whatever she pleased, draw, travel, dress. Like an adult, she would make her own choices. The life of a religious Jewish girl was so narrow and circumscribed by a million prohibitions—not the Law, but social conventions all meant to keep her in line. One could not go alone on the bus, or travel without a chaperon, except up and back to school, and even then she was escorted to the plane by her parents and picked up by the family with whom she boarded. Even on Simchat Torah, when the synagogue was filled with joyous dancing, one could not join a circle of other girls and dance with abandon, but only sit behind the curtain and watch the men dance and enjoy themselves. It was vicarious pleasure. What you read was scrutinized carefully. Would Shakespeare impinge on your purity, fill your head with lewdness and nonsense? Never mind D. H. Lawrence.

And she loved Lawrence. No one could understand that he was such a prude, such a moralist. Married all those years to his fat Frieda. Lawrence believed in passion, in having every fiber of one's being caught up in passion. He believed in honest passion devoid of social conventions and thought it was a purely good thing that connected men and women, that it was a holy connection.

Batsheva trusted him and believed that was the truth. When a man and woman married, nothing they did together had any shame or immodesty. It was all in the name of God. There was fruitfulness and joy in it, and it followed the Creator's own plan for continuing the human race. It was a commandment, a *mitzvah*. In fact, she knew that a husband was obligated to fulfill his wife's sexual needs, or she had valid grounds for divorce.

And she had remembered learning that one was held accountable in the World to Come for not having enjoyed all the permissible pleasures of this world.

She looked at herself undressed in the mirror. What value did her soft shoulders, her firm breasts with their deep cleavage, have unseen? What value her long slim thighs, her shapely calves and tapering ankles? Like a flower on the summit of a mountain never climbed by man, did its beauty even exist at all unseen? It could have no value, no meaning, until it was given over to the appreciative hands and lips of a lover.

She looked at the dress the saleswoman had brought in. It was silver, a soft silver-blue silk that fell in a graceful straight line until her thighs, then dropped in small pleats. As she walked out of the dressing room, the saleswomen stopped talking and stared. A modest little dress, who would have believed it? It had long sleeves, a high neck, revealing nothing. Yet it revealed everything about the girl beneath, hinting at her fragile young slenderness, her deep-breasted womanliness, her fertile willing hips. And when you were all through digesting that information, its color directed you toward the unbelievable eyes, eyes full of promise, of maidenly shyness and hidden passion.

Batsheva saw in the eyes of the men and women in the store who stared at her the confirmation she had been seeking. Yes, she said, I'll take it.

Mrs Ha-Levi stood watching her daughter and caught her breath. She could not believe this was really her child. She was like the expensive paintings and fine silver and crystal that filled what she couldn't help thinking of as her husband's house. As she viewed those objects like a visitor in a museum, so she viewed Batsheva as being his child. She saw nothing of herself in so exquisite a creature.

Even when she had thought Abraham Ha-Levi just a bricklayer, she had still thought him too good for her. For he had always been a fine, distinguished figure of a man while she had never been more than a shy, rather plain butcher's daughter with blood on her hands from helping in the store.

As a young girl, she had often cried into her pillow imagining a future married to a man such as her father, tied to a butcher shop or a grocery, growing gray and fat behind a counter serving demanding housewives. She could never see any beauty in her face or body that should single her out for a different fate. And yet, strangers had often told her father she was beautiful. Her hair had been black, though now it was salted with gray, and her middle-aged body had once been softly rounded and inviting.

And when her husband had revealed his lineage to her, it had cast a permanent state of anxiety over her life. She almost felt it would be just and fitting for him to leave her for the kind of woman he should have married in the first place: the fine daughter of a prominent rabbinical family with wealth, scholarship, beauty, accomplishments, and manners. She had nothing.

Always quiet and shy, passionately in love with her husband, she had faded into a shadow since the wealth and the revelation of the Ha-Levi dynasty. She redoubled her efficiency as a housekeeper and manager, subconsciously hoping to prove her usefulness and be kept on a little longer.

Thus, when her husband had announced his plans for Batsheva without discussing it with her, she did not resent it, nor did she feel she had a right to interfere. She was merely a spectator, part of the household help, and she was grateful to be that. The only time she had ever felt like a true wife was when she gave birth. She could not bear to think of the babies lost to her. It was God's will and she accepted it. She thought only of Batsheva, her perfect child, full of life and beauty, created in partnership with God and her husband. She remembered the last pregnancy, so full of hope . . . But then late in the fifth month the fetus had suddenly died. It had been a boy and having him removed from her body had destroyed all possibility of bearing other children.

Abraham had never blamed her, but she felt in her heart it was her fault. If only her body had been more perfect, her soul more deserving . . . And now only Batsheva was left, her only insurance for her husband's love. As Batsheva's mother, she had accomplished something. But the girl was so far from her. She could read complicated books and take wonderful pictures and play the piano! She dared to talk to Abraham Ha-Levi as an equal, discussing the Talmud and Mishnah with him, actually arguing with him! Disagreeing with him! It made her so proud, even frightened.

She did not want to think of this marriage in Jerusalem. She would lose the girl altogether now, even the little bit that remained, the physical closeness, the small talk.

What kind of man would satisfy this spoiled, beautiful, intelligent child, she wondered. She would have her own way in everything, like her father. Neither teachers, nor parents, nor rabbis had been able to do more than guide her reluctant steps down the right roads, and she had kicked and screamed and protested all the way. But she was just a child, a headstrong child. Had she grown up enough to understand what marriage meant? One traded one's father's rule for one's husband's rule. There was no in-between period when you were totally free, the way American girls were during college. Marriage was the beginning of the most serious business in a woman's life. There was her greatest joy in building a home and family that would be pleasing in the eyes of the Creator. Yet it was full of pain, too—childbirth and molding yourself to your husband's will. A part of you had to die to be reborn as a wife. You had to carve away those parts of yourself that did not fit in with your husband so as to form two parts of a perfect whole. Had anyone suggested to Mrs Ha-Levi that the man could also do some carving, she would have gnawed her lip in surprise and consternation, considering such a thing for the first time, and probably discarding it as unholy and highly improbable.

She closed her eyes and prayed that God would, by some miracle, allow the man her husband had chosen to be the right man for Batsheva.

Holding her breath, Batsheva pulled back the delicate French lace curtains of her room and watched the silver Rolls-Royce drive through the black-and-silver gates of the Ha-Levis' long palm-lined driveway. The butler hurried to open the front door as the chauffeur bowed slightly, opening the passenger door. She saw one man get out and her heart fell inside her like a stone. He is so old! So short! But then she remembered there would be two men and let out a long sigh of relief.

She watched amused as the older man lifted his head in wonder at the white mansion's tall Doric columns. He has a nice fatherly face, she decided. Next her father got out. Her stomach was tingling, almost sick with anticipation. She bit her lower lip so hard it began to bleed. There, one foot out . . .

"Shevi darling . . ."

Oh no, Ima! Of all the terrible timing. She let the curtain fall and hurried to sit down by her bed, taking up a magazine in her shaking hand. Her mother smiled at her and beckoned to the window and then they both laughed and hugged each other, their arms intertwined, their faces full of childish excitement.

She could not see what he was, just what he was not. Not short, thank Hashem, not fat. Dark (like Vronsky!). His clothes fit well, though he looked like a typical Hassid.

She hugged her mother. "When will I speak to him?"

"He has had a terribly long flight. We must let him rest so that he will be fresh and ready for you, difficult child!"

She threw herself petulantly on the bed. "I want to see him now! I won't live until dinner. I shall die of curiosity!" But she saw that there was nothing to be done.

The afternoon passed like an eternity. At four she took a long, luxurious bath full of expensive bubbled perfume and sweet oils and thought of the Book of Esther: "And they anointed themselves with sweet oil for six months . . ." Imagine! At five she patted herself dry and put on new silk undergarments, and finally, she pulled the silver silk over her head and let her hair fall free. No, she would not pin it up! He must see her like this, with only a silver ribbon to hold it back from her face. She pulled silver stockings over the long, smooth stretch of her calf and thigh and slipped into shoes that looked almost like lacy silver filigree. The mirror shone back at her. Never had she looked more ravishing, more innocent, or more desirable. At least, that was what she told herself. But she was not a man! How could she know, really, finally, how she would look to him?

It took all her courage to descend the long staircase with slow dignity while her trembling hand clutched the banister and her heart pounded foolishly. There at the bottom stood her parents and two strange men. The short fatherly one and a tall dark one. As she reached the first landing, the tall one suddenly looked up, and their eyes met for the first time.

She stopped and held her breath, lowering her eyes in confusion. His dark eyes, glimpsed for a fraction of a second, gave her a blank canvas on which to paint with all the colors of her imagination. Eyes full of hidden passion, she told herself. Adoring eyes, smitten eyes, so sharp and clear that they seemed to cut through her, reaching in after her hidden thoughts so that she felt almost physically violated. To her great mortification, she felt a hot blush spread from her forehead to her cheeks.

There were introductions, and some laughter, and much awkwardness on all sides, and all the while her heart felt heavy with hidden secrets. She almost did not dare to look at him, so afraid was she of his scrutiny. Yet during dinner, seated across from him, she waited for his attention to be drawn to his rebbe or her father in answering the difficult questions of Talmudical interpretation they posed for him, and then, with his eyes busy elsewhere, she studied him, finishing the blank canvas she had begun earlier, filling in all details to her satisfaction.

He had a handsome head, she thought, wondering how the thick curls would feel if you ran your fingers through them. Kinky or soft? And his beard, how would that feel on your face, brushing over your cheek? His long aristocratic face, half hidden by the dark curly beard, nevertheless seemed pale and fraught with seriousness. She felt humble thinking of the lofty thoughts, the immense scholarship, that must weigh upon him. To know so much was wonderful. She, who felt she knew so very little, admired that more than anything. He would be a wonderful teacher, too, she imagined, with his troubled, caring eyes and delicate hands. He would be a leader, with his powerful shoulders, his clear, penetrating gaze.

His eyes, she told herself, had seen the mysteries of the Torah, the very mysteries of the Kabbalah. He had been on that treacherous journey to the center of truth hidden to most people because of their ignorance and cowardice. He had been there, she would swear it. She could tell by his eyes that mirrored his magnificent soul. He would be able to lead her there, step by step.

Her eyes focused on his hands. So white and long and fine. She wondered how these hands would feel, those gentle, understanding hands. Wondered how it would be to touch those hands, to have them smooth her hair back, to touch the small of her back. All through dinner she heard almost nothing, smiling uncertainly, hoping the pounding of her heart would not sound as loud to others as it did to her. But then after dessert her parents got up with Reb Avigdor and just disappeared, leaving her alone with Isaac.

It was an awkward, almost terrifying moment. She was afraid he would read her thoughts, and if he did, she might just as well die. He got up and smiled pleasantly and began to ask her questions in Yiddish. She was startled. Yiddish! But of course, his English was almost nonexistent and Hebrew was the holy tongue not to be used for everyday conversation. She knew so little Yiddish, just what she understood from her teachers and from the private conversations of her parents.

"I must answer you in Hebrew or English, Isaac," she explained, feeling stupid and inadequate. He nodded sharply and she interpreted it to mean, very well, we will make allowances. What had she studied most recently in school, he wanted to know. "Secular studies, and the Book of Kings, the Book of Ruth, and Deuteronomy with the commentaries of Rashi, Rambam, and Ramban." He nodded approvingly. "And privately, I have been tutored in Mishnah and Talmud." He looked at her sharply, with disbelief and disapproval.

"It is not the custom to teach women Talmud."

She was not sure he had said that. Actually, she was sure, but she couldn't, didn't want to, believe it. It poured such cold water over everything. Perhaps he didn't understand that it was all right, her father approved. "But I enjoyed it and benefited from it."

There was a moment of silence while Isaac Meyer Harshen looked over Batsheva Ha-Levi. What he should tell her, it occurred to him, was that women were not given the intelligence to study the Talmud as it was supposed to be learned. Their minds were too flighty and inconstant. But most important, women had other things to do that were their role in life—and learning Talmud wasn't one of them. Isaac, a product of his environment and education, was not naturally bigoted or insensitive. He sensed very clearly that if he should tell this particular woman his philosophy of the division of labor between the sexes, woman's role in life, her limitations and responsibilities, the wondrous eyes that sought his now with such shy interest would cloud over with resentment and irritation.

Orthodox Jews believe that each human being is possessed of a good and an evil inclination that stand like close friends beside one every minute of one's life. At every crossroad in life, they are there, pushing in one direction or another, advocating the long difficult road to heaven or the short, pleasant one to hell. At every turn, they whisper advice that a man may heed or disregard, thus deciding his own fate.

At this moment then, Isaac Meyer Harshen's Evil Inclination, so long suppressed and trod upon by his strong conscience and the power of his vast knowledge, suddenly breathed fresh oxygen and sprang up with unbridled strength at his side.

He had never seen a woman like Batsheva and had no knowledge that such a creature could exist. She made him think of Esther, the matchlessly beautiful Jewish girl chosen as queen by the king of Persia over every other woman in the kingdom; or Rachel, for whom Jacob had worked fourteen years and they had seemed "but a few days" because of his love for her. Honestly, he didn't give a damn what her views on study were, her views on anything. He was lost in her eyes, in the beauty of her body, her glistening hair and skin. And, though it was an unworthy thought, he considered how much material comfort she would bring him as a dowry. He would never have to worry about money again. But most of all, he thought of her as the successor to the Ha-Levi dynasty, a position of such power and prestige in the Jewish world, a position he would step into because of her with unquestioned authority. It would give him enormous power, power he, of course, would exercise with the greatest care.

He saw her exquisite face looking up at him with a puzzled look, waiting for his answer. Almost against his will, a smile flashed across his face and she saw his eyes glance over her body. "It doesn't matter, then, if you enjoy it." She relaxed and smiled back, glad to have been mistaken.

He made her feel so shy, so young and ignorant. But he

was kind about her mistakes in Yiddish. He seemed so pleased with everything she told him. She loved to take photographs, to play the piano, to read everything and take long, wonderful nature hikes in the hills. She revealed everything to him. How she planned to travel and study and pursue her photography as an art. And all the while he sat watching her attentively, his eyes keeping hers captive, looking, she thought, into her soul, approving everything he saw there.

Actually, Isaac Harshen, at that moment, was not the least bit interested in Batsheva Ha-Levi's soul. He looked at her beauty, at the the fine carving on the chair that framed the back of her head, and beyond at the man who was the last of the Ha-Levis. He let her speak on, telling himself that she was a young, innocent creature who needed guidance. But this was not the time for it. Instruction could and would come later. It would be harsh and unrelenting, as he had experienced all instruction must be. She would no doubt suffer, as he had suffered. But in the end, she would arrive at a much higher spiritual plane, and she would view him as a husband, a teacher, and a benefactor. But now was not the time to talk of these things, a voice whispered to him and he felt himself mightily propelled down a definite road by a strong, implacable force. He smiled at Batsheva, smiled and said nothing.

The week passed with incredible, breathtaking swiftness. There were long walks in the garden, trips to Disneyland and Universal Studios. Hikes in the mountains. It was almost as if she had found a dear new friend. True, he spoke very little, but this she interpreted as a result of the language barrier between them. She didn't listen to his long silences for what they were—a refusal to deal with the issues—which at the bottom line, was plain dishonesty. He would not have agreed to this interpretation. He meant to have this girl and to mold her into the kind of wife she had to be. She was a given. Her opinions, hopes, dreams, desires were not relevant. He would become the undisputed leader of the Ha-Levis and she would be his wife, with all that entailed. He would have the Law, history, and all the pressures of society on his side to help him. And so he let her talk.

His long silences gave her an opportunity to fill in the blanks, to imagine what he would say if he had the words. She took each small incident and interpreted it, the way Rashi took each syllable in the Torah and gave its hidden meaning: The wonder and deepening smile that began in his eyes and ended in the corners of his mouth told her how very beautiful and special she was to him, that hers was a transfixing beauty. The hand that had accidentally brushed against her arm when they walked through the garden at sunset, her parents right behind her, whispered to her that he longed to touch her, to hold her, whispered that he would be gentle and passionate and wonderful and loving. The soft glow in his eyes every time he saw her shouted to her that he found her adorable and intelligent and special beyond imagination, with no hint of anything but complete delight in everything she did and said. And most of all, the way his slim, powerful body arched, bending to catch each word she uttered, told her she was totally in control. He was her servant, her helpless, adoring lover.

It had been decided that at the end of ten days, he would have to leave, as Reb Avigdor had to get back to his students. As the time drew to an end, so did the carefree moments of exploration and indecision. He would be leaving in a few days and she realized that she would miss him. He had been someone to confide in, to be close to, the way one could never be with a parent or a girlfriend. He was almost a total mystery to her, and yet that only increased his appeal. How boring to know someone completely, she told herself. How wonderful to discover him slowly, the way an explorer happens upon the beautiful mysteries of the strange exotic places he visits, with no forewarning. Of course there was so much more to him than met the eye. But that was what marriage was for. Long days in the sunshine side by side talking and laughing; long intimate nights of wonderful, soundless discovery. Gentiles did this on dates, perhaps. But that was denied her. To discover Isaac (and she had no doubt he was worth discovering, just as she had no doubt he longed to discover her) she had no choice but to marry him.

She awoke early, almost delirious with joy at how easy the decision had been, how happy it would make her and her parents and Isaac. She went down to the breakfast room, bursting to tell someone, when she unexpectedly saw Isaac sitting in the garden, stretched out on a lounge chair, a Talmud propped up in his lap. Curly, the butler's little Yorkshire terrier, was sitting and watching him, its tongue and tail flapping. She smiled, watching the dog approach Isaac from behind. It loved to bark, little ridiculous thing, like a tiny ball of fluff, under the delusion that it was a fearful terror. It barked at Isaac, then jumped up and nipped him in the arm. Isaac kicked out at the animal, his face contorted with a coward's fear and anger, becoming a face she had never seen before and could not have imagined. Then, when the animal stood cowering in a corner, she saw Issac get down on one knee and beckon it with a smile, cooing softly to it. It approached again, with a hesitant wag of its tail, until it was at arm's length. She was pleased and relieved to see that. Anyone startled by a strange dog might react with initial fright. She forgave him that and waited to see his kind, gentle hand reach out and pat the whimpering little thing. Instead, she saw Isaac's arm shoot out, grabbing it by the collar. He dragged it away and locked it in the pool shed, ignoring its terrified barks. Settling himself comfortably back into the lounge chair, he took up his book once again, ignoring the animal's pitiful wails.

She leaned back against the wall, hidden from sight, all her good feeling suddenly gone. She felt as if someone had pushed her in the chest hard, taking away her breath, and a blade of sharp fear cut through her stomach.

She needed to talk to someone. She realized who it was that she really needed. Who it was that would wipe away the opaque cloud of her confusion, the way one cleans a dirty window, leaving the view crystal clear. Elizabeth. She mourned her loss for a few moments, realizing that she had no one who could take her place. Her parents were indulgent strangers. She was a little afraid of her father. Even her friend Faygie had become "one of them" since she became engaged, spouting pieties as if she had never hung a bra on the back of Rabbi Elimelech's chair. It was the end of the summer, and almost all of her friends were either engaged or on the verge.

She had grown up in splendid, pampered isolation and there wasn't anybody she knew whom she trusted, the way she did Elizabeth, to tell her the truth without ulterior motives, without pampering her, or worrying about the consequences. Elizabeth was probably having a wonderful time in London. It was selfish of her to wish that the scholarship hadn't come through quite so soon. She didn't want to be mean, it was just that Elizabeth had said it would probably take months. She just wasn't prepared for the huge gap that had been torn suddenly in the small circle of people she loved and trusted.

Ironically, the only other person she felt would understand her was Isaac. He would bend his large head down, giving her his complete attention. She had spoken to him as she had never dared speak to anyone else. She had so loved being with him, pouring her heart out to him, feeling his utter approval. And now it must all end, mustn't it? She was so confused.

She went out to the pool shed, hoping to talk to Isaac, but he had already gone. She let the dog out. It bounded over to her with a yelp, jumping up and nipping her arm. She felt annoyance at the small, painful pinch. This was the big deal, then, over this ungrateful, wretched animal? She shook her head, relieved, her heart lightening a little. How could she have considered such a thing so important? And yet the look on his face . . . perhaps it had just been a shadow, or the way the light had hit him. As a photographer, she knew the sleight of hand light and shadow often played with real images. Or perhaps she had really imagined it. He had been annoyed and startled, as anyone would have been. Merely that. And of course he had been right to lock the silly animal away, she told herself, denying the revulsion that had come over her at his slyness, his clever deception, his disregard for the animal's suffering. The whole morning, which had begun with such marvelous clarity and pleasure, was spoiled for her now.

"Ima." She knocked on her parents' bedroom door, knowing that her father was already downstairs saying his morning prayers. She climbed into the warm bed and laid her head down on her mother's softly padded, comforting shoulder.

"What's wrong, *maideleh?*"

Batsheva opened her mouth to speak, then closed it. What could she say that wouldn't sound childish and perfectly ridiculous, she thought, hearing the conversation take place in her mind. Isaac kicked the dog and locked him in the pool shed, she'd say, and her mother would answer: *Vey is mere!* What did the dog do to him? He barked at him and nipped him, she'd answer, and then her mother would say: *Oy,* I hate that little dog. Such a mean personality. I'll have to tell John to get rid of it. And then she'd say: Ima, please, try to understand. It wasn't the dog. It was how meanly Isaac did it. I was so surprised. *Oy,* her mother would answer. This is what you worry about! A dog you worry about? A fine handsome man like Isaac, a brilliant scholar, a *tzaddik*, and you worry about the dog? Why don't you worry about your future husband? She would laugh.

So Batsheva was quiet for a while, the irritation growing

inside of her at the imagined exchange until it burst out with irrational force: "I'm not going to marry Isaac, Ima. Nobody can force me to."

"What? What's wrong, everything was going so well . . ." Her mother sat up in alarm. "He said something to you?"

She shook her head. Her mother patted her hand. What do I know, Mrs Ha-Levi thought to herself. I am so useless. But she felt obligated to fulfill her role and that role, as far as she understood it, was to further the goals of her husband, who was so much wiser than she. The way she followed the laws of the Torah, even when she could not understand their purpose, believing her understanding too limited to perceive the grand design in which such small particulars had infinite meaning and worth, so she followed her husband's advice. "Of course you must look into your own heart, Batshevaleh, but trust Aba. Aba knows best." The words came out almost automatically. "Talk to him about it. He will know what to tell you. You know we both only want your happiness."

"I won't, and you and Aba can't make me!" Batsheva said, furious at her mother's inability to even give her token support, feeling like a little kid throwing a tantrum. She was ashamed of herself, and at the same time enormously relieved, as she jumped up and ran to her room, slamming the door behind her and locking it securely.

Stunned, immobilized by the familiar indecision and panic she had always felt whenever caught between her husband and daughter's strong, conflicting wills, Fruma Ha-Levi sat on the bed thinking. To contemplate her husband's fallibility had never before been within her range of possibilities. But touched by her only daughter's misery, she began to wonder.

She held her bathrobe to her cheek. Tell him. Must know. Be all right. Settle everything. She slowly put her arms through the sleeves, feeling little waves of comfort at her snatches of thought. But in between the waves were long stretches of dangerous uncertainty and fear.

She knocked on the door of his study and waited for his permission to enter. He looked up at her with a smile that soon turned to puzzled concern.

"What's wrong, my dear?"

She gripped the back of a big leather chair.

"I'm . . . not sure about . . ." She stopped and started again, taking a deep breath for courage. "Perhaps Isaac isn't the right one for Batsheva, Abraham. Perhaps we should look some more." Encouraged by his silence, the way he paced the room, giving her all his attention, the rest just poured out. "After all, he is just the first boy she's met. Perhaps there are other boys out there who would be a better *shidduch* for her. After all, learning isn't everything. Perhaps she needs a boy who is more worldly. A doctor or a lawyer. Someone who lives in America . . ." She stopped, appalled at the transformation that had come over him. Appalled and terrified. It was that old nightmare coming true. Her worst fears materializing: His face, contorted in rage and bitterness, looked at her like a stranger, an enemy.

"YOU . . . YOU DO THIS TO ME? I had expected that tutor, that Elizabeth. Even Batsheva herself . . ." He paced the room with dangerous energy, talking to himself. Then he stopped once again and looked at her with thin, tight lips and narrowed eyes.

"But you?" he whispered, and the incongruous softness of his tone was a hundred times more frightening to her than his shouting. "Yes." He nodded, his tone thick with ridicule. "Let her marry a tailor or a movie producer then. Or some American *yeshivah bucher* who'll specialize in examining the lungs of dead chickens. That will be a fitting end to the Ha-Levis . . ."

She began to weep softly.

And then he suddenly slumped into a chair, covering his

face with his hands. Hesitantly, she walked over to him and placed her hand on his shoulder. He grasped it and held it for a moment, then kissed it. "Help me. You must," he said thickly. "This is the most important thing in my life—in our daughter's life . . ."

"I only want her to be happy, Abraham." Her tears fell in a steady, soft stream. "For you both to be happy."

He stood up and took her in his arms, taking out a large, clean handkerchief and wiping away her tears. "My dear wife. Look at me." He held her chin up. "Look at my eyes." She stared, frightened, into the dark depths of his eyes, which seemed so strange and unfamiliar to her. But it was her husband still. The man she had loved, trusted, almost worshiped, from the moment she had first set eyes on him. The man who had been the source of every happiness she had ever known, who had showered her with kindness and consideration, who had overlooked her inadequacies, her weaknesses, her stupidities, who had asked for almost nothing in return.

"Do you believe I could ever hurt Batsheva?" The long Sabbath afternoons, the Sunday outings, the gifts, the child's head pressed into his shoulder, her hand in his . . .

"Of course not. Never." She shook her head vehemently.

"I have spent much time with Isaac. He is . . . I cannot even describe his qualities. He is like a rare diamond. Only once in hundreds of years do the Jewish people receive a precious mind like his. His potential is so great it is unimaginable. And Batsheva. She, too, is a rare jewel. Together, think of the children that will be born, what they will inherit. It will be a new beginning . . ."

She was hardly listening anymore, all her senses filled with unutterable gratitude that she had not smashed it all to pieces; that his tone was now loving again, that his hand stroked hers kindly, affectionately. She felt as if she had moved back from the brink, glimpsed the abyss. "Do you really think he will make her happy, Abraham?" she whispered.

"Trust me, my dear wife. Can you do that?"

In response, she merely returned the gentle squeeze of his hand. Yes, she thought. Trust him. After all, what other choice did she really have?

Batsheva, locked in her room, was deaf to all entreaties "to at least come down and have a little bite."

Then, toward evening, another knock came. Solid and forceful.

"Go away!"

"It's Aba." His voice was firm, without compassion. No. She would not let such a voice in. Period. The silence grew. "Please, Batshevaleh. You are not a child. Must we talk like this, with a door between us? Must I stand on my poor old legs until morning?" he said gently. He heard the key turn in the lock and smiled to himself. She opened the door.

"I'm sorry, Aba." She looked down, too ashamed to face him. She felt so foolish. She couldn't even explain, that was the maddening part. Her whole body tensed, ready for the fight she knew would come. But to her surprise, her father said only: "It's such a lovely evening. Please come for a little drive." She looked at him suspiciously, and he made a small, disparaging sound with his tongue, a kind of click to the roof of his mouth.

"Of course, just the two of us."

It *was* a lovely evening and she was delighted to be out of the house, a safe distance from any accidental meeting with Isaac. She had not seen him since the business with the dog and didn't want to. She was afraid to face him, afraid he would see how much and how unfairly her feelings had changed. She kept waiting for her father to bring up the subject. But he said nothing, leaning back comfortably, looking out of the window at the setting sun. She began to relax, to let down her guard. When he spoke, he did so mildly, as if he was just making light conversation.

"I want to tell you something, and then I will leave you alone."

Here it comes, she told herself, gripping the sides of the seat.

"I want to tell you that I love you more than my life," he said hoarsely, reaching out for her hand and patting it. "If I ever thought you were in danger of being hurt in any way, I would gladly give my life to prevent it. You believe that, Sheva, don't you?"

She nodded, feeling so ashamed at her mistrust. "Yes, Aba. I do."

"I have spent this whole last week, day and night, talking to Isaac and his rebbe. Isaac is a remarkable man. Once in a generation only does such a mind exist. And he is not only brilliant, but pious to a degree that makes me feel ashamed of myself for all my faults. I could love him like the son I never had. You could do this for me, but most of all for yourself, my dear child. No matter where else in the world I will search, I can only find men who are almost as good as Isaac Harshen. If you refuse him, we must both settle for second best." For the first time he looked at her with all the force of his fatherly love and authority.

"Think of it, Batsheva. All of our family has been slaughtered—grandparents, uncles, aunts, cousins. All gone. Only you are left. Only you carry the living chain, the genes, that can bring the Ha-Levis back to life. I know you are a good child. You have always given me nothing but *nachas*, happiness and pride. You have eased so much terrible pain from my heart. You've given me hope, Batshevaleh, that our family will yet survive, will yet defeat those murderers and lunatics." He took out a handkerchief and wiped the sweat from his forehead. Batsheva reached out and squeezed his hand. She felt her heart ache with love and pity for him.

"You see, you are not like other girls who can choose

according to their hearts alone. You are like Sarah, or Rivkah—the matriarch of a whole new generation. To marry the wrong man would accomplish just what Hitler set out to do: It would destroy us. You cannot know, dear child, what kind of men the Ha-Levis were. You have only me as a poor example. Ah, if only you could have known your grandfather, your uncles . . ." He wiped his eyes.

In another moment, she felt, her heart must break. "Aba, don't, please."

She had never seen him cry. She was shocked and horrified to the roots of her being, wanting only to comfort him whatever the price. "Please, Aba, don't," she whispered. "Is Isaac really like Reb Yerachmiel?" she asked shyly.

"In brilliance, very like. And also in his goodness. I am a perceptive man, an experienced man. I can see that. Can't you trust me, my dear child, believe me? He would make you such a wonderful husband, Sheva. And he loves you dearly."

She sat up very straight. "Did he . . . tell you?"

He smiled at his daughter, his little girl who liked to be flattered and petted. "Of course, such a man does not come out and say such things. But I see it in his eyes as he looks at you. He adores the ground you walk upon, my dear child." He took her hand in his large one, softly, but firmly, leaving it no escape back to the cold, detached freedom it had known before by her side. "Do you remember the promise you made me to give this a chance? Well, that is all I ask. I see that something has upset you. I won't even ask you what. But you must promise me that you will have a talk with Isaac before he goes, to see if you can't straighten all of this out. And if not . . ." He shrugged and lifted his hands to the sky. "No one will force you. We will simply look some more."

Gratefully, and of her own free will, she gave him her other hand. He accepted it without surprise.

*   *   *

She got into bed, weary in body and soul, and considered her options. If she refused, they would bring her someone else. Only this time, maybe it would be some fat fellow from Borough Park in Brooklyn who had never traveled. Someone like Rabbi Elimelech, who thought bras were "dizzzgusting." At least this way, she would get to travel and live in an exotic place like Jerusalem. Her heart did a little dance. She had seen pictures of the hills, the camels, the ancient stone walls. So interesting to photograph. And from there, Europe was just a stone's throw: Paris, Rome, Amsterdam. Just a few hours by plane. And when she was a married woman, her parents and teachers halfway across the world, who would tell her what to do then?

As sleep began to creep over her, all her rational arguments faded away and she was left with two very different, very contrasting, states of emotion. On the one hand the terrible blackness of sleep seemed too frightening and mysterious to face, and she fought it. With horror, she felt herself losing, drowning in the blackness that washed over her. But soon she felt herself throb with the gentle rhythm of familiar warmth and comfort. She was being held between her father's large, loving, protective hands, being saved from all harm. And then suddenly, it was not her father at all, but Isaac, caressing her with his long, elegant hands, holding her securely, passionately . . .

Isaac awoke earlier than usual, too tense to sleep. He would be leaving the next day. He paced through the garden, oblivious to the gorgeous riot of late summer flowers, their almost stiflingly thick fragrance. He was in a panic, totally confused. It had all come so close to him and he had let it slip through his fingers. How? Why? he thought desperately. What have I done? It was not just the power, the wealth, he admitted to himself. It was the woman. He wanted her so badly, with all the force of his repressed love and lust and youthful imagination. How, after seeing her, being so close to her, could he ever go back to Meah Shearim and marry a dull girl with short, mousy hair and thick ankles? She had opened his eyes to women and now he would be lost forever. Just as the Ha-Levi home had opened his eyes to the pleasures of soft, comfortable chairs, obliging servants, and excellent food. It was not fair, he thought, to have shown him all this only to deny it to him! It was pure torture. A small hope still flickered inside him. She had not said no. Ha-Levi had firmly, if cryptically, assured him that he would have some additional time alone with Batsheva to—how had he phrased it?—"sort this thing out." Or some such very American phrase.

He sat in the garden thinking of all this when he heard a sudden rustle and when he lifted his eyes, she stood there, shyly, holding a flowering branch in her hand. She lifted it to her nose to breathe in its sweet fragrance, covering her face so that only her eyes were visible, shy and searching, full of doubt and hope. And suddenly he saw with crystal clarity, as desperate men sometimes do under the terrible, abject fear of their need, what he must do.

"Batsheva," he held his hand out to her, "please. Come sit by me." He spoke in English, carefully measuring every word.

She walked toward him slowly, reluctantly. When she got near him, he reached out and lifted her chin so that their eyes met. He hid nothing from her. She saw the depth of his despair, the strength of his passion, his incredible longing and his unbearable fear. She saw it all, but perceived none of its tortured complexity, looking as she did through the filtering lens of youth, vanity, and inexperience. She had never looked into someone's soul that way. She was appalled but at the same time excited. The intimacy of the act touched her quivering, sensitive, innocent soul the way nothing else could have.

Slowly, clumsily, he got down on one knee. She had to keep herself from laughing out loud, he looked so ridiculous. But also boyish and touching and very loving. He took both her hands in his—an act they both knew was totally forbidden. A man was not allowed to touch a woman until they were married. The daring unexpectedness of the act thrilled her, sending shivers up her spine. It made her see him as one of those desperate romantic lovers who must break all social taboos, being true to his passion only. A very Lawrentian lover.

"Is this how they do in America?" he said earnestly. She burst out laughing and lifted him to his feet, getting up with him. His face turned beet red, and he turned away, mortified, her laughter ringing in his ears.

She touched his shoulder gently. "Isaac. Please. I am not laughing at you. I am laughing because I am so happy." He turned around to face her, full of apprehension.

"Yes, it is true," she answered the question so clearly written on his face. "I have decided." That was a lie. She had not decided anything. She had agreed merely to talk to him. But suddenly he had her in his arms, the first male arms that had ever held her hinting of the joys she knew were her birthright as a woman. And she knew it was too late to turn back, even if she had had the strength or the inclination to do so.

Chapter six

The extravagance with which the Ha-Levis prepared for the wedding of their only daughter was comparable in style, if not entirely in scope, with that of royalty. A famous designer was flown in from Paris to design the wedding gown and trousseau, and materials were ordered from all over the world—the finest silks and satins from China and England, the softest wools, the most warming flannels (for sheets and pillowcases in the icy Jerusalem winters). It was a grand shopping extravaganza. Even for Batsheva, used to the quick and easy flow of money that answered her every need, the sheer scale of purchases made to furnish her first home was overwhelming in a dreamlike way. She found herself surrounded with beautiful choices: which pattern of shimmering crystal? Which fragile, almost transparent china? Which exquisitely carved silver? She began to lose her doubts. It was so easy, was it not, to fill one's life with happiness? All the choices were open to her, laid at her feet, awaiting her pleasure: the most elegant furniture and the latest appliances, works of art, bedding and wallpaper in delicate Laura Ashley patterns. And all the while, her father stood at her side, with a checkbook in his open, indulgent hand, and a pleased smile that never left his face. He let her choose, but guided each and every choice firmly with his quiet, almost offhand suggestions, so that she never even realized they were really his choices. Then it was all packed and shipped to Israel to furnish the expensive house he had purchased for the newlyweds. And it had all been done in an incredible three months from the moment she had left the garden with the memory of Isaac's warm hands on her own.

Sometimes, amidst all the excitement, Batsheva found herself simply forgetting about Isaac, about the wedding, caught up in the sheer power and joy of being a bride-to-be. Never had she been consulted so carefully, been catered to so wonderfully. She had made the right decision then, she told herself. Yes. The freedom was beginning already. But every once in a while, she would feel, inexplicably, a cold shiver run down her spine. More often, she would wake up in a sweat, dreaming she was being kicked or that animals were biting at her flesh, their mouths attaching to her painfully, sucking her blood. She would try desperately to pull them off. But they would not come off. She would try to scream, but find that she couldn't do that either. She was totally helpless.

But in the daytime, she was herself again, happy and full of plans, directing the servants to pack up crates and crates of her English books, her cameras and darkroom equipment. All her daytime dreams were bright, covered with a wondrous pink glow, like advertisements for engagement rings or photos taken at sunrise. Awake, she thought of her marriage as a wonderful, exciting adventure, but one that would take place in a safari park, where nothing really dangerous or unpleasant could actually happen.

In the large, lavishly furnished living room of the ostentatious home his father-in-law had acquired for him and his bride, Isaac

Meyer Harshen walked silently, his hands clasped behind his back in the attitude of a pleased explorer, surveying the longed-for new world. In the background, he heard the vague click of pots and pans in the kitchen where his mother and sisters were examining the riches from America.

"This is a kitchen for a princess. One could cook for twenty children with such a big oven," Mrs Harshen announced, pulling her head out of the large American appliance, adjusting her wig over her forehead. It was an old wig and looked almost like straw. It covered a head that had long ago been shaved to prevent stray hairs from escaping into the light of day. In case anyone should mistake the wig for hair, she wore a kerchief with ugly brown and blue flowers on top of it. Her heavy, shapeless legs were covered with thick, almost black stockings with seams, and her shoes were wide, dull orthopedic leathers made to order by a tradesman in Meah Shearim who had learned his trade in the Ukraine in 1924 and had found no reason to update his styles or his claim of being able to cure every ailment with his shoes. There was nothing on Mrs Harshen that was not practical and functional; even her earrings were merely small gold dots to keep the holes open. No trace of adornment for so frivolous a reason as beauty could be found anywhere on her stern, uncompromising person. "A young bride with such a kitchen," she scoffed. "Does she know how to clean a chicken, to bone the carp for gefilte fish?" She looked at the new refrigerator greedily. Such a big American one. Her son deserved only the best. But this girl, a spoiled American, would she be able to keep it clean, full of decent, kosher food? "They buy everything canned there, I hear," she told him. "Even the kugels come frozen. And what is this?" She opened up all the cupboards and fingered the shiny stainless-steel pots, the pretty porcelain serving dishes, with envy. One especially. She held it up to the light, her stubby, practical fingers tightening around it with avarice, even as her eyes surveyed it with contempt. A fragile, translucent white bowl trimmed in tiny, hand-painted blue flowers.

Leah Harshen, seventh-generation born in Jerusalem, was a product of generations of men and women who had learned to live on the edge of poverty with dignity and resourcefulness. They had learned how to cut a chicken into fourteen portions that could serve a family of twelve children for Sabbath dinner; learned how to mend and let out a pair of sturdy pants so that it might serve four growing boys in succession; learned how to bargain to fill the house with quantities of fruits and vegetables just at the edge of rotting to make up the sparse menu. There had been no money in the Harshen family now for generations, save for that which brides and grooms and fathers-in-law could contribute. The Harshen men all went early to the study halls to begin a life of scholarship; they did not learn professions, expecting to be supported in their quest for knowledge by their yeshivoth, their wives, their fathers-in-law, and eventually their students' families. They were never supported in more than a subsistence existence, since most brides and grooms worthy of marrying into the Harshen family came from large families in which many sons and sons-in-law had chosen a similar path to holiness, and thus the only people employed, usually the mothers and sisters, or a father who headed a rabbinical academy or taught there, had to spread whatever money there was among the many. That, and a small stipend from the yeshivah that came from charity from abroad and, occasionally, a rich relative from America, made up the difference.

In Israel it is very unpleasant to rent an apartment. There is no rental housing as such, and apartments are usually the private residence or the house-bought-for-the-children of a very particular landlord who at the end of each lease may ask the tenant to move. He may want higher rent, or may need to turn it over to a child who is marrying. And since mortgage terms are almost impossible to meet, in order to own an apartment one must be able to come up with almost the entire sum in cash—the equivalent of forty thousand dollars for a small one-bedroom place in a walkup to five hundred thousand for a luxurious villa such as Isaac Harshen and his family now surveyed. The Harshens themselves lived in a tiny two-bedroom house with a back porch covered with corrugated tin that served as a bedroom. At night, the entire house became one large sleeping area with mattresses unrolled in the living, dining, and even kitchen areas for the parents, unmarried sons and daughters, and any guests.

Thus, face-to-face with wealth for the first time in their history, the Harshens had two immediate reactions: an appreciation bordering on stupefaction that such riches were in their grasp, and, more subtly, a contemptuous disdain for those whose spiritual level allowed them to waste time and effort on the worldly pursuit of such extravagances.

Leah thought of the future daughter-in-law she had never met. That spoiled child. Her poor son would have his hands full, teaching this American girl what it meant to be the wife of a *talmid chacham* in Jerusalem, the holy city. They said she was a *frum* girl, a pious girl, but what did they know of piety in America? She had seen the American religious girls on their trips to Israel, traipsing through Meah Shearim in thin dresses that clung to them, outlining their legs. Dresses in bright colors that called indecent attention to them, like *prutzas*. With stockings the same color as their legs and no seams so you couldn't even tell if their legs were naked or not, and shoes so open you saw the cleavage between their toes.

She walked through the living room and opened the French doors to the terrace. From there the whole city lay before one, sparkling white stone that had an other-earthly look. The sun was just setting, casting a pink glow on the white stones that, by law, all buildings in Jerusalem new and old shared, giving the city a continuity and purity. Nestled in the hills, the whole city seemed to rise toward heaven, buoyed by the clouds themselves.

"This would be a good place to hang the laundry," she told her Isaac.

He looked at his mother as if seeing her for the first time. Fat, ignorant woman. "We have an electric machine that dries the clothes." His tone was barely respectful and she looked at him carefully, but did not say anything. Something strange was happening to Isaac Meyer Harshen. A slow and subtle transformation of soul that even he was not fully aware of and would not be until it was far too late. Had his fate decreed differently and he had taken as bride a plain, simple, and pious girl brought up like his sisters, whose straight and narrow mind never wandered, and who would have brought with her into the marriage the same austerity and near-poverty he was accustomed to, he would have no doubt continued his upward striving in the houses of study without distraction and led a satisfied pious life, enjoying what he could of the severely rationed material things of the world that would come his way. But like a beautiful piano of fine polished wood, if one moves it from a dry, hot climate into the full, moist air of the seashore, it will retain its beauty, learning to live with its new environment. But try to bring that instrument back to its dryness, and rot will immediately set in. And so it was with Isaac. He fingered the thick, down-filled velvet pillows of his couch, running his hands over the cream-colored material, enjoying its luxurious softness. He sat down and leaned back, closing his eyes, remembering the house in California with its silver gates and liveried servants. Although he should have been hurrying back to the house of study, he could not bring himself to move. He was trapped by the comfort, the luxury. If one believed in such things, one might say that Isaac Harshen's Evil Inclination had his hands full on his shoulders, pressing him down with all its might.

There she was, as in a dream. A queen sitting on a throne surrounded by her court. He was walking toward her, the bridegroom she barely remembered. Behind him thousands of Hassidim, a sea of black and white, frothed toward them, creating a roar of sound. He walked solemnly, his eyes barely open, reciting psalms. He was frightened, no longer himself. He felt God peering into his soul and he was ashamed. He closed his eyes tighter and trembled for all the sins he had committed since his youth. On either side his arms linked with his father and father-in-law. They, too, were serious, walking toward the bride. She was a vision like no other so that even the most pious men could not but stare at her. The dress glittered in a soft glow of light as moonbeams bounced off the tiny pearls embedded in the precious duchess silk satin.

The bride, calm, feeling herself a kind of performer, wished to please everyone and did not think of the man advancing toward her, because if she did she might tremble. She might cry out, bringing up a primal scream of fear. She tried not to think of his thick dark hair and the firm skull, precious, underneath. Of his long, gentle fingers. She tried to remember she did not know him. And her mind did not conceive at all the serious bond she was about to create. She was young and had always been able to get what she wanted of indulgent parents and outwitted teachers. She was sure of her beauty as a magic tool that would open up that which was closed to her, turning all noes to yeses. The bride, barely eighteen, looked up at the groom, who was now not to be ignored, standing before her intimately in front of thousands of the faithful. Their eyes glimpsed each other's souls for a moment, then retreated, afraid. He brought the veil down over her face. The procession continued under the vast, eternal sky of Jerusalem, holy city, the angels rejoicing and weeping at the ability of human beings to make their own choices, even if they defy God's.

Her mother and mother-in-law led her, lighting her way with candles. Her mother's step was cautious, hesitant, her mother-in-law's heavy and determined—she stepped on the bride's white train and left the imprint of her sensible shoe. They delivered her to the men, standing beneath the wedding canopy. She took small careful steps, circling the bridegroom seven times. Seven blessings were read out and the cold rim of a silver goblet filled with wine was pressed against her dry, nervous lips. She sipped, tasting nothing, and the wine traveled down her throat with a burning, irrevocable clarity. It was done! The crowd erupted in an avalanche of stamping feet. The voices of joy, of thanksgiving, sang out, filling the vast empty space, bouncing off the ancient white stones. "Still will be heard the voice of the bride, the voice of the bridegroom in the hills of Judah and the streets of Jerusalem." "Still the flame glows, my Father yet lives."

How many had been the destroyers in this place, Abraham Ha-Levi thought. Yet the Jews survived, they came back to Jerusalem to fill the city with the sound of weddings, of continuation. The father looked up to heaven and felt in that dark interminable space a presence that filled him with forgiveness. He could forgive himself now, for not being a true Ha-Levi, because he had done his role, like a true servant of God. He had fulfilled his mission by bringing his daughter to this place to marry this man. He could forgive God for standing by silently, for withdrawing His protective wing from his father and brothers in the flames of the burning synagogue, from his mother before the gas chambers of Auschwitz, from his dead son. God had allowed this marriage to take place, had given him a daughter and now a new son. In his deepest soul, he whispered: Hallelujah.

And then, as all the guests filtered to the huge banquet halls for a feast that only kings could afford, the bride and bridegroom, as tradition and law required, walked alone into a small room, the door closing behind them. They faced each other, two strangers. Boldly, she took his hands in hers. They were cold and moist with sweat, making her own hands damp. Ashamed, he dried them on his suit and lifted back her veil. A small shiver of expectation ran along her spine. He took a step backward and offered her a drink and a piece of cake. They had eaten nothing all day and watched each other break the long fast. And too soon there was a knocking on the door as the Hassidim demanded them. Reluctantly, and perhaps a bit relieved, too, to be forced from the sudden intimacy, they opened the door and were led out, he to the men, and she to the women, the long partition that ran the length of the room separating them for the rest of the evening.

The dancing took on a frenzied, riotous joy. Circle within circle moving with a step inward, and a step outward, creating a rhythm that was at once of this world and of the next. It was a celebration of an earthly happiness but more, a celebration of a heavenly decree now fulfilled. Men balanced bottles on their heads, balanced chairs on the tips of their nose. To please the bride and bridegroom was a *mitzvah*. To see them laugh was a *mitzvah*. The bride, surrounded by the women, sat enthroned as they danced around her with the pretty, delicate grace of women. Understanding and pity wet the eyes of the married women, envy and joy the eyes of the young girls who surveyed the bride. Her own eyes were blind, seeing only her own inner confusion. Whatever happened outside her went by in a white rush, a blur, almost as if her eyes had gone suddenly nearsighted and she was forced to see without glasses. "Serve God with gladness," the men's voices intoned, beginning slowly and growing louder and faster with each beat. *Streimels* and earlocks bobbed and wove in unison; hundreds of bodies pressed together, sweaty hands were clasped. Their eyes were closed, deep in thought, and their teeth were clenched together, their bodies straining to realize the significance of God's awesome mercy in bringing back to life that which was dead.

The food and wine were served up in huge platters—the most delectable and glatt kosher of meats and chickens, the finest pastry, delicious kugels and tzimmes, wonderful aromatic cakes and cookies. Special tables were set for the poor and the hangers-on. The meal lasted three hours. And then, when the last dessert was served, and people began taking greedy handfuls of flowers from the enormous centerpieces and walking out the door, only the most immediate family and friends remained. A watchful silence descended and someone got up and announced in a loud, awe-stricken whisper: *Mitzvah tanz.* The long partition separating the men from the women was dismantled.

"Come," Mrs Harshen urged a startled Batsheva, leading her across to where the men had celebrated in supreme isolation all evening. This crossing over was shocking to the bride, who felt she had overstepped some terrible boundary. But seeing the cheerful faces of everyone around her, she was reassured and relaxed. There was Isaac, already seated in a chair, waiting for her. He looked so tall and handsome, immaculate in his white *kitel.* She sat down next to him, the women behind her and the men before her. Now the "inviter" stood up. "Now we call a father to dance with the bride in the *mitvas rekide*, the *mitzvah* dance!" Abraham Ha-Levi moved slowly in front of his daughter. He wiped the sweat that poured down his forehead and someone handed him a handkerchief. Batsheva looked at her father, her eyes suddenly focusing with a smile of love. She caught hold of the handkerchief and her father danced before her like a young groom, full of laughter and merriment. The joy in the room swelled out like a balloon and she thought: It must burst, it cannot contain any more, just as my full heart cannot. One by one, the grandfather, father-in-law, uncles, brothers-in-law, took hold of the handkerchief and danced before her with slow, shuffling steps. And then, when they had all had their turn, Isaac got up.

He walked toward his beautiful bride with small, unbelieving, hesitant steps as the "inviter," the self-appointed master of ceremonies, sang out, half serious, half laughing:

And where are you going?
To the place of dust, just that wouldn't have been too
bad.
Worms, just that wouldn't have been too bad either,
But to go to the place of dust and
Worms and on top of that, moths!

Always the reminder of death, even in the midst of life, of joy. One must be reminded that there is a Creator and around the corner darkness lies in wait for us. Batsheva heard the words of the song and shivered. What did it mean? She could not move her eyes off Isaac's as he slowly came to her and lifted the corner of the handkerchief from her trembling hand. He took tiny, mincing steps before her, his eyes closed. She tried to sway with him, to follow his steps, but could not. She didn't understand where he was going, or why. So she followed him blindly, hopefully, as he led her around the floor. And all at once, his steps grew slower and more meaningful as he moved near to her and then backed away in a slow, deliberate rhythm that she could anticipate, moving toward him as he reached toward her. For a single moment, his eyes opened and met hers and she felt an unfolding inside herself, almost indecent, a raw, naked longing that made her legs too weak to hold her.

"*Hot mir a gutte nacht,*" the "inviter" intoned suddenly. Have a good night. And the wedding was over and their life together took its first tentative step forward.

Chapter seven

Then suddenly, almost shockingly, they were in their home, totally alone. He did not carry her over the threshold, for that is not a Jewish custom. Batsheva, who had seen Hollywood movies and (secretly) television shows, and had read *Women in Love* and *The Rainbow*, felt somehow diminished stepping into the house in an ordinary way. Her first home, her wedding night. Her imagination had dwelt on these things like any sensitive young girl's, turning both into magical moments on another plane of existence where somehow all of her experience of reality would no longer prove relevant.

But there it was. The floor was hard and cold beneath her feet as she kicked off her pointy, pinching high heels, worn out from dancing in circles with the women. She was weary but exhilarated too. Isaac sat in the living room opening wedding envelopes. Batsheva's heart sank as she saw the big pile still unopened.

"Isaac," she murmured, touching him hesitantly, "must we do this now?"

"Ah, yes." He let the envelope fall, and he reached up to caress her face. He saw her close her eyes and tremble and it frightened him a little. A sudden perverseness, almost a force outside his control, made him pick the envelope up again. He was avoiding the bedroom, delaying for time. And also, he really wanted to know how much money he had. It was amazing, he had never seen so much money up close.

"It vill only take, *vus*, how do you say, a jiffy. Right?" She hated him to speak his pidgin English, preferring to hear his fluent Yiddish. "I vant to add it up, put it avay inda bank tomorrow." She walked resignedly into the bedroom. A maid had already unpacked her suitcase. She sat in front of the mirror and took off her bridal veil. Slowly, she began to take the pins from her hair. The long strands fell like a soft caress down her back. She ran her fingers through it and pulled a lock across her face, breathing in its perfumed fragrance. Such soft, sweet-smelling hair. Her cheeks were flushed with the excitement of the evening, the sweet wine that had flowed like water, the dancing; and the unbearable anticipation of the night that was to come. She looked closely at herself, trying to envision what he would see. All fiery, sweet and yielding, she knew without a single hesitation that she was ravishing. She drummed her fingers impatiently, almost painfully hard, on the dressing table.

Why didn't he come?

She reached behind her and felt the endless row of tiny silk buttons that ran the top length of her gown. She remembered when her mother had buttoned them. "You will need help to take this off, but I imagine you will have someone to help you." There had been a secret smile on her mother's face, a laugh in her voice that had made her blush. She had imagined that he would do it slowly, gently, until the gown fell from her shoulders to a heap on the floor. She would then step out of it, turning modestly away from him as she took off her slip and finally her bra and panties. She had planned to come to him so, as a gift, with no separation between them. Such, she had imagined, was the way a man and his wife should be. She had planned to give herself to him completely out of love, a desire to make him happy and fill him with manly joy. For it was more than just her body she was handing to him. It was the single most precious dream of a lonely child, a dream that she had spent half her lifetime embellishing and perfecting. It was an antidote to a childhood filled with isolation and pain. She would never be lonely again, the dream said. Her mind, heart, body, and soul would have its perfect partner to fill every vacuum completely. Trembling, her hands reached back, struggling to push the tiny buttons through the holes. Finally, aching and defeated, with more than half of the buttons yet to go, she let her arms fall dejectedly to her sides.

She wandered listlessly around the bedroom, trying to comfort herself with the touch and sight of the beautiful things her parents had shipped from the States. She picked up the music box, her father's gift, and wound it up. "Lara's Theme." She watched the young couple in the sled drive round and round in the furious, blanketing snow and imagined it was something like what God must feel holding the world in His hands, seeing the lives of human beings unfold, knowing that they would go round and round until they came back to where they started. The sadness in the thought startled her.

Why didn't he come, why?

She heard the door open softly. He stood there, looming larger and more powerful than she had ever remembered seeing him, making her feel small and helpless.

"You are still dressed?"

She blushed. "The buttons are difficult for me alone."

He hesitated, then walked slowly toward her. He was terrified of this woman. Of Woman. What would she expect of him? What must he do, as a man? In his experience so far he had had only theory. The holy books taught a man everything, everything. Yet, it was still theory. They had not prepared him for her soft, beautiful face full of unreasonable expectations. He was just a virgin too, after all, who had not been expected or allowed to indulge in dreams of flesh. And now that it was suddenly a *mitzvah*, indeed a positive Commandment, he did not know how to change gears. His soul, trained in repression for so many years, resisted her soft body as if it was still a sin, as if no wedding had taken place, no blessings had been pronounced.

He was afraid to touch those small silken buttons, to see what was underneath. He began to hate her a little as she moved toward him, presenting her back to him. But what could he do? He had been taught that woman was a lustful creature that had a right to be satisfied. If he could not, she had a right to divorce him under Jewish law. He touched her small back, bent modestly and humbly toward him. Slowly, the work progressed, button after button opening, revealing white skin. Sometimes his large fingers would slip and touch the skin. Its incredible softness burnt him like coals, sending flashes of fire down his back to his loins.

The dress was open. She stepped away from him and let it fall to the floor. He could not bear it. "I will undress in the bathroom. We must preserve some *tznius*," he said with a coldness that covered sheer panic.

She felt as if he had slapped her across the face. *Tznius*. Modesty. He must preserve it. She clutched the dress to her, humiliated and cheapened. He had thrown her gift back in her face. There were twin beds in the bedroom. When he came out of the bathroom she was already under the covers in her bed, wearing a long negligee of pure white silk. She lay stiffly, still smarting from the wait and his insult. All her limbs were contracted in a pattern of resistance.

He shut off the light and she felt him climb in beside her. A stranger. Yet for all that, he was a man. She felt the cotton of his clean pajamas and smelled the soap and toothpaste. Manly, clean. His skin had a fragrance she had never breathed before. Not like perfume, but a musky, darkly pleasing odor, very male, that came from no bottle. He was so comfortingly close to her. She felt him turn toward her in the darkness and lift her nightgown over her head partly and she understood she must do the rest. Ashamed and yet excited, shielded by the darkness, she undressed completely, flinging the clothes to a soft heap on the floor. She heard him murmur, prayerlike, fumble with his own clothes, and then there was something else. Icy cold and smooth, it covered the whole length of her body. She felt him roll over and put his arms on either side of her shoulders, supporting himself. She did not feel his warm skin, but a cool separation, like material, which interposed itself between their bodies. She was confused and frightened. What should I do with my arms, my legs? He seemed to push at her, nudge her, trying to communicate something, but she didn't know what he wanted. And then she felt something hot and sticky ooze between her legs. His weight lifted from her, and he turned wordlessly away. She heard the other bed move to accept his weight.

She had expected pain. She had expected to be transported. She had expected humiliation, shame, joy, incredible excitement. But this, this nothing? This wet fumbling in the dark? This coldness? She wondered at it until mercifully the complex lines of night were erased into the simple darkness of sleep.

The hot Mediterranean sunlight slanting through the drapes woke her. She found herself alone in the bed and for a moment did not know where she was, who she was. She felt hot and dirty. She listened for a sound, a motion that would indicate someone was in the house. Hearing none, she walked naked into the bathroom. She lay in the tub a long time, trying not to think, for each time she put the night together in her mind, her jaws stiffened and her stomach contracted. She felt so incredibly stupid and confused and alone. Most of all she felt ashamed. She scrubbed herself hard, taking none of her usual pleasure in the sight of her beautiful, full breasts, tiny waist and long, shapely legs. She felt the lovely sheen of her youth had grown dull, the soft bud of her body fading like a flower that had been ripped from its roots and left without water. He, the man, had seen her, touched her, and had not validated her beauty, her womanliness. He had turned away and gone to his own bed. Like Eve after the fall, her nakedness was obscene to her now.

Filled with a sense of nameless loss, she sat at the edge of her bed, drying herself with small, mournful pats at her wet shoulders and calves. She lifted the covers. She felt it again, the cold smooth material. Picking it up, she held it full length. It was just a plain white sheet. Then something caught her eye. In the middle there was a hole. She looked at it closely. Its edges were smooth, evidence of a small scissor. It wasn't a tear. And then it hit her like a physical blow. He had deliberately cut a neat, small hole. He had prepared this thing to lay over her, prepared it consciously with full knowledge and responsibility, to prevent their bodies from touching.

His footsteps. She dropped the sheet and quickly reached for a robe. He would never see her body again if she could help it. He strode into the room. "*Boker tov*, Batsheva." He averted his eyes, waiting for her to fasten the buttons. She nodded, her fingers working with swift, nervous energy. She couldn't bear to look at him. He walked over to her bed and lifted the covers, then looked at her sharply. "Have you changed the linens then, already?" An accusation.

"I haven't done anything. I just got up." She spoke in English with deliberate unconcern for him. Let him learn a little English, he was a scholar, wasn't he? A brilliant scholar. She glanced at him malevolently. He seemed to be examining something that did not meet with his approval. His face had a pinched harshness, a face she would soon come to know well. But now, so soon after their courtship, after their intimacy, it made her feel sick and irrationally guilty.

"There is a problem," he said with cryptic understatement. She sensed the anger, barely decently covered, threatening any moment to slash through the polite words like a switchblade. Instinctively, she held her ground, looking carefully into his eyes with a kind of defiance. She didn't understand that he was beyond, far beyond, her recriminations, her wounded feelings, in some world of male pride and fury she did not begin to fathom.

He looked her full in the face. "I am not the first then."

What did he want? What was she doing in the middle of all this accusation and anger and pain? Why did she feel an irrational need to defend herself? She was filled with the panic of the inexperienced: It was the first schoolday of a child, the first day on a first job. What hidden standards had she failed to live up to? What terrible, unspeakable mistakes had she made?

"The first what?"

"The first man." His jaws flinched.

She repeated the words to herself as he had said them, not as she had translated them. Maybe there was a mistake. *Der erster mann.* No, he meant it. Man.

"The sheets are clean," he said through clenched teeth. And suddenly she understood. He was searching for proof of her virginity. There was no blood.

The doctor Isaac Meyer Harshen went to consult in his distress was also a rabbi. His office was merely a room in a rather bare apartment, with foam-rubber couches and huge bookcases filled with medical journals and Talmudical commentaries. Isaac glanced uncomfortably at the other patients—women with swollen bellies, in various stages of preparing the next generation; or thin women with pinched, unhappy faces. A few had their husbands by their side. But he could see from their sidelong glances how odd they found his solitary presence. He shifted with humiliation under their gaze.

"Are you feeling all right, my son?" the doctor asked, looking at him across a bare desk. He said it in a kindly, fatherly way. No, I feel sick, I feel angry. I want to scream with embarrassment. I distrust the woman I've married. But Isaac said none of that, nodding listlessly.

"Sit down, sit down. A new *chasan. Mazel tov* to you and may Hashem bless you. I don't want you to worry. Many a new *chasan* has come to me with such problems. Youth and inexperience. But soon they come to me to deliver their sons. So may it be with you." He chuckled.

"Has she deceived me?" he blurted out in agony.

"Deceived you?" The doctor looked at him without understanding.

"Can you tell? There was no blood on the sheets, as it is written, 'the signs of her virginity.'"

The old doctor repressed a smile. Here after all was a man in pain. A young, foolish man in pain. But he had many such men come to him from the yeshivoth. The more devout they were, the more removed from reality they seemed to be. Young virgins who were somehow expected to know everything on the wedding night. They learned something from others, brothers, the bad yeshivah boys, books. But still, they had never touched a woman in their lives before their wedding night. "My dear *chasan*. On that score I can put your mind at rest. Your lovely *kallah* not only was a virgin, but I am absolutely certain, from the look on your face, she still is a virgin."

A red flame of shame spread up from Isaac's chest to his neck and covered his face.

"Now, now, you mustn't be embarrassed." The doctor patted his shoulder. "Many come like you, not knowing. They are frightened and ignorant. And the women do not know how to help you. They, too, are pure. And forget about signs of virginity. Some women never have blood. The hymen stretches without breaking. Did you use the sheet?"

Isaac nodded.

"Ah well, *kindeleh*. That, too, gets in the way."

"But I was taught one must be modest in all ways."

"Yes, but you must also satisfy your bride." Oh, the sheet, the holy sheet! Each generation becoming holier than the next, adding to their lives more restrictions they didn't need. He looked at him kindly: "Maimonides teaches that whatever a man and woman do together after their wedding is holy. Do you intend to be a bigger saint than Maimonides?"

The anger and righteousness that had stiffened Isaac Meyer Harshen's broad shoulders left him. Like sails under a windless sky, he drooped, shrinking with remorse and humiliation. "You mean we did not actually . . . I did not . . . how can you tell?"

"*Chasan*, my dear blessed *chasan*. Do you think you are the first to come charging up here looking like the Angel of Death the morning after your wedding?" He made a tsk-tsk sound with his tongue. A sound of annoyance, of tolerance and understanding. He gripped Isaac's shoulder. "You go home to your sweet *shana kallah*. You talk to her heart, beg her to forgive your ignorance. You caress her and kiss her until she loves you again and then you do the following." He opened up a large, well-illustrated book to well-worn pages that had helped hundreds of boys such as the one he had in front of him become husbands and fathers. He explained everything to him like a doctor, reminded him of his sexual obligations to his wife like a rabbi, and sent him out into the waiting room with one final shake of the head and words of advice: "And throw away the blessed sheet!"

He walked home in silence and thought of the woman he had married. Her eyes were so beautiful, the lashes casting a shadow on her cheeks. He remembered how her skin had felt beneath the buttons. He wondered how it would feel to lay his whole hand over her, to caress her naked body? He had been such a fool, an ignorant fool! She would never forgive him. But he had just acted the way he thought he was expected to. He had denied himself sensuous pleasure in order not to give in to his body so that his soul would remain pure. Still, perhaps the doctor was right. He was a learned man.

On the way home he met people who had been at the wedding the night before, who greeted him warmly with excitement. "And where is your lovely bride?" they all asked him, in that sly, breathless way people have after weddings. He did not look up, nodding and hurrying by. He wanted to get home. What if she had left him? Oh, what a fool he was! In terror, he rushed homeward. He walked up the stairs to the lovely stone villa that was their new home, appreciating once again the taste and expense that had gone into its refurbishing.

She was sitting alone in the living room, staring out of the window. He came in softly and knelt at her feet, taking both her hands in his and kissing them. She tried to pull away but he held her fast. "Please, Sheva. Listen to me a moment. I beg you. I want—"

She broke free and ran up the stairs into the bedroom, locking the door behind her. Through the closed door, she heard him bang, then shake the lock.

"Please, my dear. I just want to talk to you."

"Go away and leave me alone."

"My dear *kallah*. Please, give me another chance. I beg you. I'm sorry." Then there was silence. She put her ear to the door. A sound, broken and guttural. What? She slowly turned the lock and opened the door. He was sitting on the floor, cross-legged, his head in his hands in a pose of utter despair.

The sight went through her, tearing at her heart. She inched closer, cautiously ready to fly to safety if he should be faking. But he just kept on, hiding his face in his hands. He looked up at her with a face broken and tearstained, all the haughtiness, the conviction, drained out of it. He was young, a boy.

"I'm sorry, my dear, so sorry. I'm such a fool, such a stupid fool. I know nothing, nothing."

In the agony of his embarrassment she saw reflected her own, and slowly the anger lifted from her, smokelike. She found herself inching closer to him, wanting to comfort him and to be comforted. She reached out a tentative hand and stroked his thick, beautiful hair. He reached up his hand and held her small one in his, bringing it slowly to his lips. His curly beard caressed and tickled her palm.

"I want to start again. Can you let me start again, to forget last night as if it had never happened?"

She didn't know really if she ever could. But in his bitter unhappiness he had turned into someone so like herself at this moment that she took comfort in the thought of sharing her misery, even if it was with the one who had caused it. "All right, then."

He got up slowly, her hand still in his, warmed between his two large palms. He took off his wide-brimmed black hat and his long black overcoat and his tie. He unbuttoned his shirt and took off his four-cornered garment and his undershirt. His chest was broad and firm, with dark tufts of hair. Batsheva turned away, embarrassed, but he held her hands and placed them on his face. He took her around the waist and very gently kissed her lips, drinking long and deep. They were so incredibly sweet, her full red lips. He kissed her again a little harder and a little longer, feeling her lips pressed up against him, part of him. Then with a fluid movement, he placed his hand beneath her and picked her up off the ground. With one leg, he kicked open the door of the bedroom and then carried her over the threshold.

Chapter eight

After the first sexual initiation of bride and groom, Jewish Law requires them to separate immediately and to remain separate for twelve days. As will be the case their entire marriage, during the wife's menstrual period and for seven days after it ceases, the beds are firmly moved apart; no hands may be held, and even the most casual of kisses must be restrained. Indeed, husband and wife may not so much as pass each other a cup of wine or a plate of food. The wife is bidden to wear a special brooch or hat to remind her husband at all times of her condition, and both must take care not to be alone together on vacations or in other circumstances that might encourage forbidden intimacy.

It is a difficult, almost inhuman custom that Orthodox Jews eventually learn not only to live with, but even, in many cases, to appreciate. For, interestingly, the forced physical distance often reawakens the longing and passion that so often die with the dull, surfeiting routine of marriage. But sometimes this separation can be a time of nerve-racking tension, a cause of misunderstandings, petty arguments, and mutual distrust—never more so than for a delicate bride and a hesitant, shy groom interrupted in their tenuous groping toward hidden knowledge. The custom of *sheva brachot*, feting bride and groom for seven nights after the wedding at dinners crowded with friends and relatives, wisely provides a wonderful distraction for the young couple during this difficult period.

For Batsheva and Isaac, however, not yet fully recovered from the disaster of their wedding night, their problems were merely exacerbated by the constant need to appear relaxed and smiling before endless crowds of well-wishers. Batsheva found her smile going cramped and false, the edges drooping and needing to be lifted by sheer force of will. At night, in long humid dreams, Batsheva dreamt she was a butterfly of gorgeous colors, netted and pinned to a board and covered with glass. She kept seeing the endless succession of people staring at her with enormous eyes. "Isn't she lovely?" they would say again and again. "Oh look, how lovely she is!"

Isaac, too, felt nervous and anxious, glancing a bit pleadingly at his bride from time to time with apprehension. He was humiliatingly aware that there had still been no blood, and that they had not, therefore—as was proper and expected—entered this period of separation. And, although they had discussed the need to put up the proper appearances, Isaac was terrified that his unpredictable new wife might forget and pass him a plate of food, or touch his arm to get his attention, thus revealing his embarrassing plight to everyone.

"Aba, please," she begged her father the night before the last dinner was to take place, "let's have just a small party. At my house—just close family."

He examined her with strange intensity and searching interest, then suddenly chuckled: "Tired of being a princess already, Sheva? All right. I'll have it catered at your house. Just the family."

It was a lovely meal. The wine sparkled with ruby light in

the twinkling crystal glasses that Batsheva had chosen with heartfelt care from beautiful Waterford patterns. The translucent bone china, as thin and delicate as a petal, which had given her such pleasure to select and own, proved every bit as magical as she had hoped: its gold rims burning with suffused fire, its deep lapis blue pattern richly satisfying. She loved everything about her new home, her new things, with a child's pure, covetous delight. Full of wonderful food and two or three glasses of fine wine, her body, for the first time since the wedding, seemed to float, detached, in a delightful distant orbit from everyone around her.

As Isaac rose to begin the *drasha*, the Talmudical explication that was as vital a part of such occasions as bread, Batsheva leaned her head dreamily on her open hand, surprised to find herself looking at him with a little of the interest and attraction of a stranger. His waistcoat, a lustrous black satin, caught and held the light in a dark, inviting sheen; the big, round mink-trimmed *streimel* hat, which had seemed so ridiculous to her at first, looked somehow absolutely right now, almost a king's crown, adding to her husband's impressive height, the manly broadness of his shoulders. The word that came to her mind was *resplendent*. He was so handsome, so imposing, commanding such respect among everyone in the room. She felt herself fill like a cup to the brim with the special possessive and uncritical joy that comes only to a young bride surveying her first home, her new husband.

"The Talmud in Baba Kama discusses the very nature of what constitutes a good problem. A squatter moves into a man's field and lives there without the owner's knowledge. Is he liable to pay rent or not? Before we can answer, we must analyze the situation. Are we talking about a field that was intended to be rented out, or one that was not? Are we talking about a squatter who would have been willing and able to pay rent, or one who would have gladly squatted elsewhere with the same benefit?" He paused meditatively, stroking his thick, dark-brown beard. "If the tenant doesn't benefit from staying in the field and the owner didn't intend to rent it out anyway, then one didn't gain and the other didn't lose. So neither is worse or better off. Thus, no one has to pay." Isaac paused, wiped his forehead as appreciative murmurs rose around him for the clarity of his presentation. He was in his element now, sharing the confident surge of pleasure that comes to a great pitcher stepping up to the plate; a great running back just handed the ball; a great surgeon peering at an anesthetized patient, scalpel in hand. "However, what if the owner intended to rent out the field and the squatter had intended to pay rent? In that case the owner loses and the squatter gains, so the squatter is liable to pay."

"But what," Batsheva's excited voice rang out as she placed her arm urgently on Isaac's, "if the squatter would have been willing to pay for staying in the field, even if the owner didn't intend to rent it out? In that case the squatter gains, but the owner doesn't lose, so again, neither is liable." Her voice had risen triumphantly.

Isaac looked at her, the blood draining from his face in surprise and mortification. Isaac's father tilted his head slightly, his mouth open. Others leaned back in their chairs, speechless. Contrary to what Isaac feared, most had not even noticed her arm on his. They were indignant and fearful of becoming forced witnesses to a perplexing, indeed unforgivable, breach of custom and etiquette that required women to sit silent and slightly befuddled on such occasions, full of respect and gratitude for being allowed to breathe in, if not understand, the words of Torah spoken by scholars. Her crime was compounded by the fact that she had interrupted her own husband, humiliating him and calling immodest attention to herself.

Abraham Ha-Levi rose quickly and patted his daughter's arm. "You must forgive the bride. She has forgotten she is not in school now, eh?" He chuckled indulgently, opening the way for others to search for the humor they had so dangerously missed.

"A real Bruriah," one of the men said, with a broad smile, invoking the legendary woman scholar mentioned in the Talmud, known also for making her husband's life a misery and for eventually strangling herself because of her brash, untoward invasion of the male realm.

"Better be careful." Isaac's father wagged his finger at her in amusement. At this signal, a welcome murmur of levity washed over the guests, like a warm wave. Small, frozen smiles of embarrassment melted into wide grins; the stern, appraising valleys crossing the face of Isaac's mother relaxed into mere surface roads. Some leaned over to whisper pleasantries to Batsheva, who sat blushing and defiant and secretly amazed at the fuss. The color returned to Isaac's face and he forced a tight smile, nodding at his wife even as an inward shudder ran through him as if at a sudden evil portent. Her eyes, confused but unrepentant, met his with a flicker of amusement that unnerved him. He looked away quickly and, as the laughter died down, took up the thread of his explication.

Keeping her head down, Batsheva stared into her plate. The calm, the acute pleasure she had felt just moments before in exercising her intelligence, was spoiled for her now. Silently tapping the plate with an impatient finger, she waited for Isaac to finish and the last of the guests to leave so she could have it out.

"What did I do that was so awful!?" she said crossly, when only her parents and Isaac were left. She flounced with careless petulance into the white, down-filled velvet couch, disarranging the pillows and pulling them into her lap like a spoiled child.

"Nothing, my child." Abraham Ha-Levi shook his head a little sadly.

Isaac, leaning against the wall, pressed his lips together, his jaw rigid with fury. "Nothing? Excuse me, Aba, but it was extremely awkward for me . . ."

"I know, my son." She's right, he's right. Everybody's right, Abraham Ha-Levi thought wearily. I can't untangle these things. I never could.

"What is wrong with a woman knowing things? I was right, wasn't I, in what I said, Isaac?"

"Of course, but that isn't the point . . ." Isaac couldn't believe he needed to explain any of this.

"Then what is wrong? I'm sorry if I embarrassed you by interrupting you, Isaac. I guess I just enjoyed what you were saying so much, I got caught up in it and forgot myself. But really, Aba," she turned her attention back to her father, aware that Isaac's expression had not budged, "when will I go back to school? I want to register at Hebrew University for spring semester. I have to do it now, or it'll be too late—"

"The university!" Isaac's shocked voice exploded. "I can't believe my ears! No religious man or woman can go to that place of incredible impurity! How could you even think such a thing!"

"But Rabbi L——has a degree from the Sorbonne. Everybody knows it!"

"Ah, Rabbi L——." He took a deep breath, suddenly conscious of his harsh tone and the startled, inquiring eyes of his new father-in-law, who sat stroking his daughter's arm. "But you see, my dear, people like Rabbi L——have spent their lives learning Torah from sunrise to sunset. They know so much, and are on such a high spiritual level, that the wisdom of the goyim can't shake their faith. They can understand and assimilate it without it harming them. But you—you will forgive me, my dear, you are very bright and know much more than most women—but you are still very ignorant and vulnerable. It would turn your head, confuse you." He looked at Abraham Ha-Levi, seeking confirmation, but got only a noncommittal, rather cold nod of understanding.

"But I love to learn. I told you that before we were married."

Isaac didn't miss the accusation that had crept into her voice and it frightened him a little. "Perhaps I could learn Torah day and night too, bring myself up to that level, or at least close, and then go!"

Isaac laughed, glad to be on sure ground again. "It's unheard of for a young married woman to learn that seriously. It would take all your time—besides, it would soon bore you." Derision, amused contempt.

"Really, Batsheva, do you want to be cooped up with Talmuds all day?" her mother said doubtfully.

"I want to go to the university," Batsheva persisted, ignoring both comments. Hadn't she weathered similar battles all through high school? She fell into the familiar, tried-and-true strategy that had never yet failed her. She turned her eyes and attention full on her father's face. "I can't see how it would hurt me. Really, Aba, do you think it would? How could it?"

Abraham Ha-Levi looked at his daughter's pleading eyes, her lovely face. He had carried them both around with him, close to his heart and mind, since the moment she entered the world. She was dearer to him than his own life. And yet, what could he do? He rose heavily, silently, his straight back bent a little as if under some unseen burden. "It is late and we should be going."

"But, Aba," Batsheva's voice rose with surprise and indignation, "can I—"

"Batsheva," he said curtly, wearily, his heart contracting, "you're a married woman now who doesn't need her father's permission for anything. You and Isaac talk it over." He turned to his son-in-law. "I'm sure you will help Batsheva to learn. Perhaps even teach her yourself."

"Why, of course, Aba, nothing would give me more pleasure."

There was ingratiating sincerity and unconcealed doubt in his voice that mingled in a way his father-in-law preferred to pretend he did not hear. Abraham Ha-Levi went to the door and as he turned to go, he felt his daughter's arms tighten with childish love around his waist. Gently, but firmly, he pried them loose and walked away, feeling suddenly very old.

Her father and mother kissed her good-bye, her mother wetting her cheek with lipstick and tears, her father, straight-backed, impeccable, shaking hands with Isaac. She didn't know how her parents felt. A balloon of fear, of anguish, that began as a small controllable bubble inside her chest, began to grow as they neared the airport. She had wanted this, to be free, and yet some invisible, almost veinlike connection between herself and her parents seemed to throb and ache. "So far away in a strange new place," her mother sighed tearfully at the airport.

Batsheva patted her mother's wrinkled hand, hiding her own discomfort, her sense of panic at being left there, alone, to fend for herself with only her husband, this stranger, as family. "I will be fine." She smiled brightly. The Good Daughter, saying all the right, expected things. Did they notice how hollow and false the words rang? Did she want them to? Did she want them to say: Ah, we have made a mistake, come home with us? Her mind fantasized on it a moment: the silent, disgraceful trip home. Endless mortifying explanations to friends, teachers, and relatives. And then the stream of darkly dressed suitors, endless boring conversations, endless cups of tea, and by the end of the year, yet another attempt at matrimony with someone who would probably be no better (indeed, probably infinitely worse) than Isaac. God, the Torah, her womanly role. They all pointed in one immutable direction. Stay the course. Pray for a child. Rejoice in your home. Besides, there was one large compensation—Jerusalem. "I love Jerusalem, Mother," she said sincerely. "Let's think of it as just my going away to school in New York." Aging, worried parents.

"You must write us, Batsheva, as Isaac will be too busy to.

And you must call every week. If there is anything you need, anything at all, please let us know," her father said with a formality that hid his helplessness. He rubbed his hands together nervously. Batsheva wondered at the huge beads of sweat that slipped from beneath his black hat down his forehead to the sides of his cheeks. His hands were wet from wiping them away.

Ever since her wedding night, the bond between them had slackened. She felt grudging toward him, like a child promised a present and then denied it. An adult would have sensed that there was a score to settle, but in her feelings toward her father, she was still not an adult. You have hurt me and I am mad, was as far as she could define her attitude, which made her feel silly and childish.

Yes, she told herself. I am glad they are leaving. It will free me from playing the role of Isaac's dear, dutiful little bride. She had made this calculation with a cynicism that both appalled and delighted her: While her father was still around, she would do as she was told. Her reasoning was simple. The time was approaching when she would have to teach Isaac Meyer exactly whom he had married. It would be painful for him. It would hurt him and humiliate him. Like a doctor preparing a patient for surgery, she preferred the operating theater to be closed to close relatives who might sway her judgment and cause the knife to be held back, or to slip.

"Dear Aba, of course I will write." She wrinkled her nose at him, like a child.

His hand went instinctively to smooth back her hair, then he pulled it back a little foolishly, touching the wig, mark of the pious married woman. He wiped the sweat from his brow and patted her shoulder instead. The comradely touch of an equal.

Batsheva lay in bed a long time. She didn't bother to feel the place where her husband had been, familiar now, after several months of marriage, with its emptiness. As always, the empty bed continued to offend her like a sudden, unexpected slap across the face. Gone to the yeshivah already. But there beside the bed was the tray with a hot Thermos of coffee and a red rose he had left for her. She looked at it, her annoyance softening. She picked up the rose and let its fragrance wash over her. Just typical of him. She didn't like coffee and never drank it and what she needed was him beside her, not a tray. But still, it was awfully nice of him anyway, she told herself, trying and failing to work up the appreciation she felt she ought to have. Nice and completely unnecessary.

She washed her hands three times as the morning ritual required and began to recite her morning prayers. But it was no good. Her eyes brimmed over with tears of regret for the stubbornness of her soul, its recalcitrance. She had everything a woman could want, didn't she? And here she was, unable to thank God, to praise Him.

A child's confusion and anger reigned in her heart. She was not used to being told what to do on so regular a basis as she was with her newly acquired husband. He was even worse than her parents, who at least spoiled her most of the time. But Isaac Meyer Harshen walked a straight-and-narrow path and he didn't mind pushing and shoving her along with him. He told her, after consulting with his mother, which of her dresses he found acceptable (nothing with red, or bright colors that stood out) and what shoes were permissible (closed toes, low chunky heels). In his parents' house, Isaac's mother watched everything she did like an exacting and disapproving governess. She once even humiliated her in front of guests by correcting the way she ritually washed her hands before eating bread; the way she held the water, the amount she filled the cup, the position she held her hands in when she poured water over them, everything was criticized and corrected.

Isaac tutored her on when to speak and when to keep silent

when his friends—rabbis of all shapes and sizes, clothed in black and white, their faces almost hidden by beards of red and black and saintly white—filled the house. He asked her to sit in the kitchen and prepare them tea and cake, to serve them and then slide silently away when they began to discuss the weighty matters of the law, even though she understood the discussions quite well and was interested in at least hearing what they had to say. She understood that it was out of extreme piety that these men did not look her in the face, or speak directly to her. But all the same, it made her feel beneath contempt, almost as if she did not exist, as if she were just a shadow. They made her feel ashamed in a nameless, guilty, unfocused way. But most of all, it made her furious. She, who had dreamt of being looked at and admired! She felt a hot rebellion growing inside of her, gathering force like lava beneath a dormant crater.

Every day, try as she might to feel otherwise, she found herself filling with almost unbearable irritation from the little things he did to her—a mild correction in the way she said the prayers over the Sabbath candles, a barely perceptible nudge under the table to curb her outspokenness when he and his father were discussing the Torah portion of the week. These were enough for her to torture him with her silence in front of everyone. She was acutely aware of his embarrassment, the way she made him suffer. "Batsheva," her mother-in-law had said, her brow arched, "don't have the first fight and you will never have one." Old advice from old wives, long browbeaten into silence.

But perhaps, after all, she was right.

Batsheva finished her prayers and felt as if she had emerged from some cleansing ablution. She resolved to repent and try harder. She got up and looked out of the window at the deep Mediterranean blue of the sky, which never failed to amaze and cheer her. The exotic black dome of the Abyssinian Church, the spires of minarets, the black-and-white tallith shawls draped over men's coats as they returned from morning prayers at the synagogues to get ready for work made an exciting tapestry. She loved so much about her new life. Jerusalem, the subject of so many longing prayers recited by heart since childhood, the dream of every believing Jew, was now her address and it had not disappointed her. The rituals, the holidays, performed in community, instead of isolation, where they had been practiced so naturally for thousands of years, seemed to take on a richer color, to give a deeper satisfaction. It was as if in the past she had been a skin diver practicing skills in the blandness of a pool and had now, for the first time, been transported to the richness of a real coral reef. She was grateful to Isaac for having made it possible, and her gratitude brought out her guilt.

She walked listlessly around the lovely house, rubbing her fingers over dustless furniture, peering into spotless mirrors and windows, newly cleaned the day before by the cleaning girl, searching for something to do. It was beginning to dawn on her, for the first time, what a serious business she had gotten herself involved in. What, exactly, was she supposed to do all day while Isaac was in the yeshivah until eight or nine every night? Of course she knew what she was expected to do—goodness, hadn't they drummed that into all the girls at Bais Sarah ad nauseum? But it all started when you had children, all that keeping them clean and quiet and bringing them up to be good Torah Jews. What in heaven's name was a childless bride, full of life, raring to learn, to experience, to explore, to travel, to . . . live, supposed to do inside her clean, empty house?

Why not try to get involved in some charitable work? her mother had written. But she hated butting into other people's lives. Let them have her money, and welcome. But it seemed so tacky to insist on giving it to them personally, seeing them all humble and thankful. Anyhow, hadn't she learned that was the lowest form of charity, when you gave directly and the receiver knew who you were? She didn't know anyone yet who needed her help naturally—like a neighbor with six little children who was going in for an operation or, more likely, a nervous breakdown. Why, then it would have made her feel wonderful to step in, full of charity and willing, noble hands (although what exactly she could have done with six whiny, hungry kids was another story she sort of glossed over). But as it was, the neighbors had kept their distance, not out of unfriendliness, but out of awe.

Then, quite suddenly, it occurred to her. Why, she hadn't even made him a meal yet! Just cheese sandwiches when he came home at noon for lunch, or scrambled eggs. And so he had taken to eating dinner at the yeshivah or his parents'. He made no demands on her. I am no wife to him, she thought regretfully, the fragrance of the rose suddenly wafting through the room once more. I must do better.

She went into the kitchen and opened the cupboards. She took out her shiny new pots and pans, fingering their bright surfaces with pleasure, then opened the brand-new cookbooks and planned a feast. Broccoli with hollandaise sauce. Ratatouille. Baked macaroni and cheese. Mushroom soufflé. It all sounded so easy in the cookbooks. But then the white sauce for the macaroni wouldn't thicken, so she raised the flame, stirring constantly until she noticed little brown flecks in it and a burnt smell at the bottom of the pot. Unwatched, the macaroni boiled over. She lowered the flame and burnt her hand trying to mop up the hot water that dripped off the stove in rivulets. She got a little yolk into the egg whites for the soufflé, and as much as she beat them, they never stiffened, staying stubbornly in a limp, frothy mass. Then she remembered the macaroni, but it was too late, boiled shapeless into starchy globs. Patiently she threw it all out and started over. She tried making Jerusalem kugel, Isaac's favorite. It didn't seem too difficult just melting sugar in oil and mixing it with pepper into cooked noodles.

Painfully aware of her failures, she watched the pot carefully, draining the noodles into a colander at exactly the right moment and rinsing them with cold water. She waited for the sugar to melt and turn brown. But though the sugar on the bottom melted, the rest stayed in a white lump. Remembering the white sauce, she restrained her urge to turn up the heat. When finally, much later than the recipe called for, all the sugar carmelized into a brown syrup, she almost jumped for joy. But, heated to too high a temperature and poured onto the now cold noodles, to her horror the syrup sizzled and congealed into candied lumps that just wouldn't mix.

She sat down in a chair, rubbing her soap-reddened hands, feeling the burn blister swell up on the palm. Other girls had had mothers who took them in hand young and taught them how to make gefilte fish and kreplach. Now, sitting in the middle of the self-made mess, the waste, she ached with regret for the blithe way she had brushed off her mother's entreaties to spend some time in the kitchen. What was the point, she had always thought, of what you ate? A sandwich, eaten out in the hills, with the sun ready to set, was a beautiful meal, she had loudly proclaimed to her classmates and their well-nourished mothers. Anyway, Jewish cooking—all cooking—always seemed the same to her—one more way to combine eggs, margarine, flour, and sugar, fish, beef, chicken, garlic, tomato sauce, and vinegar. But now, wanting to make it an offering of her love, she remembered with sadness the proud, plump arms of the Jewish *balabustas* she had known, setting steaming platters in front of their husbands, proof of their unquestionable worth.

She sighed and took out the cookbook, leafing through it with a kind of desperate determination. She turned to the meat. After all, what could you do to meat? She opened the freezer and found she had none. It was getting almost funny now. But she put on her coat—this was a test, she told herself. Like crawling through mud and shinnying up ropes in an army exercise for new recruits, meant to ferret out the men from the boys. She gritted her teeth and found a butcher shop near the house and rejoiced once again at being in a place where all the butchers were kosher. She brought home a fine piece of rib roast and put it into the oven. Braving the heat of the stove, she basted it with marinade, her spirits lifting as the delicious smell escaped, filling the kitchen. She cut up a fresh salad, then peeled potatoes, only nicking her fingers once or twice. She licked off the blood, thinking it a fitting ingredient, considering her sacrifices this lovely fall afternoon on the altar of wifehood.

She dressed carefully, taking off the wig, which she hated, and combing out her lovely black hair. It had to be covered now completely each time she left the house, forbidden to other men's eyes. But in the house she was free, her young self again. She put Joy perfume behind her ears and between her breasts. She lit two red candles in sparkling crystal-and-silver holders and set them in the middle of the table with some red roses and baby's breath. And then she waited.

It had been an exciting, wonderful day at the yeshivah, Isaac thought with pride. He had made some discoveries that astounded his teachers, some wonderful connections and leaps of understanding between different commentaries that brought it all together. It was a rare achievement, even for one used to victories in the study hall. Time had passed so quickly, he had not even bothered to eat lunch.

Exhilarated, he had stayed on later to write it all down while it was fresh in his mind. It was after 8 P.M. when he finished. He had eaten dinner in the yeshivah with the other boys. On the way home he had stopped at his parents' and had gone over his day's work with his father. His mother, as usual, had plied him with cake and tea. Time had just flown.

It was after 10 P.M. when he finally turned up at his own door. He was a little ashamed of being so late, yet, remembering the arch of his wife's back the night before, he stiffened his shoulders and put on an air of carelessness.

He remembered how she had closed the door to the bathroom quietly behind her and let the water run, trying fruitlessly to drown out her quiet sobs. He had listened to the water running but it hadn't fooled him. He had turned over and hidden his face in the pillow, humiliated and angry. At first, remembering all the blood that had finally, righteously stained the sheets, he had been terrified of causing her further pain and had hurried to be done quickly. But later, when he felt her arms still insistent around him, he had tried to be patient, but his body, long used to the hurry sickness ingrained in him from childhood, had betrayed him. It could not be stopped. He was bitter at his failure, and angry at her for rubbing his face in it. Why must she mourn so? What did it matter, after all? Nothing of any great importance. Just the animal part of one's body satisfying itself. The important thing was that he had fulfilled the *mitzvah*. The blessing of his seed lay inside her.

He couldn't have known, and she would have died rather than to tell him, that again and again in the past months since their marriage, his gentle kisses, his hesitant exploring hands, had brought her to the edge of knowledge, to that boundary she had so longed to cross. But always too soon he stopped, withdrawing himself from her as if in a deliberate denial, so that she felt as if she were going mad with frustration and disappointment.

"You will see, my dear. God will bless us with children." He had tried at first to comfort her, startled by her pain. Now, used to it, he no longer reached out to her as she returned to bed, no longer tried to curb his resentment. His wife was an unpredictable woman, he had found out much to his chagrin. Difficult to manage. And there were still public ceremonies that required their united, smiling presence. She always tried to smile. But her eyes, bright with pain, denied it, cutting into him like knives. If he had been a different man—older perhaps, or just more experienced, or had less the tendency of all human beings to believe himself the center of the universe—he might have understood that she accused herself equally, of inadequacy, of being emotionally, even physically, at fault. He misread her sense of failure for accusation.

And as she got into bed, it became her habit to turn her back to him, not out of anger, but because she wanted to give him a chance to turn her over, to take her in his arms again and make it all come right. But he saw only the silent, stubborn set of her shoulders flatly rejecting him. For the first time in his life, he had opened himself up completely, making the ultimate, shameful concession to his physical being—he, who prided himself on his mind, the fineness of his spirit, who had spent years perfecting his denial of bodily urges! And she had looked at his offering and turned her back. It was the image of her back that came into his mind now, filling him with cool indifference. "Oh, so you are still up?"

She sat in a chair wearing the long, opaque flannel nightgown her mother-in-law had bought her, her hair pulled back carelessly. She looked at him and thought of the hours that had passed, causing the lettuce to wilt, the succulent roast to lose its juices and turn leathery, the potatoes to shrivel from tender crispness into cardboard hardness. "Where were you?"

"At the yeshivah, of course," he bristled, seeing in her eyes the same nameless accusation he thought he understood so well. "You should be very proud of the achievements I have made today," he called over his shoulder, walking into the kitchen to get a drink. "They all said . . ." He stopped, seeing the table set, the food uneaten. His heart sank with sudden understanding. But Isaac, used to parents who never, on principle, asked forgiveness from children, to teachers who had to be respected even when they insulted him, or belittled him, didn't know how to say he was sorry. Part of a man's character, he remembered learning, was formed by accepting the insults and injustices that were done to him by others as a God-given act meant to teach him humility and cause him to search his conscience for wrongs he had done others. It was Isaac's curious and fatal fault, one that many pious, intelligent, learned people share, that he didn't always know how to apply his learning. Lessons meant to teach one to forgive others' failings, lessons meant to promote goodwill and understanding among men, misapplied, as they were about to be at this critical juncture in Isaac Harshen's blossoming relationship with his wife, proved a turning point from which there was no real return.

And thus, Isaac, fully understanding what had happened, called out to his wife, not for forgiveness or understanding, not for indulgence, but for answers. "Where," he asked her sternly, "did you buy this meat?"

She appeared at the door, the lamplight outlining her long, shapely legs through the material, giving a burnished copper halo to the wisps of hair that strayed around her lovely, troubled face. She made a seductive picture that angered him even more.

"I got it in the butcher shop." She winced, pressing her lips together. She couldn't stand him when he used that tone.

"Which butcher shop?" His voice rose, pleased with her hesitance, digging, like a miner who has accidentally struck the mother lode, for guilt—guilt that would, he had no doubt, more than compensate for his own.

"Why, does it matter? It was certainly a kosher butcher. They had a certificate from the Jerusalem rabbinate . . ."

"Jerusalem rabbinate," he mocked. "Zionist appointees! It's as good as *treife*. I wouldn't have eaten it anyway."

She stood stock still, looking at him as if he were a madman. It was a look that spurred him on even more.

"Don't you know anything? Kosher meat here is not like kosher meat in America. There they eat anything. But here, we don't trust the word of rabbis that work hand in hand with the government. They're simply political appointees. Meat must be watched over by the Bet Din Tzedek, 'Badatz,' the only God-fearing . . ."

She covered her ears with her hands, then picked up the roast and flung it into the garbage. She watched the gravy splatter down the sides of the garbage can and smelled the flowers and the waxy scent of candles that had burned down to a sputter. She ran into the bathroom, shutting the door behind her. This time, she didn't bother to run the water, or to stifle her sobs.

"Batsheva." He banged on the door, filled with remorse. "Please come out. I was harsh, but it was only for your own good!" Familiar words that had so often been said to him, bedrock of his childhood! "Batsheva . . ." His voice began to grow hopeless, and the hopelessness nudged him toward his only ally, self-righteousness. All right then, let her carry on if she must! But really, it is her own fault, her own problem. What can I do but point out her mistakes to her? After all, I could no more eat that meat than I could eat pig! A man must discipline his wife, even our sages insist upon this. He went on, distorting all the things he knew were true, all the beautiful things he had learned in the Talmud about a man's loving his wife as himself and honoring her more than himself; about a man's speaking to his wife in a gentle voice, as she is easily moved to tears. He was a scholar, and in his search, he had no problem finding other quotes to justify himself. By the time he was finished, he had no trouble leaving her to sob quietly in the bathroom as he climbed into bed. Exhausted from the effort, he fell asleep immediately.

When she awoke the next morning, the sun was already high, blazing through the half-opened blinds. She had no desire to get out of bed. No reason to, she thought, turning over a little bitterly. Then, as it sometimes happens, for no reason at all, she felt herself growing warm with a kind of joy, almost physically lighter. She whistled to herself and, her joy growing vast and inexplicable, she jumped up and down on the bed. Free! Free at last! For hadn't she tried to be what was expected of her? And it had all come to nothing. In that case, she told herself, I must create my life anew, every day. If I can't be what they want—"they" being her parents, her husband, the whole suffocating world around her—then let me be what I want! It made perfect sense.

And all at once it became crystal clear to her how she would fill her endless days. How was it that she hadn't thought of it earlier! She went to the closet and took down a large case, handling it with reverence. Her favorite wedding gift of all. She unwrapped it carefully, looking it over the way most women might examine a precious diamond necklace. Her father had given her both actually. The jewels had been carefully crafted in Tel Aviv by master jewelers and were worth over one hundred eighty thousand dollars. Lying in a safe deposit box in a bank vault, she thought them quite a useless gift. She would have little occasion to wear them in informal Israel. But this—this wonderful camera! A Leica! That had been her own idea. She wound in the film, breathing in the metal and rubber and chemicals as if they were expensive perfume. She was going to take some wonderful pictures. She would go climbing hills to take pictures of wildflowers; up to Masada to photograph the Roman encampment and the Qumran caves where the Dead Sea Scrolls were found; Solomon's Pools, David's Tomb. Why, it would take months, years, to capture it all!

She rummaged through her closet to find something practical to wear and found a pair of long culottes and a boat-neck sweater that showed off her pretty neck. She remembered that her mother had been doubtful about the outfit—culottes seemed a little like pants, which were not acceptable attire for a religious girl. But there were pleats in the front that really made it look mostly like a skirt. She hesitated, then put on a pair of socks and sneakers. That was also not acceptable attire for a married woman. She looked in the mirror and pursed her lips. I will do what I want. I'm married now and Aba and Ima are old and far away, she told herself, even managing to get a little satisfaction from imagining her parents' disapproval. She looked at herself in the mirror. That awful wig! It was so hot and heavy and it was ruining her hair. She took it off and flung it to the floor. She pinned her hair up and tied a scarf around it. Only a few bangs showed.

She repeated this ritual day after day, leaving early each morning and coming back late every afternoon. Like countless pilgrims for thousands of years, she explored Jerusalem. Compared to the other great cities of the world—Paris, New York, London—Jerusalem was a little village. Often, people would give her directions by saying: "One door down from Schatz's butcher shop," or "Across the street from the main post office." There was only one department store, a handful of movie houses, and two dozen or so restaurants of note. With very little effort, she learned to know every street, every alleyway, every turn in the road. She could not get over its antiquity. In Europe she had seen homes and museums that made America seem raw and new. But Jerusalem made Europe seem like a child. In Europe, an antique might be a six-hundred-year-old chair. But in Jerusalem, something old was a thirty-five-hundred-year-old burial urn that held the ashes of men who lived and died when the Pharaohs still ruled Egypt.

Through her lens, she found a real, bustling, colorful city of incredible variety, an everchanging kaleidoscope of cultures and religions. But other times, she found a white and shining vision, nestled serene and modest among gentle rolling hills—luminous, radiant, and not quite real, occupying a space not quite in heaven and yet not quite on earth.

The month passed in a wonderful, exciting rush, the negatives piling up with fantastic accomplishment. But still there was one picture especially she wanted to take that had so far eluded her: the first morning light just as night broke and the sun appeared, revealing the whiteness of the city. It meant staying up all night, alone, out in the hills, something she would need to explain to her husband. But how could she explain this to Isaac Meyer? He took so little interest in what she did. She had once shown him her camera and he had said, "It is a sin to make graven images."

And she had just looked at him, flabbergasted. It was true that one wasn't allowed to make statues to worship, but that was a long way from taking photographs of the mountains, she told herself. She felt in her heart that the images she captured were a kind of psalm, a paean of praise to God for His incredible handiwork. How could that possibly be wrong? She decided to ignore him and go her own way as much as possible.

She waited until a few days before the anniversary of Israel Ben Dov's death, when she knew Isaac Meyer would leave at midnight to join hundreds of other Hassidim to say prayers of repentance at the Western Wall. When she was sure he was gone, she jumped out of bed. The city, which usually went to bed at ten and rose again at six, was strangely alive. Crowds of black-suited men and boys walked like a dark army up the streets toward the Old City and the Western Wall. Some wore prayer shawls whose white stripes shone lustrous and dreamlike in the silver moonlit streets. She drove toward the place the Arabs call the Tomb of Samuel the Prophet, one of the highest points in the city. The road she drove along wound its way through dark orchards and forests, thick and black-green. She hadn't expected Israel to be green. She had expected desert, camels, and shepherdesses. She laughed at herself. A sort of Disneyland Middle East. But it was nothing like that. The road took her through Ramot, a suburb that reminded her of California. Beautiful stone villas with red-tiled roofs nestled cozy and familiar in the hillside. Despite the dark, the quiet, she never felt fear. It was as if God were thick about her, the night His warm cloak. The sky felt closer in Jerusalem. God felt closer. She felt encompassed by His goodwill and protection.

She found the place just as dawn broke and she climbed to the top of the minaret. Already the muezzins at the mosque in the nearby village were sounding the call for morning prayers. Their nasal singsong blended into the fabric of the city, another thread, part of the exotic cloth she loved. Then there was only the quiet click of her camera as she captured the precious first light. She had to adjust the camera for the perfect light setting. Too much would wash it out. Too little would leave it in darkness. It must be perfect. For a few hours she sat entranced, hypnotized, enveloped by the indescribable beauty and spirit of the place, watching the sun rise and move across the sky, transforming the city, the forests, the hills, with each tiny change in the shape, or intensity, or the color of its light. As it moved, certain hills were brought forward, their white stone houses etched in bright relief, awash in red, then pink, mauve, and blue. Then a cloud would float by, and its presence would lighten all colors, like a light wash brushed over watercolors. No matter how carefully she tried to hold the scene still, to focus on it realistically, it kept moving just beyond her grasp, blurring into myth and vision. She felt awe.

She took roll after roll and felt happier than she had ever felt in her life, putting the finished rolls into her purse, taking out rolls still unopened, unexposed. She was at peace with God and man. It even made her relent toward Isaac Meyer. Perhaps she would bring him up here with her and he would feel the beauty that is not written in any book. Perhaps she could acquaint him with the God she knew—the one of kindness and compassion and exquisite, delicate creativity, who created human beings out of goodness so that they might experience the incredible beauty of His handiwork, the joy of being alive.

It came to her like a revelation: She was one of them—that crowd of pilgrims of every faith who quickened their weary steps toward an incredible lifetime goal. Jerusalem. It seemed to her that wherever else she might go, her life could never have as much meaning and depth as it had here. The beauty of the city touched her artist's eye and her loving, religious soul. Its variety satisfied her hope for adventure, and its Jewishness provided her with the greatest gift of all: normalcy. After the artificial ghettos of Brooklyn and the cultlike isolation of California—an island in a sea of people who thought her odd and strange, who didn't understand her customs and beliefs at all—she felt a magical sense of happiness at having finally arrived at the mainland; at having finally found her way home.

Isaac Meyer Harshen lay back on his wife's bed, staring at the ceiling. He was deep in painful thoughts, trying to make some important decisions. On three separate occasions that day, rebbes of rank and importance had approached him with information about his wife that each felt important enough to overrule the Divine commandments against gossip and slander. She had been seen, they told him, wearing pants and without head covering. Their wives or their students had confirmed this. Another had seen her alone in the hills at night near the Tomb of Samuel, as he led his students to the nighttime prayer of exultation beneath the light of the moon. She went for drives each day, unchaperoned, to distant places. These men, whom he respected as both learned and politically powerful leaders, looked meaningfully into his eyes and held him firmly by the shoulder as they imparted this information.

He was frightened. They all wished him to do something, but he was not sure what that must be. Ever since their wedding night, he had felt her discontent. He had wanted obedience, but he had envisioned gaining it through kindness and compassion, through gentle hints, through the respect that was due him as a scholar and a husband. But she mocked him, he could feel that. He blushed thinking at how he fumbled in bed and how she moved away from him with such alacrity, such pleasure. He was chagrined at his failure and bitter at her lack of help, her lack of sympathetic understanding. He wanted so much for her to love him, to want his body, to admire his ideas, to respect his authority. But he had no idea how to achieve all these things together. He did not understand her; she was a strange, exotic creature whose needs were utterly mysterious to him. He wanted to satisfy her but had no idea how.

As head of the family, he told himself, trying to still his panic, I am the person whose duty it is to guide her. I am responsible for her actions. I have to point out the dangers I see, warn her, exert my authority. I must stop mincing words. He got up and began pacing the floor, his hands behind his back. If I only had some key to unlock her, he thought. He was very sure the things she did during the day were harmless, but they were causing both of them to be talked about. She didn't understand that this wasn't America! Here they were both in a fishbowl. There were spies everywhere. They were in a public position. Eventually the Hassidim would look to them for guidance in everything—where to send their children to school, whom to marry, whether or not to have an operation. They—or rather he—would be the sole authority for all their spiritual and physical dilemmas. His answers would be obeyed slavishly, without question. Even his simple everyday activities—how he dressed, at what time he went to the synagogue, would be picked over carefully for meaning and object lessons.

All this would happen in due course. But now, this blind acceptance was not coming to him, to them. First they would be watched by the Hassidim like animals in a zoo for any signs of aberrant behavior, for any indication of unworthiness. Their every movement would be scrutinized and criticized, held up to the measure of past sainted leaders of the sect. And should he be found wanting, he would be ridiculed and thrown out. He would not exert any power over them. Already he was being criticized, because of his wife! Didn't she understand that because of her, his piety, his scholarship, would be held up to doubt? He rubbed his forehead in anguish. How had he allowed her to go on in this way! How had he let it come to this! He had assumed that she was home doing what all married, childless women do: cleaning, cooking, reading Bible stories in the Yiddish *Tzana Reana*. If she went out, he had assumed it had to do with shopping, or with some charitable work, or perhaps to visit his sisters. He had not thought to question her because of their strained relations and how happy and content she had seemed.

She was such a stranger to him, he realized. He knew nothing at all about her. He scoured his mind for clues to her heart, her character. Her beauty, her lineage, had blinded him. He could remember nothing of the talks they had had in America, the ideas she had shared with him. He walked idly over to her desk. Her books had come from America. A whole library. They had not even been unpacked yet. Yes, perhaps that would help. He opened the package. D. H. Lawrence. He had never heard of the man. There were so many books there. He picked up one and read the title: *Women in Love*. He sat down on his wife's bed and began to read.

It was noon when Batsheva finally came home, hot, tired, and exultant. She flung off her shoes, which were full of dust and small stones, and washed her hot, sunburnt face in cool water. She thought of the packages of unpacked books. She had shipped them last because she couldn't bear to be parted from them for long. What a perfect way to spend the afternoon, she thought, going through the pages, rereading the passages she loved. Books were like old friends, with their worn covers and well-thumbed pages that fell open at her favorite passages. She went into the bedroom and her heart did a quick, unpleasant somersault. There, seated quietly on the bed, was Isaac Meyer—and strewn carelessly all around him were her precious books. He leaned back, his elbows cutting into the thin paperbacks, bending them forever out of shape. She felt physically violated. Then something occurred to her, and a shy smile played around her lips.

"What are you reading, Isaac?"

He did not answer, but held the book up, a blank look on his face.

"Is the English too difficult for you? If you like, we could read it together. I would be happy to read it to you. It is one of my favorites." Isaac Meyer and herself in the evening discussing literature. She and Isaac Meyer watching the sun rise. She would open his eyes to a whole new world they could share.

He said nothing, but stood up, his hands held palms up, his thumbs gripping either side of the book, and in one swift, savage motion turned the pages back and ripped it in half. He threw it to the floor and ground the pages with his heel.

"No!" She threw herself at his feet, trying to pull it free. She pushed at the hard, stiff, black leather of his shoes, bruising her fingertips. It was not the book under his feet, it was herself. She felt black and blue, as if the black leather had trampled her own flesh. He grasped her arm and lifted her roughly from the floor. His face was contorted in disgust and rage. His voice was hoarse, his throat muscles strained and corded with tension.

"This . . . this filth you do not bring into our home! Every sin, every temptation made beautiful and desirable. You will have no time to read such things as the wife of Isaac Meyer Harshen. If I had known what putrid things your mind was filled with,

I never would have . . ." He stopped, reconsidering, controlling himself. "But you are my wife now, the wife of the future leader of the Ha-Levis, in the holiest of holy cities. I will wipe your mind clean of the filth of your childhood, the looseness of your education . . ."

She pulled her arm free of him and wiped the tears that streamed down her cheeks. She gathered the books together with a kind of mad energy, smoothing down their bent and wrinkled pages. He grabbed both her wrists and threw her down on the bed, his face over hers, his hot breath over her nose and mouth.

"I have seen you pretend to be asleep when I come near you. I have seen you stiffen when I touch you. You are not used to the simple touch of a pure man. These books have made you crave depravity and filth. But you will soon forget that."

She looked at his eyes, so close above her own. The pupils were dilated. His mouth was stretched into a vacant smile, as if his mind was thinking of something far away. His body lay over hers, crushing her with its inert, careless weight. A small nugget of fear fell into her stomach and shot up hot through her chest to the back of her throat, choking her with rage and humiliation and helplessness. Then he seemed to come to himself, to remember. His right hand dropped her wrist and he caressed her face. "So beautiful, so pure, but all on the outside. Let me help you, Batsheva, to cleanse yourself. To cleanse your soul."

She pulled her other wrist free and pushed him away, rolling out of his grasp. She grabbed her books and clasped them to her chest, trying helplessly to keep her tears from wetting them. "Yes, you'll have to help me. You will have to help me to find the filth, because I have read all these books and haven't found any. They are mine. You have no right to touch them." She felt herself growing calm. Let the operation begin then. "Don't you dare bully me," she said slowly, deliberately. "I don't know who you think you are, but I am Batsheva Ha-Levi. Everything around you, all the money, the prestige, the honor—it all comes from me. What are you?" She looked at him contemptuously, haughtily. "An inexperienced, uneducated man. A boorish, classless . . . I hate you. I hate having your heavy body over mine . . ." All the rage that had been buried deep inside her since the wedding night began to bubble like a hot volcano, spilling over in destructive, harsh words she did not even mean. She felt ashamed, yet full of pleasure at his stunned, humiliated face. But then his face turned dark red. She backed away instinctively toward the door.

He followed her movement with his eyes and seemed to calm down. He had meant for her to love him, and she threw her hatred and contempt in his face—she who was ruining him! He smiled unpleasantly. Her rebelliousness left him no choice. He would pull out all stops, use all the ammunition he had.

"Very good. And then you know what our sages say about husbands and wives. No? I will quote it to you: 'The sages commanded a woman to exceedingly honor her husband, to fear him, and all her actions must have his approval. He should be in her eyes as a minister or a king; she must act according to his desires, and remove all things that he hates. And this is the way of the holy and pure daughters and sons of Israel in their marriages.' " His voice got even calmer. "You have to understand that, Batsheva. I own you and everything that belongs to you. I am the final authority over what you can read, how you can dress, what you can do. This is God's Law and it is for your own good." He closed his eyes and began to quote. " 'Any woman who refuses to perform any of the labor she is obligated to do, can be forced to do it even by the whip.' I want to help you, don't you understand? To lead you down the right path, and you must not resist me, for your soul's sake." He shook his head from side to side, very deliberately. "You have been very rebellious. Do you think I have not understood your message? Do you think that I don't know you walk out every morning dressed like a *prutza*, in pants and tight sweaters, your hair uncovered, to roam the city? You have humiliated me. 'But it is degrading for a woman to be continually outside and in the street, and the husband should restrain her from this. He should only allow her to go out once or twice a month, for the only splendor for a woman is to sit in her corner of the house.' As it is written: 'The King's daughter is all glorious within.' " He clenched and unclenched his fist. "It is Eve's curse: 'And he shall rule over you.' This is God's command."

She listened in shocked disbelief as he quoted effortlessly from unquestionably sacred sources. Could it be true? She had never heard that before, and yet he quoted it, word for word. Like a pious young Hindu girl in India or a devout young Catholic bride in Italy, Batsheva Ha-Levi Harshen had no wish to break out of the framework that her birth had given her. As she had once told Elizabeth: "It's like that great chain of being the Romantics always talk about. Everybody is born to certain parents at a certain time and place for a reason. True, it puts you in a certain box, but it's more a refuge, a shelter, than a prison. It helps define what you are, and helps you to play the God-given role you were born to." What she had wanted and expected from her life and from the man she married was not to break the boundaries of that box, but to expand them, balloonlike, to include more and more. She wanted the doors and windows to be open so that she could take in everything that wasn't forbidden by *Halacha*, Jewish law, and give it its place: art, music, poetry, literature, good movies, good plays, and especially, her photography. She wanted no longer to be held back by those boundaries established by her rabbi-teachers, which, like barbed-wire fences around mine fields, often shut out a wide margin of area that was perfectly safe to trod upon, simply to ensure one's feet from straying too near real dangers. Not being a scholar, she accepted that she wasn't in a position to draw those boundaries for herself. That was what she had originally found so appealing about Isaac—the profundity of his knowledge, which she assumed would give him a wide breadth of understanding to draw the thinnest, subtlest of distinctions between the permissible and the forbidden that would lend her life new horizons. With him by her side, she had reasoned, she would no longer be hemmed in by those wide and useless margins that confined her friends and classmates. And now, to her unmitigated horror, she felt the ground shrinking beneath her, all windows locked shut, the door slammed closed, the box becoming so small she could hardly find room to stand up. It literally took her breath away.

"I have had people telling me that my wife runs around by herself. My mother has come to visit you every day this week and you have not been home. Where have you been? With other men, perhaps . . . ?" He grabbed the camera off the bed and held it.

His action seemed to wake her from her stupor. "Isaac, please, please. Be careful with it, it's a delicate instrument." How to get his destructive hands off it? Pry it away? How, how? "I wasn't doing anything wrong," she pleaded. "Just taking some pictures. Pretty pictures of the hills." She instinctively spoke to him in soothing, simple language, the way one speaks to a very small child or a maniac. "There aren't even any people in them. It took me such a long time to focus right and get the perfect lighting. How can you even . . . ?" His attack was so sudden and vicious. She had had no training in self-defense, except for a few moves Elizabeth had once shown her for fun. Her parents, her beauty, her money, had always protected her before. She felt entirely vulnerable and helpless. She had never even really disliked anyone before, but here she was faced with deliberate cruelty and narrow-minded suspicion. It was like being punched or slapped in the face. If Elizabeth were here, she thought suddenly, she would say; "Up yours, Isaac Meyer." The thought calmed her, and she felt a hysterical giggle begin. She would kick him in the behind and tell him to leave her alone with all this bull. People don't belong to people, Isaac. Wives don't belong to husbands. This is a partnership, she would say. And give me back my camera before I kill you.

But she wasn't Elizabeth. She wasn't in America, she realized almost for the first time. She was in a totally different society with a radically different set of rules. Women did not call their husband obscenities. They did not openly defy them or their wishes. His hands were big and powerful. She rubbed her wrists, which were still red and hot from his grip. She suddenly realized that for the first time in her life she was afraid of being physically hurt. She stood up with dignity and it took all her courage to say calmly: "Please give me back my camera, Isaac. I promise to tell you the next time I go. I'll put my wig back on, only it's so hot and heavy. I'll try harder . . ." She was ready to promise anything to get the camera back, to put her books away, out of harm's way. "I'm just not used to all these rules. We learned different things in school from the rabbis in America. They're more lenient there. I'll try harder to be a good wife . . . please give me back the camera, Isaac." She reached out for it.

He pulled it out of her grasp. Torture was a new experience for Isaac Meyer. So long dominated by his parents and teachers, by the million dos and don'ts of his belief, he felt acute pleasure in watching another human being squirm helplessly under his total control. He toyed with the overweening power of his male strength and authority. They were all alone, after all. Who was to see or know what happened here? Deep in his soul, he was fearless, laughing at the idea that any unseen power could judge him, laughing at God. He thought of her soft body turned away from him in revulsion, remembered the stiffening of her limbs, contracting away from him.

"I told you graven images were a sin, didn't I?"

"But, Isaac, I told you, it's only trees, hills . . ."

He flipped open the camera and ripped out the film, exposing the roll. A red and blinding light lit up behind her eyes. She imagined jumping on him, scratching his face with her nails. But she could do nothing. She was immobilized with a shaking hatred. Her tears seemed to please him. Rather than soften him, it spurred him on. The small bully in him, so long repressed, sprang up whole. "Now you will hand over the books. Come on. I'll take them eventually, so don't be foolish. Don't make me hurt you."

"But, Isaac, what do you need them for? Can't we talk about this?" But all the while she spoke, she watched him methodically pick up the scattered volumes and place them in the carton.

"No!" But with one quick and brutal movement, he snatched the books out of her hands and added them to the pile. He carried them to the bathtub. She saw him empty bottles of toilet water on them, then set them on fire. The smoke rose and billowed and crashed on the ceiling, then flattened and spread out, polluting the house. Grabbing her camera and her purse, she ran out into the street, blinded by grief and smoke and the stench of something so foul and cruel—not just Isaac, but the way he twisted all the things she held sacred to fashion a prison for her. It broke her heart. She hailed a taxi and took it to the main post office, the only place one could place a foreign call.

"Aba," she whispered, choking.

"Who is this? Batsheva. Oh, yes."

"Oh, yes"? No "My dear child, what is the matter?" Doesn't he hear that I'm crying? "Aba. I want to come home," she managed to get out before her sobs shook her body and made the words incoherent. There was silence. "Aba, please. I'm so unhappy. Isaac is a cruel man. He has . . ."

"Batsheva, listen and listen carefully." The voice was that of a stern stranger. "Isaac called me a little while ago. You must stop this nonsense immediately. How dare you parade around Jerusalem in pants and without head covering, all alone in the middle of the day? If only half what he says is true . . . Is it true?"

"I just wore some culottes and I took some pictures," she protested sickly, hopelessly. She tried to conjure the image of her young father to be her companion in that booth: his work-roughened hands digging deep into his pockets for candy, caressing her hair out of her eyes, smoothing the pain from cuts and bruises. But she could not find him. He had disappeared, and all that remained was this righteous stranger, granite hard and cold.

"So it's true, then. I can't believe my ears. That my daughter should prove such a disgrace to me and to the two-hundred-year-old name of Ha-Levi. Hitler tried to destroy our family. But you, you, Batsheva, are worse than he. Because you will finally complete his work. You will destroy everything I have worked and prayed for."

"Aba, sweet Aba, please listen to me. It's not true. He is so mean to me. He took away my camera, burned my books. He said they were filthy . . ." She sounded so foolish, she realized. Childishly foolish. But there, exhausted and heartbroken, totally alone, she needed her father's comfort and she had no words to earn it. She had been taught never to speak ill of anyone, to give everyone the benefit of the doubt. Even if it were true, it was *richilus*, slander, one of the greatest sins. How could she say he was a monster who reveled in humiliation and petty bullying? How could she describe how the revulsion crept up her skin like insects when he touched her? She did not know these things, although she felt them. She had not yet the consciousness to separate and define her feelings and trace their history. She wept bitterly into the black, impersonal phone.

"My dear child. I know how hard it is for you." His voice had softened, becoming lovingly familiar. "A new country, newly married. There are so many things to get used to. You must look to your husband for guidance. He is a scholar, I know, and probably busy with his books. But his scholarship must have given him some understanding. He will teach you what you need to know. You are acting out of ignorance. Jerusalem is not California. It's a privilege for you to be there. Only the holiest people have such a *zchus.* Try to be worthy of it, of your husband."

"But, Papa, he's . . ."

"Please, nothing bad about Isaac. I will not listen, it's *loshon hara.* I am going to hang up now. Write to me and try to make me proud."

"Papa, don't!" But the phone had gone dead and outside the door, the blond tourist in the Harvard T-shirt looked in curiously. He had a kind face, she thought. Like Elizabeth. If only she could call her! She would understand. But Elizabeth was at Cambridge and had not written so far.

Isaac had called him. She imagined him watching her run out the door, his sick smile on his lips, knowing that she would call her father, knowing what would happen. At that moment her dislike and fear and humiliation suddenly converged and metamorphosed into an emotion she had not known before: hatred.

She wandered aimlessly around the city, her mind a blank. With sunset the weather in Jerusalem turned cold. A light drizzle began to fall. She shivered, hugging herself, and did not return the stares of passersby, well-dressed in heavy sweaters and carrying umbrellas. She had rushed out of the house with nothing but a few cents in her purse, change from a soda she had bought. The rest she had already used to pay the cab-driver. Her stomach ached from hunger, and her mouth was caked and dry. She was so tired, tired. She sat down by the bus stop and watched bus after bus come and go. Her feet grew wet and soggy from the pelting rain. I have no place to go, but to him. No one at all that I know, but him. Slowly, the hunger and cold chipped away at her pride and fear until only the most basic, primal needs of her body were left. In the distance she could already hear the faraway drone of the bus, bearing down, waiting to stop in front of her and bear her away to him, to Isaac. In her heart a weary resignation began to take hold.

Suddenly, the sound of footsteps made her lift her head. It was a young girl running to catch the bus. She wore a pantsuit with a zipper down the front that hugged the curves of her pretty body. Her light, agile feet danced along the wet street, carefree and reckless. She was laughing out loud, breathless, and her long dark hair, all sparkly from raindrops, streamed out behind her, bouncing joyously with each step. Batsheva felt her heart stop. No, whatever happened, she would not do that. Go back to Isaac Harshen in that smoke-filled house. She felt her lips press together with resolve. She took her purse over to a lamp post and rummaged through it in the waning light. So little money! But then she found a zippered compartment she had forgotten about. She looked inside it and there, still shiny and valid, was an American Express Gold Card, Visa, and MasterCard, and her American passport.

Chapter nine

The bed at the King David Hotel was very large and comfortable. It was an old, elegant hotel, finely maintained, she decided, and the food, delivered hot and tempting on a tray, was wonderful. She was not sure how much she ate, or even what. But it was by turns warm and sweet and savory and filling. The aroma of steaming coffee filled the room, mingling with the heady scent of a fantastic concoction they called a Sabra—a rum-soaked cake with a baseball-sized scoop of whipped cream. She leaned back into the fluffy pillows, licking the cream daintily off her fingertips like a perfectly contented child, and snuggled beneath the blankets, toasty warm. Her wet clothes lay drying all over the room. Later, she thought, I will go down into the lobby and buy some new clothes. She went to the vanity and unpinned her hair, letting it tumble down her shoulders and back. She danced around the room and let it whip around her face and felt a joy, a youthful exuberance, bubble through her body the way it had not in many months. She didn't look too closely at her face in the mirror, afraid that it might somehow have changed, that she might look visibly older. Somehow she had expected that. She allowed herself only one quick glance in which she could find nothing different about the face or body, except that she loved it less now, respected it less. But then she smiled, and the face smiled back: sweet, sweet, pretty thing! She hugged herself.

She formulated no plans but was satisfied to drift. Later she wandered into a boutique in the lobby and flipped idly through the racks of clothes until she came to a bright-red pantsuit with a zipper down the whole front. Her fingers closed around it impulsively. "Would you like to try it on, dear?" the saleslady murmured.

She began to back away hesitantly, then stopped. "Yes," she said firmly, surprising herself. "I would like that very much."

The fit, as the saleslady gushed, was magnificent. Tastefully tight and perfect, emphasizing her generous bust and tiny waist and long, long legs. She looked at herself in the mirror, fascinated. She turned around and let her long hair swing like a cape around her shoulders. The image she saw could have been that of a movie star, or a singer, a model or an actress. What a desirable woman I am, she thought, shocked, the thought coming to her as a newly observed fact, the way one suddenly discovers one's hair is streaked with blond or red from having spent long days out in the sun. The idea made her self-conscious and shy.

She became almost painfully aware of the faces in the lobby and in the shop that had turned to peer at her as she studied herself in the mirror, and she hurried behind the curtain to take the outfit off. A certain part of her was pleased with the attention and urged her to buy it, to walk proudly out of the store wearing it, hips swinging. She had a certain urge to overdo it, to compromise even her own standards of modesty to show her utter comtempt for Isaac's. The way a put-upon teenager will say: Okay, if that's what they think of me, that's what I'll be. But even though she was just a teenager and very put-upon at the moment, she had a very strong sense of herself, a stubbornness born of years of resisting teachers, friends, parents, and the world outside her golden ghetto. She pressed her lips together. Why should I let him do this to me, make me into something I'm not? She didn't recognize herself in the mirror as herself, but as the embodiment, the confirmation, of Isaac's falsest accusations. She took it off and gave it back to the saleswoman apologetically: "It just isn't me." The dress she chose was very soft and clingy, with sleeves well above the elbows and a modest but open V neck. She looked very girlish and vulnerable in it. She put nothing on her head to cover her hair. It was a compromise she could live with. Charge it, she told the saleswoman, waving the card like a battle flag. Charge it.

Later that day, she went out and bought bright dresses and leather sandals for long, lovely walks, and high-heeled patent-leather shoes for dancing and a lovely lavender bathing suit, because its color pleased her eye. But if someone were to have asked her seriously at this time where and when and how, precisely, she would do this walking, dancing, and bathing, she would have looked up a little surprised and chagrined perhaps and given the matter some thought. But as it was, no one did and she gave the subject no thought. Like a small child stuffing herself on sweets, she could not satiate her hunger. The buying finally became wearisome to her. She wandered listlessly through the lobby, looking into the shop windows. She stopped in front of the glittering display in Stern's Jewelers, her eyes fascinated by the diamonds and rubies and emeralds heaped up like a king's ransom. She pressed her lips together as if to keep from laughing out loud.

"May I help you?"

Help me. Yes. She thought of her father's harsh voice. "How dare you do this . . ." "Yes. I am buying myself a present. Something very expensive." She bought an enormous pearl-and-diamond ring, large and gaudy. Not her style at all, like the necklace in the bank vault. She would never wear it. Waiting for the credit card to clear, she went into the gift shop and bought ten new novels: Vonnegut, Tyler, Shaw, Eco. Charge it, charge it, she told the salespeople. Then she went back and pocketed the small box with the ring she didn't want, thinking with pleasure of the justice of her father paying the bills, and her hunger began to abate. There was now only one more thing left to buy. She went out of the hotel with firm, purposeful steps and crossed the street, not allowing herself to hesitate for a second, knowing that if she did, her courage, which was not quite real, but rather forged in a dreamlike vacuum, could vanish at any moment.

"Yes, miss?" The travel agent's hair was black and thick, she noted, and his eyes appreciative. Israeli men. So many had those large, handsome heads and that dark, romantic coloring. She felt an absurd blush creep up her cheek.

"I . . . I," This was no time for weakening, she kicked herself mentally. Play the part, damn it! She straightened up and lifted her head, looking him full in the face with a mysterious smile (at least that's what she was attempting. She had no way of knowing if it *was* mysterious or simply, as she suspected, foolish and gawking, like a teenager sneaking into an adults-only bar). "I want you to please arrange some tours for me around the country."

"Of course, miss. Where would you like to go?"

"Everywhere," she said before she could stop herself.

He laughed. "How long do you have, miss?"

"Why, as long as it takes, I suppose," she said, getting a little hot, thinking this must be the stupidest conversation the man had ever had. Suspicious too. Maybe he'd call the police or medics. But he just looked at her seriously and politely, and began leafing through some books.

"A five-day tour of the country leaves tomorrow. The Galilee, Tel Aviv, Haifa, then three days in Eilat—a little sun, wonderful this time of year. How is that?"

"Fine," she said with what she hoped was adult dignity and decision. Then she took out the credit cards and held them out toward him like candy bars, defeated by the smile on his face as she let him choose.

The next day she waited in the lobby early, surrounded by tourists. She didn't check out of the hotel. A hundred dollars a day didn't seem worth bothering about, and anyway she needed someplace to leave all her new things. She took only her camera, bathing suit, a dress, and a few changes of underwear. She wore her new dress and walking sandals.

"Where's your father and mother?"

"Excuse me?" She looked over the woman who had spoken. Teased blond hair, gray at the roots, wearing an unmercifully revealing print dress that showed much more than anyone needed to see of her wrinkled flesh.

"A *maidel* like you by herself." The woman shook her head doubtfully, with a stare that began at Batsheva's toes and ended much later at the top of her head. She sighed. "*Nisht geferlich.* So I'll watch you." She patted Batsheva's arm and held on to it relentlessly. Batsheva looked around at the other members of the group and the light bounced off balding heads and little Kodak cameras. There didn't seem to be anyone under fifty-five.

"Excuse me, I . . . think I've forgotten something." She backed away politely, pulling her arm free.

"You'll miss the bus, darling," the woman called after her, disappointed.

"It's . . . brain tumor. Forgot. Just have to have it removed this afternoon. Terribly sorry. Don't wait." Batsheva babbled incoherently, practically fleeing.

She made her way to the Jerusalem Central bus station and sat down, as anxious as a little girl on her first school outing, as delighted as a runaway with her foot firmly on the steps of a Greyhound bus bound for faraway places, drunk with the heady sense of freedom.

"I hear Eilat's great this time of year."

"Yeah, windsurfing's great, and the scuba diving . . ."

Voices filtered out of the bustling crowd. Young, blond tourists having the time of their lives. Young soldiers, handsome and rested, returning from weekend passes; bearded old men; pretty, dark-eyed girls lining the platform waiting impatiently for buses to take them to clear destinations in Tel Aviv, Haifa, Ashdod, and Ashkelon. A bus would pull up and they would shift along the metal railings that kept the lines straight, moving quickly, purposefully, toward some goal: a job, family, a boyfriend or girlfriend. But where was she going to? What was she going to do?

"Eilat," the young man ahead of her in the ticket line said. He wore a Rolling Stones T-shirt and was tall and muscular with a deep tan. When her turn came to buy her ticket it seemed as good a place to start as any.

"Eilat, one way," she said. When she turned, he was standing there, waiting for her.

"I've never had any luck before now," he said with a boyish grin. "You've only bought one ticket, you're going my way, and you're the most beautiful girl I've ever seen," he said with frank admiration.

She didn't know what to do. So she looked at him, blushing, confused, with shy pleasure. She had never dated, never flirted. She was filled with joy at this confirmation of her desirability, but her sense of propriety made her stiffen and move away, carrying his face and words with her like a secret gift, to unwrap and savor in private.

The bus lurched forward in sudden stops and spurts, throwing the passengers "around like cattle," the elderly man she chose to sit next to groaned, shaking his head and opening his paper. The bus barged around corners and pulled up short at lights. It raced with something of the reckless verve of a motorcyclist on a clean stretch of road, inching into crowded spaces, calling up a symphony of angry beeps and honks all along the road.

"Now I'll tell you a story," her seat mate said, folding his paper with resignation. "A famous rabbi goes to heaven to meet his Maker. He sits in the waiting room hour after hour, waiting for his sins to be weighed against his good deeds. The line moves very slowly. All of a sudden, he sees a new fellow come in, go straight to the head of the line, get weighed and sent straight to Eden. Now the rabbi, who has been very patient, gets up, dusts himself off, and goes to complain. 'Who was that fellow that he got such treatment, while I have been sitting here for hours?' 'Why, he's an Israeli bus driver.' 'What!' the rabbi says. 'How could it be that a man like that waltzes right in, immediately gets weighed and sent right through the Pearly Gates while I, a famous rabbi, the leader of a large congregation, am kept waiting for hours in doubt?' 'Well,' the angels tell him, 'it's really quite simple. When you get up to make a speech, you cause hundreds of people to fall asleep. But when an Israeli bus driver sits down to drive his bus, he causes forty people to pray.' "

Laughter erupted all around them, the sound mingling with the muted hum of the engine. Batsheva looked out of the window at the long flat fields, the gentle hills. How lovely it all was. The admiring glances of a strange young man. The amusing tales of strangers. Batsheva closed her eyes, savoring the small, unexpected pleasures of being alive.

Then the scenery changed, the green erased as if by magic, swallowed up by the desert as the bus moved down toward the lowest point on earth: the Dead Sea. The mountains, white and stark against the brilliant blue Mediterranean sky, stretched as far as the eye could see with no sign of life. It was like being on another planet. Bedouin tents dotted the landscape, the only sign of human habitation. On the road was a Bedouin woman, dressed in long black robes that covered her from head to toe, balancing a load of firewood on her head. She walked with a slow, accepting gait behind her husband, who sat on a donkey and sauntered through the burning sands at a leisurely pace. Batsheva stared at her, almost feeling the heavy press of the wood on her own head, the heat of the sand, the rough gravel on her own feet. I know you, she thought, without surprise. She watched with almost morbid fascination as the woman moved, like a dark cloud in the billowing black dress, stately and sure, pride struggling with acceptance, as she followed her husband through the strange, deathlike setting, leading flocks of goats to almost nonexistent pastures.

And then they were gone, and mile after mile passed with no living thing. Miles of huge white-and-gray cliffs. After a while, the boredom that settled over her began to change into something else. It was as if the absolute blankness of her surroundings had entered her mind and heart, washing them clean of all pain, all worry. It made her feel pure and clean and strangely happy, full of awe and patience. The desert was uncompromising. It would not be rushed, and she began to take it at its own pace, to accept it on its own terms in all its strange beauty.

Hours later, she sat on the shores of the Red Sea in Eilat, her flesh cool and fragrant after bathing in its waters. She leaned back and let the fresh wind whip her hair around her face. The country was so small, yet the contrast enormous! After the desert this dreamlike sea surrounded by mountains that turned red in the sunshine. The young man in the Rolling Stones T-shirt sat down next to her. His name was Bobby, he said. He was such a good-natured, natural flirt. Sometimes the things he said made her want to laugh, and other times she fought the redness that crept into her cheeks. So this was dating, she thought. You sit with an attentive young man who owes you nothing but to be pleasant and agreeable. You give him the pleasure of your company. You get to admire his fine white teeth, his laugh, without committing yourself, knowing that around the corner may be another young man with whiter teeth and funnier jokes. She felt a sense of irretrievable loss as well as discovery at what she had missed. He rubbed her back casually and she gave a startled jump at the unexpected pleasantness and promise of his fingers. "I have to go now," she said. "I'll be honest with you. I'm married. I'm religious. You're barking up the wrong tree."

He let out a long sigh. "Lucky man. Unlucky me." He walked off along the beach and turned around and waved.

"Unlucky me," she repeated. But she was having too good a time to let the incident worry her. For the next three days she swam and ate wonderful fresh fruits and vegetables, and tanned in the hot winter sun, her flesh growing rosy and healthy.

On her fourth day she rented diving equipment and arranged to take a lesson. She looked a little in terror at the dark waters, but the instructor held out his hand: "Don't be afraid, I'll be with you the whole time. Do you remember the signs?" He repeated the "okay" sign, thumb and forefinger meeting in a circle, his brows arched in almost absurd, questioning concern. She pulled the mask over her eyes and nose and took a deep breath through her mouth from the oxygen tanks that weighed down her back. Letting him lead her, she found herself slowly sinking deeper and deeper beneath the sparkling, light-filled surface of the sea, plunging into gray-green shadows. A terror gripped her for a moment, seeing all that water sealing her off from the safety of familiar earth and air. How will I breathe? she thought with panic, even as her mouth sucked in greedy doses of oxygen that easily filled her lungs. The bubbles caused by her exhaling reassured her with their rhythmic, tangible proof of her continued existence. But still a little of the panic stayed with her. She felt her body floating, led gently by the hand. And then, suddenly, confronted by the living mountains of coral, she forgot everything else. The instructor tapped her gently on the shoulder, pointing out a face in the sand, almost a child's stickpoint tracing of eyes, a nose, and mouth, and shook his head no vigorously. She realized that it was a living thing, the poisonous stonefish, buried head-deep in the water. He pointed again, his hands expressive, reaching out to the living coral that throbbed and sent tentacles forward, retracting with a wondrous, quick motion, an open and close of lacy fingers. He took her reluctant hand and stretched it toward the lovely, amber-colored, flowerlike thing. She touched it hesitantly and almost laughed with joy as it snatched itself back, responding to her. It felt like long velvet ribbons.

Gradually she forgot to be afraid, taking in her breaths naturally. Every moment another unexpected wonder floated by: a school of gaudy bright purple-and-yellow fish; an eel, slithering wormlike; a spider crab walking imperiously sideways. The beautiful colors of the fish, the undulating, living coral, filled her with a foolish desire to cry. It was so beautiful. She had never imagined this whole, hidden world. Each fish with its own pattern, its own shades of color. We think we are creative, but what are we next to God? she thought. Her body was filled with a sweetness, a lightness of gratitude and discovery.

And when she emerged a thought had crystallized: This, just this, she thought, is what I thought my marriage would be. A man to guide you gently into beautiful hidden worlds; to take you by the hand and lead you past all the hidden dangers, pointing out all the hidden beauty and wonder. She thought of Isaac and their marriage and realized with a shock of real understanding its fundamental failure and the irreconcilable wrongness of her connection to him.

The next day, she signed up for a bus tour of the rest of the country. She didn't want to think anymore. To make any more decisions. The rest of the country passed by her as if in a crowded dream. She did not feel the way the other tourists did. They looked and appreciated. But they were observers, foreigners.

Already the country had become part of her the way Brooklyn and Los Angeles never were, never could be. Home. Drifting and homeless, she recognized the irony of it. It was all there, the things she had dreamt about and read about as a child: Safad, home of the mystics and artists, high in the hills, full of saintly graves; the harp-shaped Sea of Galilee; the bustling Jewish city of merchants, Tel Aviv; the kibbutzim full of Jewish farmers, and the breathtaking green lushness of their fields, redeemed with honest sweat and blood and love from the barrenness of centuries. The bus moved on relentlessly, the days passing with unbearable swiftness, to their last stop before starting back to Jerusalem. Haifa, port city. It let them off at a point overlooking the harbor, with its enormous ocean liners lined up like toy boats. They could take you anywhere. You could disappear in Sri Lanka or the Himalayas. You could wander the islands of Greece and the beaches of southern France. The men on the tour bus had sidled up to her slyly, behind their wives' backs. She thought of the boy in the T-shirt and his flashing white teeth and easygoing smile. And the world was full of so many men. But then she turned her back to the port and looked up to the mountain of the Carmel. Green and fragrant. There were higher, greener mountains like this elsewhere. But there was no place else in the world where the mountain was hers in the way this was. Mountain of the Bible, of the prophets she had learned by heart her entire life. She felt its silent claim upon her. Still, a part of her longed to climb aboard the anonymous vessel and sail away without a backward look. She thought about this as the bus made the long, quiet ride back to Jerusalem. She dozed and dreamt of sailing in the white clouds, high above the earth.

When she woke up, the bus was already in front of the King David. Her father and mother, Isaac, and her mother-in-law were waiting for her in the lobby.

* * *

"Aba, Ima," she said, her throat choking back unwept tears. She did not even look at Isaac. Her mother fell on her neck, weeping. She was so little, Ima, Batsheva thought, stroking her heaving shoulder. Little and growing old. She felt the tears sting her eyes, but stopped them. I will never cry in front of Isaac Meyer again. I would rather die, she thought. Really.

"Ima, I'm all right." She noticed her father had moved closer. He stood, straight-backed, unmoving, his face a mask. He made no move to touch her. "I am sorry if I worried you, Aba," Batsheva said weakly, feeling the heavy emanation of disapproval that seemed to sear her chest like ultraviolet rays. It took her breath away to be in the same room with Isaac and her father. She clung to her mother.

Her father turned, and she became conscious of the small, curious crowd of onlookers who had gathered to stare at this scene. Tourists and bellboys. She became conscious of her new, clingy dress and her long, bare, tanned legs and arms. She had nothing at all on her head and her hair hung down her back. Mortified, she nevertheless tossed her head defiantly and walked to the reservation desk.

"My key please."

The clerk, with a pained expression, leaned forward and whispered, "I'm so sorry. But your room has been canceled. Your things are in the lobby."

"But, why, how dare . . ."

He raised his eyebrows and cocked his head toward her father.

"I'm sorry. It was handled through the manager. There was nothing I could do," he apologized uncomfortably.

So they wanted a scene. All right then, they would get one. She turned and faced her father: "I'm not going back home with the husband you picked out for me, Aba," she said loudly, pointing at Isaac. Everyone turned to look, and she noted with pleasure the blush that crept up her husband's throat and around his eyes. She saw her father take one step toward her, and she pressed her lips together firmly, readying herself.

"Batsheva," he said in anguish, just before he clutched his chest and collapsed to the floor.

Hadassah Hospital is located at the end of a long and winding road through the mountains. It is the largest and some would say the most advanced medical center in the Middle East. Patients come from all over Israel and many Arabs sneak in from as far away as Abu Dhabi and Saudi Arabia. During visiting hours, its halls teem with the extended families of Sephardic Jews and Arabs. Dozens of brothers, sisters, cousins, aunts and uncles, grandchildren, and even good neighbors, crowd the elevators and waiting rooms, bearing aromatically spiced homemade couscous and pungent meats that are strictly forbidden to be brought into the rooms. They bring food in anyway, of course, pleading and cajoling with the easygoing Sephardic guards who turn a sympathetic blind eye. They fill the rooms, feed their loved ones, and envelop the patients with warmth and nourishment and sympathy.

Batsheva looked at them enviously as she went into her father's almost empty, silent room. She was all he had and she brought no food, and little comfort. She opened the door quietly and wanted to weep with despair. Her tall, impeccable father laid out weakly in wrinkled, striped hospital-issue pajamas. His powerful hands white and subdued, helplessly straddling his sides. When had this happened to him? She remembered how he had seemed suddenly older at the airport after the wedding. But this frailty, this gray, aged weakness? How silently it had stolen up on them all. He had not had a heart attack, the doctors said. But the twenty-hour trip, the wait at the airport, the worry, the anxiety, the confusion. Why, even a younger man would have collapsed from exhaustion, they said with meaningful glances at Batsheva.

Your family must make sure you live a more subdued, relaxed existence from now on, they warned, or they could not promise it wouldn't lead to a heart attack the next time.

"Aba." She knelt at his bedside and took his hand, so suddenly frail, in her own. "How do you feel?"

"How should he feel, after all you've put him through!" her mother burst out reproachfully.

"You don't understand what happened, Ima. Isaac is . . . a cruel man. I can't go on with this."

"Batsheva." Her father tried to sit up.

"Again you do this to him!" her mother shrieked. "Now leave us, selfish child!" She ran to her husband and gently pressured him back down.

Batsheva felt the hot knot grow again in her throat, and she turned to leave. But her father squeezed her hand.

"No, don't go, Batsheva. I must talk to you. I have to tell—"

"Not now, my dear. You must rest now," her mother interrupted.

"Do not interfere. Leave us," Abraham Ha-Levi said suddenly, with a flash of his old, commanding authority.

Surprised, and perhaps relieved, her mother shrank back into her accustomed shadowy role. "Yes, dearest. I will go." She glanced at Batsheva, raising her brows in warning. She walked out quietly, closing the door behind her.

"Aba, I must tell you the truth about Isaac," she pleaded.

"Yes, yes. You must of course. But first I must tell you something that will make you understand that it doesn't matter." He took her hand in his and patted it—the touch of a loving father to a beloved child. "We are so much alike, my dearest child, that is the problem." He sighed and ran his fingers softly along the ridge of her pale cheek. "I, too, ran away. I didn't want anything to do with my parents' destiny. I felt they had no right to choose for me . . . But—God felt otherwise." He smiled, a sad, ironic smile. "Like Jonah and the whale, my fate has pursued me, as it will pursue you." He took a deep, painful breath, pausing for a moment to reflect upon what he was about to reveal to his daughter, pained that he could not prevent it.

"When I came to America after the war, I had nothing. I also wanted nothing—but to be left alone to lead my own life. So I told no one where I came from, who my family was. Then I married your mother—I was nothing but a common bricklayer, a laborer, and your mother a beautiful woman, a storekeeper's daughter—I was shocked she even agreed to meet me. When I married, my life changed. I wanted so much to have a family . . . Oh, how can you, how can anyone, understand what it's like to have no one of your own? To have lost every remnant of your own flesh and blood? Your eyes become the only eyes in the world, your face the only face. It . . . was like being dead and without connection to anyone. With your mother, I wanted to start fresh . . . How I prayed for a child! Seven years . . ." He looked up at her with a small flash of remembered anguish. "Seven long years we waited. Your mother miscarried once, and then your brother was born."

"Aba!"

His eyes closed. "His name was Yerachmiel Ha-Levi." He nodded, in incredible pain. "And I felt I had gone through enough. That, finally, I had been forgiven for my lapses, forgiven for running away." He turned to her, searching her shocked face for understanding. "I was in the synagogue on Yom Kippur. It was a hot day and I remember being on my feet, praying, wiping the sweat that ran down my face. Big beads of sweat. It was very hot, you see. That is why I let him . . . It wasn't my fault. Your brother was three years old. 'Can I go outside?' He was tugging at my prayer shawl. I could see he was hot and bored, but I was in the middle of praying, it was forbidden for me to move or speak. So

I just nodded to him and he ran outside the way children always do on Yom Kippur, to play on the synagogue steps. And then, he must have . . . he just fell. No one could tell me how or why. He just fell." He opened his hand and stared at it, drawing a long, imaginary line across the palm. "It was a very clean break, just at the back of his neck. He died instantly."

"Aba, please, don't." She wiped the silent tears that streamed down his old cheeks. But suddenly his crying ceased and he forced himself up in bed and took both her hands in his. "I sat *shiva* in the house. I put a rag over my head and would not look at anyone. I sat in darkness for seven days and seven nights, do you understand? But on the seventh day I understood. God had dealt with me measure for measure." He nodded slowly, with full conviction. "Measure for measure. I had robbed my parents of their continuation, I had broken the chain. And so God had taken my son from me. And when I understood the reason, the justice behind it, I also understood that I couldn't run away anymore. And so I took the rag off my face and looked again into the light. I went to the synagogue and prayed. I vowed that if God would grant me another child, that child would be the Ha-Levis' new beginning. I made your mother swear never to tell you about your brother, to give you a new, fresh start. Do you understand, my dear? I promised on the souls of my dead father, mother, and brothers that their work would be continued. If I fail to keep that vow, their souls, my soul, will drift forever in the darkness, cursed, cursing me, deprived of rest." He lifted his head urgently from the pillow, his tortured, obsessed eyes seeking hers.

"You are that child, Batsheva, and Isaac is the scholar I can never be! Don't you understand? *I* did not choose him! God has chosen him for you by giving him such brilliance. He is the finest scholar in the Jewish world, a gifted man. Your children will have his genes and our genes. They will illuminate the world, as your grandfather and uncles did. It would be different, my child, if you had been a boy. Or if your brother had lived. Or," and for the first time, Batsheva glimpsed the enormous bitterness and anguish that coiled around her father's soul, twisting it and shaping it, "if Hitler had never walked the earth. But things are as they are. I have done my best. If you walk out on him, then the vow will be broken, the chain lost, and their souls will curse me in the darkness! Batsheva, please! You cannot run away, my child, believe me . . ."

"Aba, please! Don't upset yourself. Here, lie back now. Sha. It is all right. It will be all right," she murmured hopelessly, smoothing back his furrowed brow with complete devotion.

"I had no choice. You have no choice. You must stay with him and continue the role you have started." And then, slowly and painfully, Abraham Ha-Levi told his daughter about the train that had rattled on its way to Auschwitz, about vows, about God, and about fate.

She emerged an hour later, pale and weary, drained of anger and of hope. Later that day she packed her suitcase and left the hotel room where she had been staying with her mother and went back to her own home. The house was dark and cold and smelled of stale smoke. On the stove, someone had placed a kettle of soup and she thought of Esau, willing to sell his birthright for a plate of soup. She could understand him now. Birthrights. If only I could sell my birthright for this soup, she thought, I really would. I would gladly sell it, she laughed out loud, taking a large, steaming bowl and draining it. And as she crawled into the comfort of her soft bed she felt that sleep was the greatest father of them all; asking no questions, full of comfort and unconditional love. So that later that night, when her husband crawled in beside her, she did not have the strength to turn away. She thanked God for the darkness, for sleep, and for the blessed sheet.

Chapter ten

Isaac Harshen's mother viewed the door to her son's house with irritation. So much to do to prepare for the holidays, and here she was giving this silly, spoiled child all her time and attention. But someone had to take her in hand before she disgraced the whole family. With the sigh of the martyr, she used the key her son had given her to keep, opened the door, and stepped into the house. It was a little after eight and yet the room was still shrouded in darkness. "*Aztlanus ve batlanus*," she said out loud, laziness and frivolity. Thursday morning and no smells of cooking fish or chicken soup filled the air, as they did in the houses of good Jewish daughters all over the city. She herself had been up at five to say her morning prayers, to hang out the laundry, and to prepare four or five cakes for the Sabbath meal. "Still in bed?" she called out loudly. "Well, time to get up now, daughter-in-law. What will your husband eat for the Sabbath if you sleep all day?" She listened for some response, but heard none. "Fast in sinful sleep, I wouldn't wonder. *Atzlanus ve batlanus*."

She bustled about, pulling up the blinds until sunlight

flooded the room. She looked around, wiping her fingers over the shining tables. Well, at least the child knew how to dust. She was not impressed that the floors and windows sparkled; the cleaning girl did that work. All the child needed to do was a little cooking and she hardly did that. Her poor son, her poor Isaac, saddled with this skinny, useless creature. She had been watching the girl's flat stomach now for months with the eyes of a trained expert but saw no change. Even for that she seemed to have no talent. Poor, poor Isaac. With a heavy, forceful tread, she lumbered to the bedroom door and knocked loudly with fat-padded knuckles. Ever since she had witnessed that disgraceful scene at the hotel and demanded Isaac give her a key, she often came into the house in the early morning before Batsheva got out of bed. Usually the girl at least had some shame and got up when she arrived. But there was no sound on the other side of the door.

She turned the doorknob. Batsheva was sitting in front of her mirror, combing her long hair. She did not turn or acknowledge her mother-in-law in any way, but continued to comb her hair until it bristled with electricity and shone like silk. She wore a loose, shapeless polyester dress with dark gray and green flowers. Suddenly she smiled and turned to face Mrs Harshen. "Do you like it, Ima? It's the dress Isaac brought me home. He has taken all my clothes away. Did you know that? Yes, of course you did, didn't you? You must have helped him pick this out. It's your taste, isn't it?" She twirled around the room and laughed a little hysterically. "He says my clothes are too loud, too bright. I will attract men's attention to myself. So he has taken away my clothes and bought me a whole new wardrobe, my wonderful, generous husband."

Mrs Harshen stared at her. A crazy woman. For all her *yichus* and her family tree. A *meshugenah*. This was why her father and mother had hidden themselves away all these years and then bought themselves a *chasan*. *Oy vey*, my poor son. The girl spoke in English, and so Mrs Harshen understood very little of what she said. But her face, so pale with two feverishly bright spots on her cheeks, and her eyes tortured and unseeing—demonic eyes, soulless eyes such a color, so light—said a great deal. Mrs Harshen was not a perceptive woman but a shrewd, rather cynical observer of human behavior. Among her friends and her family, she was a vigilant searcher for backsliding of character revealed in hemlines that were too short, hair that strayed beneath hats and wigs, new clothing more than twice a year. At the butchers, she noted who purchased too expensive cuts of meat, or who paid the extra ten cents to have the butcher do the salting and soaking of meats, something every frugal housewife should do herself.

Mrs Harshen knew something was wrong with the young creature before her but she was incapable of attributing it to anything as frivolous as unhappiness. The girl's svelte slimness was now almost bony, her pretty high cheekbones gaunt and hollow. All that was clear to Mrs Harshen. She was just incapable of understanding how a bride with a fine husband—a scholar—a home, and money, could want more out of life. She did not imagine that her experience with life had left any gaps and so, uncomprehending, she labeled it craziness and dismissed it. Anyhow, she had come for a specific purpose this morning and she was anxious to finish with it. "I vant to speak mit you frankly," Isaac Harshen's mother said, then switched to Yiddish. "Someone told me they saw you yesterday wearing a scarf and that your hair stuck out a finger's length." She folded her arms across her ample breasts belligerently. "Is this true? No." She held up her hands, palms outward. "Don't answer." She walked over to the girl and lifted her hair from her shoulders, her tongue making a clucking sound of disapproval. "It doesn't matter. I know you want to do the right thing. But such long hair, you make it hard for yourself to cover it. Now you see me, I have no problem." She took the strawlike wig from her head. Underneath, it was full of graying stubble, like patches of poor grass on an untended garden. "A pious *maideleh* should do the same. Do you want me to help you? It will make things much easier for you. Do you have a razor?"

Batsheva snatched her hair away and backed toward the bedroom wall. She stared at her mother-in-law. "Like a caged animal," Mrs Harshen later told her son, throwing up her hands. "So I told her, 'Listen, I came to help you. If you don't want, I'll leave.' Then I guess she gave it some thought and decided to do the sensible thing. She didn't say a thing, just walked into the bathroom and brought me a razor. A mess to clean up, let me tell you, my son. Hair so long and thick. I saved it. Maybe the wigmaker will be able to use it. She'll give me a good price. Of course, I will give the money to charity." Mrs Harshen was pleased that her son nodded at her with appreciation, a slow smile spreading across his face. To turn sin into a good deed was a noble thing indeed.

"I'm worried about Batsie."

"Bats who?" Graham MacLeish chuckled, mixing the drinks and trying to keep his bathrobe closed.

Elizabeth leaned back luxuriously into the soft pillows of her brass bed. The room was still a little dark, so she squinted at the letter in her hands, rereading it. It puzzled and worried her. "Batsheva. A little student of mine from California. Actually, she's not so little. She got married about a year ago."

He sat down beside her on the bed and leaned forward, kissing the warm full place between her breasts and carefully balancing the drinks in his hands. "Fascinating stamps. Jerusalem. She's visiting Jerusalem?"

"No, she married a guy there. Never saw anything like it. Her parents are these Hassidic Jews and her father just picked her out a husband and she married him."

"Obedient girl. What I wouldn't sacrifice to find myself

such an obedient girl . . ." He had put down the drinks and climbed in beside her. His hands pushed the silk nightgown gently off her shoulders and he buried his head in her red-gold hair, breathing in its rich fragrance. "Someone who would satisfy my every lust on demand."

When was she going to stop being embarrassed at seeing Graham MacLeish without his clothes on? They had been lovers for months, and yet her image of him—tweed jacket, pipe, suede shoes that stamped the floor to make an emphatic point—the image she had carried around for four long years dogged her like a ghost. In bed, she had to force herself to remember that this mortal, this firm but aging flesh, was The Graham MacLeish, stuff of her student fantasies. It was not in bed she loved him most. She loved him most when he was fully dressed, bent over his work in the clear circle of lamplight at his huge English oak desk. She loved him best when he read her papers, thoughtfully puffing on his pipe, his rugged, lovable face drawn into serious lines of concentration. She had to admit it. She loved him still as the best teacher she had ever had. Now she pushed him away gently. "This letter has really taken away my appetite. Listen to this:

My dear friend Elizabeth, I don't know if you'll get this letter because I don't have your address, so I'm just mailing it to Cambridge.

"That's what took so long. It went to Cambridge, Massachusetts, and then some enterprising postal clerk forwarded it here.

Why haven't you written? I need your letters so much, you have no idea.

"Well, why haven't you written?"

"A long, dirty story. Her father paid me off to get out of

town so he could influence this poor child to marry a man she didn't even know." She saw him look at her queerly, eyebrows raised, the look he gave her whenever she did anything classless and American, like eating food in the street, or talking too loud.

"And you took the money?"

"Yes, Graham. I took it. A month later I sent it back though, when my scholarship came through." His face kept a kind of amused contempt that annoyed her. "I wasn't the rich mistress of an important professor then." He had very little money between alimony and child support and often they shared expenses for food and utilities. Cultured Englishmen never intimated problems with money. Too low class. The arrow hit its mark.

"I see." He stiffened.

Guilty, she reached out and drew him down to her, planting an urgent, penitent kiss on his lips. "Sorry. Please listen to the rest.

> *I am almost nineteen today. Remember the last time we spoke, how I said that I thought marriage would be an incredible adventure? I'm on a boat going down, like the hero in* Heart of Darkness, *going down the river in Africa. I just keep going down and down and it's so dark. And on the bank the natives just keep throwing stones at me. I'm so afraid and I have no one to help me.*
>
> *Sometimes I think that they are right and I am wrong. That they are trying to teach me something I don't know because I am not holy or learned enough. I used to think I knew what it meant to be a good person, a good Jew. I thought kindness was very important, because Abraham was so kind to everyone, you know. But even Abraham, my husband points out, threw Hagar and his son Ishmael into the desert to die because Sarah and G-d asked him to. He didn't want to, but he had to. My husband says that proves that cruelty can also*

be a mitzvah, a good deed. Maybe he is right. I am not sure.

My husband was chosen for me because he is a scholar and will one day head the Ha-Levi dynasty. He will tell all the followers what to do then. Everyone will have to listen to him.

Already they have started coming to the house. Men and women waiting in the living room and the hall, lining up to see him. I overheard one conversation. A man and wife came. They had six sons. The doctor had told the wife not to have any more children because she might die. But the husband said to Isaac, "I must have a daughter, otherwise I have not fulfilled the Commandment of being fruitful and multiplying." I waited for my own husband to lead them to the truth. But do you know, Elizabeth, he told him to keep trying and G-d would help. How can he know that? How can he take a chance like that? I told him this and do you know what he answered? He told me that I had no faith.

I must tell you this. I am frightened when I think that all of them will listen to him. He will tell them who to marry and what operations to have, and where to live. He will have great power and no one will be able to stop him. He has great power over me. Perhaps it is because I am weak and evil.

I don't know if you will get this letter, but you must tell me. Was I an evil person when you knew me? Was I? Is he right?

Everything I love, my books, my photographs, my clothes, he has taken away from me because he says that they are no good, against G-d's will.

Maybe you think I'm being unfair to him. I've become a very unpleasant, complaining person. I really can't help myself. I feel very sick inside—sick and unhappy. Sometimes I just want to die—to be free.

This has been the hardest year in my whole life. It was worse because it followed a year which was one of the happiest I ever had. When I was young, I tried so hard to progress—to lift myself out of my family and their life—their strange isolation. I dreamt of a lover who would take away my loneliness forever. But now I am in the same position again—in total isolation with no hope of ever getting out. I feel dead inside.

I don't know my husband at all. He is a stranger, a strict, unpleasant, demanding stranger.

I shouldn't have gotten married. I realize that now. I am too unstable. I needed to prove myself first, to accomplish something on my own. Living with Isaac, I am drowned in trivialities, burdensome and unending obligations. I will never accomplish anything living with him.

I am losing my faith also. I have never felt farther from G-d in my whole life. I can't even learn or pray or anything. I am totally unconnected—remember—dejection, the death principle.

If this is what life is, I don't want any more. I want so much to get away from him, from my house, my family. But I have no place to go. I am afraid G-d will punish me if I leave my husband. I know my father would rather see me dead. He's told me as much. "If you leave your husband, Batsheva, I will sit shiva *for you." You don't know what that means, Elizabeth. It means they will sit on the floor, my mother and father, for seven days and pretend that I have died. They will bury me in their hearts, I will be dead.*

Then I think, maybe it's not Isaac. Maybe it's me. Perhaps I'm just not ready for marriage with all its responsibilities and worries. I was such a spoiled kid, you know. I think, maybe it's just me and I have to try harder to please them, Isaac and Aba and G-d.

If I had only had a few more years to be young and to dream of a good life. Why did they rush me so?

I can't think of anything you or anyone else can do to help me. That is my despair, my hopelessness. I am being selfish, I know. I wish I wasn't such a problem to everyone.

I love you and need you, my dear friend. Please write.

Batsheva

"Clearly a basket case." He lifted his chin and sipped the drink with bored nonchalance.

Elizabeth moved a little farther away from him and examined him carefully. His voice was cold and dripping with superiority. "I can't believe this." She shook her head and jumped out of bed, putting on her robe. She wanted to cry with disappointment.

"Are you planning to interfere then? Is that it? After you took the money from Daddy?"

"Not even an honest whore, what?" she shot back harshly. She went over to the window and looked out, fighting the lump in her throat.

He walked over to her and put his arm around her shoulder and squeezed it. "You are much too harsh on yourself, Liz dearest. Your imagination is aroused. Sympathy flows in your exquisite breast. But what in heaven's name can you do? This is a different world with its own rules. Your coming in from the outside and upsetting things might make them even worse. Anyhow, she sounds so passive. Typical effect of religion on the masses." He tilted his head back lazily, swallowing the last drops from the glass.

She shrugged off his arm and turned to face him, her eyes blazing and narrowed. "Remember Wordsworth? The continuum of existence. The social obligations of the poet to reach out and touch society, to make that connection with the non-I. Remember all that stuff you taught me about how literature humanizes, how it lets us break through the boundaries of our own narrow culture and experience and to experience the shared human condition?"

"You get an A, my dear."

She stared at him. Hairy, pidgeony chest, red swollen organ flapping around comically. What had she ever seen in this man?

"I taught Batsheva everything you taught me, and we believed it! Two fools, huh? A country girl and a passive religious lunatic. What was it, then? Just some more hype? Another day another dollar from the poor-fool students, seekers of truth and MBAs?" She took off her robe and threw it down. "Okay. Here it is. Tits and ass. If that's all you want, just take it and let's not bullshit each other anymore, okay?"

He lifted the robe and gently helped her into it. "My mother told me never to get involved with the Irish. Temper, temper. Whew, my dear lady! Excruciatingly sorry for the bloody mistake. Your sentiments are indeed noble. Let me point out yet another consideration. By the postmark, this letter is at least four months old. And what if, pray tell, while it was wandering around London, all these problems have cleared up? And even if, more likely I grant you, they haven't, my question remains. What can you do?"

She closed her eyes, remembering that day in California when she had reached out and hugged Batsheva Ha-Levi. She had felt something real then, inside her chest. She had made a promise. Even a calculating climber like me has some pride, some sense of honor, she thought. That promise stood. "She needs a friend. I would have thought that a man of your artistic temperament could understand that, could scrounge up a little sympathy for a sweet, confused, and desperately unhappy child—because that's all she is."

He leaned forward and held her close, brushing the hair out of her eyes with his lips. "Do you know why I love you? You don't, do you? You think it's your stunning body, your wonderful face. I love you, you little fool, because every once in a while you make me remember what it's all about. I forget sometimes, in between food and fornication and marking papers and faculty wars. Don't ever let me forget, okay?" He made a low sweeping bow. "Sancho Panza, at your service." He picked up the phone and dialed the long-distance operator, reading the name and address off the envelope. He dialed and when Batsheva Ha-Levi Harshen picked up the phone he said, "Graham MacLeish here. Your friend Elizabeth is waiting to speak to you, dear, hold on a moment." Elizabeth took the phone from him and smiled, remembering suddenly why she loved him.

When the plane was safely off the ground and the roar of the engines had died down, Graham repeated the question.

"What did she say that has us winging our way to Jerusalem five hours later?"

"You didn't have to come!"

"Touchy, touchy. Tut, tut, a mere theoretical question. Artistic curiosity. I might write a novel about this someday." Elizabeth leaned back and looked out at the darkening sky over the twinkling lights of London, clone of New York and Los Angeles. Large, festering, and impersonal labyrinths with millions of human tragedies happening every minute. Why, just as they spoke, a young innocent girl was being raped or killed, a child was being sexually abused by its father, a nurse or doctor was killing a patient, a vile old man was giving money to a twelve-year-old prostitute. But it didn't touch them, any of them, sitting comfortably among the clouds. You couldn't make much of a difference in this world, could you? But you had to try anyway when the rare opportunity came your way.

"She said to forget her letter. She said she was fine."

He sat up bolt upright and stared. "It must be the ascent clogging my ears. Or perhaps the cabin is running out of oxygen and my brain is therefore not functioning. She said she was fine?

And this is the reason that you immediately packed and boarded a plane for the Middle East?"

Her cheeks felt hot. She cupped her palms around her face. "She is not herself. It was awful to hear her. All the life has gone out of her. She's dying, Graham."

"A bit melodramatic, aren't you? After all, it could have been a lousy connection, a water-clogged cable, a shaky satellite transmitter . . ."

She took his hand in hers and kissed it and shook her head slowly from side to side. "What they must have done to that poor child in only a year. It breaks my heart. If only I hadn't left California. If only I had waited for my scholarship to come through. If only I hadn't thrown her to the wolves. I'll never forgive myself, never. I have to make this right, Graham."

"I again applaud your noble sentiments. However, you flatter yourself overmuch if you think anything you can do will make that much of a difference. What are you planning to do when you get there, if I might be so bold as to inquire?"

"I'm planning to drag her out of there and bring her back to London."

"Surely you're joking?" He laughed.

"I fail to see what's funny. If you saw a child about to be run over by a car, would you discuss safety with him, or drag him bodily out of harm's way?"

"You are too precious and naïve. A real country girl. Don't you think her husband, her in-laws, her parents, are going to have some say in all this? Don't their opinions matter?"

"They've sold her down the river for some crazy, fanatical, cultish reason. Their opinions don't count."

The stewardess pushed the cart of tinkling drinks down the aisle and Graham looked up. "You'd better give me a stiff one." He drank it in one gulp. "Now, let us carry this fantasy to its ultimate conclusion. You have by some stretch of the imagination carted and cajoled this young heiress out of her connubial bliss and back to London, where she moves in, I suppose, with us."

She put her fingertip into her mouth and chewed on the nail thoughtfully. "I haven't thought it out that far, actually."

"That's clear."

"I don't know exactly what I'll do when I get there." Her tone turned peevish and stubborn. "But one thing I know for sure: I'm not going to let fate just chew up that child and spit her out. I'm not going to sit passively by." She put a placating arm on his. "We'll just have to play it by ear. Please, trust me. My instincts are good, and so is my education. I had one of the best teachers around."

"You know, the last time Crusaders came to the Holy Land they rounded up all the Jews and murdered them. Don't be surprised, my darling, if the Jews are ready for us this time 'round. Poetic justice?"

It was just the kind of black humor Elizabeth was in the mood for, and, had she heard it, it would have pleased her immensely. But the effects of the long day, the tension and the Dramamine combined to put her fast asleep. Graham smiled at her tilted, oblivious head framed in red-gold curls. He took his blanket out of the compartment in front of him and unfolded it, tucking it in around her shoulders. "Sweet dreams, Don Quixote."

I must be mad, he thought. All this for a woman. A lovely woman, a delicious woman, but nevertheless a woman. I'm such a pathological liar. Admit it, sir. You love this classless little American fool, this child. You have loved her for four tortured, noble years in chastity, out of respect for the establishment. You pined for her like a schoolboy and almost clicked your heels for joy when you opened that white envelope. He remembered a wonderful story he had once read. Faulkner, perhaps? Anyway, it was about a man sitting in jail after having acted out the plot of a Western thriller he had read, only to have been caught in a way not mentioned by the author. Could he sue the author, he wondered, for having lied?

What was all that stuff he had taught Liz?

More specifically, did literature succeed in humanizing the savage animal instincts native to each and every one of us? Are we kinder, more charitable, more loving because of the books we read? Could *Crime and Punishment* stop us from murdering an old lady whose money we needed? Could *Lord Jim* stop us from jumping ship and saving our own necks and letting everyone on board drown instead? Total bullshit, of course. And yet this was precisely the lofty message he conveyed to his students.

He was a cautious man, a man of thought and very little action. He was pleased and rather alarmed at the insane impracticality of the mission he was currently embarked upon. In truth, he had very little sympathy for Batsheva Harshen, whoever she was. Along with D. H. Lawrence, he believed that for every murderer there is a murderee, a person who consciously or unconsciously chooses his own fate, no matter what protests he makes to the contrary. He did not believe that fate tolerated interference. Indeed, if they ever got the girl back to England she would no doubt attach herself to a man just as awful as her present husband. Once a victim, always a victim. Of course, he would not say any of this to Elizabeth. He would stand by her side, playing the good mentor, the moralist with the heart large enough to encompass all the music, poetry, literature, and history of Western civilization. He would not say that Coleridge was wrong about each of us constantly changing and evolving, creatively reaching our potential in harmony with some organic creative principle. He would not say that he had long ago lost faith in his scholarship, and that it had ceased to have meaning save for that given it by the young, impressionable students who copied each word feverishly and even, on rare occasion, took them seriously. He leaned over and planted a gentle kiss on Elizabeth's forehead.

When had he lost his faith? Maybe it was just a gradual wearing away over time. Literary criticism had become a kind of game, sifting through the books for patterns of meaning, for thematic significance in concrete details. Proving the author had meant just such and such by a certain word or phrase because of letters he had written. And always there was some bright young scholar who came along and could prove just the opposite with other letters, and other facts, until it became a meaningless game, a search for higher meanings where none existed. After all, literature was not the Bible, words of God that had holy significance, or were placed in such and such an order for Divine reasons. Authors just wrote to make money or to point out some brilliant, original new slant on the human condition, which no doubt had been pointed out zillions of times before, usually much better. But even though his scholarship was empty, he kept going through the motions. He could not abandon it, because he had nothing else to take its place and he abhorred vacuums. He attached himself parasitically to Elizabeth because her young belief somehow made up for his own corrupt lack of faith. She gave his life some meaning because she still took his long-abandoned values seriously. She had enough faith, enough youth, enough love for them both. And this would be true as long as she didn't find him out.

He gestured with his glass toward the passing stewardess, who stopped and refilled it. He lifted it in a silent toast to Batsheva Ha-Levi Harshen, wherever she was, thanking her in his heart for making him look good.

Chapter eleven

Only when the plane touched down at Ben Gurion did Elizabeth feel a sense of panic. A strange country, a stranger mission. What if Batsheva really *was* all right? She'd feel such a fool dragging Graham all this way, spending all this money. Worse still, what if she really was as bad as she sounded? Not actually dying, but physically sick or flipped out? The thought terrified her, as did the idea of who would answer the door when she knocked. She shuddered just imagining the possibility that she would have to meet Isaac Harshen. The man sounded positively insane. And then a small unworthy idea entered her mind: What if Batsheva had become one of them? Graham was right about this being a totally different world. She had never understood Batsheva completely, Jews like her completely.

Graham steered her efficiently by the elbow through the crowds toward the taxi stands, where they waited for four other passengers to fill up the cab before it headed into Jerusalem. She was comforted by the familiar atmosphere at the airport. Like airports everywhere, it was crowded full of one-minute human dramas, partings and meetings, hugs and tears. Children running everywhere. No matter where you went, people were people. During the forty-five-minute drive to the capital, she tried to concentrate on her next step. Find a hotel? Or straight to Batsheva?

Reading her thoughts, Graham leaned over to talk to the driver: "Can you recommend a nice hotel?"

"*Betach*, sure. You want for . . . uhm . . . many dollars?"

"Sure." If we are hell bent on making brownie points, Sheila can just wait for her alimony this month.

"Go to Hilton. Best food. Best, you know . . ."

"This your first visit, darling?" an elderly woman with several shopping bags and a strong Brooklyn accent asked Elizabeth. "Oh, you gotta see all the sights. The Old City, Meah Shearim, where the Hassidim are, you know—with the long black coats and hats straight out of Poland in the Middle Ages. Even the kids dress like that and speak Yiddish. Little kids, imagine. So cute. But what they're gonna do with Yiddish when they need to earn a living, you should tell me." She stopped and examined Elizabeth carefully. "But you have to dress a little different when you go there, darling, you shouldn't be offended I'm getting so personal. Otherwise you could get stoned or something. Put on a blouse and skirt, darling."

Elizabeth was suddenly conscious of her nipples showing through the thin material of her halter top and of the tight cut of her jeans.

"Stoned! Do you mean that literally or figuratively?" Graham interrupted, his eyes wide with concern.

"I never went to college, mister, but what I mean is a rock in the head." She settled her shopping bags about her more comfortably. "And don't try to drive a car in there on Friday night or Saturday neither. They don't like people messing up their life-style. So listen, everybody has a right to live their own life. So I just put on a skirt and a blouse and a head scarf."

"I think we'll go to the Hilton first and call her to meet us there, what, Elizabeth dear?"

Elizabeth took a deep breath and shook her head like a stubborn child. "I'm going straight there. But why don't you go to the Hilton, darling? I'll meet you there later."

"And let you brave the natives alone? What kind of chivalry are we discussing here? No, no, my dear. Wherever Quixote goes, Panza follows."

She put her arm gently on his. "Please, Graham, I need to do this alone. I'm not afraid." She gave a little brave toss of her head. "Besides, I'm just a shiksa. As long as a local boy doesn't invite me home to meet his mother, I'm perfectly safe."

"Gallows humor. A bad sign." But he heard the determination in her voice and knew that there was little point in arguing. Besides, he needed a hot bath and a drink and could live without becoming embroiled in yet another tiresome domestic drama on this long, exhausting day. So he threw up his hands in what he hoped was a graceful gesture of surrender. "But if you don't show up at the hotel in two hours, I will come after you, sword unsheathed, I warn you." Hell hath no fury like a miserly professor blowing for a night at the Hilton and spending it alone.

She pulled Graham's sweater around herself. Last-minute concession to strangers' morals. It was almost dark and growing cool. She started toward the house, then turned around. I need to walk around the block. I need to think, she told herself. She tried to remember the phone conversation that had sent her off to the airport. She had not told Graham all of it and could not be sure if it was because she was ashamed for Batsheva or for herself.

"How are you, Batsheva?"

"I am healing, Elizabeth. I am ripped open, but I am healing." She remembered Batsheva's penchant for the melodramatic. But the words had terrified her. Ripped open. Ripped. Open.

What did that mean? Physically hurt? Tortured? I wish I knew more about these people. I wish I understood. She tried to piece all the bits of information she had together to get some real understanding of the situation. Batsheva, coerced into marrying a man she didn't know. Browbeaten, probably, into a narrow and suffocating existence, gasping for the air of freedom, slowly dying without it. I am doing the right thing. I am saving a human life. It will not be easy for either of us, but I must make this plunge. For once in my life, I must think about someone else.

Am I thinking about someone else?

Or am I just doing penance for my own soul, to make up for my own corruption?

Circling the block, she had kept her eyes down. Now she looked up. Men in Hassidic clothes passed her by, lowering their eyes as they approached her. Though it was early still, the streets were almost deserted, all the stores shuttered for the day. It was as quiet as a church and as dull. She pulled the sweater around herself more tightly. She thought of London awash with the light of street lamps and brightly lit storefronts in Leicester Square; the National Theatre blazing with light and music beside the Thames, crowded with people in evening clothes, humming with witty, pleasant conversations. They would be standing drinking long cool drinks around a pianist in a tuxedo and a beautiful cellist in an evening gown who were playing duets. She must take Batsheva there! She would show her the British Museum, and the National Gallery—rooms full of masterpieces! She would take her to Stratford-upon-Avon and Bloomsbury. She would go down to Cambridge with her and show her E. M. Forster's room, and the students—hatless boys with bright red cheeks and long woolen scarves riding bicycles. She owed that to her, at least.

Yes, she told herself, gaining courage from the images of a delighted Batsheva, a beautiful, animated Batsheva alive with interest. She would give her a taste of the great world outside her ghetto. Then she could decide for herself what to do. Where to live out her life. She would only be a teacher, opening possibilities. She would not coerce, not rush in like a fool, offering her own beliefs and life-style as a perfect model. Lord knew it was far from that. She had come full circle and found herself in front of the house again. She looked up and saw a single light burning in Batsheva's window. With something close to the exhilaration and despair of soldiers before the dawn of battle, she pressed the bell on the beautiful carved oak door, her mind bursting with words and plans.

But then when the door actually opened, she found herself face-to-face with a reality that canceled all of her words and all of her plans. For as Batsheva Ha-Levi Harshen reached out with a gasp to hug her, she felt the swell of the girl's stomach and the ripple of the unborn child that had taken possession of her body, moving and growing inexorably in her womb.

Batsheva held her tight for a long time, then finally grasped her hands and stepped back. "Is it really you, my friend?"

"I'm afraid it is." Elizabeth let the girl lead her into the dark house where only a reading lamp glowed. She was a little afraid, and hugged the sweater around her, her eyes darting in all directions.

"Don't worry, Isaac isn't here. He won't be here until midnight, or later. He learns, you see. At least that's what he says." Bitterness and resignation. That's what it had been on the phone. Totally uncharacteristic, it was frightening. She didn't know this woman dressed in the ugly scarf low down on her forehead and loose brown dress.

"You look so . . . different."

"You can say it, Liz. I look old. I look ugly. You of all people have always told me the truth."

"Let's put on a light, then I can tell you."

When the room was illuminated, its richness took

Elizabeth's breath away. The polished ebony of a grand piano. The diamond sheen of a magnificent chandelier. Another gilded cage. Slowly, reluctant with fear, she looked at Batsheva. The tall body was a little stooped now, the proud, lively shoulders rounded with humility and shame. The clothes were awful. Cheap cotton housedress, long-sleeved, high-necked, and almost down to her ankles. But the face was still the face of a beautiful nineteen-year-old. The light, magical eyes were more exquisite than ever but tender, like a badly hurt child's whose trust has been betrayed for the first time. But the face still glowed. Maybe it was all those hormones coursing through her bloodstream to keep the baby alive. Or maybe, she tried desperately to believe, there was still some hope. No, it still had that sweetness, that reaching out for life. But she looked so different. It was the hair, the absence of her beautiful black hair.

"Your hair. What have you done to it?"

Batsheva instinctively put her hand to her head as if someone were threatening to remove her scarf. "Nothing. Don't let's talk about it, please! Tell me what you're doing here! Tell me about London." All the old eagerness she remembered. Encouraged, Elizabeth told her about her studies at Cambridge, about the city of London. She saw Batsheva drink it in like a drunkard who, despairing of getting a drink, suddenly comes upon a full bottle.

"But you still haven't told me what you're doing here," Batsheva suddenly interrupted.

"I'll tell you. But first talk to me about yourself. Tell me what's been going on. You scared the daylights out of me with that letter, you know. And over the phone. You sounded so ill."

"I know," she whispered, laying her cheek on the back of her hand so that it partially covered her mouth.

Elizabeth reached out and gently took her hand away.

"Don't stop yourself. You can tell me. Your big sister, remember?"

She had tried so long, tried so hard, to be brave. The tears that Isaac could not wring from her with all his cruelty came rushing like a torrent with the first words of kindness and understanding she had heard in months from someone she loved.

"Liz, I've been so unhappy. I want to go home and I can't. I want to learn, to take photographs, to travel, and I can't. I hate Isaac. I hate him!"

She gathered the girl in her arms and for one sweet moment all the plans and words she had rehearsed came rushing to her lips. But it was all changed now, wasn't it? There was another innocent person in the picture. Elizabeth, for all her open-mindedness, believed in families. In fathers and mothers and Thanksgiving dinners, and little baby booties knitted with love. She suddenly felt her role as rescuer transformed into that of homewrecker. But then she looked again at the miserable young girl in front of her. Batsheva. I . . . want you to come back to London with me. Go and pack. We will leave right now. I will save you from Isaac, from your father, from this life . . . but the words would not come, they stuck in her throat. She swallowed hard and said instead, "There is the child to think of, isn't there? Isaac may change with a child. Some men do, you know. They get softer, kinder." I wish I was dead, Elizabeth thought sharply. I wish I could just die right now instead of saying these things. But some deeper moral had taken over.

"Do you think he might?" She shook her head doubtfully. "You don't know him. He is so cold, sometimes I think he has no heart. All day he sits and learns about being a good person, about doing God's will. But he comes home stiff and cold as metal. Everything I want is no. Everything I want is a sin. He thinks, he truly believes, he can do anything he wants to me and no one will see." Her shoulders shook uncontrollably with sobs.

"Oh, sweetie. Poor, poor child." Elizabeth rocked her in

her arms. What to do, what to do? "Don't cry, it'll upset the baby. Sweet baby," she crooned.

Batsheva sat up suddenly and held her stomach, smiling through her tears. "Sweet baby. I wouldn't want to hurt the baby. It makes me so happy just thinking about it. Soft, sweet little thing. My baby. Oh, it's moving, just feel." She took Elizabeth's hand and pressed it over her stomach. A tiny lump passed under it like a soft running animal. Alive. A life. "My parents are so happy about the baby. They will all come when it's born. And if it's a boy, they will make a circumcision ceremony with thousands of people. He will be the next leader of the Ha-Levis. A little crown prince." Her eyes glazed with sorrow, staring into the future.

Elizabeth understood what she was seeing in the girl's face, but not why. To be the mother of a little prince was not a sad thing, after all. She felt totally lost. After all, Isaac didn't drink, he didn't gamble. He was a bastard who liked his own way. (A man. So what else was new?) But that was not a reason to leave a child without a father. Maybe she just needed some cheering up. "Let's go out for a drink. You'll show me the town, okay?"

"I can't. Isaac doesn't let me go out alone at night."

"You're not alone, sweetie! Come on. Just tell him an old friend blew in from out of town."

"I can't, Liz. You don't understand."

"You're right. There is something going on here I don't understand. Where's the Batsheva Ha-Levi that did anything she damn well pleased? The one who jumped into the swimming pool with all her clothes on? The one who longed for a lover like Vronsky? The one who told her rabbi-teachers where to get off? Where's your courage, your spunk? You can't let this guy walk all over you! Tell him off, for Christ's sake. Kick him in the ass. Where's your courage? You're not afraid of him, are you?"

Batsheva looked at her friend's soft, curly hair, her softly rounded woman's body. If only Elizabeth had been a man—a man with broad shoulders and thick forearms—she would have confided in her. But she was a soft, slight woman who could not help. Elizabeth would only feel more ashamed of her, so ashamed, perhaps, that she would feel the pity and contempt that takes the equality out of friendship and sounds its death knell. You think I am a coward now, my friend. But if I lifted my dress and showed you the black-and-blue marks on my stomach and back, my husband's discipline, fruit of his hard fists, then you would have no respect for me at all. Not telling, that was the supreme hold she had over Isaac. It was a shiny, sharp blade, the treasure of her collection of things she held against him. He was terrified of her telling someone what he had done. But still, he would do it again. She needed to be very careful. She had no one to protect her. No one she could tell. Her father and mother had made it clear to her, had they not, that they didn't want to know. "Married religious women just don't go out drinking in the evening. But I can meet you in the morning." I'm so afraid of him, Elizabeth, and afraid of your eyes if you knew.

"I'm not sure how long I'm staying." Elizabeth's voice was formal, offended. Graham was right. Passivity. What a fool I've been! And I was going to convince her to come to another continent with me!

"Please, don't be mad. Please, Liz. Come with me tomorrow. That is, if you can. What are you doing here anyway?"

"International conference on literary criticism at the Hebrew University of Jerusalem. Graham MacLeish is speaking." She lied easily. She was furious at Batsheva, at Graham for being right, and at herself for having accomplished nothing. Then she relented. Poor kid, what had happened to drain out her fire so completely in such a short time? "Sure. We're at the Hilton. Meet me at eight A.M.?"

"Yes. I mean, no. That is, can you make it a little later?

I have something I want to do first." Isaac would not have to know.

"I guess so. Call me when you're ready to come."

The Jerusalem Hilton is an elegant continental hotel. Surrounded by date palms, its modern tower can be seen from all over the city, much to the dismay of many old Jerusalemites who feel high rises have no place in the ancient capital of the Jews.

"More wine, monsieur, madame?" The waiter, Elizabeth noted, was very dark and slim. Omar Sharif-ish. He spoke French with a definite accent. Arab? Israeli? But my, the wine was very, very good.

"Yes indeed, indeed." Elizabeth lifted her glass.

"Gamla. A locally grown and processed wine. Very fine, no?"

"I'll say." Elizabeth felt her lips tingle as the dry white wine touched them. Smooth, light. She leaned back and stared at the ceiling. It was covered with dark wood-framed mirrors. Tiny lights in the shape of grape clusters gave the room a soft, luminous glow.

"Feeling better, pet?" Graham leaned over and lightly rubbed his hands up her arms from her elbow to her shoulder. The soft light burnished her hair and skin with a dull gold fire. "You're ravishing, you know. If only you would smile."

"I feel like such a fool, Graham. A big damn fool." She threw her head back and his appreciative eyes followed the graceful curve of her throat as she drained the glass. She had told him what had happened and, while he agreed with her—a big fool was right—he was shrewd enough to understand that women in the doldrums of self-criticism do not want to be agreed with. Anyhow, he was playing the broad-minded, generous-hearted man of learning, *n'est-ce-pas?* Besides, now that the whole plan of taking the little bride back to London was called off, he could afford to be relaxed and generous. "Perhaps she isn't telling you everything.

There could be mitigating circumstances, after all," he lied convincingly.

"Do you think so? Oh, I hope so. But why won't she tell me what they are?"

"Lots of reasons. First, maybe it's one of those Jewish things, you know. Like suffering through Yom Kippur without food or eating those indigestible flat crackers on Passover . . ."

She eyed him doubtfully. "This has nothing to do with religion. I think. Oh, boy, what do I know? Everything with Batsheva has something to do with religion. But still, she would tell me if there was some law that said she had to suffer in silence. She's not like that, Graham. You'll see. Tomorrow when you meet her. But she's changed so. She was such a lively, beautiful girl, it used to take my breath away. And now . . . well, you'll see tomorrow."

"I take it we're staying then, my love." Expensive hotel. But still, he looked at her again, it might be worth every penny.

"Just another day or two," she entreated. "Something isn't right, but I can't figure out what. It's like those black-and-white pictures by Escher where things seem normal up to a point and all of a sudden they're all sideways or backwards and you just can't figure out how they got that way, even though the evidence is staring you in the face. She isn't passive. She isn't stupid. She is desperately unhappy. And yet she doesn't talk of leaving him. You see, if she would bring it up, then I could offer . . . But this way, I just can't suggest it to her, not now with a baby on the way . . ." She looked up at Graham's relaxed, indifferent blue eyes gazing at the menu, his neatly combed graying hair, with sudden insight. "You don't give a damn, do you, Graham? You're doing this for me, aren't you?"

Leave your guard down for a minute and undo miles and miles of work. "It's you I care about, and I won't pretend otherwise. But your little Jewish friend does interest me," he protested weakly. "I'll tell you what. Tomorrow I will undertake to find out whatever it is that's going on. But tonight, please," he reached out and threaded his fingers through her hair, "let us just have a simple, romantic evening."

The alcohol had already spread out in warm concentric circles through her body. Her head felt heavy. He was handsome, wasn't he, in a sophisticated, mature kind of way. He was a scholar too, a brilliant scholar, and she was so lucky to have him, wasn't she? "All right," she relented, not completely trusting him.

Batsheva slept badly, her body tense with anticipation, listening for Isaac's footsteps. He came in, as usual, at about midnight. She heard the water running in the bathroom, the open and close of the medicine cabinet. He took all kinds of pills that he claimed were for allergies. Sometimes they made him fall heavily into his own bed in an immediate deep sleep, and sometimes he seemed newly awakened, full of terrible, frightening energy. The first time he had hit her had been after taking them. He had wanted her to come to the bank with him and take her name off the joint account her father had set up for their household money. It was against the Torah for a woman to have her own money, he said. A husband was the legal owner of everything she brought into the marriage. She had said she needed some time to look into it and he had grabbed her and pulled her out of bed and told her to get dressed. She had looked at him very deliberately and climbed back into bed, pulling the covers over her head. She had not understood at first what was happening. It felt like something had fallen heavily on the bed, a book, or a piece of metal. But when she looked up it was Isaac pounding away with clenched fists, his face red, almost, yes, quite insane. In the end she had done as he asked. And now she was totally dependent upon him for spending money. On his insistence, her credit cards had been canceled. She had no checkbook, only the cash he saw fit to part with.

She wanted some money now to buy some clothes and a wig so that Elizabeth wouldn't be ashamed to be seen with her. She considered whether it would be better to approach him in the morning or now. He might leave before she got up. But then again, he had taken some pills, and she didn't yet know which kind. "Isaac," she whispered, sitting up. She saw his large dark shadow move toward her. He had grown much heavier in the months since the wedding, his slim waist bloating up and spilling out over the waistband of his pants, white, unappetizing flesh. "Isaac, would you please give me some money. I need to buy clothes and a hair covering." She didn't say wig, because she didn't know if he would approve or disapprove. Even though his mother wore a wig, she knew that the more strictly pious women wore only scarves or hats, and lately he had begun to lecture her about using only one of those big ugly scarves all the time. She felt his weight pull down the mattress as he sat down beside her. Wordlessly, his hands reached beneath her nightgown. She fought her revulsion and tried to keep her voice normal—the modest, pleading whisper that she had learned worked best with Isaac. "The baby is growing inside of me and all the clothes I have are getting tight. I need a new dress and a head covering to match." She felt his hands move up and down her thighs roughly.

"Yes," he said hoarsely, his breath hot. "Yes, of course, my love, my dear wife." He groaned and lay on top of her for a moment. Dead weight, unmoving. She did nothing, listening to the tick of the clock, the creak of the bed. Then finally he rolled off and got into his own bed.

In the morning, she found the money on the table.

"I'll get it, pet," Graham called over his shoulder. When he opened the door he stood still for a moment and blinked.

"Dr MacLeish. Batsheva Harshen."

With a real effort he wrenched his eyes away from hers—

what an extraordinary color, mesmerizing—and realized that she had been extending her hand. He took it warmly into both his own and led her into the room. It did not take him long to see that despite the wig, despite the loose dress, she was a woman of rare and delicate beauty. Perhaps the most beautiful he had ever seen. "You must forgive me. I'm at a total loss for words. I had no idea you'd be such a charming young lady."

She smiled. "You expected someone fat and squat and bald, I'm sure. Not every Jewish *hausfrau* fits that description."

"Not at all, not at all," he shook his head, feeling at a sudden loss. He was not a man who easily rebounded from the disruption of his expectations. And he had expected just that: an ignorant, pregnant, pious girl, heavy with suspicion and inertia, rejecting the outside world. He was not prepared for her vitality and intelligence. Certainly not for her beauty.

"Batsheva, sweetie! You look like a little doll!" Elizabeth hugged her, immensely relieved. She did look much better this morning. She felt a weight roll off her chest. Maybe it was all going to be okay then. Maybe there wasn't any deep, dark secret. Just the typical rough and tumble of newlyweds adjusting to each other. Batsheva was very young and full of impossible expectations, Lord knew the kind of books she got her information from. "Let's have a great time today, I'm just in the mood for it!"

They wandered the city. Batsheva led them to all the places she loved, giving them history and folklore, imbuing them with her infectious enthusiasm. They saw the Knesset and marveled at its art and sculptures; the Dead Sea Scrolls in the curious cavelike exhibition at the Israel Museum. Graham was mildly interested in the antiquities, especially the little stone Astartes, fertility goddesses with pointed breasts and round stomachs. But his attention began to wander as the women examined the shards of pottery and diligently listened to the recorded explanations in earphones. He leaned back and looked at them together. Snow White and Rose

Red. The exotic Jewess and the flaming colleen. They had nothing in common in culture, history, life-style. A little smile played around his lips. And yet, look at them, the intentness of their expressions, their naïve pleasure in learning. Why, their eyes, unfocused and intense, were shining. The younger girl was so sweet, he thought. Elizabeth had lost that already, that adoring look he so loved in female students. Already he had seen that questioning furrow in her brows, that slight doubt that he knew was the beginning of the end in his relationships with nubile coeds.

They all eventually figured him out. Therese, his first wife, had lasted the longest. But then she had never been more than a C student to begin with. No matter. When she left him, there had always been some other sweet, adorable, impressed young thing to take her place, and then another to take that one's place. He had avoided the relationship with Elizabeth precisely because he sensed her quick intelligence, her shrewdness. But then he had succumbed to her, to opportunity, to his own vanity. Perhaps he had changed. Perhaps she would find something underneath the veneer worth looking up to, loving. The women defined him to himself. Without their adoration, he was nothing. He looked closely at Batsheva. A face like a Raphaelite Madonna—all sweetness and light. Oh, what he could do with a child like that! I'm a vampire, he thought dryly, constantly in search of new blood to renew myself. He felt a small twinge of regret that she wouldn't be moving in with them.

"Ready to go, ladies?" he finally asked, growing impatient. "Maybe we should be heading back to the hotel, dears. It's been an exciting, rewarding, but awfully tiring day." Graham half groaned in mock exhaustion. A hot bath, some wine and thou, already, love. I've paid my dues today. "And we have to leave early tomorrow."

"Just one more stop," Batsheva pleaded. "Please."

She had saved the ride to the Tomb of Samuel for sunset. She had never been back since that first time. They hailed a taxi and sat in the back, three across. Elizabeth on the right, Graham on the left, Batsheva in the middle. As Batsheva got into the car, her dress brushed against the seat and rode up her thigh. Graham glanced down briefly, appreciatively, and was about to say something, then thought better of it. All through the ride he stared at it, puzzled. Black-and-blue marks. Welts. He had once been in an emergency room and seen a child with marks like that. A badly abused, molested child.

The sun was setting. They stood entranced looking at the hills, the white stones, the whole other-worldly ambiance of the city at their feet. "Where is your camera, Batsheva?" Elizabeth suddenly asked her. She asked it casually, but then saw a shadow of pain pass over the girl's face. Batsheva shrugged.

"I don't have . . . much . . ." She seemed to be searching for words. "Time. Yes, time."

Elizabeth looked at her carefully, but decided not to pursue it. "I'm climbing up to the top of the minaret. Anyone game? Come on, Graham!"

"You go on up, youngster, and leave the old and pregnant to their well-deserved rest," he called out to her. She waved and was gone.

They were alone on the darkening hill.

"You know, that letter you sent really worried Liz. She cares a great deal about you, my dear. Actually, we were both surprised to find you so well. All your marital problems on the mend then, eh?"

"Yes. Yes. On the mend then," she said absently, picking up strands of grass and tearing them into tiny bits.

"He's beating you, isn't he?" Graham said very quietly.

She turned her head and got up, walking away from him. He walked after her and caught her arm. She struggled briefly against him, then finally laid her head on his chest and wept. He stroked the length of her back, in long comforting strokes, from shoulder to waist. Soft, long strokes. "Can't you tell me? Eh?" He led her to a soft mound of grass.

"It's only happened once or twice," she lied. "I'm probably just as much to blame." She shook her head helplessly from side to side.

He lifted her chin on his finger and looked deeply into her eyes.

"You hate him, don't you, my dear. You despise him."

She let out a long-held breath and looked away, ashamed.

"Then why don't you leave him? The Hebrews have always been a lot more liberal than we Catholics about divorce. Is it the baby?"

She shook her head, unable to speak. No one had spoken to her about this, and she felt in another moment she would burst, the long-held scream, the primal, awful in-held scream would rip her apart.

"Please, tell me. I won't tell Elizabeth unless you want me to."

"Have you ever read the Bible, Graham?"

"Well, yes, as literature."

"And do you know the story of Jephte?"

"Let me see, from the Book of Judges, yes? It inspired an oratorio by Carissimi: *Plorate, filii Israel, plorate virginitatem meam, et Jephte filiam unigenitam in carmine doloris lamentamini*," he sang. "Lament and weep, ye children of Israel, for a hapless maiden, yea, weep for Jephte's unhappy daughter with wailing notes of sadness."

"O my father, thou hast opened thy mouth to the Lord and hast returned to thy house in peace, therefore offer me for a burnt offering before the Lord," she said to his surprise, continuing the lovely chorus, her voice breaking. "Well, I am Jephte's daughter, sacrificed to God." She laughed bitterly.

"I don't understand." He shook his head. "Please, can't you . . . ?"

"My, my, don't the two of you look cozy! I swear, if it was anybody else but you, Batsie, I'd wonder," Elizabeth laughed. Batsheva jumped up, a confused smile spread across her face.

Graham cleared his throat.

Elizabeth looked at them, puzzled. "What did I interrupt?"

"Nothing my dear. Just a Bible lesson. Book of Judges, what, Batsheva?" He reached out and patted her arm. "I promise to look it up." Batsheva returned his meaningful glance gratefully.

The sky moved from the dark red fire of sunset to the pale silver radiance of the rising moon. Realizing this, Batsheva started to walk toward the taxi, frightened. "I must get home. My husband, Isaac . . ." She gnawed her lips nervously.

"Of course, we'll take you home."

"No! I mean, you'd better not trouble. You can just let me off on your way to the hotel."

Elizabeth put her arms around the shivering young girl. She was sure now that her first impression had been right. Something was terribly wrong. She was shivering from fright, terrified.

"What is it, kid? Can't you tell your big sister Liz?"

Batsheva rested her head against her friend's shoulder to still her trembling. But it was slender and delicate. She could not lean on it.

"You can't help me, Liz. No one can." She reached up and kissed her friend's soft cheek. "I've had such a wonderful day. Thank you so much, so very much."

"Must you get back now? We have to leave early tomorrow. When will I see you again? I have to talk to you. Something is wrong, isn't it?" Elizabeth pressed.

"No, please, please, Lizzie. Everything is fine. It's the way it must be. I must get home before Isaac sees I'm gone."

"Can't you just explain to him that you forgot the time and had some dinner with old friends?"

"No, please. I have to go home before he gets there."

"Likes his supper hot and on the table, eh? My kind of guy," Graham broke in suddenly, taking charge, wanting to see things finally settled. "Well, the cab is waiting for us. Let's just get in and go."

Elizabeth turned to him angrily. "Graham, I want to get to the bottom . . ."

"Yes, you do. Of course you do. You can talk in the car." He hustled them both in and gave the driver directions. He had hesitated for a moment, but had made his decision swiftly to leave Batsheva Harshen to her fate. She was young and beautiful and, perhaps, just his type. But she was also very pregnant with an insane husband and a rich, influential father. Things were complicated enough without private detectives and policemen staking out one's life. It was true that he had wavered for a moment, but he was old enough to know that taking in stray dogs and cats gave a momentary satisfaction in exchange for a long, drawn-out mess, inconvenience, and expense.

As long as he could help it, Elizabeth wouldn't have to find out about the black-and-blue marks, about the passage in the Book of Judges (whatever that meant anyway). When they reached Batsheva's address, they all got out.

Graham took Batsheva's cold hands in his and kissed them. "Good-bye, my dear."

"Good-bye, Graham, and thank you." He had given her words of kindness at a time when they were rarer than diamonds in her life, and she would always be grateful.

He held the door open for Elizabeth to get back in.

"You get in, Graham. I'll be there in a minute." She grabbed Batsheva's arm and walked off with her.

"Tell me what it is."

"I can't." She caught herself. "I mean, there isn't anything to tell."

"Now, you listen to me carefully. I know you, and this person I see in front of me, this shivering, frightened kid, isn't you. What has he done to you? Won't your parents help you?"

Batsheva shook her head helplessly. "I can't tell you, please. It doesn't matter. Soon I'll have the baby. My own sweet baby. I'll be all right. I'll be fine."

"Batsheva, please."

Batsheva's eyes glittered with undropped tears. She hugged her friend for a long time, tightly. She thought of the open cab door, and the rush and lift of an airplane soaring up into the sky. But in the middle there was her father's face, white on the hospital pillow, his unforgettable words. "Jephte's daughter," she whispered and shook her head, releasing Elizabeth from her embrace.

"What?"

"Nothing. I have a present for you. Wait here." She returned, breathless, moments later, with a bulky package tied with a red bow.

"What is it, Sheva?" But the girl just shook her head.

"Don't open it until you're on the plane, promise me?"

There was something strange in Batsheva's face that Elizabeth didn't like, a tightness, almost a martyrdom that didn't sit well. But there was no time. The cabbie had begun to honk, and Batsheva was already backing away, saying Isaac would be in any minute. The prospect of meeting Isaac Harshen frightened Elizabeth more than she was even willing to admit to herself.

"I will promise, but you've got to promise me something." She grabbed Batsheva's hand tightly. "Promise me if you change your mind, if you want to talk to me, you'll call me, write me, or just come. You're not alone. You have me, for better or for worse. Friends. Remember? You were the one who made me promise." They were quiet, looking at each other, warmed by the memory of that fragrant spring day when they sat weaving plans into a beautiful fabric to cover their lives. So many hopes, so many plans . . .

"She wouldn't promise. She just shook her head and kissed me," Elizabeth told Graham, who was already deep into his second drink and was motioning the stewardess for a third. She began to unwrap the gift, then sat looking at it unbelieving, as the tears flowed unheeded down her cheeks.

Graham gasped and sat up straight: "A Leica. Whew. Have you any idea how much one of these costs? Now, that's what I call a good friend."

"Don't touch it, Graham! Don't you dare touch it!" And suddenly her soft, unfocused sadness became sick with real fear. She wiped away her tears. "I'm just going to save it for her. She'll ask for it back one day. I have to believe that."

Chapter twelve

There was a certain rhythm to the pains. Like music, they began gently, then rose to an unbearable crescendo. She thought she would die. And then, suddenly, they melted away again. Pianissimo, pianissimo. The midwife dabbed her forehead. Batsheva had decided to do without heavy anesthetics, as was the custom among the women of Meah Shearim—and Israeli women in general—out of zealous regard for their babies' well-being. Instead, she whispered psalms: "*Achas shaalti may ace Adonai, oto avakash* . . ." This thing I ask of the Lord, that I might dwell in His house all the days of my life . . . Over and over she whispered the words silently, terrified of the next crescendo.

"*Yehiyeh tov, maideleh. Od me at, od me at,*" the woman told Batsheva. She had a kind, soothing voice. It will be all right, just a bit longer, Batsheva's mind translated the Hebrew words. It was all right now. Restful. Then again the pains started and all at once they gripped her with horrible force from which there was no escape. She screamed, a loud animal noise that frightened her. Can this be me? Can it? She flailed her arms and legs, trying to escape from the torture. "I can't, I can't do it," she sobbed.

"Yes, you can. Of course you can," the midwife's gentle, encouraging voice soothed her. "Just a little bit more, and it will be out. See, already I see the head. Come, sit up and push."

"Really, the head." She had forgotten about the baby. It had been erased by all the never-ending, wrenching pain. She had thought of death, of any kind of escape, but she had forgotten the baby altogether. Remembering made her smile. She pulled herself up and began to push, straining with each contraction and surprisingly, it did not hurt anymore. It was work, hard work, yes, the pushing. Animal work. But it was satisfying, not painful. She held her breath and pushed and pushed and pushed.

It moved.

"Yes, beautiful, dear. Yes, here it is, yessss," the midwife cheered. Spectator at a football game.

A terrible weight suddenly pressed down on her. She screamed. Incredible pain. And then, miraculously the tiny cry.

"A boy, a beautiful, perfect son." The midwife laid the warm, moist infant on her breast. Part of her body, yet not part. The pain was over and there was her child, her baby son. An indescribable relief and happiness swept over her that had no precedent either in her experience or her imagination.

"I have a son," she wept with unknown joy and it was as if the pain had never existed. "A baby son." She touched his long, thick black hair and knew she would die for this creature, to protect every silky hair on its head. For him who a few moments before had not existed, she would unhesitatingly give her life now. She wondered at the strange fierceness of her love. And in her heart she thanked God for His gift.

They had all come for the circumcision ceremony. Her father and mother, all the Hassidim. She dressed the child with cold, shaking hands. She had been to so many Brit Milas in her life. They were joyous occasions, like weddings and Bar Mitzvahs. But now it was her own child and she thought about how they would clamp his foreskin and cut it off with a knife. Her little baby! He would bleed and cry. Yet, this must be done. God had decreed it and they must obey.

The women were given a separate room and then Isaac came in with her father and all the Hassidim. A flood of black and white. Isaac put his hands out and she had no choice, no choice at all, with her father there and all the men at his back. She gave the child to her weeping mother, and her mother gave the child to her father, who was beaming with triumph; her father gave the child to Isaac, who took it with cold ceremony and bore it away into the next room. The laughing, joyous voices of the men drifted back to the women, who stood silently, their faces puckered with anxiety. The men's loud prayers reverberated like a clap of thunder, but the women's lips moved silently. Amen, they whispered with resignation. Then there was silence as the mohel did his work and then the heartbreaking cry of the infant. Batsheva's heart contracted. She felt her mother's hand patting her own. They could hear the songs of the men rise up, loudly, in happiness as they danced with the crying infant, welcoming him into the covenant. The women smiled with relief. The men had finished. When the mohel brought him back to her, the baby was quiet, sucking on a piece of wine-dipped cotton. His eyes were tightly shut. She winced at the bloody diaper. But the wound was very clean. The mohel, a pious man more expert at his craft than any doctor or surgeon, for he did hundreds of such circumcisions a month, had been carefully trained. He smiled kindly at the young, worried mother, understanding her ache of helplessness as she examined her tiny son. Dear little boy, precious child. She counted his tiny toes, kissing each one and then the arch of his soft, plump foot. Sweet, so sweet. They were not going to hurt him anymore, she vowed, deep in her soul, deeper than she had ever thought possible. Her lips pressed together, drawing upon reserves of strength she did not know she still had. Never again, she thought, her anger irrational, her bitterness misplaced. She would not stand by idly, helplessly. Let them try, she thought, feeling her insides harden like a stone.

"My dear Batsheva," her father came up behind her, his face radiating such incredible happiness that for a moment its reflection caught hold of her own face, imparting a vicarious glow. "I am the happiest man on earth! My cup runneth over! Here, darling. Take this. It can never bring you a hundredth part of the joy you have given me. But take it, with my love. A little token."

She didn't like to look at her father's face. It was so painful to see his deliberate blindness, his willed ignorance. So she opened the box. The diamonds and emeralds glittered against the background of green velvet like drops of water caught forever under the sun. A magnificent necklace.

"I bought it from Shershon, in Tel Aviv. They designed it for you especially. But if you don't like it, they will happily exchange it . . ."

"Thank you, Aba," she said, not looking at him. "It is very beautiful." No hug, no dancing feet, he mourned, wanting to cry for the little girl he had lost. He searched her face but saw only the love and overwhelming joy of a mother for her first child. The other things—the sadness in the corners of her mouth, the dull luster in her once bright eyes, he could not and would not see.

Like many bad marriages, Batsheva and Isaac's settled into a period of resignation, a modus vivendi of shared unhappiness. The baby gave Batsheva a new willingness to look for good in the man who was her husband, her baby's father. She tried so hard to find something to focus on. He was, after all, a brilliant scholar. He taught the Torah, the Talmud, to younger students, leading them on to a good life, she told herself. He was very clean. He dressed immaculately, groomed impeccably, and was still, despite his gaining weight, a handsome, imposing man.

In the bedroom, he made few demands and in return gave little. She knew it was because she had radiated her dislike so clearly, her repugnance at his touch. She felt guilty about that. Maybe I should have tried harder. She prayed to God so often, asking him to help her, to forgive her. To help her be a better wife, a good mother, and she felt that He heard her prayers. Since the baby's birth, Isaac had stopped hitting her. Perhaps, she thought, I gave him reason to before. Perhaps all men did that to their wives when they passed over that invisible line. She knew she was not the kind of wife he had wanted. She hated to cook and clean the way his mother did and could not bear to spend the hours in the kitchen needed to bone and grind fish for gefilte fish, or roll out thin strudel dough. She made macaroni and cheese, pizza, guacamole, and Isaac grimaced and went to his mother's for dinner. She tried to dress the way he seemed to want, suppressing her distaste, avoiding the mirror. She kept her wig on day and night and tried not to care that, underneath, her own hair was growing dull and matted for lack of sunshine and fresh air. Outside, when the sky over the white city was particularly brilliant with white radiant clouds and blades of sunlight filtering through like an artist's conception of holy light, she tried not to frame in her mind the wonderful photograph it would make. She tried to forget the person she had been, becoming quiet and without needs or desires. She tried to be what was expected of her.

Isaac saw the subdued obedience in his wife with satisfaction. Yet he regretted, too, how quickly she had been subdued. Her meekness took away his pleasure in seeing her bend to his will, but it was valuable, too. It was necessary, with the baby to care for, to keep her well, to keep peace between them. The child was important. He had been chosen as successor, but the child was the blood of the Ha-Levis, the undisputed heir. Already he had heard rumblings among the Ha-Levi Hassidim questioning some of his judgments. The woman he had advised to have another child against the doctor's order had died. Marriages he had approved of had failed. Operations he had advised against had turned out to be critically, irreparably, necessary. And so it was now more important than ever to have his wife firmly by his side, their child paraded through the streets each day.

In the past, Isaac had not approved of her visiting other women. "It leads to the sin of gossip and slander," he told her. But Gita Kessel was Rabbi Magnes's daughter and the wife of Rabbi Gershon, already respected as his father-in-law's successor. Isaac had introduced them himself. Batsheva had been reluctant at first. She had made acquaintances among the women of Isaac's students and fellow teachers—young, pretty women who cared about their clothes and their hair. She learned that most young women had to work full- or part-time to support their husbands in the yeshivah. They gave their babies over to daycare centers, older women, or mothers with small children at home. Only women with the wealthiest fathers could afford to stay home and care for their own children while their husbands studied.

Most of the women she met were good people, teachers of small children, secretaries, seamstresses. It was a great source of pride and status to them that their husbands spent all day bent over a Talmud in a yeshivah. As young brides they sacrificed gladly to keep their husbands learning. But after the first child was born, the hardships and constant tension over money made them careworn and dull. They never read, never went to the movies, had never been anywhere farther than Safad or Bnei Brak. If they learned, they learned only the little books of Bible stories with moralistic messages at the end. The fate of the young women was reflected in the lives of the older families. For with the years, the families grew. Ten, fifteen, even twenty children were not unheard of, for birth control was considered wrong, even though it was permissible according to the strict letter of the law. And no matter how large or poor the family, the children were immaculately dressed: the little boys copies of their fathers all in black and white, the little girls in pretty, old-fashioned, home-sewn dresses, with long braids and bows in their hair. How hard these women must work to keep their children like this despite their poverty, Batsheva thought with admiration. Still, she could not bring herself to befriend these serious, sacrificing women who had no room for anything frivolous or extraneous in their difficult lives. They seemed so much older than she. Perhaps if she had been poor, if she had been able, like them, to feel the accomplishment of achieving some noble goal through her suffering and self-negation. But she had everything, and was left with the boring housework, the cooking. She wanted to have some fun and these women didn't know what the word meant.

But Gita was different. Tall, slim, and aristocratic looking, she navigated with confidence through the narrow streets of Meah Shearim, her impeccable lineage and social position surrounding her with an almost impenetrable shield of approval. If Gita wore red, well, then, it must be all right to wear red. If Gita wore stylish hats with feathers that covered almost all of her hair, well then, the women took heart, it must be all right to cover almost all of your hair. If Gita went to symphony concerts in the evening by herself, well then, the social buzz rang out clear with approval, well then, it must be all right then.

Batsheva, swept into Gita's company, found herself joyously released from the prisonlike structure Isaac and his mother had built for her. Putting their babies in backpacks, she and Gita would travel to museums and art exhibits, shop for fashionable clothes, and try on hats, giggling like school-girls.

With Gita as her guide, she also opened her eyes and was

amazed at the sheer variety of ways Hassidic women chose to observe the same law. There was so much room for individual taste and style. Some wore ugly scarves pulled tight over hat forms; some wore stylish kerchiefs and let their bangs hang out; some wore scarves that reached almost to their eyebrows, covering every strand. And some wore pretty colored scarves that matched their clothes. Some wore only long, black kerchiefs over shaved scalps. And those who wore scarves considered themselves more pious and chaste than those who wore wigs, because if the intent of the law was to make a married woman unattractive to other men, the wigs sometimes did the opposite. She thought of her mother-in-law's straw hairdo. There were women who would not consider her devout enough!

Among those who wore wigs there were also many variations: some wore expensive human-hair wigs done up in the latest style at the beauty parlor, and some wore strawlike acrylic. And some even went so far as to wear scarves or hats over their wigs to obviate any and all criticism!

On their legs, the same variety persisted: The Daughters of Jerusalem, with their black scarves and dresses, wore thick black stockings; others wore thick flesh-colored hose with seams, to make it clear that their legs were indeed covered. And some, perhaps most, wore regular pantyhose in different, fashionable shades.

And some wore beautiful designer clothes in bright colors, modestly, but not severely, covering their slim bodies, clothes Isaac would not let her wear. And some were fat and wore only wrist-length sleeves and mid-calf skirts.

And through it all, she finally realized, to her amazement, there was an element of taste, good taste or bad taste, which had nothing at all to do with God's will.

And so, Batsheva began to think, there must be different kinds of men among them, too, different kinds of husbands, not modeled on Isaac Meyer Harshen, who allowed their wives to dress so differently. But this remained only a theory. She could not meet any young men. For the men of Meah Shearim walked with their eyes cast downward, avoiding any contact with a woman's gaze. And those who did look, did so surreptitiously, from behind doors, through the slats of partly closed windows. They would not sit next to women on the bus, but crowded together in the back. They would not agree to take an intercity taxi that needed at least six passengers to begin its journey, if a woman insisted on sitting with them in the back instead of segregating herself in the front seat beside the driver. When they came to Batsheva's home to speak to Isaac, they avoided being alone in the same room with her, and if they said hello at all, it was without their eyes meeting her face. She knew it was out of modesty, to preserve their distance from her, a married woman, whose very touch was the essence of sin. But still, it made her feel unwanted, unclean.

She began, with Gita as her guide, to explore and understand the place in which she had lived from the beginning as a stranger, an outsider. The houses of Meah Shearim were built around inner courtyards, long row houses piled one on top of the other with all kinds of temporary add-ons to increase the unbearably limited space: glass enclosures, plastic and even cardboard nailed down over balconies to keep out the cold winter winds, the intolerable summer sun. Long staircases wound around the old buildings, almost hidden by rows of laundry, countless diapers hanging everywhere. And in the courtyards were always the riches of the poor, the pathetic clinging to worn-out, useless junk that is the surest sign of unbearable poverty: old rubber basins, dried-up palm fronds from a long-ago booth erected for the Feast of Tabernacles; a cabinet that once held a sewing machine. It made her realize with shame, for the first time, how much she had and how little she shared or appreciated it. She had always taken her home, her wealth, for granted. But now, face-to-face with the unrelenting poverty around her, she felt ashamed. With Gita's help, she began to make the long climb up the steps, entering into homes so bare it made her want to weep, and yet so clean and honest and proud, it filled her with envy and humility. She gave, from the small allowance Isaac permitted her, more than she could, and found herself happy to go without things she wanted. It was a new experience that made her feel as if some change had taken place in her soul for the better.

Her own home was one of those old stone villas erected by rich men at the turn of the century, full of Old World charm. Her father had completely renovated it with every convenience of modern plumbing, air conditioning, and electrical wiring. He had had craftsmen painstakingly retouch wonderful hand-carved doors and mantels, lovely hand-painted Armenian tiles, keeping all that was original and irreplaceable. From its windows she saw the mysterious black dome of the Abyssinian Church, with its black priests, dressed in black flowing robes, its riot of birds, walled in in utter isolation. Sometimes she tried to imagine how the black priests must feel and thought perhaps she felt something of the same thing: outsiders amidst the people and streets that surrounded them—women in bathrobes and old worn black boots climbing up thirty steps to run-down, crumbling homes; old men in wispy beards and old clothes, walking slowly down narrow cobblestone courtyards that could have been in a little village in Poland.

Their babies grew. Dina, Gita's little golden-haired girl, and Akiva, black-haired, blue-eyed little boy. Little Akiva, little boy! He loved to laugh. Whatever silly thing Batsheva did—wink at him, or hide her eyes for a moment and then reveal them—made him double up with belly laughs so infectious she found herself smiling all day long. She kissed his round, perfect knees, his pudgy thighs, drinking in his delicious sweetness like wine. Sometimes her love swelled up inside of her with a fierce, hopeless ache and she would hold him and hug him, burying her face in his soft, fat stomach. He smelled so fresh and fragrant, redolent with baby shampoo and powder. He would grab her wig with both hands and tug it off, screaming with delight, delighting them both. Once he did this to her out in the park and Gita saw.

"What have you done to your hair?" She was appalled.

"My mother-in-law does it for me whenever it gets grown in. Aren't you supposed to? Don't you?"

"Don't be a nitwit! God forbid! A woman is supposed to look attractive to her husband. Crazy to cut it off at all, beautiful hair like that." She smoothed down Akiva's thick black hair. "Tell your mother-in-law that Gita said it is forbidden to shave off your hair, and that you only have to cover it when you leave the house. In the house, I never cover my hair." Batsheva blushed, embarrassed by her own ignorance. She had accepted Isaac's word, his mother's word, believing herself ignorant of the law. What had her father said? "Let him teach you." Isaac had said it himself so many times. He would lead her. He would instruct her in the ways of the Lord. She had never, until now, questioned if what he said was indeed true, was indeed God's will.

"I went to Bais Sarah, but we never really learned the source of the laws. They just told us—pious women do this, and do that. I never learned to question anything. I don't know what is law, or what is custom, or what is just social pressure, and passing fads."

"Well, you can read Hebrew, can't you? And Aramaic?"

She had learned both in school and had even had private tutors. "A little."

"So open up the Talmud, or the Code of Jewish Law. Read Maimonides. It's your life. What good is observance if you don't know what you're doing, huh?" She winked. "I think you're in for some surprises."

"What kind?" Batsheva was puzzled and amused by Gita's laughter. But Gita just patted Batsheva's wig and helped her pull it back on.

Gita's suggestion and, ironically, Isaac Harshen's stern insistence that she read none of her own books, had led the way to her studying his books. Left with no other reading material, she had taken to struggling with the big set of Talmudical literature that now comprised the only books in the house, and she had learned, beyond a shadow of doubt, that Isaac Harshen was no scholar. The private lessons she had taken in Talmud to please her father and the Hebrew and Aramaic of her school days enabled her to decipher the difficult passages very slowly at first, and then with greater ease. To her shock, she found that Isaac Harshen was making up a lot of what he piously quoted her or seriously misconstruing it. There were laws he half fabricated, or twisted just to keep her under his thumb. For the Talmud, she learned, was full of discussions where scholars passionately disagreed with each other over the interpretation of laws. And yet, Isaac always acted as if everything was engraved in stone. Isaac, she had learned, was a man who memorized words but had little understanding of their meaning. He lacked the ability to assimilate knowledge that makes a man or woman a wiser human being, or the gift of making intuitive leaps of understanding between concepts that constitute true genius. If anything, the opposite was true. While the clear intent of the Talmud, she had learned, was to make men kind, charitable, generous, loving, forgiving, hospitable, and honest, Isaac, because he was dishonest and without understanding and even real faith, used his phenomenal recall for detail to prove through the dry letter of the law that cruelty and narrow-mindedness and petty unkindnesses and even untruths were permissible. He constructed a whole way of life that was a perversion of everything pious Jews strove for.

Once Batsheva realized this, once she understood totally that what she had taken as God's word was only Isaac Harshen's word, it gave her a wonderful inner freedom. But she did not confront him with this knowledge. Instead, she saved each lie, each inconsistency, hoarding them up like a prisoner who rejoices over each rusty scrap of metal, dreaming of creating an instrument capable of cutting through to freedom. Isaac Harshen was a liar and a bit of a fraud, a hypocrite certainly. He acted as if he had some special access to truth. But she had uncovered the most wonderful secret of all. He didn't really believe in God. She saw this in the cruel lines in the corners of his mouth when he bullied her, careless of all the laws that said a man must treat his wife better than himself. He bullied her because he had no fear that God was looking over his shoulder preparing a reckoning.

She began to stay out later and later with Gita. Sometimes she would ask, embarrassed, if Gita's own husband ever minded. Gita laughed. "Why should he mind? And if he does, so we talk about it, we discuss it." This was incredible to Batsheva, the very thought. She began to understand how abnormal her relationship with Isaac really was. She was not his wife, but his child, his terrified child. She more and more wanted to see Gita's husband with her own eyes, to study him and contrast him to the husband she knew, to be sure it was not a misunderstanding on her part. The opportunity came on Succoth, the Feast of Tabernacles. It was Batsheva's favorite holiday. She loved the sukkah—a little hut built of wooden slats with large palm leaves or bamboo for a roof, where they ate their meals for eight days in the almost summery autumn air. She spent the morning helping Gita to decorate it. Akiva and Dina played happily with strings of brightly colored ribbons and paper and baskets of plastic fruits. Newly risen from crawling, Akiva tottered like a happy drunk, his stomach out, his back arched, falling as much as he stood. The women laughed at him and tickled him.

"Ah, my dear Gitaleh, hard at work!" Rabbi Gershon walked in briskly, sweeping Dina off the ground and throwing the delighted child up in the air. She grabbed his thick brown beard and pulled. "Ay, as it is written: The raising of children is painful." His brown eyes were full of warmth and laughter.

"Gershon, meet Batsheva Harshen."

"Ay, Isaac's wife. A great privilege." He did not avoid her face, but looked at her pleasantly, full of friendly curiosity. "I understand your parents are considering moving to Jerusalem permanently?"

"Yes, my parents love it here. But my father has so many business interests in the States, I don't know when he'll be able to come."

"It must be hard for you here alone, without your family and friends. You must take good care of her, Gita," he called over to his wife, who stood up on a chair tying apples and grapes to the roof. She looked down at him and nodded, her eyes meeting his with a click of understanding.

Batsheva's eyes wandered from the man's to the woman's. She drank in how their lips parted in happiness, how their faces lit up with pleasure when they looked at each other. She felt with the surety of sudden instinct that no sheet, or anything else, had ever come between them. The man's long fingers held the child's back firmly, but so kindly and carefully. It was so easy to hurt or frighten a small child. A careless pressing in of the thumb and forefinger, a sudden loosening of support beneath the tiny arms. But she could see that this man would never do that. His hands were strong and reliable and intelligent. He set the child down carefully, with just the right whoosh of swiftness to delight her without jostling her into fear or rejection.

"I understand that Zubin Mehta will be conducting the Philharmonic in an all-Mozart program tonight. You must go, of course, Gita. Do you enjoy Mozart?" He turned to Batsheva.

"He is my favorite, next to Beethoven," she answered shyly. She was not used to speaking to men as an equal.

"Gita adores Mozart. She says he makes order out of chaos. He is predictable, yet wildly unpredictable. Just like my dear wife," he teased fondly.

"But how can I go? I haven't even prepared dinner yet. I don't have a babysitter . . ." Gita remonstrated.

"Now, now. I will make myself a few eggs. I'm not completely helpless, you know. And Dina will be perfectly safe with me, unless of course, you don't trust her to me?"

Gita laughed. "And what about the yeshivah? And what about all the students who will be waiting there for you, full of questions and problems . . . ?"

"I'll tell them there is no greater *mitzvah* than *shalom bais*, domestic harmony, and that they should go home to their own wives. Disgraceful how these newlyweds roam around the yeshivah until all hours! I have made up my mind to kick them out at seven o'clock at night. I will tell them I don't want to see them after that. That they should go home and spend the time with their new brides."

Batsheva looked at him, trying to hide her surprise. Isaac was never home.

"Oh, you want to create a revolution then?" Gita looked at him with excited pleasure. "You know what the others will say, that you are taking them away from learning, corrupting them . . ."

"If they were home with their wives they wouldn't have time for all this dirty business. It's a *chillul hashem*—a blasphemy, a desecration of God's name." His tone rose angrily.

Batsheva had heard rumors that certain yeshivah students had been involved in "disciplining" other boys found talking to girls, watching TV, or reading newspapers. They had picked one up on the ruse that they were driving him to his parents' and instead had taken him to a deserted stretch of beach and beaten him up, making him eat sand, burning his hand with cigarettes, and exacting a promise from him that he would never repeat his "crimes" again or tell anyone. The same shadowy group had also gone on a rampage of burning down bus shelters because they disliked the advertisements that featured pictures of young models in bathing suits. While people in Meah Shearim condemned the activities, many were afraid their houses and cars would be next if they openly voiced disapproval. No one was sure who was leading the attacks. The police, nonreligious and antagonistic, held the whole community guilty of the violence and were not effectively able to search for the ringleaders.

"Let them say what they will, right, Dina? We must raise one worthy of being my little Dina's husband." He took the child into his lap and played an elaborate game with her fingers and toes, counting them off and walking his fingers up and down her arms, and tickling her beneath the fat folds of her little chin. Akiva, attracted by the laughter, toddled over to them and pulled himself up, holding on to Gershon's pants. He stood watching them, stamping his foot and clapping his palms and spread fingers together. But when Gershon swooped him up with one arm and the child saw the man's beard, his hands tightened into fists and his little body twisted, struggling to get away. He screamed with fright.

Batsheva felt a sudden leaden weight fall down from her throat to her stomach with a hard thump as she gathered her baby into her arms. She understood only too well the child's terror and agitation. He had mistaken the man for his father.

Human beings are strange and wonderful creations. They have been known to accommodate themselves to the barest conditions of survival. As survivors of Auschwitz and prisoners of war will testify, one can survive deprived of love, respect, home, warmth, sustenance, family, even God; be subjected to torture, terror, and daily degradation. As long as everyone around one is subject to the same conditions, men and women can cling to life, the way desert plants survive for years waiting for one rainy day. But let a man in Auschwitz see a man in the next bed receive a crumb of bread more than he, he will not be able to live one more minute without that crumb. His life will become meaningless without that equalizing crumb.

And so it was with Batsheva. Her meeting with Gita and Gershon made her realize with profound shock that Isaac Meyer Harshen was not inevitable. That there were different kinds of men, different kinds of marriages. The circumscribed and holy lives of the people around her, which she had asssumed had the same inevitable shape and form as her own, were in fact as individual and eclectic as the people themselves. Her observation of Gita and Gershon's relationship gave her a model by whose clean and wholesome lines she could finally contrast with certainty the grotesque deformity of her own marriage. There was no love, there was no passion. She had reconciled herself that these things did not exist in the world her father's vow had condemned her to. And now, suddenly, she saw it in front of her and wanted to die if she could not have it.

Each day, she grew paler and thinner. Only the baby gave her strength to go on. Only darling little Akiva, who had to be cared for. She gave him all of her pent-up love, all of her passion, sublimating it all into one great rushing stream of caring and kindness for her child. He was a little boy, climbing, running, scraping his knees, bloodying his chin. She took every fall personally. If only she had been more careful, if only she had been faster to catch him! Gita laughed at her, then worried about her. Children fall. Their wounds heal. But it wasn't right, Batsheva silently told herself, that Akiva should ever cry because he had hurt himself when she, by being wiser, faster, or more understanding, could have prevented it. Whenever he fell, she felt the pain in her own body, sharp, like a knife wound. With his birth, and that desperate, helpless cry of a newly born human being who recognizes neither the weary small hours of morning nor the rightful, earned rest of night, had come that revelation that changes every young girl into a woman and a mother: the total dependence of another human being on one's generosity, one's love and kindness.

The brilliant, harsh light of summer slowly faded into the cool burnished gold of autumn. Batsheva watched her tiny son grow with something like awe. Each word he learned filled her with pride and an inner conviction that he must be a genius. A word—Ima. He, who had lain helpless on his back, without sight or understanding, now expressed himself.

"No nana" he would say, throwing bananas on the floor, and she laughed with delight. She learned to know him as a person with tastes, opinions, hobbies, likes, dislikes. That he favored noodles and disliked cheese. That he hated to be wet but could live quite comfortably being dirty. That he loved water, in his face, in his hair. That he needed to be tickled, but liked it under his armpits, not his chin. That he loved best to be outdoors. He ran, climbing recklessly up stairs on all fours, kicking balls into the gutter. He would lean back and close his eyes, feeling the hot sunlight on his face. He would stretch out his hands and watch the shadows dapple his skin.

They sat down to dinner, Batsheva, Isaac, and Akiva. The child sat with them in a chair that attached to the table. He banged the plate with his spoon. Isaac looked up at him sharply and took the spoon out of his hand.

"No!" the father said with cold authority.

"He's just a baby, Isaac. For pity's sake."

"It is never too early to teach him respect for his father." The child reached again for the spoon, picking it up in his fist, whamp! down it came again.

Batsheva rushed over and took away the spoon. Isaac grabbed her wrist.

"Put it back."

"Please, Isaac. But why, if it annoys you, he's only a baby."

"Put it back, I told you." His voice was menacing.

She gave it back to the child, who examined it carefully for a moment, then threw it across the table.

Isaac rose up. "No!" he shouted, and drew back his hand, open-palmed.

Batsheva grabbed the child into her arms. "Don't you dare touch him. Don't you dare. I'll kill you, I vow to God I will. Don't you ever dare!"

His eyes narrowed, but then something about the firm brace of Batsheva's body, the slight hysteria in her voice, amused him. He laughed. "A man who spares his discipline hates his son."

"Another quote, Isaac, brilliant scholar? Teach me, yes. Wife beating, child abuse, why, you must have one for murder too, I bet." She spoke bitterly, beyond caring about the consequences. "Even murder or suicide. Give me a quote for that, Isaac, dear. To show that it's all right, that it's a *mitzvah* even."

"Why, as a matter of fact, it is permissible, even laudable, under particular circumstances. For example, Pinchas was blessed by God for killing the Jew who was whoring in public with a woman. Ran them through with a sword. As far as suicide, if someone asks you to take another's life or he will take yours, you must submit and have your life taken rather than be party to a murder." His voice had that prissy, instructive singsong he used in the yeshivah. Poor students, she thought, molded in his perverted image. A corrupt teacher could damage so many lives. And Isaac was not just to be a teacher, but a leader to thousands. It was sickening.

When Akiva had been a baby, Isaac had taken no interest in him. He refused to hold the child. "A scholar who has a spot on his clothes is deserving of death," he quoted to her. The baby was not clean enough, important enough, for him to deal with.

But as the child grew, he began to go into the nursery each morning and evening to recite prayers to him. Batsheva would hear the Hebrew words of the Shema—Hear O Israel, the Lord is our God, the Lord is One—and Modeh Ani—I am thankful before you, King everlasting, for Your great compassion in returning my soul. The prayers, which she had always found so touching and beautiful, echoed darkly through the house in Isaac's stern voice. "Shema," he would say to the child, "now repeat it. Shema." The child would turn his beautiful, curious little face up to his father and reach out his hands to be picked up. "Say it, Shema," Isaac would repeat, like a machine. And the child, frustrated, would cry for his mother behind the closed door of the room until Batsheva was permitted to swoop down and rescue him.

Thus, the shaky contract, the modus vivendi of Batsheva and Isaac's marriage began to crumble with her bitterness over his treatment of Akiva, and her new understanding of her husband. Suddenly she felt she could not bear to be with him one more minute. His step in the hallway made her heart sink, the touch of his hand made her physically ill. Often she daydreamed that a car would hit him full speed. She imagined the funeral, his dead body swathed in a winding sheet laid deep beneath the earth and covered forever. She imagined herself as a blameless widow raising her child alone in secret joy. Sometimes watching the daily ways he maliciously hurt the child made her suffocate with rage so strong, her hands would tremble with the need to squeeze his throat, to see him choke, and to stop the flow of his words forever.

Once, when the child had just finished eating meat and therefore would have to wait six hours before having any kind of milk or cheese, Isaac opened the refrigerator and deliberately took out a carton of ice cream. He eyed the child carefully as he filled up the bowl, piling in scoop after scoop. The child walked over to him and pointed to the icy rainbow of colors, the delicious creamy stuff. He pointed to his mouth and began to whimper as the father, unmoved, deliberately ate spoonful after spoonful. The child, breathing in the tantalizing aroma of chocolate and strawberry, the sweet irresistible odors, rubbed his tiny fists into his eyes and began to weep in earnest. He reached up, trying to stick his fingers in the bowl. The father looked down at him and said calmly: "You have just eaten meat. You can't have ice cream for six hours." His eyes twinkled with sadistic amusement as the child threw himself on the floor, hysterical with the denial.

Batsheva, immobilized by hatred, watched the man in front of her. The big tablespoons of ice cream were spooned in so rapidly that they did not fit and some slobbered slightly down his chin. He dabbed it away before the drop fell onto his clothes, staining him with evidence. He was so successful at that, she thought. Hiding the evidence. If I could kill you now, I would gladly do it, she thought. But she could not, and so she turned the rage inward. If I could only die, she thought. If I could only die. She ran to her baby and lifted him, straining him to her breast. "Sha, *tateleh*, my baby. Sha," she crooned, her heart splitting with the child's pitiful rage and frustration and her own helplessness.

"Batsheva, you look awful." Gita took her by the shoulders and peered carefully into her face, her downcast eyes. "What is it? Are you ill? Come, sit down."

"It's nothing. A cold perhaps."

"It's Isaac, isn't it?"

Batsheva looked at her friend, startled. "But how . . . ?" She kneaded her fingers together. "Is it that obvious?"

Gita nodded sympathetically. "You are from different cultures, different worlds. You've been all over, read, studied. Isaac knows so little about your world. Perhaps you should both get a good marriage counselor. Now, don't shake your head no. It's nothing to be ashamed of. You have no idea how many *frum* couples I know have needed this kind of help. It's hard to live with anybody else, and Isaac is basically a stranger."

Batsheva opened her lips to speak, then pressed them together. How could she explain? To say that she hated him, body and soul, she knew would reflect badly mainly on herself and might even damage her friendship. How could she discuss his petty cruelties to the baby or tell Gita that she would have gladly seen him dead over such trifles? "It's true, I don't understand him at all," she finally whispered, ashamed.

"There's a woman, Mrs Schrieber, who is known for her help to young couples like us. I've never personally been to her. But rumor is that she does help. Why don't you call her?"

The room had a musty smell, like old curtains in the attic. The furniture, heavy with elaborate carvings, seemed to place them in another era, long ago. Batsheva stood stiffly, awkwardly.

"Come, dear child, sit, sit." The woman patted a chair facing hers. She was in her mid-fifties, Batsheva guessed. Despite the warmth of the rooms, Batsheva noted that she wore a high-necked blouse that buttoned to just beneath her chin, and long sleeves. Her wig was plastic-looking, stiff with spray. But her gray eyes seemed intelligent and kindly.

"Now, you must tell all about yourself first. You are a new immigrant, yes? From America."

Batsheva nodded. "My accent always gives me away."

"That and your face. Americans have such pretty little faces." She smiled. "Your dear parents are still there? Ah, yes. So lonely to be separated from one's family. I myself lost my family in Europe." She sighed.

"My father's family, too, was lost," Batsheva said sympathetically. "I am an only child."

"You are newlyweds, I suppose? I am so glad you came to me," she reached over and patted Batsheva's arm intimately, "so glad. You have no idea how many hundreds of couples I have helped. Hundreds. It is not easy for me. I am a poor widow and I take no money for what I do. But I feel this is God's will, why He has put me here on earth, to help His children Israel live in harmony. You know marriage is very hard. You must work at it, every minute. My mother, she should rest in peace, used to say: 'Don't have the first fight, and then you will never fight.' But nowadays, the girls especially are so forward. They want so much and right away. Patience, I tell them. Patience. Now please, child, what was your problem?"

The problem, Batsheva thought, is that I hate my husband and wish him dead. But she said only: "My husband and I are not getting along. I find his ways . . . difficult. He does not let me do any of the things I enjoy. He is cruel to my son. To our son," she corrected herself. It was a mistake she often made.

"Can you give me examples, dear?"

"He took all of my books and burnt them."

The woman raised her eyebrows. "What kind of books were they?"

"English literature. Forster, Lawrence, Virginia Woolf . . ." The woman stared at her blankly. "Well, they were important to me."

"And what kind of things does he do to your son?"

Batsheva thought—how can I put it into words? He tortures him with stupid tests of discipline. He watches him cry and doesn't reach out his arms to him. He is constantly molding him into his own image, denying him the right to be himself. But what, specifically? "He wouldn't let him have ice cream," she said helplessly, and was not surprised that the flicker of a smile crossed the woman's face. "You don't understand. He took out ice cream deliberately to eat it in front of the baby. Just to torture him because he knew he had just eaten meat and wouldn't be able to have any for hours . . ."

The woman shook her head vigorously. "I can see the problem already, my dear child. Yes, I see it so clearly, as if the scene were right in front of my very eyes." She leaned forward urgently, taking both of Batsheva's hands in hers, searching her eyes. "You must not jump to conclusions. *Havey don call adam l'kav zchus,* give everyone the benefit of the doubt. Now, how do you know your dear husband realized the child would want the ice cream? Or perhaps he thought you were planning to take the child into a different room? After all, a husband is allowed to eat a little ice cream in peace, no?" She chuckled, just filled with the comic possibilities of the scene: the husband and baby in childish competition for the sweets; the overprotective, indulgent mother. "And a father, after all, must teach his children the laws."

Batsheva felt herself blushing with fury at the portrait painted of her in the woman's scenario.

"Do not be ashamed of yourself, my dear. You are so young. I expect you even wanted some of that ice cream yourself." The woman gave an indulgent chuckle.

Suddenly Batsheva had an irresistible urge to wipe the smile off this woman's face. "And what would you say if I told you he beats me?" she asked and had the satisfaction of seeing her goal immediately accomplished.

"That is serious, serious," she sighed. But there was no shock on her face, as Batsheva assumed there would be, and as she continued speaking, Batsheva understood why. "You are not the first and the last to tell me this. I'll tell you the truth—men will be men. They will be obeyed. You are not thinking of divorce, are you?" She looked up sharply.

"I don't . . . well, know."

"You must forget about that. Think of your poor innocent, fatherless child! And do you think the men that are out there are any different, any better! You might wind up with no one, and then where would you be? No, I'll tell you the whole secret, my dear child. Do not make him angry. Obey his wishes, even if they seem a little strange or foolish to you. The man must be the head of the family, otherwise the family crumbles. Be a Woman of Valor, bear up under your hardships as a good Jewish girl must. What you have—a Jewish family—is a holy thing. You must not tear it apart. Give him love and patience and he will certainly change and become the man you hope for. God will help you, my dear. He always does."

Chapter thirteen

The winter rains came, short and heavy, washing the summer dust from the white stones of the city, making them glisten with light. Then the winds grew gentle, blowing the clouds away and bringing the clean bright days of Passover and spring. Before she would have dreamt it possible, the golden summer had come and vanished and preparations began again for Rosh Hashanah, Yom Kippur, and Succoth. The year had come full cycle, she thought, and was back to the beginning again. Nothing changed. The sun went up, it came down. The pots were washed, then filled again with food and washed again. Clothes were laundered, then worn, dirtied, and washed again.

Only in Akiva did she see the beauty and wonder of growth and change. He had grown so much, his fat baby feet and hands thinning out slightly, turning him into a little man. He was a wild, happy child. He could pass no ball without throwing it up into the sky. He could see nothing with screws and bolts without longing to take it apart. His curiosity was insatiable and with him Batsheva rediscovered the world. The hours they spent alone together or with Gita, hiking up through the hills, picnicking in the grass, were the only happiness she had. Away from the house, she forgot about her husband, her joyless marriage, and lost herself in her child's delight. A long-tailed lizard's swift climb up the rocks was a cause for celebration, for shouts of excited happiness. A drink of cool raspberry-flavored water after a long hot walk a reason for total contentment. The heat of the sun on one's upturned face a reason for living. But all through the long, cloudless days a dread so deep she could not name it lingered just beneath the surface. Our last summer like this, she thought. How will I stand it? After Succoth he would turn three, the age when Hassidic boys started their education in the *heder*. They would go from year's end to year's end with no summers, no time off at all. Isaac scoffed at the idea of summer vacations. "Time off from life, from learning, from performing God's will?"

Sometimes she would wander down to the places where the little ones sat learning their *aleph-bais* and listen to their loud, childish voices repeat the letters in singsong unison. She would peer through the dusty windows with their rusting iron bars into the sunless rooms filled with sweet, pale children and hug Akiva to her, kissing his rosy, sun-kissed face, and ache at the thought of him inside with the others. She discussed it with Gita, who sighed, but agreed with Isaac that boys needed to begin their education early. "But," she admitted, "I'm so glad I have a girl. At least she will be able to wait another year. But you know, the rabbis are pretty good with the little ones. They dance with them, sing with them. It's more of a kindergarten than a regular school. Just be careful not to send him to Betsher's." She gave a shudder of distaste.

Where had Batsheva heard that name before? Isaac. It was the school he had gone to as a little boy. "Isaac went there, you know."

"Really? Awful place. The teachers still use canes on the children, like something out of Europe in the last century. It is so wrong. They make the children so afraid they can't see straight, let alone learn anything. Isaac wouldn't send him there, would he? After all he suffered himself as a child?"

Batsheva turned away, ashamed to admit she knew so little of her husband and the workings of his twisted mind that she could not even begin to guess his plans for their son. What she was certain of was that she would have little or no say in their son's education. Her father would be consulted. Isaac would discuss it with his rebbes. But no one would talk to her about it. She wanted desperately to ask Isaac, but each time she began to, she remembered the shoes in the attic.

She had gone up there to take down the special dishes used for Passover—two sets, one for meat and one for milk, used only one week a year. Beneath the cardboard box she found his shoes in a plastic bag. They were almost new. She took them out curiously and turned them over. Sand littered the floor. Beach sand. Other than that she could find nothing wrong with them.

But when she began to polish them she noticed some dark stains she hadn't seen on the top. They turned the cloth a dark blood-red. Dried blood. She replaced them, terrified he might notice they had been touched. Putting them back, she noticed other things—half-filled cans of kerosene and spray paint. But her mind did not wish to know any more. It stepped back into the darkness of wishful thinking and dark day-dreams.

A listlessness had come over her, a kind of welcome, deliberate ignorance. Unable to control her life, she began to retreat into a world she created each day, day by day. She told herself the long, carefree days would never end, that Akiva would be her baby forever.

His third birthday came in between the New Year and Yom Kippur, during the time known as the Ten Days of Repentance, when pious Jews believe that charity, prayer, and repentance can change any evil decree written down for one in the Book of Life.

Batsheva woke at dawn after an hour of fitful sleep in which she had turned from side to side seeking some relief from blackness. But it was so dark everywhere she looked. She tiptoed into Akiva's room and opened the door very softly so as not to disturb him and sat down in the rocking chair next to his bed, her eyes wide with despair. His long, dark eyelashes, too pretty for a boy, made a soft fringe of shadow on his full, soft cheeks, and his long curly hair framed his face. Sleep softened his alert, mischievous face, making him look like a helpless baby again. She fought the urge to take him in her arms and hug him hard, to rest her hot cheek against his cool, sweet one. Instead, she closed her eyes and prayed: "God, I know that I am full of sin and I am ashamed to ask anything of You. I ask You because You are our Father, my Father, and I am in such terrible pain. I know that You are good, God. Whatever Isaac says, I know that Your ways cannot be hurting and cruel, without pity or understanding. Please. Help me to save Akiva from his father's cruelty, from his grandfather's obsessions. Give me strength to protect him and wisdom to keep him from all harm. I promise to bring him up to serve You, to know You and love You. With all of my heart I vow this." Her tears fell unheeded, wetting her hands, her nightgown, her cheeks. She rocked and rocked, repeating her prayer.

In her dream, a growing shout began in the distance, then traveled like thunder, rolling and crashing through her eyelids. It was like an army marching toward her with knives and sticks and guns, and only she stood in its way, barring it from reaching Akiva. It came closer and closer and she saw it was not soldiers at all, but scholars in long black coats with twisted sidecurls. One had her husband's face, the other her father's. Gita and Gershon were there. No! But yes, they were there with the others, marching relentlessly toward her. "Give us the baby," they chanted. "Give him to us!" They held out long grasping fingers with punishing pointed nails. NO! she screamed, but no sound came. They ignored her and marched right through her as if she were a ghost. She woke with a start and realized the noise was real, out in the street. She went to the window and drew aside the curtain. Thronged below were hundreds of Hassidim in Sabbath finery singing and dancing. They had come to witness the first step of the future leader of the Ha-Levis on the road to greatness. It would become the stuff of parables and myths, she knew. How the child had looked, what he had said. They would have the joy of telling all this to their grandchildren. They had come, she understood, to take possession of her son, to take him forever from her into some dark male enclave where she would be allowed only to hover at the outskirts, like a beggar.

She pressed her lips together and clenched her fists, but then Isaac was already at the door in his immaculate satin waistcoat, a mink *streimel* on his head. His beard, newly trimmed, came to a sharp point. Behind him were six or seven Hassidim. Isaac held a scissor in his hands.

"What are you going to do?" Her voice trembled with fear.

"Just cut his hair, as is the custom."

She sat Akiva on her lap, hugging him tight. The child's eyes were still partly closed, hovering somewhere between sleep and wakefulness. She watched with a kind of silent madness as his beautiful curls fell to the floor and they shaved his head so that only his long sidecurls were left. He whimpered when the cold air hit the unfamiliar bareness of his scalp. "It's all right, my angel, my baby. Sha, sha." The men handed her clothes and she dressed him: a little black vest and knickers with white stockings and a black skull cap. And when she was finished, her heart seemed to break: He looks like a stranger, she thought. Like one of those children I see in the streets of Meah Shearim: little old men speaking Yiddish, their backs bent from the weight of heavy books, their eyes fearful, terrified of punishment.

Then they took him from her. They fed him apples with

honey, making him lick the honey from the pages of a book where the Hebrew alphabet was written so that the words of the Torah would be sweet to him always. The child, still half asleep, suddenly woke. He felt the cold air on his shaved scalp and touched it uncertainly. He looked for his mother, and seeing her far away, began to whimper: "Ima, Ima." He held out his hands to her. She pushed through, making an urgent swathe through the crowd. They parted for her uneasily. She reached out her hands toward the child, but her husband stared down at her in cold fury, whispering harshly: "Still in your nightclothes, in front of all these men! Dress yourself quickly. We must leave now."

One of the men took his prayer shawl and wrapped the child in it gently, covering his face. He would be carried this way in his father's arms, protected from the Evil Eye, to his first day in school. The child, cranky from the sudden wakening, frightened by the roomful of strange men, the unwelcome press of his father's arms, and the sudden envelopment in the cloth, screamed: "Ima, Ima!" He kicked and bit in a tantrum of grief and terror until finally she was allowed to take him. She held him close to her, murmuring comforting things she did not feel. "It's all right, darling. Ima is here. You will go to school like a big boy. And I will come with you. You'll dance and sing with lots of other children. You'll like that, won't you?" She smiled at him brightly. His hands reached out, touching her cheeks.

"Crying?" His fingers felt the tears that had overflowed from her bright, almost manic eyes.

"No. Not crying, baby. Ima's just happy for you. You're such a big boy now. You will make me proud of you? You will be a big boy now, won't you?"

Isaac, bending down, swiftly took the child from her. The child's eyes, perplexed and wide with uncertainty, did not cry anymore, but clung desperately to his mother until he was borne away in the relentless tide of men.

Batsheva dressed quickly and followed the crowd, which swept like a parade through the streets. Forced to linger on the fringes, she was far behind and could not get close to Akiva. A woman fell in step beside her. "Where are they going?" she asked, and Batsheva realized, for the first time, that she did not know. A kind man, overhearing the question, in rare friendliness turned to answer: "To Betsher's, to begin the education of the heir to the Ha-Levi dynasty."

Betsher's. Batsheva did not move, and the crowd surged around her, parting for her still, rocklike figure. She stood very still and closed her eyes. *Her life blood seemed to ebb away from her and within the emptiness a heavy despair gathered.* The words came into her head. But from where? *Her passion seemed to bleed to death and there was nothing. She sat suspended in a state of complete nullity, harder to bear than death.* It was as if someone were talking to her, telling her how she felt . . . It was Ursula, the words of D. H. Lawrence in *Women in Love*, she realized.

She turned and ran home, knowing she had stumbled upon the answer to all of her questions. She took out the book, bought secretly and hoarded, and read:

> Unless something happens, I shall die.

It was as if Ursula were her, thinking and planning within her.

> *Obliterated in a darkness that was the border of death. She realized how all her life had been drawing nearer and nearer to this brink, where there was no beyond, from which one had to leap like Sappho into the unknown. The knowledge of the imminence of death was like a drug.*
>
> *There was nothing to look for from life—it was the same in all countries and all peoples. The only window was*

> *death. One could look out on the great dark sky of death without emotion, as one had looked out of the class-room window as a child, and seen perfect freedom in the outside. Now one was not a child, and one knew that the soul was a prisoner within this sordid vast edifice of life, and there was no escape, save in death . . .*
>
> *How beautiful, how grand and perfect death was, how good to look forward to. There one would wash off all the lies and ignominy and dirt that had been put upon one here, a perfect bath of cleanness and glad refreshment, and go unknown, unquestioned, unabased . . .*
>
> *Whatever life might be, it could not take away death, the inhuman transcendent death. Oh, let us ask no question of it, what it is or is not. To know is human, and in death we do not know, we are not human. And the joy of this compensates for all the bitterness of knowledge and the sordidness of our humanity. In death we shall not be human, and we shall not know . . .*

Batsheva closed the book with a kind of joy. This then was what she had been seeking. A way out. The beginning of a new form of existence. Death. She would go to it gladly, beautifully, choosing it with all the intelligence and imagination she had never been allowed to use in planning her life. She took off her wig and let her hair fall to her shoulders. She had let it grow back. It was duller now, with a strawlike stiffness from the hours spent beneath the wig. But as she brushed it, it crackled, sparkling with electricity, and framed her face with a dark halo. She took out a box with a dress her mother had just sent her that Isaac wouldn't let her wear. A gray silk. Soft, so very soft. She put it on and felt it caress her skin. From the top drawer of her dresser she took out the diamond-and-emerald necklace, taken from its safe deposit box for her to wear to a wedding that night. She put it on, together with diamond earrings she had gotten just recently from her father and then slipped on the big pearl-and-diamond ring she had bought herself on that wonderful day.

She took her purse, but packed no bags. Empty, she thought. Clean and empty. For the last time, she went through the house and thought: This has never been my house, my home. Everything in it, all the beautiful furniture shiny with wax, the polished crystal and silver, has the cold gleam of objects in a museum. Like her mother, she, too, lived in a house where nothing was hers. She was merely another one of the objects put into the house, like the curtains or the piano, to fulfill someone else's dream, someone else's needs. My bridal bower and love nest. A young bride's first home, she thought mockingly, with a final ache, giving up the dream of her youth. She had imagined it so differently as a young girl! But that did not matter anymore. She was past caring, past regrets. She closed the door quietly, finally, behind her.

The police received the missing-persons report the same evening, but did not feel it necessary to do anything until the next day. By that evening, they had already located a clerk in a shorefront hotel in Tel Aviv who remembered the young, beautiful rich woman and the little Hassidic boy—an incongruous pair. He remembered thinking it odd, too, that they had no luggage, and that with such a small child she should ask specifically for a room on the highest floor overlooking the sea. Usually people with small kids avoided the high floors. She had registered late in the afternoon and spent the night and had gone out twice the next day. The second time, about three in the afternoon, she had not returned. Oh, yes, she had asked him about boat rentals at the marina.

By the time the police got into the room and found the suicide note addressed to Abraham Ha-Levi, Los Angeles, and located the rental service with the missing motorboat, the gray dress and the child's black vest, covered with tar and seaweed, had already washed up on the beach. They found the boat capsized far out at sea, whether drifted or driven there, they could not tell.

In Jerusalem, the Ha-Levi Hassidim ripped the pockets off their black waistcoats and covered their heads with ashes. They could hold no funeral because there were no bodies.

Part Two

Chapter fourteen

"We're going to be late, pet," Graham said impatiently. "Can't you call her tomorrow, for pity's sake?"

"It's her little boy's third birthday. Actually it was, I'm already four days late," Elizabeth said calmly. Lately Graham had been getting on her nerves. He's getting fussy, she thought. A fussy old man. The unspoken insult made her look at him brightly and smile. She had been on the phone for twenty minutes, getting busy signals from Jerusalem. "I'll try once more and then give up," Elizabeth pleaded, pressing the redial button. He sighed and turned on the television. She heard the phone connect and the long, slow rings—nine, ten, eleven . . . "Hello!" she shouted; the connection was terrible, like speaking to someone on the moon. "I'd like to speak to Batsheva, please. This is her friend . . . Yes, Batsheva Harshen . . . Could you put her . . . What's that?" She put her hand over the receiver, "God! Shut that thing off! Please, this is a terrible connection, could you speak a little . . . God, no! No, oh, please, dear God, she couldn't have. Please say it again. Batsheva, God, no!" She let the phone smash to the floor. Graham dove for it.

"Hello, who is this? Are they sure? How did she? When? Could you speak up a little? All right. We'll call back later. Good-bye."

Curled up in a fetal position on the couch, Elizabeth rocked, hugging her shoulders. Graham sat next to her and she hugged him, sobbing into his shoulder. "Why, Graham, why? She was so happy the last time I spoke to her. She loved that little boy so much. How could she do that to him? To herself? How? Why?"

"Drink this, here. Down the hatch now, that's a good girl," he said soothingly, handing her a brandy and pouring himself a vodka as he spoke. When she had finished, he refilled the glass. Then suddenly, she sat up.

"It's my fault."

"Good heavens!"

She got up and paced the floor. "I remember now. We were discussing Anna Karenina and I said . . . oh my God, Graham! It's my fault! I put the idea into her head! We were having this stupid discussion about why Anna did it and I told her that I thought suicide was a way of taking control, an act of courage. My God! I did it," she screamed hysterically. He slapped her sharply across the face and grabbed her arms, holding her tight.

"Now you listen to me, you silly fool! That girl had a husband who was beating the daylights out of her. She was black and blue all over. I should think that that had a little to do with it." He felt her stop struggling and go limp.

"She never told me that. How do you know that?"

"I saw the marks when her skirt accidentally rode up when we were getting into a cab. I spoke to her about it later. She said there was nothing she could do. Something about being Jephte's daughter." He was feeling a little uncomfortable now and beginning to realize he had made a serious mistake.

"Why didn't you tell me about any of this before, when we were in Jerusalem, when I could have done something?" She got up and paced the floor, pulling painfully on her hair. "You knew, yet you kept it a secret."

He avoided her eyes. "I thought you knew . . . I . . ." he faltered.

"Liar!" She pounded his chest with her fists. "You knew she was married to someone who beat her, and that she was desperate, and you let me leave Jerusalem without trying to help her. What was it, Graham? Were you afraid she'd move in with us and spoil your love nest? Was she too pregnant for a threesome?"

"I'm getting a little too old for these theatrics, pet," he said, grabbing her wrists and holding them a little tighter than necessary to keep them away from him. "I'm also a little too tired and too bored with Ms Ha-Levi Harshen—may she rest in peace—to pretend anymore. Yes indeed, I knew that if I told you about the black-and-blue marks you'd go running off to kidnap her and I wasn't about to be saddled with hiding a pregnant Jewess from her monied Hebraic clan, who wouldn't hesitate to have me fired from Cambridge. Trust the Hebrews, my dear, their money allows them endless liberties."

"You never did care anything about her, did you? It was just a way of impressing me, keeping me believing that you were really—"

"What? What do I need to be for you? Good, decent, moral—no, more than that!—a rock of moral strength, a giant of spirit infused by the best in Western culture and civilization. While you, my dear, were not above taking a bribe that resulted in this poor, misguided child's eventual leap into the sea. So please, don't look at me all fire and brimstone." He drained his glass. "We are the same, my pet. Empty inside, waiting for someone else to do the heroics so we can latch on to them and take some satisfaction, some sense of being alive. We're two phony hypocrites, selfish and indulgent, who care for no one, for nothing. But I at least have one thing you don't: self-knowledge."

Stricken, she stopped struggling and let her hands hang helplessly at her sides. "It's true. I let her marry him—that monster! That brute!" Then a certain light came into her eyes, a flash of intuitive understanding. "A scholar," she said with quiet contempt. She looked up at Graham. "Another scholar, learned in all things, trained in the pureness of philosophy, in the delineation of the most delicate shades of emotion, the highest categories of truth." She shook her head. "I'm not like you, Graham. I may have done selfish, immoral things, but I care. I want to be a better person. I haven't given in yet to all the ugliness in my soul. I'm a country girl, and yet I was sitting right on a pile of it and never smelled it." She laughed low—a harsh, tortured sound. "Get out of here, Graham," she said softly.

"A splendid idea." He rose, picking imaginary lint off his neatly pressed gray wool slacks and tweed jacket and getting into his overcoat. "I hope to return when you've come to your senses, pet," he called after her as she disappeared into the bedroom.

"You don't seem to understand, *pet.*" She came back to him, holding a valise in her hands. "I mean get out of my life, for good. You can get the rest of your things later. Now give me back my keys, you bastard."

"Elizabeth, dearest, you don't mean this. You're upset about your little friend, as of course you should be. You'll feel better in the morning, darling, and I'll be there to share it with you." He spoke calmly, but his years of experience with coeds told him that this chapter was ending. His panic rose.

"The goddamn keys, Graham," she said sharply, her palm upturned. He reached into his pocket and dropped them finally into her hand. She pocketed them.

He walked out of the door, the youth gone from his step, his shoulders suddenly stooped, heavy with the burdens of middle age. "You'll change your mind. Won't you let me help you? I can make you feel better, I know I can."

"You're so right, Graham. I feel better already," she said, slamming the door in his still-pleading face.

She walked slowly back into her bedroom, crawled beneath the covers, and buried her face in a pillow. She thought of the sunlight glinting off the polished brass fireplace screen at the Ha-Levis', the smell of roses fresh from the garden in little crystal vases on brightly polished wood. She saw Batsheva, a little ninth-grader, her hair braided with red bows, her gray-blue eyes wide with friendliness and excitement, bending over clean, new books, Penguins whose pages had never been turned before. How her face had looked up with curiosity and pleasure, asking, asking, asking, seeking to understand a whole world denied her, wanting to be part of it, yet struggling to keep faithful to her own world. She had struggled so. Why had she finally given up? What had pushed her over the edge? She would never know. If only I could talk to her, beg her forgiveness, Elizabeth cried inside herself.

The gray wash of insomnia kept the blackness of sleep always a little at bay. And then a word came to her: repentance. She remembered once Batsheva had told her the three stages of repentance: recognition of the evil deed, sincere regret, and finally a deep-rooted change that would allow one, in the identical circumstances, to act differently. Slowly, in the dark reaches of the the endless gray night, she passed through them. When she awoke, she felt fragile and clean, as if she had spent the night in fasting and prayer. And deep in her soul she felt some change had taken place.

She found a church and lit two candles. And on her aching knees, she watched their small, brilliant, fragile flames flicker, illuminating the darkness.

Abraham Ha-Levi, sitting on the floor, his exquisite suit ripped to shreds by his own hands, heard the door open and more voices enter. He closed his eyes wearily, waiting for the people to come in and sit down and offer condolence. For seven days, as is the custom among Jews, he was forced to receive the comfort of friends and strangers. He wanted desperately to be alone, and yet just to prevent that was the object of *shiva*, the seven days of mourning. After the loss of a child, or a mother, father, sister, or brother, husband or wife, one was not allowed to be alone.

Voices. So far away, and suddenly he heard the whispers of his classmates and felt the icy, cold breeze of a Polish winter come through the smashed windows of the university. Go home, the professors shouted. Your grades will be sent to you. The Germans are in the streets. Be careful. No Jews allowed on the train. Jews not allowed to travel. The valise wrenched from his hands. Helplessness. Rage. Hide. Do not be caught. The train's acrid smoke, the strange palpable silence of the passengers. And every new face that boarded: A policeman? A soldier? An ache in the stomach, a spasm of death-fear. Midnight. Silent steps with no backward glance and then, suddenly home! Running footsteps, pounding on the door. Mama, Mama. Silent tears in rivulets down her dear face. But I am home, Mama. I am safe, why do you cry? Where is Papa? Where is Aaron, and Joseph and Gavriel? Her soft caress. Sleep, she says. In the morning you will see them. But now, sleep child, dear child. Her warm caress, the waxy smell of the burning Sabbath candles reaching their end. But I will only kiss them, Mama, and wish them goodnight. In which room does Papa sleep? Running through the silent house. Empty, soundless. Mama's piercing, manic cry. Mama, Mama, where are they, what has happened? The synagogue, she cried. It was not my fault. I was not home. I would have gone with them, gladly.

Aching, tired legs pound the streets, and when they arrive, the smell of cold smoke. Burnt wood. The white-and-black cloth of a prayer shawl, singed. Two Hebrew letters from a Torah scroll. And then . . . then . . . the bones—white bones in the rubble. The smell of burnt flesh. The heave, the heave of nausea. A death-longing.

He opened his eyes and heard the voices around him discuss the weather, the high price of tomatoes, the fall in the stock market. Well-dressed Jewish matrons of Los Angeles and their solid, comfortable husbands. The sunlight bouncing off an alligator purse and well-shined shoes pierced his eyes like a knife. He shut them again.

Give him the money, Mama pleads. The guard grins, his heavy fist circles a gun. The first time I aimed my gun at a small child, the guard says, I had to close my eyes. The second time I looked with one eye. By the third I did it with both eyes open and enjoyed it.

Give him the money, but not the tools.

Why do they push me? I am going into the train. But there is no room. Do not move or you will crush a child. Someone has vomited. Airless, suffocating.

At the end of the line, they will kill us all. We must escape.

Shut up, fool! You lie, little fool. We will tell the guards about you when we stop. Shouting voices, enraged voices. Mama, they will not listen, come with me. I will cut open the barbed wire that seals the windows. We will jump. I will go first, then you must follow. Mama, Mama.

You are the remnant, son. You must continue in your father's footsteps, your brothers' footsteps. You must wear the crown of the Ha-Levis. I am not worthy, Mama. I can't, Mama. You must promise me, son, you must vow it to God that you and your children will continue this, it is God's will. A sacred vow. Make it. Make it. Now, on your father's holy grave. Your brothers' holy graves. Slowing down. The train moves into the mountains. Clip—one gone. Clip, and the second. Then the third. An opening. Jump! A crack, a thud, a piercing pain in the shoulder and the back. Down on the ground. Mama, jump! Mama!

A scream. She will not follow.

Vow it! Her pale lips mouth the words.

I swear it, Mama, Mama. On my father's holy grave. On my brothers' holy graves. I vow it.

The rumble, the soft rumble of the cattle cars. Gone. Alone. Forever.

"Do you want to eat? You must eat, my darling."

He opened his eyes and looked at his wife. Her tearstained face. Still tears left, he wondered. Fortunate woman. He closed his eyes and shook his head.

He was in the garden now, Batsheva on his lap, her soft cool lips on his cheek, her arms thrown trustingly around his neck. And what have you brought me now, Aba, dear Aba? I have brought you a great gift, little princess. And where is it, Aba— the tickle of small hands thrust deep into his pockets, the cry of joy, the ecstatic hug, the wet urgent kiss on the cheek. He felt no tears well up. He was dry, he thought. Nothing human was left him. No human emotions. He was simply a drawing, a still life, all emotion frozen and long past. A memory. Not all, he thought. Out of all the things human beings feel in their short, tortured time on earth, out of all that joy, sorrow, compassion, love, respect, honor, awe, surprise, gratitude, and judgment, only one emotion had been left him: anger. But it was so strong, so deep, it made up for all the others. He felt he could destroy the universe with it. But he didn't know who or what he was angry at, so it stayed locked up within him, an atom bomb deep and silent in an underground silo.

At first he thought it might be Batsheva. It should be her, he thought. But then he thought of her letter and he knew it wasn't. He had memorized it, word for word, and whenever the voices grew too intrusive, he would simply repeat it to himself, drowning out everything else.

Aba, my dearest,

It is the Ten Days of Repentance and I must ask all those I have harmed throughout the year for their forgiveness. I must ask you and Ima through this letter. I am sorry that I will not be able to hear you say "I forgive." But you must say it, as I have said it.

I want you to know that I forgive you. I forgive you the way Jephte's daughter forgave her father for making the vow that ended her life. I looked it up in the the Book of Judges. It really wasn't Jephte's fault, he was just a foolish man. When he vowed to God that he would sacrifice the first thing that came to greet him on his return from victory, he thought it would be a cow, perhaps, or a sheep. He didn't think it would be his only daughter. His beloved daughter.

I know you are thinking that I have committed a mortal sin. But I asked Isaac about it once, and he told me that under certain circumstances taking one's life was not only allowed but actually a good deed, like when someone asks you to save your own life by killing someone else. Isaac and the others—they are asking me to kill my baby, to kill his spirit.

I thought about only taking my own life, but then how could I leave my baby in my husband's care? I can say no more. I would not like to have loshon harah, *slander on my conscience. I feel clean now, pure and holy. I am sure He will gather me and Akiva in His arms and shelter us forever.*

Dear Aba, dear Ima. I forgive you both.

All my love,
Batsheva

Jephte. Am I? No. I was forced to promise. I also had no choice. Her face above his in the hospital room. Promise me. Swear a sacred vow to me, Batsheva, that you will not leave him, your husband. That you will not bring disgrace to our name. That you will keep the vow, so that my mother's soul will rest in peace. But it could have been a good life for her. What had he asked of her that was so terrible. To marry? To have a child? To follow God's law?

Isaac, he thought suddenly. "How could I leave my baby in my husband's care?" Her voice on the phone: "He is so cruel to me." Isaac, Isaac, he thought, and felt the silo within him slowly open.

The Hassidim, who crowded around the house throughout the day and night, looked at Isaac Harshen's straight back, his impeccably clean clothes, his calm face, and were filled with awe. He was from another world, they told each other. He was on such a high spiritual plane he could already view the tragedy the way the angels did in the World to Come, where death was simply the beginning of the real life. But then some began to look at him slightly differently. A wife, a firstborn son. They thought of their own women and their own small children and their souls shuddered and their awe turned to fright. It was not human, they thought. That calm acceptance, that unbending, tearless grief. If it was grief . . .

Then after the first rush of shock died down, others began to ask in whispers: And why did she do it? What suffering was so terrible that she needed to end it in such a way?

He had been the caretaker of the real heir to the Ha-Levi dynasty and he had not watched carefully enough. The last legitimate Ha-Levi was gone, some began to grumble. They remembered the woman who had died in childbirth bringing the child into the world Isaac Harshen had insisted God wanted. That and other stories gathered like tidal waves far out in the sea. And just when it seemed that nothing could stop them from crashing down on Isaac Harshen, an idea was thrown into the still, dangerous water that spread in concentric circles throughout the world of Meah Shearim.

It began with Mrs Harshen. "She was insane, a crazy girl.

That is why her father was so willing to give such a dowry. To buy such a house. Insanity." She dried her dry eyes with a handkerchief. Her poor son. Her poor Isaac. Such a light of the generation. Such a *gaon*, a scholar of such talent and promise. This crazy girl. Why, she would lie in bed till all hours. She had to be watched all the time, like an infant, so that she would not go off and disgrace the family. They had been so good to the ungrateful girl. Taken her into the family like a daughter. Spent more time with her than she did with her own daughters, God help us, and this was the thanks. This was the reward. Then, her eyes lowered, taking shrewd stock of who was in listening range, she whispered of wedding-night problems with signs of virginity and rendezvous with Gentile men in expensive hotels.

My poor son, my poor grandson, she wailed, her eyes truly misting. Evil, insane girl! My poor son, my poor grandson. And the fears and the anger that had come to the surface like bubbles from an underground volcano, burst somewhat, and the calm surface of the water began to return. Insanity. An insane, evil girl, they repeated, hesitantly at first and then, by the fourth or fifth time, with more conviction. And Isaac was a saint who had had untold trouble with her and had borne it like the yoke of heaven.

Isaac Meyer Harshen was patient with his Hassidim, and understanding to his mother. He decreed that those who had decided to fast over the tragedy should now stop and eat. And he had the satisfaction of hearing them whisper, "He thinks only of others," and seeing their wonder, their awe of such compassion, such saintly calm. Only he knew how long and hard he had traveled within himself to reach such calm.

The gray dress, the tiny black vest, covered with seaweed, rancid with salt water, had hit him full in the stomach, numbing all his senses. He had come home and thrown himself across his wife's bed, nuzzling her soft pillow, inhaling her lingering fragrance. He had staggered like a drunk into his son's room, filled with the echo of his childish laughter: sturdy, stubborn little boy! He had sat down and wept with bitterness and horror.

Then, suddenly, his tears had dried up. She had won, after all. She had freed herself and the child and he was left behind, helpless, an object of pity and derision and cruel speculation. She had defied him this one last time and won an irrevocable victory. What would his Hassidim think? The thought had terrified him.

From the very beginning, they had not trusted him. He had seen it in their calculating eyes, in their raised eyebrows at his decisions concerning points of law and ritual. He had felt, from the beginning, that he must prove himself worthy. He must lead the battle against the *Tumah*—the impurities—of the outside world, its encroachments: the women tourists who sauntered into Meah Shearim bare-armed, bare-legged, teasing the boys from the yeshivoth. The government of black-hearted Zionists whose dirty deals compromised the Laws of God. The bus shelters, for example, which had been built by an advertising company in exchange for permission to put up advertisements—posters depicting depraved women almost naked in bathing suits, young girls posing with young boys for Kodak pictures. To burn, burn, burn. It was the only way to restore the purity of the holy city. And the young boys in the yeshivah who had been led astray. They were found talking to girls on street corners, or going to the forbidden movie houses, or the theater—the filth of Roman amphitheaters! He had led the faithful and had not spared the rod! He had helped to beat the *Tumah* out of them and return them to purity. And his wife, his Batsheva, he had tried so hard to teach her! To remake her in the image of the women he knew—his mother, his sisters—silent, holy presences that did what was needed and slipped quietly away when men gathered for important Torah matters. Yielding presences that made no demands. Listeners willing to sit at the feet of scholars and drink in their wisdom.

Her beauty had always frightened him—tempting and voluptuous, she was the essence of sin. But he would have yielded totally to her, to it, if she would only have accepted him! But she didn't want him. He bit the tight, white knuckle of his clenched fist. That was the great stone he had needed to crush to have her spring newborn, meek and clean for him. Her silent negation of him, of everything he stood for and believed in. He had felt it emanate from her with the power of a searchlight, uncovering all his hypocrisy, his petty cruelties. She hated him and he loved her so . . . It had been a hatred that threatened his life, his very sanity. He had come to understand that he had to destroy that hatred, even if it meant destroying her.

She would tell everyone he was not a scholar, not even a man. She dangled the keys above his head, taunting him. They all looked at him and knew: All the wealth, the position, it all came from her. He was nothing. A calculator, a rememberer of facts and figures. She alone had questioned his faith and his scholarship. She alone had seen him sink into the soft velvet couches and luxuriate in the wealth and comfort and power she had brought him. Dangerous woman.

He thought of his son. It had been hard for him to feel the child was really his—the blue eyes, the raven-black hair—he was Batsheva totally. He had seen no hint, no reminder, of himself in the child in looks, character, or temperament. If only Akiva had had his own brown eyes, or the shape of his nose—some reminder that he was not totally a Ha-Levi, *the* Ha-Levi. He had had mixed feelings at the child's birth: triumph at his success at providing a fine young son and despair in the knowledge that he had created his own rival and successor. A real Ha-Levi, a male Ha-Levi, now lived. He shuddered. Had lived.

"Would *kavod harav* like a drink?" someone asked him deferentially, softly.

He shook his head with a wan smile and returned his gaze to the open Talmud before him. Calm, they thought him. Saintly calm. And some thought, he knew, that he just didn't care. But that was not true. He simply felt that on some fundamental level it had nothing to do with him. The woman had never been his wife in any real sense. She had always sought to separate herself from him, from his ideas. She had scorned him with her soft, polite words, her false, calculating meekness. He had felt the sting of her contempt and fear and disgust. So, being separate, she was responsible for her own actions, which were so horrible as to negate any petty bullying or unkindness on his part. With her death, his love turned quickly and totally to hatred. She was totally responsible, and he, like the High Priest in the Temple after sacrificing the red heifer on Yom Kippur, emerging from the Holy of Holies dressed in pure white linen, felt his forehead beam with purity, totally absolved from all past sin.

In time, when the body was found, he would send out hints that he needed a new wife, and sweet, local girls, fresh young virgins who had never left Meah Shearim, would be brought to him. He knew that the one he chose would consider herself quite fortunate.

Chapter fifteen

At Bloom's in London's East End, the lunchtime laughter and conversation rose to almost deafening heights. The voices spoke a rather odd mixture of proper British English interspersed with Yiddish expressions. White-coated waiters with sad European faces gave the menu of the day in Yiddish-accented cockney. The photographic mural running the full length of the wall showed racks and racks of clothes, bringing some of the bustle of the wholesale garment trade of Aldgate into their midst. Certainly the boisterous, friendly atmosphere of the kosher restaurant was a far cry from the staid, muted tones of other English dining establishments in the city.

The noise seemed to disturb a little blond girl sitting with her mother? sister? aunt?—the curious businessmen waiting for their gefilte fish, kishke, mutton and chips could not decide which, although they had studied the stunning young woman from the moment she had stepped through the door. A movie star from Hollywood, some conjectured. The flowing blond hair, the dark glasses and gray fur coat. The little girl was also dressed stylishly: a velvet jumper and frilly white blouse.

"Don't be afraid, darling," the woman whispered, of necessity loudly to be heard above the din of voices and clatter of rolling serving carts and dishes. "Here, do you want me to cut your meat for you?"

The little girl nodded, scratching her head.

An American accent, the men all agreed. And definitely not Lower East Side of Manhattan. An actress or a dancer, they agreed, studying the long legs in fine knee-high calf leather. Then someone noticed the small suitcase. Tourists, perhaps? In need of guidance, perhaps?

They nudged each other, and finally, the boldest, a salesman with dark red hair and a friendly paunch, got up amid guffaws and pats on the back and strode over purposefully.

"Excuse me, miss, is it? I wonder if you wouldn't be so kind as to settle a little dispute among the fellows." He gestured vaguely in the direction of his tablemates. "Some of us are certain you're a famous movie star out of Hollywood, or a stage actress perhaps?" She smiled, confused, annoyed, and shook her head no. "You don't have to hide from us, you know. We wouldn't even ask for an autograph," he continued aimlessly. "We also couldn't help noticing your American accent and suitcase and wondered if you might need some guidance in finding a place to stay in our fine city? A nice Jewish hotel, perhaps? Golder's Green has several . . . I just happen to be headed that way myself. The car's parked a minute away . . ."

"Thank you so much." Her eyes were blanks behind the smoky lenses, giving no clues. "But I am not Jewish."

The man took a step backward in confusion and his eyes met the laughing, expectant faces of his tablemates. "I'm sorry. I simply assumed—eating kosher food here at Bloom's—that you would be."

"Moslem, actually. My mother was English, married to a Palestinian. Moslems eat no pork, you know. My husband and father will be waiting for me outside when I finish. They are very protective."

"Palestinian, as in PLO?" He swallowed hard, and his face turned a dark red, matching his hair. He stumbled back to his table.

"Finish quickly, darling. Here, take your drink." Careless, careless! The woman berated herself, suppressing a small smile around the corners of her mouth. I must not take these chances. From now on, they would eat at home, or only in vegetarian restaurants. The Jewish world was too small. The child scratched her hair and pulled at the soft, blond curls. The woman reached over and gently pulled the hands away. She would have to learn to deal with men who looked her boldly in the eyes, who made clear offers of themselves and their property. She would have to stop blushing and take these things matter-of-factly, the way heroines did in novels by Judith Krantz and Rosemary Rogers. She chuckled thinking of the way she had handled the last one. Not bad for a beginner.

She breathed in a glad breath of surprise and pleasure as the waiter set the steaming platters of food in front of her. Hot, tender lamb chops with new potatoes. Potato kugel. Hot apple strudel. She ate greedily. There had been nothing but lettuce and tomatoes to eat in Cyprus. Unwashed lettuce and tomatoes. She wrinkled her nose in disgust, remembering the foul dockside fare. She searched the child's face for some sign of damage, but there was nothing but the blank, careless concentration on stuffing as much of the frankfurter into its mouth as theoretically possible. As she ate, she tried to plan, but always her gaze would wander off and settle on some quaint Dickensian storefront, or an Englishman in a bowler hat and tweed jacket braced bravely against the ice-cold London dampness. It was as if she had been born yesterday. Every sight, every sound, seemed new and full of pleasurable discovery. As the warm, hearty meal eased the sharp pangs of hunger she had carried with her for several days, she felt a deep contentment with everything around her. It was all new and yet familiar from the books she had read in her girlhood.

Still, she recognized she had serious problems. She needed to rent an apartment, to furnish it. She needed a job and someone to care for the child while she worked. How does one rent an apartment, she wondered. Or find a job? It was a total mystery. She felt the confusion of a young baby, newly freed by its maturing limbs from immobility, who realizes with elation and panic the possibility of movement. But where to go, but what to do with this enormous freedom? She had been in London less than twenty-four hours and she had no idea where she was. She had asked about a kosher restaurant at the tourist information center at Heathrow and had given the cabbie the address. She could be on the other side of the moon, for all she knew. Or on a small island.

She got up from the table and smoothed the new cashmere dress with a deft, soft movement from her waist to her knee. She put the gray fox wrap around her shoulders and walked over to the table of laughing men, seeking out the red hair. As she approached, the voices died down to a whisper and then died altogether. She smiled.

"I wonder if you gentlemen couldn't recommend a good hotel in a central location?" The men cleared their throats nervously and peered toward the door. She had played her role too well. She threw back her head and laughed. "The PLO are busy tonight, gentlemen. Don't worry," she told them in her best Yiddish.

Nigel dropped her off at a quaint little hotel in Mayfair. A kind fellow, Nigel. A little like the young man in Eilat—full of easy laughter and pleasant manners. This must be what they call flirting, she thought, thinking of the complimentary banter that had gone on between them, the broad hints at a shared future, the almost embarrassingly sweet flatteries. I had not known it was so easy to attract men. It had always seemed so very deep and complicated before, a contact with a man. She pulled the hotel's thick towel around her and sat down in front of the vanity. No bathrobe, no slippers. She would need to shop tomorrow.

She looked at her child fast asleep in the big double bed, back to being a little boy again. The top of his head was covered with dark stubble. She smiled. He looks like a—what were they called? A punk rocker. The latest style. He had no pajamas, but then he was warmly covered and the room was overheated, as were most places she had been in the city. She looked at her own dark hair. It had been two years since she cut it, ever since Gita had told her it wasn't necessary. It was long and straight, and beginning to get back its former shine and thickness.

She had not told Nigel her name. She must have a name. But she couldn't change it legally until they stopped looking for her. If they were looking. Perhaps it was all paranoia and they were already getting up from sitting *shiva*, already beginning to forget. She thought of her mother and father and the guilt and pain tore her stomach. She took a deep breath and her mind wandered back to the open window of the Tel Aviv hotel.

The ledge had been very narrow and the chair she rested one foot on tottered each time she tried to leave it. Akiva's clasping, trusting arms pulled heavily down on her neck and shoulders. She inhaled the salt of the sea and felt the hot blue Mediterranean sunlight dapple through her eyelids. Fifteen stories down, tiny men and women walked as if it were an ordinary day. Cars honked. Buses careened awkwardly to stops. She closed her eyes remembering the moment before her death—for even now, alive, she still thought of it that way. No one knew she was there poised above them, a twenty-two-year-old who had so rarely been permitted to experience the ordinary pleasures of life. If she jumped, the stream of people would stop for a moment and gather. But soon they would go on again, a careless, flowing river accepting the sacrifice of her blood, her baby's blood, with calm indifference.

Why couldn't she be one of them, anonymous and ordinary, her life flowing easily toward the end that awaited them all? She looked out to sea and saw the big ships crossing the horizon and remembered that day in Haifa and thought again of boarding one and taking off to Timbuktu. Anywhere. But it was too late to turn back. She had no home. She was already dead and she could not see her child murdered by them, his spirit slowly beaten down, repressed into a carbon copy of his father. She felt his tiny hands shift restlessly. One swift jump. Closing her eyes, she thought back to the first time she had plunged, headfirst, into deep water. Down, down she dove, terrified, into the dark, bottomless underworld. But then, swiftly, had come the exhilarant rush, as she surfaced into the light again. Yes. One must plunge into the ultimate darkness in order to reach the light again. And suddenly all fear left her and she kissed her child's sweet head, feeling the shaved scalp. And she had vowed to protect every hair. It was that kiss that gave her determination.

And then she jumped.

That she remembered. She remembered the child's sharp intake of breath and her own horrified, final scream as her feet left solid ground. What she did not remember was how she got back down into the room again. There had been a brushing noise, like flapping wings, that had pushed her back, and a flash of gold fire. Or perhaps it had all been a dream and she had not jumped at all, had not even meant to jump, had not even stood up upon that chair, looked out over the ledge into the street . . . But she knew the rational explanation was also a lie. Something extraordinary had happened to put her feet down again on solid ground, with the boy safely clasped to her, unharmed. And she, in an epiphany, had realized profoundly that explanations simply didn't matter. Whether God had plucked her physically back, or simply given her the strength to resist the devil at her back, she had survived and was blessed.

"Abraham, Abraham. Lay not your hand upon the child, neither do thou anything to him, for now I know you are a God-fearing man." She had paid her debt to God and man. Jephte's daughter, some commentators said, had not been sacrificed bodily, but had simply been sent off to live her life in exile. That would have to be enough.

The rest had come easily. The idea to sell the jewels and buy passage on a private yacht bound for Cyprus. The idea of renting a motorboat and having the yacht pick her up out at sea. The careful planning, the desperate secrecy. The pure luck of having her American passport in her purse, recently renewed, Akiva added to it. It was as if the naïve Batsheva Ha-Levi Harshen had jumped and lay there dead. This new, fearless, enterprising woman she did not recognize. She let the towel fall around her and touched her white, soft shoulders. She liked this woman, this blissfully free woman who had sprung fully grown, not from the head of Zeus, but from her own head. She was creating her as she went along. She tried to see herself as Nigel had seen her, as other new, exciting men would see her now in this foreign, magical city. Her eyes stared back at her—innocent yet wide with expectation, as if she wanted to know everything, to experience everything, and could not wait another second. They were not as friendly as they used to be, and some lingering pain around the edges made her look her age. She felt very sophisticated, sitting there naked. What was it about hotel rooms that made you feel like you could get away with anything? Perhaps the strangeness of everything, the anonymity of the very towels, the sheets that did not know you and thus could never bear witness that you were not acting like yourself.

The blond wig looked good, she admitted, giving her a kind of obvious, Barbie-doll charm. Frivolous, that was the word. She looked ready to dance, to have silly, flirty conversations with handsome, attentive men who drove sports cars and never read books. But it was not her.

When, she wondered, would she ever be herself again? And which self did she really want to be? The little rich girl, the naïve bride, the sacrificing daughter and wife? None of them. She swallowed hard. It was no fiction then. She really had died up there on the fifteenth floor. And was this not, then, a delicious dream come true—to be born in the spring of one's youth, full of strength, health, beauty, and intelligence and without the restraints of parents and even, for a little while at least, of money? She had gotten fifty thousand dollars for the jewels, nowhere near their worth. And she still had the pearl-and-diamond ring, symbol of her freedom. It would be enough to tide her over until she found work.

She reached for the phone, then put it back again, resisting for the tenth time that day the impulse to call Elizabeth. If her father had any suspicions, Elizabeth's would be the first place he would send detectives. They would not, after all, ever be dead and buried as long as there were no bodies. Her father, she thought, and the ache in her chest returned. Fear? Regret? Both, perhaps? She tried not to imagine him opening the letter, his pain. She did not wish him any harm, him or her mother. But neither did she wish them reunited with their daughter. They had used her, both of them. She had never been a person to them, but simply an example to the world of what they had accomplished, like the big house they lived in, and the clothes they wore. She glanced at Akiva's small fists, curled in deep, blissful sleep. You cannot own another person. Even carrying one inside your body, giving him life, doesn't give you the right to dictate his future. The moment he is out and inhales that first independent breath, he is gone from you forever, a separate life with its own dreams, its own failings, its own right to experience joy and pain, success and disappointment.

She shuddered with a sudden coldness. Up there on the fifteenth floor she had almost done the same thing—taken her child's life as if it were her own to dispose of as she saw fit. The insanity of it. No, she owed her parents nothing. Akiva owed her nothing. From now on, the love she gave him, the love she received, must be unconditional love, the only real love there is. She could just see the mourners—her parents, Isaac and his mother, flattened by the shame of it, not grief, but embarrassment. What would the Hassidim say? What would happen to the family's illustrious name? How will Isaac hold up his head? She smiled to herself. How wicked I have become! How much pleasure their pain gives me. Her father had come after her once before. When would she feel safe, she wondered. Seeing confirmation of her death in the newspaper, a few lines in the *Jewish Chronicle* or the *Jewish Press*, would help. She would look for an international newsstand tomorrow. Tomorrow, she thought, and for the first time in many years her days stretched out before her as her own book of clean blank pages full of endless, delightful possibilities. She crawled in quietly under the covers and felt the warm, solid press of her son nestled safely against her chest. Beautiful tomorrow.

Chapter sixteen

London in winter. Sparkling Christmas trees and the rosy glow of pub windows bedecked in ivy. Golden leaves fallen from large, old trees, making a lacy pattern over old streets. The houses of Mayfair, carefully preserved, seemed to say: "We are a testament to the calm and gentle passing of time." Their ornate wooden banisters and doors, their old brass nameplates, glowed from what seemed a special patina of time, the faithful succession of caretakers, dustcloths in hand, all propelled by the same values, the same clear sense of order and duty, rubbing and dusting, oiling and polishing.

Through the parted French drapes of a townhouse, she glimpsed a delicate white-and-gold boudoir, a bed whose luxuriant mauve and powder-blue quilts had been gracefully thrown back. On the thick, powder-blue carpeting a dainty pair of silver-and-pink slippers seemed to rest with romantic expectation. Unable to resist, she looked into the next window, as if turning the page of an enthralling story, and saw the polished gleam of a table surrounded by exquisite small dining chairs upholstered in powder-blue silk and the glint of an ornate silver centerpiece.

Order and elegance and Old World charm. There were all her beloved stories and characters out of Dickens, Forster, Conrad, and Lawrence, finally understood and come to life in their proper setting, as they never could be amidst the incongruity of California sunshine or Brooklyn drabness.

There were the magic golden gates of Buckingham leading to palaces with horse-drawn carriages and soldiers resplendent in red uniforms. There she could imagine Clarissa Dalloway flinging open her French windows and loving ". . . the swing, tramp, and trudge; . . . the bellow and the uproar; the carriages, motor cars, omnibuses, vans . . . the triumph and jingle and the strange high singing of some aeroplane overhead: life, London . . ."

The air was as cold and crisp and sweet as the first bite of a winter apple. On the ground, the newly cleared first snow was still white and sparkly with diamonds. Batsheva walked as if enveloped in a delightful dream.

"Look, Akiva, the double-decker buses! Oh, look, there are policemen on horses!" Two children, she admitted to herself. The stores intimidated her a little. Rodeo Drive seemed so long ago, such a dream. Had she ever walked into such stores full of rightful confidence? They seemed so elegant and the shoppers and salespeople were so well-mannered. She had never thought about her manners before, but wondered now, with the flashy blond wig, if she would stand out like a country bumpkin. And then, to top it off, in Harrod's polished showrooms, Akiva dropped his thermos and glass and chocolate milk went spurting in all directions. Batsheva watched in horror as the brown liquid spread in muddy rivulets on the immaculate floors.

"Oh, dear me," a saleslady said mildly. Batsheva held her breath. "All that good milk. Such a shame. Here, let me clean it up."

"I'm so very sorry," Batsheva murmured, wanting to sink

into the floor. She was pale with gratitude as if she were apologizing to the mistress of the house, who had the power to forgive her.

"Not at all, madam. I'm sorry you've had the inconvenience of losing the child's good drink."

This, Batsheva thought, is real class. The woman does not know if I am rich or poor, a princess or a secretary. She contrasted it to the fawning snobbery of the saleswomen of Rodeo Drive, who would have made her, a stranger, feel tacky and unwelcome. Real class is simply good manners. Kindness and consideration for the feelings of others. She would try to remember that. "I wonder, since you've been so kind, if you could help me select a winter wardrobe for the boy?" She bought a great deal, happy to repay the woman's kindness, and the clothes were so delightful. Good English wools, soft cashmeres and sporty tweeds, all solid, well-made stuff. Such pretty bright colors and red, lots and lots of red.

She loved adding her own step to the happy, determined trudge of the shoppers as they rushed with a secret, restrained joy through the exciting shops of Regent and Oxford streets; the beautiful young men, disdainfully and absurdly hatless, their faces ruddy from the sharp wind, their gold hair carefully cut and combed, their dark-wool overcoats perfectly tailored; the young women, graceful and slim in beautifully cut suits and coats with bright scarves, shawl-like around their shoulders.

And yet, although there was a determined, forward rush to the movement of the people around her, there was still a control, a restraint she had not felt in Manhattan. They did not crowd or push. There was a wonderful civilizing process that seemed to affect everyone. A certain calming force, a correctness and self-control blanketed the crowds. She noticed the small dark men of the Third World, uncomfortable in English wool coats, casting anxious eyes on their small dark sons, in secret terror they would raise their voices and call attention to themselves. Even the punks, in their outrageous leather outfits and wildly colored hair, traveled in groups, needing, perhaps, to shore up each other's identity, so strong was the mesmerizing, almost magnetic pull of London's social strictures, its sense of clear order, refinement, and tradition.

On the way back they walked through Hyde Park. There was something reassuring about the slow, happy glide of the ducks, the rolling lawns. A man in a riding cap and jodhpurs, his back straight, rode in slow, controlled circles around the edges of the park, directing his magnificent horse with just the slightest lean to the right or left.

It was a scene that seemed timeless in its beauty. And for a little while, Batsheva felt all the tension, the pain, the uncertainty that had filled her for so long, simply leave her, like an exhaled breath, to disappear smokelike in the cold air. She lost track of time. But by the time she returned to Mayfair, she was grateful for the overheated warmth of the hotel. In the lobby, a roaring fire danced, delighting Akiva. They watched it a while; then, growing drowsy, Batsheva asked the hotel clerk for her key. To her amazement, he handed it to her together with a note, which she opened nervously:

A movie tonight? Will arrange for babysitter.
Pick you up at eight.

Nigel

So this is what a date is, she thought, her arm through Nigel's as they walked to the movies. She glanced at him shyly. If only he weren't so . . . pudgy, she thought. If only his hair weren't so very red. Still, she loved the freedom of saying yes to him, of actually going to a movie that had not been censored and approved in advance.

"Did you like it?" he asked her later over hot apple cider in a red-brick and brass pub. She loved the pub, which made her feel warm and mellow and forgiving. She was glad the place was dark with a red glow. Her face was still burning with embarrassment. He had taken her to see *Last Tango in Paris.* To see such things on the screen in full view of so many people. She had been so ashamed. How could they do such things, such incredibly private, vile things up there, blown up so large? It would not have bothered her perhaps, she thought, to have read it in the private spaces of a book. There is an intimacy, a one-to-oneness in a book that takes you in discreetly. But seeing it displayed on the screen was voyeurism, like walking with a crowd into someone's bedroom. Perhaps he had not realized the kind of movie it was. He certainly didn't seem bothered by it. Nor did he apologize. She decided she didn't like the little dark hairs on the back of his knuckles.

"I'm not sure," she told him, for she had been taught never to hurt anyone's feelings.

The next day, a large bouquet of flowers arrived. He would pick her up again at eight, the note said. She wasn't sure if she had to go, or if she could say no. All the things girls learn when they are fourteen. Dating etiquette. So she went. This time he took her to the theater to see *Evita.* She felt the pleasure of the large audience around her enjoying the songs, the story. But the heroine was a streetwalker, her husband a corrupt politician. The tunes were catchy, but the lyrics strained too hard to fit the music. It really wasn't to her taste. And she decided she didn't want any more dates with Nigel.

Afterward he took her to dinner and to another pub. It was much darker than the first one had been and she didn't like the way the single men looked at her. When she tried to order cider, Nigel waved his hand and told the waiter to bring her a daiquiri. She had no idea what that was. She was embarrassed by her ignorance. A drink meant a little wine on Friday night. A little hot, tasteless liquor in a paper cup in the synagogue after Saturday services together with herring and sponge cake. Drinks in a bar she had only read about in books. The heroines either drank a few and felt very sophisticated, or got roaring drunk and did all kinds of awful, exciting things they either deeply regretted, or didn't. She wondered which one was in store for her. She began to blush; then, after the second drink, she began to feel she wasn't going to blush anymore that night.

"Won't you tell me who you are? Who the child is? What happened to the little blond girl? Where did the boy come from?"

"I will tell you everything, Nigel, my dear and good friend." He looked so much better now. Almost handsome, she thought. A dear good friend. Funny, she hadn't felt sleepy at all a moment ago, now her eyelids drooped. Vaguely, she remembered him telling her to drink up still another drink. Then they were walking. And then they were in a car. It was so nice, his arm around her back, supporting her. Sweet. But she didn't like his breath, hot on her mouth, then down her neck. His cold fingers touched her nipples. She looked down at herself in shock and clutched her open blouse together and pushed him away.

"You want me. Don't fight it. You know you do." His hands were on her thighs, pressing them apart roughly. She hit the heel of her hand upward against his nose and heard his sharp cry of pain.

She opened up the car door and ran into the night. The cold air helped her wake up a little. They had eaten dinner at Bloom's and the pub was nearby. She looked around at the forbidding alleyways of Aldgate East, once the Dickensian embodiment of human wretchedness. The alleyways and courtyards, where Jack the Ripper had once stalked and disemboweled his pitiable victims, were still as frightening in their foul-smelling darkness. Large, bleak tenements in ugly, red Victorian brick, where once, less than a hundred years before, more than half the children born never reached age five, dying from cold, disease, and hunger; where hundreds of brothels full of wretched, hopeless young women had once served up their tawdry pleasures to the aristocracy, hemmed her in from all sides.

She pulled her coat around her and felt the tears roll down her face. The city, which had looked like a birthday cake full of brilliant candles before, now seemed dark and dangerous. She had no idea where she was or how to get home. Suddenly she heard footsteps. In terror, she turned and saw a dark shadow moving closer. She walked a little faster. She heard the steps keep up. There was no point in running. No place to hide. It took all her courage and faith to stand perfectly still. She opened her purse and held her keys between her fingers, the second thing she remembered Elizabeth once teaching her, as a joke long ago (for when would the sheltered, protected Batsheva Ha-Levi ever need to defend herself?). She closed her eyes and said a little prayer, waiting.

"Evening, miss." The policeman tipped his cap, looking her over. "You all right, luv?" She went weak against him. "Whoa, now, steady there you go." He caught a flash of white breast inside the fur coat and smiled to himself, knowingly. "Now I've told you girls not to be roaming around my beat anymore. Call it a night, luv, please." He shone the flashlight in her eyes and saw that he had made a terrible mistake. "Well, I'll . . . Sorry, madam. It's just so dark here. Are you all right? Who did this to you?"

Police stations. Questions. She shook her head. "Can you tell me where I can find a taxi, please?" she whispered.

"Certainly, here, let me help you. A bit too much to drink, eh?" She leaned gratefully on his steadying hand. She changed hotels the same night and left no forwarding address.

She had not had to search long in the papers. For throughout the Jewish world, the apparent double death of the young Ha-Levi bride, heiress to the Ha-Levi name and fortune, together with her small son, made headlines. Fortunately, though, thanks ironically to Isaac's manic dislike of photos, the only accompanying photograph was that of her father surrounded by mourning Hassidim. The articles were pitiful: young wife and child in double murder-suicide. She almost cried when she read them, pitying the poor girl who had done that awful thing. It gave details about the family, but no description of her or the child. There was no mention of Isaac. He had sunk back into anonymity again. She felt a small twinge of satisfaction. How he would hate that. The article did say that the bodies had not yet been found and that the whole matter was being investigated. She hadn't expected it to be so open-ended. The secrecy weighed upon her heavily.

As the weeks went by, she learned how to cope. She rented a small apartment in Bloomsbury, near the British Museum and the University of London. An expensive area, but she felt she needed the safety it afforded. The experience with Nigel had taken some of the exuberant glow out of the city for her and she stopped going out at night. But during the day she never tired of exploring. The amazing indoor grave-yard of Westminister Abbey, the crown jewels in the Tower of London, the breathtaking National Gallery with its rooms full of Rembrandts, the wonderfully musty Victoria and Albert Museum. Only the nights were lonely.

Then a neighbor, an older woman, asked her if she would be interested in hearing some lectures on twentieth-century English literature at London University's extension service and offered to babysit for Akiva. The university was practically in their backyard. Batsheva accepted gratefully.

She sat down a little awkwardly in the back of the room, feeling anxious that someone might come in and throw her out. It wasn't a college crowd; she looked around disappointed to see so few people her own age. But then as the lecture began she pulled herself forward and sat at the edge of her seat, her eyes boring into the beautiful blond woman who stood so confidently at the front of the room.

Her hair was longer than she remembered, a shaggy tangle of curls pulled severely back. The face was wan and older—definitely, visibly older. Kinder too, perhaps. A face that had learned sympathy through personal tragedy. Dear face, Batsheva thought. And when she finished explaining Conrad's *Heart of Darkness* as a journey to the darkness of one's soul, an exploration of self, Batsheva felt the sting of hot tears well up in her eyes as she remembered the good, full days of her youth, curled up with Elizabeth, poring over the books she loved.

There was no way she could go up there to her, she thought. Why, nothing had changed. The detectives could be there right now in the lecture hall, waiting for her to make just such a move. It made no sense to come out of hiding now, no sense at all. But her feet, no longer under her control, went down the long aisle. Just to get a closer look, she told herself. She will not recognize me. I will turn away long before. But she knew the familiar face had pierced through her shell of loneliness and she could not go back inside again.

When the lecture was over, she waited patiently outside the building. A light drizzle had begun to fall and she put up her umbrella. A moment later she saw Elizabeth emerge, her head bent against the rain. She walked up to her rapidly.

"Excuse me. I was in your lecture now and I wanted to ask you a question if I might."

Elizabeth didn't look up. "Ask away, but you'll have to hurry along with me. I'm going to the dining room for some coffee. Come along then." Now where have I heard that voice before? Elizabeth thought vaguely. She shrugged, defeated. "Now, what was it you wanted to ask me?" She hurried along, thinking only of the sheltering warmth ahead of her.

"I wanted to ask you about Anna Karenina. Why, why did she do it?"

"But the lecture was about Conr—" Elizabeth stopped

suddenly and looked up, drawing the girl over to a streetlamp. The women looked into each other's eyes. Elizabeth reached up, touching the familiar face, wanting to feel it solid beneath her hand, afraid it might vanish. She hugged the girl's delicate, slim back and was reassured by the fragile presence of real bones. "Batsheva?" she questioned, feeling the presence of the thin line between reality and fantasy, between sanity and insanity.

Batsheva took Elizabeth's cold hands in her own warm ones and kissed them. "My dear friend."

Wrapped up in bed in warm flannel nightgowns and holding hot cocoa, they talked deep into the night. Elizabeth would ask and Batsheva would answer, her voice sometimes tearful, sometimes earnest. And sometimes their voices would tangle, a question and answer interrupting each other with urgency as they reversed roles and Batsheva asked. And as the night wore on, their voices grew louder and less serious, joining in shouts of girlish laughter like teenagers at a pajama party. With Elizabeth beside her, so many things began to seem funny. Isaac's demanding discipline and self-control from the baby while he stuffed himself with ice cream. Getting drunk with fat, redheaded Nigel and his hairy knuckles. Isaac's thing getting stuck in the hole in the sheet, his demanding signs of her lost viginity when he couldn't keep an erection long enough to deflower her. This Isaac seemed less a monster and more a poor buffoon, or, as Elizabeth put it, a real space cadet.

That comforted Batsheva somehow, reducing her ordeal to more human, forgettable dimensions. And the laughter was very good, very healing to them both.

They woke late the next morning, curiously full of energy when Akiva climbed into bed with them, his face full of cookie crumbs stolen from the cupboard. He put a tentative hand on Elizabeth's soft, ample breast and, liking its softness, squeezed with both hands.

"Men. They're all the same." She giggled, tickling him. "And you, my fine young man, so carefully brought up in the Holy City." She wagged a mock-angry finger at him. "And how are you set up for money?" Elizabeth asked, turning her attention to Batsheva.

"I've got enough for a year or two. But I need to . . . I want to work. I just don't know what I can do."

"You could go back to school for a while then? Oh, just as you always wanted to! Remember your dream? We could go to Paris during the spring break, and ski in Italy during the winter break. I have such a fun group of friends, really interesting people."

"What happened to Graham?"

Her face clouded; then a glimmer of a smile broke through. "Off with the old, on with the new," she said, with forced gaiety.

"I'm sorry, Liz." Batsheva lowered her eyes, regretting the pain in her friend's voice. "You loved him so."

"Years ago you would have said: 'I'm desperately sorry, dearest, you loved him passionately.' A definite improvement, there. No doubt from the complete lack of my tutoring for a few years."

"No, actually, it was Isaac's Yiddish lessons that did it," she said with a straight face. And then they both started to giggle again, thinking of Isaac and Graham, suicide notes and trips to the south of France, until their stomachs ached and the laughter became hysterical. Elizabeth left, taught class, and returned late in the afternoon. She brought a package with her.

"What's in it?" Batsheva asked her, tentatively tearing off the wrapping paper.

"What you asked for. A job."

Batsheva held the Leica, stroking it as she would a beloved human thing. "But I gave it to you."

"My dear, I already have a little Kodak to match my talents. Take this back and make some money."

"Doing what?"

"What!" Elizabeth exclaimed, exasperated. "Why, taking pictures of course. Weddings, Bar Mitzvahs, confirmations, baby pictures, passport photos—for starters. And then some really artistic things for magazines. You could even set up a darkroom in the potting shed out back . . ."

"I don't know. Do you think I could, for money?"

"Why not? You could set up a small studio in your living room with a few different backgrounds and put up notices on the bulletin boards at the university. Students are always doing foolish things like getting married and having babies and getting passports."

"I think," Batsheva said suddenly, startled by a sudden vision, "I think that my life is finally going to start."

Chapter seventeen

His name was Robin Pernell. He had dark-blond hair that slanted across his forehead and a way of tossing his head to get it out of his eyes that made him squint with laughter and look charmingly boyish, Batsheva thought, trying to capture the look on film. He wore scruffy-looking jeans and an old sweater with a long red-and-white knit scarf around his neck. He was a young graduate student in economics, about twenty-five or twenty-six years old, she estimated. He had been one of the first of her clients to respond to a handwritten notice on the university's bulletin board.

Getting just the look she wanted had turned out to be difficult, and she had had to keep asking him to come back, feeling rather embarrassed and assuring him that it wouldn't cost him extra—a point that by his clothes she felt would be important to him. He hadn't seemed to mind, though, which struck her as very kind at first, and then later, as rather odd. He just kept coming back, listening dutifully to her instructions, as she fumbled with the lights and the umbrellas to set the shot up perfectly. All the while, he sat there quietly, watching her with keen interest and an ironic smile.

When she finally handed him the last print—a really excellent portrait they both agreed—she sighed with relief. But the next night he turned up again. "I'm running out of excuses," he said, flicking his hair out of his eyes and letting the little laugh lines around his mouth deepen. "Won't you please go out with me tomorrow night?" She was was shyly pleased, surprised, and a little uncomfortable.

She had not gone out alone with a man since Nigel. But he had stood at the door, a little pathetically, she thought, waiting for her answer. So she said yes because his face pleased her, and his manner seemed gentle and controllable. He showed up early and she hardly recognized him in a new tuxedo, forcing her to excuse herself while she hurried upstairs to change out of her skirt and sweater and into evening clothes. He took her to a private staircase at the Royal Opera House that led to box seats.

An old gentlemen dressed in a fine tuxedo leaned out of the next box and smiled at them. "Robin! Haven't seen you in ages. How's the earl?"

"Fine, Sir Richard," Robin answered, and the man nodded at Batsheva with approval.

She felt the blush rising from the modest high neck of the pretty gray-velvet dress she had purchased with so much pleasure so recently. The other women wore low-cut satins with sparkling jewels brilliant on their white skin. She felt prissy and old-fashioned. She would buy such a dress. Tomorrow, she vowed.

"'Sir Richard'? 'Earl'?" she questioned, but he laughed and tossed his head, his very handsome boyish head, until her attention was called away by the magnificent rise of the heavy red-velvet curtains that pulled back into unbelievably lush folds to reveal the fairyland of Swan Lake.

The dancers, in love with their own bodies, lifted by the

entrancing music, told a story of pain and love, betrayal and renewal. Batsheva watched Odette move with the graceful flow of a swan's effortless glide across water, an almost bodiless spirit molding herself to the music, following the dancer's agony and happiness, and her final ecstasy. She was delighted with the good box seat and the wonderful view. The gilt that adorned the theater, the magnificent old chandeliers that illuminated the huge hall, enfolded her in a splendid richness and excitement that made her almost feel like crying with pleasure. She glanced at Robin gratefully. The most expensive tickets around, no doubt. And a rented tux. Poor boy, to spend all his money to impress her, money he certainly could have used to buy himself a new winter coat.

She looked at him secretly in a sidelong glance. He made her think of Gerald in *Women in Love.* He, too, "had a glisten like sunshine, a gleaming beauty, a maleness like a young, good-humored, smiling wolf." She hid her smile in the back of her hand. He caught the smile and the gesture and gently took her hand away and kissed it. "What is so amusing? This is supposed to be the tragic part: Siegfried vows eternal love to Odile, mistaking her for Odette, and now Odette is stuck forever as a big white bird. But I'd never do that to you. Betray you." His eyes were serious and tender.

The kiss sent chills up her arm. No man had ever done that before, she thought, missing the wonderful irony of such a thought. Isaac must have done that to her. Once. But curiously, though he had battered her body, he had not touched her dreams. He had never been her lover, and thus whatever he had done could not prove or disprove those girlish dreams of love and romance that lay cocoonlike deep inside her, waiting for the right conditions to emerge. And so she faced each new man with more hope than fear. It was all new, without precedent. She wondered if she liked it.

She pulled her hand away gently and turned her hot face

back to the stage. The lovers leapt and turned in perfect time to the music, becoming the visual embodiment of the soaring notes. Every gesture, every curve of every finger, spoke of years of discipline and training.

How wonderful to have such an art, such a talent. To be trained for it. To know who and what you are and to always be able to push yourself up a little further, to be a little better, year by year. I am so useless, she thought. I don't know how to do anything, except take pictures. Maybe.

The next day she went out and tried on some evening dresses with no back and very little front. She looked at herself in the dressing room, thinking of Robin, the slow, boyish smile breaking over his face, his wolflike pleasure. It gave her a delicious shiver of panic. She looked at herself doubtfully, surveying the long smooth stretch of skin that went from her throat to the soft rounded beginnings of her breasts and deep between them.

"It is what they are wearing to the theater this season," a saleswoman told her decisively. "It looks perfect on you." She bought the dress.

On the weekend, he took her to the National Theatre. They sat in the stark, excitingly modern lobby and listened to a pianist in an evening gown and a cellist in a tuxedo play Mozart and Bach. All around them well-dressed people held drinks and listened quietly with real interest. It was all so . . . so . . . civilized. Yes, that was it. Civilized. She felt a calm invading her body, streaming through her like the warming alcohol. Did one need anything else? Pleasant company, wonderful music and theater, fine liqueurs? What did one need with all the heavy burden of tradition, of family, of religion weighing one down?

She looked at Robin's long, smooth fingers that held her bare arm solicitously, as if she were a precious, delicate objet d'art, and she remembered Isaac's heavy insistent hands, his firm grip of ownership. She had gotten free of him! Perhaps she should get free of it all, religion, tradition, heritage, birthrights. Throw it all overboard like so much extra baggage. She felt it all holding her down like an anchor of lead when she wanted to rise, like a hot-air balloon, bursting and expanding with untried possibilities. She wanted to rise and soar above it all. And up there, she would find a different stratosphere. She would find calm, wonderful, peaceful, civilized calm.

They took their drinks out onto the balcony and watched the lights on the boats resting on the Thames illuminate the dark silken ribbon of water. The theater was a beacon of light in the dark night, full of music and exquisite shades of feeling. Afterward he took her to the Dorchester for a late supper.

"Are you sure you can . . ." she began delicately, looking around at the elegant lobby, full of marble statues and jewel cases.

"Afford it?" His perfect white teeth gleamed with pleasure. "Yes indeed, my dear."

"Good evening, Lord Haversham." The maître d' approached them hurriedly.

"Good evening, Albert," Robin replied calmly.

She didn't have time to dwell on her confusion, because a moment later she was face-to-face with a menu such as she had never encountered before. She put it down nervously. She had never been to a nonkosher restaurant. There listed before her was a cornucopia of forbidden foods: beef slaughtered without rabbis testing the sharpness of the blades to ensure the animal felt no pain; beef unsalted and unsoaked to rid it of blood; forbidden mixtures of meat and milk or cheese; ham and pork and shellfish. She shivered. Even the wine, brought in a gleaming silver decanter by a deferential waiter, was forbidden. For wine, unlike liquor or beer, also had to be supervised by rabbis for the entire process, from picking the grapes to the final product.

"Shall I order for you?" Robin looked up, amused at what he interpreted as her endearing childish delight in such a selection, her inability to choose among such tantalizing possibilities.

She hesitated, feeling trapped by a combination of her own desire to try everything, and a deep-seated fear, an almost terror of straying from the familiar path. Was she ashamed of who she was? "Please," she finally whispered miserably.

Misunderstanding completely, he ordered for them both. "You really haven't told me much about yourself, Betsy," he began, leaning back and sipping the wine. The waiter had just filled her glass. She held it, feeling the smooth globe moisten and cool her palm. Betsy had been Elizabeth's idea, but she had trouble relating to it. Betsy Wetsy. Sweet Betsy from Pike. She smiled. "There's nothing much to tell. I'm divorced with a three-year-old son. I've enrolled for the spring term at the university and I take photos to earn my keep."

"No alimony or child support?"

She shook her head. "I have no wish for contact of any kind with my ex-husband."

His brows arched. "That bad, was it?"

She smiled. "Worse."

He reached his hand across the table. "My gain, the fool." His hand covered hers so warmly. "You haven't touched your wine. It's wonderful. Do."

"Yes. I'm sure it is." He was being so nice. She wanted so much to fit in to the beautiful place. To feel at home in the calm, cultured room. She brought the shimmering liquid to her lips and saw his eyes rest on the smooth curve of her neck. She closed her eyes, gulping it down, and felt it burn through her body, hot with accusation.

"But you haven't told me anything. Where were you born? Who are your parents? What kind of flowers do you like? Do you sleep on your back or your stomach?"

She laughed. "Are you sure you're an economist, not an anthropologist?"

"You're always laughing at me," he reproved her, hurt turning his features serious. "I am mad about you. I want to swallow you whole, to know you completely."

The wine was beginning to work, making her reckless and sleepy. "I am a runaway princess, a barefoot heiress. I was born and raised in New York, and I lived for a time in California. During the school year I went away to boarding school where they filled my head with important information about God. My parents were very conservative and didn't like the Hollywood influence on their pristine, virginal offspring, reader of dirty literature and dreamer of wild dreams."

"Say, this is more like it! What kind of literature?"

"D. H. Lawrence mostly, who, incidentally, was a terrible prude. Ran away with the mother of children he was tutoring, a fat German *hausfrau*. Insisted on marrying her. He tried to beat her, you know, except that he was so frail and she was so big that just a mild defense on her part laid him out flat. Poor David Herbert." She shook her head, commiserating.

"Let's drink to him, shall we?" Robin laughed, tossing his handsome head. "To David and Frieda." He lifted his glass and drained it.

She was beginning to feel slightly woozy as she lifted the glass to her lips and sipped again. Each time the liquid touched her lips, she felt polluted, poisoned. When she finished, to her horror the waiter brought the first course. She stared at it. Prawns on a delicate bed of smoked meat.

"Smoked ham, a delicacy the way they do it here. Frightfully good." He ate heartily.

She picked up her knife and fork decisively and cut the meat. She wound it around her fork and lifted it to her mouth. She saw the accusing faces of her father and Isaac rise up before her, the shocked and horrified faces of the kindly bearded men who had been her teachers at school. She touched the meat to her lips and felt her head swim. The fork dropped to the floor. The waiter rushed to replace it.

"Are you all right, dearest?" Robin's voice was full of concern.

She pushed back her chair abruptly. Her legs felt like rubber. "Will you excuse me for a moment." Without waiting for his murmured concern, she wound her way with as much dignity as she could through the softly humming room and felt the eyes of the men turn and linger as she passed. In the ladies' room, all green and white like a lovely spring garden, she heaved miserably. She touched her face with cold water and washed out her mouth many times. She spent a long time drying her lips and replacing the lipstick. She stared at herself in the mirror. The red lips. The white, shameful cleavage. The red dress that clung to her tiny waist, her slim hips.

Who are you? she wondered. No one I know, or like very much. A woman trying once again to please a man, the way I tried to please my father, to please my husband. I don't know who I am yet, she thought. But surely, I am not the same as the people sitting here in this room enjoying this meal. Perhaps one day I shall be. But not now, not today. She went back to the table. She was tired of playing games.

"Feeling better?" he got up and helped her into her seat.

"Yes. Thank you." She saw the dish had mercifully been removed. In its place, the waiter brought a large lobster. Red and ugly. She breathed deeply. "Robin. I have a confession to make. I can't eat any of these things, or drink the wine, because I'm Jewish."

Robin's placid face puckered in confusion. He pushed back his hair with his hand, trying to concentrate, to assimilate the information. "But what's that got to do with the food?"

"It's not kosher," she said simply and went white when he burst out laughing.

"Don't tell me people still believe in all that rot? I mean, didn't that go out with the Middle Ages?"

"You mean like ghosts who are holy and virgins who are mothers?" she said with cold fury.

He swallowed hard, aghast. "Jewish beauty. My downfall. Well, then, dear, what would you like to eat?"

"Fresh fruits or vegetables. Cold. With no dressing," she said with defiance and shame, as if she had shown herself odd and unworthy. She felt his laughter, his contempt, burn into her forehead. And yet, she was still grateful that he reordered for her and sat across from her with quiet dignity. She didn't know what people did under such circumstances and so would not have been entirely surprised if he had walked out on her.

"My dear, your wish is my command," he said lightly. But his eyes were a trifle less friendly than before and gleamed with a colder light. That night, he kissed her longer with slightly less tenderness. His kisses began as a quiet question and ended with an answer, without involving her at all. She finally pushed him away. His boyish face turned sour. "I've heard about Jewesses," he said drunkenly.

"Good-night, Robin," she said wearily. He turned on his heel and left her standing at her entrance. She thought about him long into the night and walked around in a daze the next morning. Each time the phone rang, she jumped. She was impatient with Akiva and hurried through her photo sessions. A week later, when she had finally felt the wound congeal, he called again.

"I'm sorry," he said simply. He sounded thoroughly contrite and miserable. "I miss you. Would you consider going out with me again? I won't touch you, I promise."

She held the phone away from her, her heart beating with confusion, pleasure, anger, and a little panic.

"Hello?" she heard his far-off voice murmur. She brought the receiver back to her ear.

"Robin? I . . . I'm not sure."

"Look, darling. I won't blame you if you never speak to me again. I was such a total, bloody fool. But it was all such a shock to me and I was more than a little drunk. I'm learning. And you must know how much you mean to me. Please, don't cut me off. Try me again. I've grown up, really."

She closed her eyes and saw the glisten of his blond hair, his handsome young face. "I forgive you, Robin." She was not entirely sure that she did. But she did miss him and the calm, superior world he had introduced her to. He came by an hour later in a small, expensive sports car and cajoled her into finding a babysitter, dropping everything, and taking a drive. At first she refused to get in. "Won't you get into trouble, Robin? I mean, I don't need you to do these things for me, renting tuxedos and cars . . ."

"I've a few pennies left," he said almost seriously, opening the door for her and waiting for her to get in.

They went into the English countryside, through green fields hemmed by ancient bare-branched winter trees and towering lush evergreens, all covered in a silver-gray mist. They passed silver granaries and Tudor farmhouses and glimpsed lovely, solid Georgian homes. Sheep made their slow, playful progress in paddocks, and there was the glisten of trenches filled with fresh rain. Gray birds lifted off the ground in the hundreds, rising smokelike in the gray air.

The people, too, lacked the sophistication of their London counterparts, animated by a country friendliness in their old boots and raincoats. In a country pub, by a roaring fire, served by an able lad and a blushing lass, Batsheva thought with delight, she felt her body slip into a trance of warm, heedless pleasure. How wonderful to forget who you are! How wonderful to shed all the heavy load thrust on one by an accident of birth! She envied the serving girl her red, uncomplicated cheeks, her basic uncomplicated drives for love and food and shelter. The setting sun and the hot flames of the fire turned the icy windows a brilliant red, making her feel as if she were enveloped in a ruby light, like an actress bathed in stagelight. Playacting, she thought uncomfortably, hating herself for honesty. They had hardly spoken and nothing had been resolved.

"I promised the babysitter I'd be home early, Robin," she said, reaching for her coat.

He rose reluctantly and helped her put it on. He had been very quiet, content apparently to let sleeping dogs lie. Content just to sit with her in the soft, glowing firelight, just to watch her face. She had been both grateful for and resentful of his quiet. He had not tried to order food or drink for her, or brought the subject up at all.

"Can we make one more stop? It will only take a few minutes." He had been so unpushy, so considerate, she owed him that. "Of course, Robin."

The small car, expertly handled, took the long winding road with confidence and familiarity. The dark trees swayed, encompassing them on both sides like a dark bower, and then, suddenly, there were massive grillwork gates stopping their way. Robin pressed a button inside the car, and, to her surprise, the gates swung open. They entered a circular driveway and stopped before a magnificent Tudor mansion. Robin jumped out and opened the door for her. She stepped out and almost gasped at the stunning house—a castle in a storybook.

"But won't the people mind? Really, Robin, shouldn't we just stay in the car?"

His white teeth gleamed, handsome and wolflike. "But my dear, if we do that, how are you going to meet my family?"

The butler opened the door with stiff courtesy and took her coat. At least she had dressed carefully, she comforted herself, looking down at the soft plaid wool skirt and the azure cashmere sweater. Robin took her cold trembling hand and led her into a large, ornate living room. Its antique charm had a priceless, indefinable aura of quality, of riches cared for and watched over, passed down intact from generation to generation with absolute confidence. It was a huge room with fourteen-foot-high ceilings. Exquisite plasterwork, ornate gilded moldings, covered the ceiling. Two graceful marble columns framed the entryway. Built-in bookcases lined the walls and the light glinted off rare gold bindings.

"My mother." Robin held his arm out and a short, very thin woman with tightly sprayed gray curls rose graciously from one of several large, comfortable gold-velvet couches.

"How do you do, my dear," she said appraisingly, a real question. Batsheva took the extended limp hand. Its diamonds glittered from the reflected overhead light of an ornate gold-and-crystal chandelier.

"And my father." A gentleman in a blue-silk smoking jacket and a pipe, straight out of a magazine ad, got up and patted her hand.

"A pleasure, I'm sure, my dear. Won't you come sit by me a moment, Betsy? Robin's terrible about bringing his friends to see us. It's such a pleasure to actually get up close to one. He's told us a little about you, but not much."

"Really, Father, none of your Parliamentary inquiries, please," Robin interjected. "Anyhow, she has got to get back to her little boy and I wanted to show her the house."

"Little boy?" Robin's mother said slowly, with an inquiring nod of the head toward Robin.

"Please, Mother, not a word more. Come help me show her the house. There's an angel." He kissed his mother's hand. His smile was charming.

"Robin, really!" his mother capitulated, leading the way up the staircase.

"It used to be an abbey, you know," Robin pointed out,

"before Henry the Eighth got rid of all the monks. Two hundred and fifty years ago my ancestors lived in the north wing. I don't know how. Beastly cold in there. That's all closed off now. Come in here. This is my favorite."

"There must be thousands of books in here," Batsheva gasped. Robin smiled. The smile of ownership.

"Look at these tapestries," Robin's mother said. "They were woven from designs by Raphael in 1500 for Pope Clement the Tenth to decorate the walls of the Sistine Chapel." Batsheva did as she was told, an agony of discomfort filling her. The picture showed a Christ-like figure prone, bleeding from wounds. Men in robes with halos surrounded him. She hated it. The whole glorification of suffering, of death.

"A bit gory, what?" Robin laughed. "Come next door then. If you like Disneyland, you'll love this."

She smiled, relieved. A Chinese room.

"Of course, two hundred years ago China was so unknown people were entranced by anything they thought was Chinese. The wallpaper is probably more gaudy than anything the Chinese would be caught dead with."

"It is rather overwhelming," she agreed. It was full of shrubs, rocks, and colorful birds and butterflies.

"The chairs are Chippendale's 'Director' of 1793," Mrs Pernell sniffed, offended by the uncalled-for levity.

"The tables are beautiful," Batsheva offered contritely.

"They're from around 1800, mahogany with Chinese porcelain plaques for tops and shelves. All the porcelain is Chinese. These blue vases are painted with the marks of the Emperor Chia Chi'ing. We just recovered the chairs in this red silk." The corridors seemed endless. Like magic mirrors, they took one on and on. There was a sporting room filled with hunting trophies and portraits of dogs and horses. A blue drawing room, covered in blue-damask wallpaper and filled with ornate French commodes and desks (the Yiddish word *ungepatchkaed* came into Batsheva's head. Overly dressed up, tasteless really). The rich inlaid wood, the thick gilt overlay, would have been described as gorgeous by some. It seemed heavy and boring to Batsheva, who was nevertheless dazzled by the combined magnificence of the setting and perfect condition of the priceless antiques.

"This bedroom was only used by visiting royalty. Charles the Second stayed there and Queen Victoria and Prince Albert slept there when they were newlyweds. They were both delighted with the house and the gardens. It's recorded in the queen's journal," she added, haughtily. Behind his mother's back, Robin took Batsheva's hand and squeezed it, pushing his nose up with his finger. She suppressed a giggle. There was something hilarious about the woman's seriousness. "My father had the design of the old wall hangings copied in a new red-and-gold brocade that was specially woven for the room. I don't use this very much and the shutters have to remain closed most of the time. Light is the great destroyer of fabrics." She sighed.

The rooms were endless. Green drawing rooms, a state salon full of gilt and Murillos and Van Dycks, Reynoldses and Caraccis; murals depicting the glorious history of the Pernells: kings served, naval victories achieved. They arrived at their starting point through a museumlike labyrinth of staircases.

"It's magnificent, thank you so much," Batsheva said courteously. So this was where Robin Pernell packed his bags with scruffy-looking clothes and old scarves. And I was worried about him spending too much money on me! She was overwhelmed, but curiously unimpressed.

"Now, my dear, you must stay to dinner. Now, now, not another word." Robin's father shook his head as she began to protest. "You haven't really told us a thing about yourself," he coaxed.

Batsheva glanced into the dining room at the table already

set with fine silver and china and looked at Robin a little desperately. He shrugged helplessly.

Before she could think of an answer, the front door slammed and lively footsteps pounded into the room. She found herself face-to-face with a tall, blond teenager in jodhpurs and riding boots.

"Really, Grace," the mother remonstrated. "Such a racket."

"Sorry." The girl tapped her riding crop against her long leg, staring at Batsheva.

"Good Lord, Grace," her father intoned. "Is that what passes for manners these days?"

"Sorry," she said, lowering her gaze. She had Robin's good white teeth, his charming smile. But there was a callousness about her, a cutting sharpness that was almost brutal.

"This is my friend Betsy," Robin said, looking uncomfortable. "Now, try to behave yourself, Grace. I thought you were away at school."

"Got back early," she said. "And so glad that I did." She held out her hand. "How do you do, I'm Grace Pernell, the sister Robin is so ashamed of. I am blunt, you see. Totally unacceptable. I usually say what everyone else merely thinks. Robin said you were beautiful and you are. Are you going to marry him?"

"Grace!" Robin said, a deep, dangerous growl of protest. Batsheva saw Robin's parents exchange embarrassed, questioning glances.

"Dinner will be ready momentarily, Grace, so do get changed. In the meantime, Betsy, you must try this wine. Special reserve 1942." The earl filled a crystal goblet and handed it to her. She took it helplessly, searching for Robin, but he just avoided her stare. He wasn't going to help her then. She was on her own. She took a deep breath. So be it. She placed the glass carefully on the coffee table.

"But, my dear, you haven't touched it. You aren't a teetotaler, are you?" The earl chuckled. "Mind you, there is nothing wrong with that. I wish some of Robin's other friends would be able to pass the bottle by as easily. But surely, one little sip before dinner . . ."

"I'm not a teetotaler and I'm afraid I won't be able to join you for dinner because . . . (There were so many things she could say, 'because my child is expecting me home for dinner, because I am a strict vegetarian, because I promised the babysitter I'd be home early . . .' a million excuses she could have made had she been too ashamed to say the truth. As it was, she saw no reason to lie.) because I am an Orthodox Jew and drink only kosher wine and eat kosher food," she said with simple dignity.

She saw the earl examine his drink with sudden fascination and Lady Haversham shoot an almost imperceptible look of shocked disapproval at Robin, the kind of look a very well-bred mother might give a child who has begun to pick his nose at a dinner table full of guests. "Well, is there anything else we can offer you at least to drink, my dear?" she asked Batsheva with extreme politeness.

"Just some brandy would be fine," Batsheva said miserably, the woman's overconsiderate tone making her ill with embarrassment and nervousness. There was an uncomfortable silence. A fine old clock chimed perfectly on the mantelpiece. There was a sense of timeless order in the room, things cared for and in place, Batsheva thought. Even the people—Robin, Grace, the parents—had faces that mirrored those of ancestors that hung in gilt frames along the graceful banister. If only I could disappear, she thought.

She was the eternal outsider. She was the stone thrown into the calm pond that destroys the beautiful reflection, turning it into a turbulent muddle. That was it. She craved the civilized calm, and yet the moment she entered it, her presence seemed to destroy it. She just didn't fit in anywhere. Except for one place, now lost to her forever.

"When I was younger, I had a friend at school who was Jewish," Grace interjected suddenly. "She invited me for dinner and I asked for a glass of milk with my meat. Well, her father went into a long explanation of why it wasn't permitted, and what it all meant. I was awfully embarrassed, although thinking back now, I don't see why I should have been. It was rather odd, after all." She smiled sweetly at Batsheva, with just a hint of malice.

"The Hebrews are an ancient superior race. Why, look at how many Nobel prizes they've won! Look at Disraeli!" Robin blurted out. "They're basically the same as the rest of us. It's just that we don't know very many since they travel in such different circles. Now, if we could just get to know them better, they wouldn't seem odd to us at all . . ."

"That's not true, my dear, strictly speaking," his mother corrected him. "I mean about not knowing them. There was that family from America—the Goldshmidts, was it?—that bought the Clemens estate. They must have poured enormous amounts of cash into it, which they never seemed to run out of. We had them here a number of times. You do remember, dear, don't you? I personally found them charming. But I'm afraid most of our neighbors didn't think so. They wound up moving away in the end," Lady Haversham said a little abstractedly, as if trying to remember. "Back to a place called Scarsdale, if I recall correctly."

Batsheva winced. Jewess, Robin had called her.

Looking at it with strange objectivity, it was incredible to her that the sheltered, wealthy, beautiful Batsheva Ha-Levi should be looked down upon by people whose own culture and education, whose own heritage, went back a few hundred years, while her own went back thousands. An old house full of tacky antiques her father could buy and sell in an afternoon, she thought meanly. And the calm she so treasured, that came with real manners, real culture—certainly Grace had been brought up with precious little of it. I come from a real aristocracy, she thought with sudden pride. Generations of people whose achievements in scholarship, in pious leadership, earned them a princelike status. And each generation had to contribute, to rise up to its heritage, not simply hand down old clocks finely polished, old houses and old bank accounts.

All my life, she thought, I have been sheltered by wealth and family and community from understanding who I am, what it means to be a Jew. Now, stripped of everything, vulnerable and alone, she experienced the raw pain of blind prejudice and unthinking cruelty that had been her people's lot for centuries. And these good, cultured people perpetuated it, instilling it in their children, giving it posterity through their complicity and—she glanced at the earl—their accepting silence. She pressed her lips together.

"Will you please stay to dinner, dearest?" Robin implored, ignoring his mother's raised eyebrow. "I'm sure cook can arrange for something—a salad, fruits . . ."

"No, thank you, Robin. I'm afraid there is nothing here I would be able to swallow." She stood up and wiped off her dress, as if shaking off centuries of foul dust. And when Robin took her home, she answered his good-night with a good-bye.

Chapter eighteen

"Sheva?"

"Back here, in the darkroom, Liz," a voice said faintly. Elizabeth looked around the room and shook her head in amused shock at the chaos. Books were piled everywhere. Blooming flowers and plants, green, sprouting things, spilled over out of old bottles and milk containers, creating a hothouse atmosphere. The dull-gray walls were covered with blown-up prints of photographs: the cryptically lined face of an old woman selling flowers in Covent Garden; a beautiful chameleon caught changing colors. Akiva weaved through the happy disorder, ferrying blocks back and forth in a little red wagon he dragged behind him. Elizabeth rumpled his curly bent head, and he looked up at her briefly and seriously, then broke into a careful smile.

"Close the door quickly. I am so glad you're here. Wait until you see this one!"

"I don't see how you can stand it in here." Elizabeth wrinkled her nose at the sour odor of chemicals rising from large plastic basins. "It's as dark as Hades."

"Just look . . ."

The women stared down at the large blank sheet. Batsheva held it carefully with plastic tongs, shaking it gently from side to side in the clear liquid. Around the white spaces gray, then black began to form. Batsheva grew quiet, staring at the developing print. When it had set, they took it out into the light. It was a picture of hills with tiny white houses nestled within valleys under gray billowing clouds. At its center, a magnificent ray of light was just breaking through, the embodiment of benediction. The light was perfectly caught within the darkness.

"It's magnificent," Elizabeth said, breaking the silence. "It reminds me of Ansel Adams's pictures in *Yosemite and the Range of Light*. Where'd you get it?"

"It was one of the first pictures I took in Jerusalem. I thought Isaac had destroyed it, but then I found this undeveloped roll of film that was stuck under some papers in my purse." Her face grew sad staring at the picture.

Elizabeth watched her, startled. Everything was going so well. After a short period, word of mouth had inundated her with customers. One of them, an art professor, had been so pleased with a series of portraits of his little girl that he had introduced Batsheva to a gallery owner, who had asked to see her portfolio with a view toward a one-woman show. She had developed a large, lively group of friends: Indian scientists, local poets and artists, young dancers. She especially seemed to attract rich young members of the upper classes. But she very seldom dated anyone. Elizabeth was amazed (Envious? She sometimes wondered.) at how many invitations the girl had to turn down every week. There was this fascinating innocence, yet a mystery, a world-sadness, about her that attracted the romantic interest of men. They all wanted to protect her. To make love to her, too, no doubt. Elizabeth's mind wandered for a moment, wondering: Does she? She looked at the girl again. There were actually tears in her eyes.

"What is it? Come on, tell old Lizzie."

"You'll think I'm sick in the head."

"We all know that. Spill it."

"They'll be preparing for Passover now. The sun is already summer-hot and so close to you, it's like a layer of clothing. The windows will be open and people will be banging dust out of carpets and pillows. Curtains and sheets will be billowing on clotheslines, dancing in the breeze. The men will be carrying matzohs home from the factories. Everything will be white."

Elizabeth followed her gaze out the window to the gray buildings, the gray sky of London. I always forget how different she is, Elizabeth thought, looking her over. Most people would lump everything together in their mind. They wouldn't be able to sift the good from the bad, blaming the place in addition to the man, the society. She had come out of hiding and her hair hung long and thick and black with an almost Oriental silkiness. She looked like a rare bird.

"Hey, this is supposed to be the happy ending. Beautiful young maiden flees wife-abusing fanatic and finds freedom and fame in the big city."

"Freedom, yes. Fame, maybe. But there is something missing."

"Yes, and I know exactly what it is, my little chickadee. *Romance!*"

"That's not even funny."

"It wasn't supposed to be. You need the Big Love! Lady Batsheva's Lover. I can just see it now. Directed by David Lean, music by Michel Legrand, a script by . . ."

"Moses." She laughed.

"My dear, that would be no fun at all."

"Exactly. As long as I'm married to Isaac anything I do with another man is a mortal sin. Do you know what the punishment is for adultery? It's like committing murder—you lose your place in the World to Come, your eternity. Can you see making that kind of sacrifice for any man?"

Elizabeth chewed her lip pensively. Well, *now* I know. She doesn't. Where have I had this conversation before? Flesh versus spirit. Heaven versus hell. Ian's brother, David. A wicked smile lit up her face as a thought crossed her mind. "You sound just like a man I know. Very spiritual type. You'd like him, you know what! Just exactly your type. Very dishy too. I'm going to have a little get-together tonight with some friends. You must come over and meet him."

Batsheva shook her head with an ironic smile. "I don't know. Men are such a problem. I go out with them and really enjoy their company. And we see wonderful plays, or operas, or ballets. But it's never enough for them. They always want something more from me that I can't give them."

"Do you want to give it to them? Are you suffering in denial? Or is it just a great excuse?" They looked at each other and giggled.

"Not such a big sacrifice," Batsheva admitted. "You see, I like them all up to a point, and then they kiss me. It's sweet, but . . ."

"No bells, no hot, thunderous red flashes of lightning?"

"You're making fun of me."

"My dear, I know the feeling well. Graham was a fully tuned thunderstorm for many years." Her face got a fixed, pensive look.

"You miss him, don't you?" She was anxious to change the subject, as well as curious.

"Yes, and I hate myself for it. He isn't good enough for your pure, dear friend."

"But I thought Ian and you . . ."

"Ian is a well-known poet, while I'm a mere lowly Ph.D. candidate. We travel in the same circles, that's all. He is ten feet deep in women. It would be a long-distance romance."

"Will Ian be there tonight also?"

"Dunno. Haven't asked him yet." Her stomach got butterflies, just thinking of it. Years go by and nothing changes. Still waiting for the man. Well, at least the man had changed to a considerably higher variety. That was a progress of sorts, she comforted herself.

"Will you come?"

"All right. But only to check out Ian, to see if he's worthy of you."

The soft noise of music, cultured laughter, and ice tinkling in tall glasses wafted gently through the windows, reaching Batsheva as she stood undecided in the street before Elizabeth's apartment house. It was a friendly noise, but still, it implied a certain cohesiveness, a group. She had come to be wary of such situations. You never knew when you'd run into more Grace Pernells. Elizabeth had invited her a number of times, but she had always felt awkward. They were such an educated, sophisticated crowd. She felt like a stupid child among them. She let out a deep breath and climbed the stairs, knocking quietly with an absurd hope that no one would hear and she could go home. The door opened immediately.

"Well, hello."

She stood there dumbly, looking into the man's laughing blue eyes, his large and very handsome face. There was something so familiar and comforting about him, yet at the same time something compellingly different. He wore a soft, well-worn blue sweater and a kind of funny white collar beneath it. He was tall enough for her to have to lift her chin to see him smile down at her. His eyes had a searching, penetrating intelligence, a brightness that was almost frightening.

Mercifully, Elizabeth came along and rescued her. "I see you've met David."

"Not really. But I'd be eternally grateful for an introduction," he said warmly.

"David Hope, Bets—"

"Batsheva," Batsheva interrupted her impulsively, suddenly unable to bear the thought of this man calling her Betsy.

Elizabeth covered her confusion well, hardly losing a beat. "Batsheva Levy. Batsheva is a soon-to-be-famous photographer and one of my dearest friends, David. She has lately been fending off the entire young male wolf population of London, just as you have been fending off the sweet foxes. You two actually have much in common." She smiled and left them.

His large hand held her small one so warmly and comfortably that she did not even consider that she might ask for it back instead of following him to the quiet corner near the fireplace where he led her. He seated her carefully on the most comfortable available chair. "I'll get you some wine."

"No, please."

He looked at her curiously. "A teetotaler?"

Here it comes, she thought with dread, the beginning of another beautiful evening in London. "Actually, it's against my religion to drink nonkosher wine. But a beer will be fine."

"You must tell me all about it, it sounds fascinating." He handed her the beer and sat cross-legged at her feet. She looked into his eyes and searched for the usual criticism, surprise, and contempt, but found only clear openness, and the pure interest of a scholar.

"Please, I'd rather not," she said. "I just don't want to be a specimen tonight. I hate talking about my religion and all the things I have to do because of it. Orthodox Jews have two million things they can and cannot do. If I get started, I will bore both of us stiff. I just want to feel like everyone else tonight. To relax and laugh and flirt a little." She took a long drink. "I don't mean to offend you."

"Ha!" he gave a sharp snort of laughter and stretched out.

"Offend me!? I can't believe it! You sound just like me! That's what I keep telling all my friends! It gets so awful sometimes I just want to scream! The same questions again and again—about God, about religion, about sex. They refuse to believe I am just as normal as the rest of them. They think I must be some kind of throwback to the Middle Ages, or repressed or just a fool."

Batsheva closed her eyes for a moment. Perhaps I am dreaming, she thought. But when she opened them, David was still there at her feet, his friendly eyes searching her face, proving that she had not conjured him up out of her desperate need for companionship and understanding.

"All the time I have been here," she began quietly, "I have felt so alone. Religion has to be shared. Friday nights and Saturdays. Sabbath meals. I have learned to keep this to myself. People are so prejudiced against religious Jews. They find us so queer because we cannot eat with them, or join them on weekends. But I didn't know that Elizabeth had any other Jewish friends—" She smiled at him with such excitement and pleasure.

For the first time, his honest eyes seemed to cloud with doubt and then with sadness. "My dear," he said, taking her hand, "she doesn't. I am not Jewish."

"But, you said . . ."

"I'm not Jewish, but I know all your feelings well. I'm a novitiate. I'm going to be a priest."

She got up abruptly, but he took her hand in his and gently pulled her down. "Now, you're not going to treat me the way people treat you, are you?"

Her heart was beating so fast and so loud. I am frightened, she thought, hating herself for her youth, her inexperience, and her prejudices.

"Or, for that matter, the way people usually treat me!" He

laughed, an open, generous laugh. She found she could not help joining him.

"How could I? It would prove that I was the same as all those people I have been telling myself I am superior to all these months." She laughed.

"You mean you've been harboring this humble sense of superiority against the world even as it attacks you with its contempt? Heavens. Just like me." He shook his head. "Now," he took her hand again, "having gotten that out of the way, can we go back to your original plan, which sounded, I must say, very good to me."

" 'Plan'?"

"Yes, you know. The part about relaxing and laughing and flirting." He saw her eyes widen just a fraction with shock. "You're thinking: 'My Lord, flirting and laughing and he almost a priest!' " He saw her face relax. "Please, each religion has its pluses and minuses. Right now, I'm not breaking a single vow. Are you?"

"Well, I can't think of any, but I must be."

His eyes rolled upward: "Well, heaven be thanked for that at least." Someone had put on a record, and the room was reverberating with dancing.

"Shall we?"

She shook her head. "I never learned how."

"Good. It'll be the blind leading the blind then." Again, his warm, kind hand enveloped hers and she felt herself lifted up against her will, all her struggle gone. He took her hand and put his arm around her waist. He was very slim and graceful for such a tall, powerful man, she thought. He pulled her carefully toward him and for the first time in her life, she danced. She felt the strong muscles of his chest and thighs, and she breathed in the warm male fragrance that rose from his beating heart as he bent his body considerately to hers. They danced until all their stiffness and reserve melted away into the music. She felt him rest his cheek delicately against her hair. For some reason, she was not afraid. Perhaps because there was no insistence in him, no demands. He danced with her, leaving her free, but sharing generously all that was best in him. When the music ended, they stood still for a moment, neither wanting to move. When they parted, they both felt a new shyness that had not been there before.

"Batsheva and David, you must come here and give us your opinion," Elizabeth called to them from across the room. Batsheva walked over gratefully, glad of the distraction. She felt as if she had been on raging white water thundering toward the edge of a precipice.

"Batsheva, I want you to meet Ian, David's brother," Elizabeth said, her face alive, almost glowing with pleasure and pride.

She looks so very lovely, Batsheva thought, studying her friend's gold hair burnished by the dancing flames in the fireplace. Her body was soft and voluptuous in a long emerald cashmere dress that fit her like a tight sweater.

"Now, David, we need your opinion about this. We are discussing the moral imperative of poetry. Now, my good friend Roger," she nodded at an intense young man with dark, nervous eyes, "maintains that all art is removed from life. That it has no purpose except to exist. The way a rose is a rose is a rose is a rose. However, I maintain that there is such a thing as moral and immoral art."

"For example?" Roger interrupted.

"Well," David's deep voice broke in, "what if one writes a compelling poem about the rape of a small child, from the point of view of the rapist, which absolves him of all guilt, which shows the utter rightness and beauty of the action? It might be wonderful art, perfect verisimilitude, but totally immoral, don't you agree?"

"No, I don't." Roger shook his head. "Once you start preaching in art, once you put shackles on the artist, you are lost. It isn't art anymore. It's some preachy sermon. The artist has one responsibility. That is to his art, to make it as perfect as he can, a criticism of life. To do this, he must be free, totally free. Every culture is full of taboos. If the artist adhered to them all, we would never have real art."

"I agree with David." Ian shrugged. "The artist, because of his power, has to accept responsibility for the moral consequences of his art. We don't work in a vacuum. We are dealing with real minds and hearts that are profoundly influenced by what we do. That doesn't mean I think we need outside censorship. We must discipline ourselves. Artists, priests, scholars, and teachers are all in the same boat. We are molding minds, hearts. There are so many fakes around."

"Oh, I agree totally." Roger sneered, his eyes shifting from one brother to the other. "The priest and the poet. Two sides of the same coin, wanting to change the world to their own spiritual calling. Rarefied humans, too good for the rest of us." He walked off with a shrug.

"Roger paints erotic pictures of large, elderly nudes." Elizabeth giggled. "So I think you've offended him."

"Do you know what the most beautiful poetry in the world is? It's the Bible, because it combines the perfection of feeling with the perfection of words," David mused, when the laughter over Roger subsided. "It follows Milton's prescription, it's 'simple, sensuous, and passionate.'"

"I had no idea there was any poetry in the Bible." Elizabeth looked up, interested.

"Well, there hasn't been a great deal of understanding of biblical poetry. It started with Lowth, an Oxford poetry don, who gave a series of thirty-four lectures that were published in 1753 under the title: *De sacra poesi Hebraeorum pracelectiones academicae.*"

"*Nahamu nahamu 'ammi, yo'mar 'Elohekhem, daberu'al laev Yerushalaym we-qire'u 'eleha,*" Batsheva said softly.

'Be comforted, be comforted, my people, sayest the Lord, speak to the heart of Jerusalem and call unto her that her wars are ended, her sins are pardoned . . .' Isaiah, Chapter Forty, verses one and two." David smiled at her. "It's so beautiful in Hebrew, the comforting *oo* sounds, wonderful onomatopoeia. You can just feel the soft comfort of the words."

"Wow. I'm impressed!" Elizabeth said, more than a little impressed.

"David never ceases to amaze me. The man is a walking storehouse of knowledge on every topic on earth. He is an incredible scholar with a mind like a sponge—never loses a drop. He is interested in everything from pre-Columbian art to the mysteries of the Trinity. Puts me to shame." Ian grinned.

The mention of the Trinity seemed to pour cold water on Batsheva, who was basking in the joy of having spoken Hebrew and been understood, having met someone who not only knew Hebrew but the Bible as well. He was so familiar, so close to being like her and yet so intrinsically alien and strange. He was forbidden, much more than any food or drink. He represented a whole culture that was in locked opposition to her understanding of the world. The old combat of Jew against Christian. Three could not be one, and one was not three. The Jew, still waiting for the Messiah to come and end all suffering, could never be reconciled to the Christian, whose Messiah had come and gone, leaving the world to suffer on.

She was afraid to look at him. So she looked at Ian instead. He surprised her. She had expected someone dark, ascetically thin and tall with the high, hollowed-out cheeks of the poet, dressed in tweeds. Instead, he was solid and square-shouldered with a broad chest and powerful arms and legs. He was very fair with a strong square chin and a high, intelligent forehead. His light-brown eyes exuded a lively energy. He was dressed like a farmer—soft red-flannel workshirt open at the collar, faded jeans and workboots. She looked from brother to brother, startled at David's dark, almost Italian coloring, his tall, slim body. They were so totally, startlingly, different in looks. What must their parents look like? she wondered. Yet there was a similarity of spirit: They were both aggressively alive, intensely part of the world, yet floating above it all, in some calm, superior sphere of the universe reserved for the real aristocracy of this world, people who possess generosity of spirit, intelligence, and knowledge.

As her eyes rested on David, she felt a shock of fear go through her. She wanted, she realized, to touch him, to smooth back his straying thick hair, to trace the broad dark brow to the crease of the laugh lines around his eyes, to feel with her lips, the tips of her fingers, the soft throb of the pulse in his temple. "I . . . I have to leave. Thank you, Elizabeth. It's been wonderful meeting you all. David, Ian." She nodded quickly, panic taking hold of her, and turned abruptly, almost rudely, to go without looking up at him again.

"I'll get your coat, Batsie." Elizabeth rose, puzzled. They searched for the coat under the mound on the bed and finally retrieved it. "You just got here. Why are you going? Didn't you have a nice time?" Elizabeth asked, mystified.

"I . . . the babysitter has to leave early." She didn't look up, but plowed on toward the door.

But David was already there, waiting for her.

"I'll take you, Batsheva." He held the door open for her.

"No, really. I live so close by . . ."

"Please," he said, his eyes forcing hers to meet his. "I have to get back to the seminary early. My car is right outside. I would dearly love the pleasure of your company, if only for a few more minutes. Please."

"I can't," she whispered miserably. But he had already tucked her arm comfortably through his and she knew there was no way to escape even if she had still wanted to.

Chapter nineteen

She closed the door behind the last guest, kicked off her shoes, and padded tiredly back into the living room. She was weary from the responsibility of hostessing, of being bright and cheerful and witty. He had come. The thought exhilarated her and filled her with despair. She wanted to close her eyes now and savor every moment, remember every glance exchanged, decipher every remark for subtle hints, the way schoolgirls do with their first innocent crush. There had been women around him all evening, but he had sought her out. But maybe he was just being polite—after all, it *was* her party. He was that type, gentlemanly, courteous. Old-fashioned in so many ways, like the soft shuffling country boys of her youth, except with a mind and talent that she could only admire, the way one admires in awe any natural wonder.

She tasted the triumph once again. Ian Hope had accepted her invitation. He had been in her house, sat on her sofa. She looked toward it with pleasure, remembering, and a sudden shock pierced through her. "I thought you'd gone." She looked at him almost horrified. He had been stretched out there all along, and she hadn't known it! An irrational disappointment flooded her. She had wanted to revel in the illusion, the daydream, and here he was, dangerously, uncompromisingly real. Did she really want that?

"I wanted to be alone with you, Elizabeth." The words thrilled her to an extent that made her feel foolish and uncomfortable. She began to be afraid, to wish he would go, or that he would never, ever go.

He got up and paced the room, running his hands roughly through his wild shock of hair, disheveled as a lion's mane. "I'm no good at this sort of thing at all. No good at all." He seemed to be talking to himself. He stood in front of her, his hands gripping the sides of a small glass of brandy. "You see, when I am alone, just me and a pen and paper, I have all the words in the world. But when I need to use them to communicate face-to-face, I am as speechless as a newborn baby." He put down the glass and clasped his hands behind him in frustration. Elizabeth watched him carefully, dreamily. His energy frightened her. She was used to Graham's sophisticated calm, his lifeless, cheerful wit that he used as clothing to cover up the appalling emptiness of his soul. This man hid nothing. His willingness to wear his heart on his sleeve was wonderful and confusing to her. It was a challenge she was unsure she could meet.

He sat down on the sofa and looked into the dying embers of the fire and let his hands fall helplessly between his knees.

She couldn't bring herself to sit next to him, so she sat at his feet. He smoothed the bright gold-red of her hair, threading his large, vibrant hands through the hair at her temples, then massaging them backward, spreading her hair around her shoulders.

"You are the most beautiful woman I've ever seen and I would love to make love to you," he said with simple honesty that took her breath away. She felt her body shiver, her back arch from the soft massage of his hands over her shoulders and back. She closed her eyes, almost afraid to breathe, waiting. But he did not continue. He drew his hands away and pushed them deeply into his pockets, stretching out his solid, handsome legs.

"But I won't. I can't."

She opened her eyes, a shock of fear going through her. He was standing by the fireplace now, his chin resting on his closed fist. "Why not, Ian?" My God, how foolish and needy she sounded! How obvious! She hated herself, but felt that she had no choice. She forgot how to play games with him, or she didn't want to remember.

"Because I want more than that from you. I want everything or nothing. I want you to know everything about me—every awful, rotten thought I've ever had, every unkindness I've ever done. I want you to be perfectly clear. I am a serious man who wants serious pleasures." He took her hands in his and kissed her fingertips, gently, softly, each one in its turn. "I am more vulnerable than any woman—most men are. We are fragile, really. I am terrified that you would find out something you couldn't bear about me. So I want you to know me first; then we will decide together."

"But I want you now, Ian," she pleaded like a little lost girl.

She understood him perfectly and it terrified her. It would be so much easier to go to bed with him now, to feel his body cover hers, to keep herself closed off and hidden from him, giving him only the obvious. It had been enough for Graham, for every other man she had ever known. She was terrified of what he was asking her and wanted to seduce him, to take the easy way out.

He understood that, and resisted her, though she could see it took all his strength.

"No, I don't want that." He shook his head and moved

away from her. "We must be friends first. Like little teenagers." He smiled. "Boyfriend and girlfriend. We will date. I will show you all my terrible poems that I keep hidden from everyone else. I will tell you the unacceptable feelings of jealousy, avarice, and gluttony I feel in the middle of the night." He smiled at her, a self-mocking, revealing smile. "And then, when you know it all, you will tell me if you can love me the way you have never loved another man." He understood her, she saw. Her suspicions, her callousness. But also her ability to criticize, to demand quality. He frightened her. Commitment frightened her.

"You are like your friend Batsheva, you know."

"Like her? How?"

"You are both pure souls that life has just washed over, tossing you around but never really changing what you are inside, essentially."

"And what is that?"

"There is a diamond-hard purity in you. An innocence. I'm afraid no man could ever live up to it. Certainly not a poor specimen like me." His face fell dejectedly.

Her hand touched his face and he saw the smile spreading her lips. "And you are like your brother. A saint. He was very good to Batsheva, wasn't he? I hope it wasn't wrong of me to ask him to cheer her up. She's been so depressed lately." She felt herself on safer ground now. She had just been steering blindly, but now she was grateful to have reached this impartial ground. She saw he was disappointed at having been deflected, but he brightened with sudden interest.

"Is that why he paid her so much attention? He is usually so shy with women. I wondered. But now I understand it all. He considers it a ministry. Perhaps even a conversion ministry."

"It would be very wrong of him to see Batsheva that way. Anyhow, he'd be wasting his time, believe me. Why is he becoming a priest anyway? He seems such a normal, sensitive person. How can he shackle himself to such a . . ." her nose wrinkled in distaste, remembering the hard, stern men who had been the priests of her childhood, "such a . . . limiting profession?"

"Don't ask me to explain David."

"But you are brothers! You must know how this happened to him."

He had moved closer to her as she spoke and she could feel his breath move the wisps of hair near her eyes. He put his arms around her and held her for a moment.

"Please, Ian," she whispered, running her hands with a subtle pressure down the length of his back and feeling him breathe in sharply. He led her to the sofa and sat down, pulling her down to his lap, and pressed his head against her shoulder. "No. I am a greedy man. I want more than that. Much more, if you will have me."

She felt the insistent pressure of his solid flesh against her soft shoulder and stared ahead, frightened, into the dark glowing embers of the fire. The glowing unpredictable wood could, at any moment, leap out with a passion of flames hidden deep beneath its soft light, or die altogether, burnt out until the end. She sat there, afraid to move, watching and wondering how it would all end.

Getting into the car with David seemed an act of such intimacy that Batsheva turned rigid with embarrassment. She couldn't stand being near him, she told herself. He made her impossibly uncomfortable. The ride with him was agony, her whole body held in a stiffness of resistance. He said little, but spoke in a soft, joking way, making fun of himself, confessing all his sins, telling her how his thoughts would wander during prayers to soccer and the pimple on the tip of the Father Superior's nose. He told her how he disliked the bare, simple room in the seminary and longed for colors and pictures and wonderful clutter. He told her about his childhood in the estate near the Lake District, and the wonderful hikes through the woods he'd take, trying to figure out where Wordsworth had stopped and taken inspiration.

Slowly she felt her body relax, all the tension flying away like air from a punctured balloon. He was harmless, how could she have thought otherwise? Slowly she began to interject sentences, interrupting him to share scenes from her childhood. She told him about Faygie, the butcher's daughter, walking advertisement for her father's strict *kashrut*, whose defiantly rolled-up skirt had once cost her father hundreds of dollars in unsold pounds of meat. She explained to him that the photos she took were carefully chosen, a way of thanking God for the beauty of His creation. Sometimes they would finish each other's sentences, interrupting each other in agreement and approval, and their voices would dance together in confusion and pleasure.

Neither of them wondered when he passed her house and continued to drive. They found themselves at the other end of the city and rejoiced at how far away they had gone and how long it would take them to get back to where they had to go. And more and more it became apparent that there was still so much more they had to say, and no time at all left to say it in. They kept discovering things about themselves in the other's words, ideas about life, and people, and the world they had thought but had never heard expressed aloud by another human being until that moment. And each time it happened, they were silent, trying to make sense of it. They seemed to know each other so well. And yet, when they thought about it, there could never have been two human beings so far apart both in where they had come from and where they must go.

David felt himself in a state of almost shocked incomprehension. He had come to Elizabeth's to minister to another human being, perhaps even to start the long process of winning her over to the beliefs that sustained him. He had begun the evening with a wonderful glow of calm righteousness. Christ was within him, and he would reach out with Christ's mercy to aid a suffering fellow human being, for Elizabeth had told him a story that paralleled the truth of Batsheva's tragedy, but left out the true details. He knew that Batsheva had escaped from an unhappy marriage and from a suffocating society that had taken her freedom of expression from her. He knew that she was a deeply religious Jew, but had, in the righteousness and purity of his earlier state, believed that could only be a mistake forced upon her by a lack of understanding. She did not know Christ, and therefore, she rejected Him. She did not know the freedom He could bring her, the joy and kindness and light of salvation that would be hers once she reached out to Him.

But then he had met her, and his rigid sense of mission had lapped out of him, petered out. He had listened to her speak about her God, about Jerusalem, and he had seen the fire illuminate her face.

"What is it like, Jerusalem?"

She hesitated, wanting to be precise. "It is like having God move in with you. He is so close, you feel Him in the air, the clouds, the mountains—especially the mountains." She closed her eyes, remembering the soft lines of the hills that rose up and faded in the distance, becoming an experience that led your eyes straight to heaven. "I used to feel all day that He was by my side. When I brushed my teeth, when I dressed, when I sat down to eat . . . there was always a prayer to be said, something to be thankful for."

He listened to her and grew more and more confused, almost angry. She accepted her relationship to God with such simplicity. She was so close to Him. He thought of his own heartbreaking struggle for faith. Nothing was natural to him. He was never sure, perfectly sure, there was a God. A doubt, like a small crack in a wall, entered the solid armor of his persona, and he began to question the sincerity of his ministry, his worthiness to comfort and lead her.

He was not sure of anything, anything. But then, when he opened the car door for her and saw her radiant eyes, her beautiful, graceful movements away from him, movements that ended with her agonizing disappearance behind the closed door of her home, he became absolutely certain, as certain as he had ever been about anything in his entire life, of one thing: that he must see her again.

Batsheva leaned against the door for a moment as it closed behind her, steadying herself. It was late and the babysitter was curled up on the sofa, asleep. She decided not to wake her and walked softly into Akiva's room. His small, bright face, framed and made white by the dark mass of hair, looked so angelic. Usually, when the ache of homesickness wracked her, his face was drug enough to still the pain. But now even as the sight of her son filled her with happiness, it left the yawning chasm of her loneliness unfilled.

She undressed slowly. How her body pleased her tonight, the elegant, firm stretches of her soft skin; the wonderful slimness of her waist and hips that rested on long, white legs. She was astonished at herself. She had not felt like this since . . . she tried to remember, and her memory seemed almost fictional, like a dream she had once had. But then she did remember—that day, thinking of Anna Karenina and her lover Vronsky, thinking of the strange and wonderful lover who would cover her body with his. She hugged herself, wanting to weep with the aggravation of it, the pleasure of it! A man who had touched her so deeply, so physically and spiritually! A man of such alien, dangerous belief, opposed to everything she held sacred! She felt the hot tears of anguish and joy rise, blurring her eyes. Yet she could see clearly, so very, very clearly, her inner vision. David, his body lean and beautiful, bending close to hers, enveloping hers with its warmth;

his open, generous face, his dark-blue eyes looking at her full of kindness and gifted intelligence. Those warm, beautiful, unforgettable laughing eyes.

She got into her wide, empty double bed. Since leaving Isaac, she had learned to treasure it as a sanctuary where she could revel in the comforting silence of privacy, the immeasurable pleasure of uninterrupted, protected sleep. But now, for the first time, it felt cold to her, an uninhabited and unfriendly place. She was frightened at the chaos inside her and terrified she would not be able to put it right, to straighten the sails of the carefully constructed craft that had allowed her to float safely along for these eleven months. She felt the waves of desire and anger and disappointment, of pleasure and joy and love, crash against her chest like the waves of a hurricane.

She felt so alive again, like the young Batsheva who had jumped headlong into the cooling pool of blue water to still the fever rampaging through her veins. Only this time, she understood clearly, she would drown. Her mind, overcome with sleep, felt no fear, but the irrational pleasure of losing control, of being enveloped by the blue, immaculate water that shone like crystal. She felt the surging joy of helpless pleasure as she sank, unable to resist, to breathe, deeper and deeper into that blue, laughing, kind, intelligent, blue water.

Chapter twenty

To her surprise, Batsheva carried on very well. Yes, extremely well, she told herself several times a day. She took the pictures of teachers and students carefully, moving the little umbrellas and floodlights painstakingly to set up just the perfect lighting conditions. She was a conscientious mother, playing with Akiva even more, teaching him the Hebrew and English alphabets, reading him stories.

But each time the phone rang, she felt her heart leap up uncomfortably in her chest, and goose bumps rise on her flesh. And when she heard the stranger's voice on the other end asking for a portrait sitting, she found herself filled with a bitter disappointment that was almost too much to bear.

She ate too much, or forgot to eat at all. And all day long, she went around with a bright, hard look in her eyes that bordered on despair. She began rehearsing for his call, going through her part all over the house, watching her face reflected in windows, the glass frames of pictures, and mirrors, as she mouthed the words: "David," she would begin, oh, simply, very simply. "I think it would be best if we didn't see each other anymore. It's wrong for us to get involved in something there can be no happy ending to." She never questioned her ability to deliver those lines, or that their relationship must end because it could never be a casual, platonic friendship. She began to count the hours. Sunday all day was twenty-four. Monday all day, forty-eight. Tuesday, all day, seventy-two. And then, finally Wednesday, at 1:10 P.M., eighty-five hours and ten minutes after she had seen him last, he called her.

"I can't believe you're actually calling me. I've waited so long," she blurted out, then froze up in utter horror at hearing her thoughts spoken. She heard his wonderful, generous laughter come like magic through the hard, ugly plastic of the phone. So, what is to be done now, she thought, lost completely. The last thing in the world that had occurred to her was that she would actually spill out her honest feelings to him, feelings she had yet to admit to herself. She felt her cheeks burn with humiliation.

"You're wonderful," he said. "You've saved me from lying through my teeth about portraits I desperately need done, about misfortunate children I want you to help me with . . . Eighty-five hours and . . ." he paused, ". . . eleven minutes."

There was silence on both ends of the line as they reflected on what had happened. They had bypassed a whole step of false casualness and been brought face-to-face with the reality of the depth and uncomfortable strength of the attraction between them. I must see him once and for all to end this insanity. He cannot look as wonderful, be as wonderful, as I imagine him, Batsheva thought. I will find that his ears are too large, or his face is too ruddy. He will say something offensive (bound to, eventually, a priest!), she thought somewhat desperately. It's best if we spend time together so that I may see these things sooner, so that they may hit me harder.

I must see her, he thought. I must finish my ministry, or

at least prove to myself it was a hopeless challenge. I must reach out to her in Christ's name. I must test myself to see if I can relate to her as a soul, if I can quell my desire for her as a woman. I must elevate and purify my carnal love into pure spiritual love. But this I can only do with her by my side. It is the only way to end this obsession.

"I must see you," they said simultaneously, and then didn't know whether to laugh or be appalled.

"I'll pick you up in an hour. We'll feed the ducks in Hyde Park. Your little boy will like that."

"Yes. All right. In an hour then."

Her hands shook as she brushed her hair so hard it crackled like an electric wire. She tried on dress after dress, rejecting one because it made her look young and innocent, another because she seemed old and worldly. She looked in the mirror and racked her brain to understand how she should look, what exactly she was trying to accomplish. Did she want to look ravishing and unforgettable? Or businesslike and unapproachable? Did she want to make it easy, or impossible, for him to accept her farewell? Was she going to say good-bye at all, or was that simply beyond her? She kept going round and round and coming back to the same point. She couldn't, wouldn't, decide. She finally just grabbed the sweater and skirt she had worn to Robin's house. It was a little frayed now, after much use, but the color had remained just as beautiful and rich.

He hung up the phone and lay back on his narrow, hard bed at the seminary, staring at the ceiling. He felt himself in a total state of chaos. He thought of her, trying to concentrate on ideas. But her face, her soft body, would intrude. She had touched him, reaching in deeply to his mind, his heart, his loins. He felt ravished and destroyed, all his beliefs brought into doubt. Ever since he had been a small child, he had been tortured by questions that never occurred to anyone else—not to his father or mother, Ian or his classmates or teachers. Why are we on earth? What does it mean to be good, to be evil? What does God want of us? They had all treated the questions lightly, the way one reacted to a why-is-the-sky-blue-and-the-grass-green kind of question. Perhaps they had all had these questions themselves but had been able to resolve them with pat answers from catechism.

It was funny, when he thought about it. The Church had never given him the answers that satisfied him. It had only enticed him forward with more mysteries, more questions, until he felt that it would take him his whole lifetime to find the answers. That was why he had decided to become a priest. He wanted to find the answers, to live out their truth undeflected by any false, time-consuming sidetracks through ordinary life. And so he had thought until he met Batsheva.

She was not the first woman who had attracted him. He loved all women, in the abstract. In high school, he had felt himself drawn to pretty young girls, wanting to touch them the way one feels one must caress a fluffy little kitten. They had touched his body with their sweetness, but he had grown tired of it. They satisfied such a small part of his incredible hunger, like a little piece of cake without the whole meal that goes before it. He had realized then that in order to satisfy his hunger, there would have to be an endless stream of women, and still the main part of him would remain unfed. And so he had decided to have no woman, but to seek something more solid and difficult to satisfy his soul.

But in Batsheva he had sensed some indefinable essence that drew him like a magnet. It was more than just incredible womanly beauty. It was an inner radiance, a glow. She seemed to have answers that he had never dreamed of, answers the Church had kept from him. Or, more truly, it was his love of questions. She posed the most incomprehensible combination of questions of all: added to the eternal mystery of Woman was the eternal question of the Jew. And so, he told himself, he would minister to her needs. He would reach out to her and let Christ offer her salvation. Yes, it was his duty to sublimate this desire, to turn it into a service to the Lord. He would save her soul, the unbaptized soul of the unbelieving Jew who has denied Christ. He would be her salvation. This would be his gift to her, out of the growing love he felt for her.

She opened the door and let him in, afraid almost to look at him. An indefinable thrill ran through her that was almost frightening.

"And so this is Akiva?" He didn't bend over the child, but squatted down so that they were almost equals, face-to-face. He put out his hand ceremoniously. "So happy to meet you, sir." Akiva put his little hand out and giggled as David tickled him under the arm. "Laughing at me, are we? Well, we shall have to see about that, yes indeed." He was about to pick the child up and swing him, but thought better of it. After all, he was a stranger and very tall, and the height might be frightening. He would do it later, when they got to know each other, he thought, somehow never questioning that there would be a later. "And how do you feel about feeding the ducks, sir?"

"I like ducks," Akiva answered thoughtfully, "but I was in the middle of reading a book." He looked at his mother doubtfully.

"And what is the book about?" He loved children and thought Akiva the most wonderful little thing—so bright and mischievous and handsome.

"About how the world began. It was dark, oh, so dark, and then light . . ."

"He'll keep you here for the whole seven days of creation," Batsheva laughed. "Come on now, up we go, Akiva. You can read your book later."

The child skipped between them on the grass, chasing the ducks. A current flowed between David and Batsheva that was so strong it seemed to fill up the empty space that separated their bodies. It swirled around them like fine steel wires, pulling them together without their willing or understanding it. Slowly, to her utter amazement, Batsheva began to tell David everything. She described her childhood, so isolated and filled with religion and custom, and how she had loved the rituals and felt herself close to God. She described her dreams as a young girl, her desire to travel, to read, to learn, to become a wife and mother and to lead a good life, fulfilling all the demands of custom and religion, yet being herself as well. She hesitated when she came to the part about Isaac, knowing she was opening a door that would be impossible for her to ever close again; knowing that she would risk his disgust, and his condemnation. But it could not be helped. He had to know everything, every detail she had not yet admitted to herself. An instinct told her this.

She described Jerusalem and he saw her eyes shine with love. She described Isaac, and he saw the glow fade and harden and disappear. "It was as if Isaac cut me up into little pieces and kept taking one piece and then another away until there was nothing left, until I was almost totally destroyed. And worst of all, he did it in God's name until I almost believed they were the same, Isaac and God, until I almost hated God." She took a deep breath, trying to keep her voice steady. "I know that I am young and still ignorant, but I have learned through everything that has happened one thing: that God does not want that. I understand—oh, not everything, I will never understand everything—but enough to know that He gives us lives that are separate and beautiful and expects us to develop whatever there is inside us. Isaac cannot imagine anyone who is not a clone of himself. There is no room in his heart for forgiveness and understanding for the things that make us individual and human—our weaknesses, our desires. I used to think he was both evil and ignorant. I don't anymore, I don't even hate him anymore. I feel sorry for him and everyone like him. They want to do the right thing, but they think the right thing is to crush themselves, to stuff their lives into tiny, tiny cubbyholes and to cut off all the parts that don't fit.

"When I was young, I had so many questions, so many doubts about what we are doing here, being alive. I thought—if I marry a scholar, I will have someone to teach me, to explain things to me. I see that was wrong. You can't give over your doubts to someone else and ask him to hand you the answers on a silver platter. That's like handing him over your soul. The best you can do is to struggle with the questions honestly and try to be a good person."

"You're so good!" he said softly.

She looked up into David's eyes and quickly looked away. No, she did not want his compassion, his understanding. She was afraid it would soften her, take away her courage to tell the whole truth. She took a deep breath. "You don't know anything about me. I am a wife who abandoned her husband. A daughter who brought grief and shame to her parents. A mother who almost killed her son." She saw his shocked face stare at her sharply, but she plunged forward, describing the way they took Akiva from her; the tottering chair and the open hotel window.

"Good God!" He gripped his hands together painfully.

She was bent over and her shoulders trembled. He took her in his arms, his hands caressing her head and humbled shoulders, blindly, with a blind instinctive love and tenderness. He held her until the trembling stopped, then used his large hands to wipe the tears from her face.

"But you see, I am not dead. So there must be a purpose to my life, which I . . . I don't know. I must find it somehow, on my own. He wants us to live, you know." She nodded with perfect conviction. "That's the reason we are here, to go through it. That is why He pulled me back to life. And so I live, trying to reconcile all the opposites—to be myself, and to make that self pleasing to Him. And now you know everything." She looked at him full of pain and unhappiness. "I am a runaway. An outcast from my family, from my people. An eternal foreigner condemned to live among strangers."

This was the moment, his rational mind cried out to him. Offer her Christ's comfort. His guidance and friendship, to ease her burden of loneliness. Ask her to join you in a new life, to become one with a new people. The words caught in his throat and he felt a disgust with himself that almost nauseated him. Never had he felt more inadequate, more humiliated and small, thinking of his earlier arrogance. He felt heartbroken and yet incredibly elated, as if at the edge of an enormous, life-shattering discovery: I cannot offer her Christ's forgiveness, he thought with a flash of frightening clarity, because she doesn't need it.

She had been at the edge of spiritual and physical death and both times, through her own strength, had pulled back. Her pain, her incredible struggle, had purified her. She was a purer soul than he would ever be, he knew. She was drawing her strength and her conviction from a deeper source—a source that as yet evaded his comprehension. He cupped his hands around her beautiful face and stared into the radiant light that filled her wet, shining eyes. She had pulled back from death and was filled with life, with faith, with forgiveness, and with understanding.

While he . . . he felt such contempt for himself. He had been no woman's husband, no child's father. He knew God only vaguely, filtered through books, through mysteries, through other priests. He had, until now, he thought bitterly, lived vicariously. It was a miserly, selfish life. A coward's life.

Batsheva, misunderstanding his bitter silence, felt the full weight of his imagined contempt wash over her. Now he knows it all. It will be over now. He will hate me now. She tried to find some satisfaction in the thought of the total rupture of their relationship, the break that she knew had to come. But instead, she felt an emptiness, a loss almost like the death of a loved one.

"Ah, this wee one must be yours, then," a stranger's voice interrupted the tense silence. The man, who held Akiva's muddy hand, looked shrewdly at David and then at Batsheva. "Yes, I knew he must be yours. Spitting image of his father."

"Akiva!" Batsheva exclaimed, horrified and amused. He was so incredibly wet and dirty and wore such a big smile.

"He just took in after the ducks. Thought he was a duck too, hey, little fellow?" the man said with a chuckle, patting the child on the head. "I'd get him into some dry clothes if I were you, luv."

David wrapped him in his jacket and walked him quickly to the car. He looked at the child. Spitting image of his father. It was a cruel irony that the child could be mistaken for his. For the child he would never have. The beautiful little boy. They took him home in a strained silence. David had not said a word. He knew she was waiting for him to say something, but he was so miserably confused. Despite the unbelievable complexity of their relationship, his mind kept offering up the most exasperatingly simplistic solutions. I just want to hug you, he thought foolishly. I want to hold you close to me and never leave you. I want to go home with you and stay, to wake up in the morning with you, to feel you next to me when I sleep. But what can I offer you? How could you ever love me, a fool like me, a poor confused coward like me? And even that offer was a false one. He did not belong to himself, but to the Church. So he could not honestly even offer her that.

So he said nothing.

Batsheva, respecting his desire—as she thought—to be rid of her, was too proud to plead. They would part in dignity, if nothing else. She hugged Akiva close to her and giggled. She just couldn't help it. She giggled.

"What is it?" David turned quickly, not understanding.

"He smells . . . he smells like . . ." She burst out laughing, uncontrollable laughter that made her shoulders heave. "He smells like a swamp," she finally said, barely understandable through her laughter.

David took a deep breath and let it out. He smelled the awful swampy, muddy odor of the wet clothes. "And it's all over my jacket. Hmnph. Ha—" He guffawed once, loudly, trying to restrain himself. But it was no use. He was caught up in the laughter. He laughed until his eyes blurred with tears and his stomach ached.

David carried the child into the house, swinging him, and felt satisfaction and relief as Akiva squealed with laughter. He undressed the child as Batsheva got the bath ready. He got pleasure from looking at the firm, pudgy body still plump with baby fat and from the press of the child's small, trusting arms around his neck. He handed him over to Batsheva with an unconscious reluctance.

"Can I watch, please?"

"Of course." She smiled at him. She was absorbed in the child, soaping down his sweet little body. There is so much love and gentleness in her hands, David thought. He watched her strong, capable arms, her beautiful long fingers take the washcloth across the child's smooth back, down his little arms and legs. She was on her knees, her slim, graceful back arched over so vulnerably. I want to protect you, he thought irrationally. She shampooed the child's hair carefully, her fingers caressing the shining, fragrant bubbles into his small scalp. David felt his own scalp begin to tingle with longing. He felt a warmth go out to her from somewhere in the middle of his body—his heart, his groin. It was all mixed up together—love and lust and tenderness. They flowed together seamlessly, and there was no way to tell where one began and the other ended.

Batsheva wrapped Akiva in a large towel. The room was hot and moist, filled with the intimate fragrance of warm, clean skin and soap. David made no move to leave. She didn't understand. Why? She felt as if she were balancing something very carefully that might, even with the most delicate movement, come crashing down upon her head. His presence filled her with a silent, unfathomable joy.

"Shall I put him into bed?"

"Thank you, David, but I don't know if he'll go . . ." But even as she spoke, to her surprise, Akiva reached out his arms to David.

"Swing me. Hard," the child demanded.

"Ho, ho. So that's it, eh? Well, I don't know about that. You just hold still, now, don't you dare go swinging around," David said with mock sternness that delighted the child, and he swung him high up, almost to the ceiling. Akiva screamed with pleasure. "Let me down, let me down! Mama!" But as soon as David brought him down, his face, flushed red with happiness, beamed up at him. "Again, David, again!"

"What, you again? Now, didn't I tell you not to go putting your feet off the ground?" He lifted the child, all the while delighting him with that mock-stern voice: "There you are, off the ground again. Now, under no circumstances are you to go swinging . . ." He swung him up. "Now, there you go again. My, my."

Finally, he laid the child down in bed and kissed him, breathing in his clean child's sweetness and warmth—the warmth of home, of family, of deep, meaningful connection to life.

"Good-night, son." It sounded so good to him.

Batsheva stood in the doorway and watched them. Did Akiva remember his father, she wondered, with a sudden, aching longing to be held in the arms of her own father and mother. A child needs parents. A father and a mother. He closed Akiva's door.

Without the child between them, the intimacy became unbearable.

"I'd better be going," he said with a heavy heart. Nothing had been resolved. It was all worse than ever.

"I'm . . .(in love with you—God! don't say it out loud!) . . . I'm afraid that your jacket will need to be cleaned."

"It doesn't matter."

"I'll . . . let me clean it. Or, that is, have it cleaned. I'll call you when it's ready."

They were both aware that this meant a continuation of their relationship.

"Well, all right. Thank you," he said awkwardly. They were downstairs, in front of the door.

She was inches away from him. "Well, good-bye then."

He turned, in despair, peering outside at the empty, impersonal street that rose up to swallow him. But then he turned and caught her around the waist, his lips finding hers. "Oh, dear God, I love you so much," he whispered.

"Can you, after everything I've told you?"

"Did you really think anything else? You are so brave and wise and good! How could I help it? But I have no right. I can't offer you anything." He stepped away from her, his back against the door, his head lowered in defeat.

She reached out to him, putting her arms around his neck, pulling his lips down to hers. They felt themselves filled with an unbearable joy, a happiness that swelled so large they felt they could not contain it, that they would burst. It was totally new and strange, a happiness that neither had ever known before. Then spontaneously, they pulled apart and looked at each other hard, remembering that he was to be a priest, and that she was a married woman of a different, irreconcilable faith. They forgot who they really were, and remembered only the social labels, and the labels made it impossible. And all the joy they felt turned rapidly to despair.

"It's impossible," she told him.

"Utterly hopeless," he agreed, reaching out to her and hugging her to him for dear life.

"We must never see each other again. I don't think I could stand it."

"Yes, yes, you're right." He shook his head in agreement, feeling as if she had torn into his stomach with a scalpel.

"Nor call either. I can't stand it, waiting for the calls."

"Nor call either," he repeated in a hopeless, dazed way, his face still tingling from the touch of her hair on his cheek.

They felt themselves slowly parting, their flesh becoming cold and separate again.

"Good-bye, David," she said softly, holding out her hand.

He took it in both of his and kissed the palm.

"Good-bye, Batsheva."

Chapter twenty-one

"Forgive me, Father, for I have sinned." Father Paul Craven looked up, recognizing the voice. It was one of his most promising novitiates, a student of rare brilliance. "Speak, my son."

"I question my ministry. I question my faith, my future as a priest."

Father Craven, who had heard so many things in the dark of his confessional, nevertheless found himself shocked. He, of all his students? He had pinned so many hopes upon David. He would make a wonderful theologian, a sensitive and caring parish priest . . . "What has caused you to question your calling, my son?"

"I have found love and question the Church's answers."

"The love of a woman?" He held back a sigh. It was the wall for novitiates, the way athletes, driven beyond their strength, encounter that wall of fatigue, of despair. It happened to almost every one of them, if they were normal. It was the critical hurdle. What worried him more was the intimation of a fundamental loss of faith, to which there was no antidote.

"Not just a woman. A child, too. A family. She is a woman of a different faith. A Jew. She is a married woman who has run away from her husband, a man who was very cruel to her. My intentions, at least at first, were pure. I was asked to help her and intended to reach out to her in Christ's name. But I found myself doubting she needed help or forgiveness. Her own faith is so strong."

Father Craven threaded his fingers together carefully. "And this has caused you to question your faith, your calling?"

"I am so confused, confused. I feel small and unworthy. She does not know Christ, and yet her faith is so strong, so deep. I don't understand it. I have doubts in my heart that betray the Church. I have reached out to a woman whom I cannot offer anything honorable. I have questioned my worthiness," the voice paused for a moment, lowering in shame, "the foundations of my love and obedience to Christ and to the Church."

"All these are very grievous sins, my son." There was real sorrow and disappointment in the old priest. A sense of deep personal failure. "But God is merciful and understands human weakness. He tests all of his servants, the way he tested Abraham by asking him to sacrifice his firstborn son, as you are being tested now." Then he looked up sharply as another thought occurred to him. "Have you committed adultery?"

"No, Father. But this is more to the woman's credit than to mine. She has sent me away. I did not, I do not, want to go. I want to be with her. I think of her constantly."

The priest felt himself relax. Not as bad as it could be, Father Craven thought, his fingers weaving in and out as his crafty mind sought an answer. "So, even if you were to leave the Church, she could still not marry you since her own faith forbids it, not to mention her own still-unbroken marriage vows?"

"That is true, Father."

Father Craven's generous heart went out to the terrible pain he heard in the young man's voice. Yet, he could not help feeling relieved. He proceeded cautiously. "And can you not convince her to divorce and accept the Church?"

"As I told you, Father, her own faith is very strong, stronger I'm afraid than my own. It has nourished her through terrible hardships, taken her back from the brink of death. To ask her to abandon it would be like asking her to destroy herself."

"Do you mean to say that asking her to accept Christ, to accept her only eternal salvation, would be an evil in your eyes?" he said coldly.

"I told you, Father, I am confused. But that is how it seems to me now," came the honest reply.

"Pray to Jesus Christ our Lord to grant you wisdom, to strengthen the weak fabric of your faith, my son," he began sternly. Then, remembering something of the agony of doubt of his own novitiacy, he softened. "Our Savior sends trials to each of us, to test our love. Who of us hasn't felt the sharp pain of doubt over our vocation? Pray that you may yet overcome these obstacles and bind yourself to the Church. I will pray for you in your struggle."

"Do you recall one of the novitiates in your theology class, David Hope?" Father Craven asked Father Gerhart over lunch.

"Fine young man. He'll prove a treasure to the Church," Father Gerhart said, shaking his large, graying head emphatically and cutting his meat. He was a big man with a ruddy complexion and a robust appetite. He had a reputation for handling problems with novitiates head-on with both sleeves rolled up. Sometimes this approach was quite disastrous, while at others his shock tactics proved more effective than delicate, subtle reasoning. Taking all this into consideration, Father Craven continued the conversation somewhat hesitantly.

"Well, I'm afraid we might be losing him."

Father Gerhart put down his knife and fork deliberately

and folded his arms across his chest. "We certainly can't afford to lose any more novitiates, especially someone of David Hope's caliber. He is my star pupil, with a mind so sharp, so retentive. A rare intelligence. Gives me the devil of a time in class, keeps me on my toes. My old answers just aren't good enough for him." He shook his head, looking down into his plate thoughtfully. Then he looked up with narrowed eyes. "And what's at the bottom of it, Paul?"

"I'm not at liberty to say. But I would be grateful if you could perhaps find a way of having him leave here for a while. I think a change of place would be very helpful to him at this stage."

"I understand completely. Rome, America, Jerusalem . . . round out his studies, give him time to think." Father Gerhart picked up his fork and knife once again, cutting vigorously. "Excellent. We mustn't give up without a fight nowadays, eh, Craven?"

Chapter twenty-two

As is often the case with human beings who find themselves grated raw against the sharp, merciless ironies of life, Batsheva thrashed around looking for someone to blame her troubles on so as to lighten her own load of guilt. And finding that it was no comfort to blame anything as amorphous as fate or God, she settled on Elizabeth. After all, she told herself almost convincingly, wasn't it Elizabeth who had introduced them? If only she had never met him, if only the clock could be turned back! But now, if she closed her eyes, his blue ones stared lovingly at her, as if etched indelibly on the back of her lids. If she walked in the street and saw someone tall and dark-haired, her heart began to knock angrily in her chest. And each time she gave Akiva a bath, she could almost feel the presence of his lean, beautiful body inches away from her in the hot, moist room. It was physically painful, exhausting, and draining.

And so, the way one eases a sharp physical pain by pinching another part of one's body so as to distribute the concentrated agony, Batsheva began to think back and remember how Elizabeth had not been there when Isaac had proposed and she had desperately needed to talk to her. She began to blame her for that and for not taking her back to England with her when she came to visit, painting over the rational objections of her fair mind with the black brush of her despair.

She became distant and cold when Elizabeth called. She made up excuses to avoid going to see her or having her visit until Elizabeth finally showed up at the door, her face lined with worry, and begged her: "What's the matter, what's going on?"

Batsheva gave her a bright, false smile and said, "Nothing. Why should you think anything is wrong? I'm just busy, that's all." And she bustled around, ignoring her, making her feel in the way until Elizabeth finally just walked out, deeply hurt.

Having no father confessor, and no close friend who could appreciate the awful hopelessness of her situation except Elizabeth, Batsheva condemned herself to suffer in terrible silence, until all her anger dissolved and turned inward, settling into a dark, heavy depression. She would lie in bed deep into the morning, her head turned to the window, studying the clouds, taking meaning and omens from their random movements. There, she told herself, as a soft white one was overtaken by a dark gray one that moved like smoke, muddying the sky. There it is, the darkness overtaking the light!

Her body felt heavy, leaden. She could find no reason to lift herself out of bed each day except for Akiva's care. Her days centered around his meals, his bath, reading to him. She did her work lifelessly. In the evenings, she sometimes forced herself to accept invitations for parties she knew would be full of people she didn't like or respect—immoral, careless people. She would go and drink and parry the foolish come-ons of the men, dancing with them, laughing at their sordid double entendres, then leaving them hot and chagrined outside her locked door. They disgusted her. All men did, she told herself. She would live like a nun, like

Jephte's daughter, sent away in her virginity into the wilderness to live in isolation, loved by no man. Nothing, nothing helped. She felt herself motionless, in a state of suspended animation. Something must happen, she thought. It must.

She had not seen him or heard from him in two weeks.

"She refuses to talk to me." Elizabeth flung herself into a chair, holding her head in her hands. "She's like a stone wall. What have I done? If I could only know that!"

"You know what you've done, dearest," Ian said dryly.

She couldn't stand it when he did this to her, taking away her little defenses, making her stand there nakedly, all her petty sins exposed. He was right, of course. She knew it was David. "But I only thought it would be amusing for her . . ." she said weakly, almost begging, hating herself.

He sat down on the arm of the chair and pulled her toward him so that her back rested up against his chest. She leaned against him gratefully. He folded his arms over hers and rested his cheek against her hair.

"Why do I do such terrible things, Ian?"

"Because deep down in your heart you want a happy ending—but an ending that is happy by your standards. You can't believe that Batsheva can be happy without a man, or that David could be happy as a priest. You're a meddler, a dear, unprincipled, kind-hearted meddler."

"A yenta, as Batsheva would say," she said morosely.

He hugged her and smiled. "Precisely, my dear love."

She turned around and looked into his face. "Ian, I love Batsheva like a sister. She is making herself sick over this. You should see her face—pale, almost transparent, and those eyes are . . . are . . ."

"Don't tell me. I've seen them." He shook his head.

"You've seen Batsheva?"

"No. I've seen David. It's awful. He's in total chaos. He's going . . . or being sent . . . away, you know."

She sat up straight. "No, I didn't. My God, poor Batsie. Oh, Ian, what have I done!? What's to be done?"

He shook his head, exasperated. "You'll never change. What makes you think you have to do anything? What makes you think you're involved at all?"

"But of course I am! I started this whole thing, thinking it would be an amusing diversion. I think I did it for myself, most of all. Just to see the two opposites clash . . ."

"Tut, tut, tut, there you go again, dearest. Honesty, honesty."

"Uffff. You never leave me alone!" She jumped up and paced the floor. "Yes, all right. I thought they would be perfect for each other. And they are. Perfect. They are madly in love. What's wrong with that?" She saw that look on his face of dry amusement. He was a hard teacher. She clasped her hands together, prayerlike, and rested her lips on them. "They should be together. They must overcome the obstacles."

"Why don't you call up the pope and ask him if he's interested in dating Mother Theresa?"

She wouldn't be deflected. "When is he leaving?"

"On Monday. He'll be gone six months."

"That gives us the weekend." She tapped her forefinger against her lips.

His mouth dropped open. "The weekend for what?"

"Why, to get them together of course."

"You know, you're . . . you're . . . incorrigible, really hopeless! What possible good could come of that?"

She walked over to him slowly and put her arms around his waist, resting her face on the soft, worn wool of his comfortable sweater. "I feel it's right. I can't explain it. It would be wrong for him to leave without their seeing each other again. It would be too awful for them both. Please, Ian, trust me!" She looked up at him and he threw up his hands and looked up at heaven.

"I am in love with a madwoman," he shouted.

"And you weren't good enough for me, remember?" She dug her finger into his armpit, tickling him. He squirmed, like a big, confused, sweet-natured child, unsure whether to laugh or cry.

"The Church isn't going to let him go so fast," Ian pointed out. "Novitiates, especially of David's ilk, are rarer than unicorns, you know. They're dropping out like flies. And it's going to be difficult for her, as a corpse of over a year, to get a divorce from the patriarch." Now he was pacing the floor. He had never wanted David to be a priest either.

"And there's no reason she should accept an invitation from me now. She isn't even on speaking terms with me," she added glumly.

"And I'm not even sure David is free this weekend, or if he'd come if he was."

"It's totally hopeless," they finally agreed, hugging each other. Their eyes met in perfect understanding: "So let's do it."

"I know you're furious at me." Elizabeth spoke quickly, afraid she'd hang up the phone. "But please come. The countryside is so beautiful this time of year. Akiva will love it, and Ian asked especially that you come. His father will be there and his mother and some friends. Maybe David, maybe not. Please, Batsie!"

"Why are you doing this to me? Don't you know how ill I am? I can't!" She dropped the phone back into its holder as if it had suddenly turned into a black, live thing. It rang immediately.

"I'll pick you up on Thursday morning. He's going away for a long time," Elizabeth's disembodied voice said quickly and then she hung up before Batsheva could do it for her.

Chapter twenty-three

Batsheva filled Thursday with appointments for client sittings. And then she canceled them. She took all the clean clothes out of the closets and washed them and ironed them. She rearranged all the cans in the kitchen cupboards. She cleaned out the refrigerator and scrubbed the inside of the stove, in a panic of nervous energy. Ten times she packed her weekend case and ten times she unpacked it.

Thursday dawned bright and clear and warm. A perfect spring day. One could almost see the tender new grass shooting up through the soft, moist earth, the light-green buds lifting their heads toward the radiant sun. She put her head outside her bedroom window and breathed in the fresh, fragrant, sun-warmed air. Everything seemed to her to be softening and sending out new shoots, sure they would be nourished and allowed to grow strong and beautiful. On such a day, she thought, it was so good to be alive. Anything was possible on such a day, she told herself, packing again. She packed light summer dresses in bright flower colors. She packed her Sabbath candles and a bottle of kosher wine for Friday-night *kiddush*.

The wind blew through her hair and Akiva squealed in delight in the back seat as the convertible tore up the highway. There was still a strained silence between the two women. Elizabeth, feeling the full weight of her accumulated guilt, did not presume on the tentative reconciliation Batsheva's presence next to her represented. Who knew why she had agreed to come? She wisely decided not to probe, but to make believe everything was all right.

Batsheva leaned back, enjoying the fresh air, the freedom of rushing swift and windlike through the countryside in the little topless sports car. Just being out in the open, after so many days holed up in her bedroom, made her feel that something positive was already happening. She looked gratefully at Elizabeth and reached out impulsively to pat her hand.

"Thank you."

"For what, Batsie?"

She had meant just for the ride, the excursion, but now she remembered that she would have never come to London, never have met David, without Elizabeth. She gave it a moment's swift thought—never to have met David! "For everything, Liz. For opening up my life. For letting me experience it. For David."

Elizabeth let out a deep sigh and glanced at her cautiously. "Do you mean it? Even after everything that's happened? All this misery?"

"When I was in the last year of high school, I remember we had a discussion on whether or not it was worthwhile for man to have been created at all, since he is bound to sin, to fail, and to be punished. At that time, I thought it would have been better never to have been born. But I don't think that anymore." She returned Elizabeth's smile. "I'm glad I'm alive. I'm glad I've met him. I used to think that love was a fiction. A lie. But it isn't, Liz. I know that now."

"But I feel terrible, seeing you suffer like this!"

"I can't see any possibility of peace of mind ahead, that's true. I can see hopelessness, pain for both of us. But I can also see happiness, such incredible happiness, if only things were different."

"Is it really so impossible?" Elizabeth asked softly.

Batsheva didn't answer, but gave her a look filled with terrible despair, terrible hope. But then an idea, almost a joke, occurred to her and she was glad to say it, to lighten the atmosphere. "There is a saying that since God created the world, He has lots of time on His hands and He spends it playing matchmaker." It was not such a joke, she thought. It really was God, His laws, the love they both felt for Him, standing in their way. "He will either bring us together or keep us apart. It is in His hands." And once she had said this, she felt her heart grow lighter. She had given the whole package of insoluble puzzles back to God. She must stop trying, straining for the answers. She would be quiet now and wait.

It was a long drive, but a beautiful one. Still, they were both grateful to enter the big iron gates of the Hope mansion. It was not as large or as ostentatious as Robin's house, Batsheva thought, or as her own back in California. But it was far more homey and comfy looking. A servant opened the front door and took their luggage. Batsheva looked around, delighted. It had such a warm, elegant charm. There were period antiques, fine paintings, and fresh flowers everywhere.

Ian came bounding down the stairs and Batsheva watched his eyes fill with excitement and tenderness as he caught sight of Elizabeth's curly blond head.

"Liz," he called.

She watched Elizabeth turn and saw her eyes widen with

serious pleasure, her face light up with uncomplicated happiness. Batsheva felt her stomach ache with unworthy envy.

"Batsheva, I'm so glad you could make it." Ian's voice reached out to her, opening the circle of warmth and friendship to let her in. She took his hand gratefully. "Come out to the garden, both of you. My parents are waiting for us. We'll have some tea."

David's father, she thought, looking into the bright familiar blue eyes of the tall man who got up and grasped her hand firmly. But he was so light! Blond like Ian. Ian's mother too, was light-haired, light-complexioned. She saw nothing of David in the woman. David was not there. The realization hit her like a stone full in the soft center of her body. It was not so easy to give problems back to God, she thought wryly.

They drank hot tea out of translucent bone china with a delicate rim of gold. The table was generously full of delicious little cakes and sandwiches and puddings. Batsheva drank the tea and gave Akiva some cookies she had brought with her, amusing and distracting herself by watching Akiva stuff the cookies into his mouth. But then when everyone laughed at him, he became shy and came to her shamefacedly, laying his head in her lap. She stroked his hair gently, feeling some of his discomfort at being the center of attention. She was relieved when the conversation shifted to Elizabeth. Batsheva remembered that this was her friend's first meeting with Ian's parents. From the uncharacteristic way that Elizabeth was nervously answering the friendly questions, she realized, too, how serious an occasion her friend considered this to be. She said a silent prayer for her, but was relieved that this was the case, hoping it would mean that no one would bother much about her and she would be able to deal with whatever feelings were in store for her this weekend without constant scrutiny.

And as she watched Elizabeth, she did not feel the eyes that were carefully inspecting her, inch by inch. She did not realize that Ian's parents were extremely aware of who she was, and terribly concerned about the turmoil she was bringing David. Ian had not gone into detail, but they knew she was a married woman of a different faith.

Lord Hope, who was as concerned as his wife about this puzzling, and—to all appearances—unsavory relationship, was shocked at the reality of the girl. He scrutinized her carefully from under half-closed lids even as he bantered with Elizabeth. He had expected to find someone coarse and grasping. Instead, he found her refined, sensitive, and shy. Her long, slender body was as graceful as a dancer's and her face radiated an incredible spiritual and physical beauty. There was something familiar about this girl, something he had experienced once long ago . . . he could not put his finger on it.

"Come with me, my dear," he said in an offhand way when they rose from the table, tucking her arm comfortably under his. "I'll give you a guided tour."

Batsheva noticed the deliberateness of his steps, which belied the impression of a random stroll through the house. He led her through the lovely high-ceilinged living room, the large, light and flower-filled dining room, opening a side door that led into what must have been a music room. It was a romantic room, she thought, admiring the old, polished upright piano with its brass candlestick holders. She was about to say so when he stopped and looked up at a large oil painting above the fireplace mantel. He glanced at her and back again, as if making some kind of comparison. His eyes flashed as if with a sudden, remembered passion. Her eyes followed his, confused. She studied the painting carefully. It was a young woman, with black hair and eyes and a dark complexion that was certainly not English. She admired the skill of the painter who had captured the singular expression—neither smiling nor stern, but questioning. Her eyes shone with a clear, fine intelligence, but not the kind that can turn to cunning even if forced to. They were wide with a trusting simplicity that seemed to leave her defenseless against deliberate cruelty of any kind.

The rich, red fabric of her dress fell over her long, slender fingers, which held a book. Batsheva strained to see what kind, but the letters were indecipherable. Then her eyes were drawn to the curious jewelry that hung around the woman's neck. Was it a cross? She peered closer, straining. Then she smiled to herself, a sad, wry smile, acknowledging the manipulations of one's heart on one's mind as the little brush-stroke of gold suddenly transformed into a *hamsah*—the little golden hand worn by the Sephardic Jews of Israel, as common a Jewish good-luck charm as the Star of David.

"Something amusing, my dear?"

"No, nothing." She felt foolish and embarrassed. This kind of thing had happened to her numerous times: seeing the back of her father's proud gray head on strangers in the street; seeing signs in the distance that she could have sworn were in Hebrew. It was, she supposed, no different from a man dying of thirst in the desert who conjures up mirages of waterfalls.

"Who is she?" Batsheva asked quickly, wanting to change the subject.

"Gracia Mendes Cresas, my first wife and David's mother. Ah, you didn't know David and Ian are half-brothers?"

She shook her head, trying to hide her shock. "I wondered at his dark complexion, his black hair, after meeting you and Lady Hope. Now I understand. What happened to her, David's mother, I mean?"

"She died in childbirth." His clear, calm brow furrowed. "She was a very special, very lovely woman, with a rare mind. David takes after her so much." He gave her another one of his strange, searching looks. "Forgive me, my dear, for hurrying you off into here. It's just that I wanted to be sure who you reminded me of."

Startled, she looked up at the picture again. There was no physical resemblance between them, yet he was right. Their faces were suffused with the same elusive spirit. Something of what stared back at her from the mirror looked back at her from the portrait. They could have been distant cousins, or members of the same extended family.

"She was from a very old, noble Spanish family. She came to England as a refugee from Germany during the war. She had been a student and then a teacher at the University of Heidelberg and had even managed at her very young age to complete a remarkable book on philosophy. Her death was so sudden." His voice thickened. "David is so like her. The coloring, but also the intelligence, the reflectiveness."

He turned to her, his friendly face full of unhidden discomfort. "I must be honest. My wife and I are both very upset by his relationship with you."

She felt the blood rush to her face. "David and I have no relationship. I am not free to have any relationship with him, or any man, as a married woman, an Orthodox Jew."

Lord Hope was taken aback by the simplicity and directness of the honest answer, which earned his immediate respect. He felt confused as the scenario he had built up in his mind of the conniving, exotic stranger suddenly dissolved, leaving only blank pages in its place. "But surely," he protested, "you must know David was seriously considering leaving the priesthood because of you!"

She looked at him wearily. "You don't, you can't, understand. I love David, and I believe he loves me. But I asked him to go away some weeks ago because we have no future. I haven't heard from him since and I know nothing of his feelings or plans. I have no right to."

"But surely you've considered divorce, conversion . . ."

She winced. "It has taken me a long time to recognize who I am and to come to terms with it. We can't do anything, become anything, that we want. There are certain limitations, boundaries, to each of us. Going beyond them is like jumping out of the window or under a train—it just destroys the self. To change my faith, I would have to deny and betray everything I believe in. It would kill me. It would kill whatever love I have." This, too, surprised him and again he felt an unexpected surge of liking and respect for her.

"I have to be honest, too. I never wanted David to be a priest, but neither did I want to see him involved in a sordid, demoralizing affair, or to throw his future away on a . . ."

"Designing Jewess," she interrupted coldly, turning away, suddenly sick with anger and mortification. Pernells, everywhere. And she had liked this man so much.

He took her shoulders gently and turned her around. "You have no idea how incredibly mistaken you are . . ." He seemed to want to say more, but stopped himself, glancing up painfully at the portrait. He took a deep breath. "I was going to say, on a whim. And having met you, I know now that, too, was wrong."

The stiff resistance in her body relaxed. She felt comforted. "Forgive me. I'm so sick of people's prejudices that I just anticipate them."

"No, we aren't prejudiced. But we are very concerned about the damage this is doing him and—as I can now see—doing you. He will tell you himself, no doubt, when he comes home."

Her heart skipped a beat. "You expect him to come, then?"

He hesitated. "He knows that you're here. I expected him to come *because* of that. But now that I've spoken to you, I hardly know what to think." He watched a visible dejection contort her features and his natural good-heartedness and hospitality asserted themselves. "Now, no more of this depressing talk! What a terrible host I am! My dear, I've promised you a tour and you shall have it!" He tucked her arm under his, patting it with real affection.

The tour confirmed her first impressions: It was an elegant, charming home of real quality. She was delighted with the guest room, all delicate lilac flowers from the wallpaper to the ruffled bedspread. There were fresh lilacs in a vase on a dressing table that was covered with little crystal decanters of perfume. From the bay windows, one could see miles down the flat meadows and newly plowed farmlands. She looked out anxiously into the distance, feeling the familiar straining, the terrible anticipation, grip her heart like a vise.

"Ima, come see," Akiva called from the room. It was filled with wonderful old toys—painted toy soldiers, rocking horses. It would keep him busy for days. She gave him dinner and put him to sleep, then began dressing for dinner herself. She put on a gray-silk dress she had bought because it reminded her of the one, long ago, that had made the shopgirls on Rodeo Drive stare in envy. It was simple and graceful and served as a background, setting into fine relief the sheen of her lovely skin, the light, incredible color of her beautiful eyes.

She looked into the mirror. She had changed so since the first time she had worn this kind of dress. She no longer felt there was any power in her beauty, or joy in her womanliness. Instead, there was a recognition of limitations, an acceptance of gifts. Her beauty could bring her good things and bad, as could her name and lineage. What she made of her life, finally, would be affected by these things, but not decided by them. She had control over the raw materials that made up her life and not the opposite. But then, how little control any of us has in this life, she thought. It is just an illusion, the careful plans we make, the choices we agonize over. A drunk driver, a certain man at a certain party one happens to go to, and it is all over, for better or for worse. Elizabeth knocked.

"Come in."

She opened the door. Her face was flushed with excitement and her eyes sparkled. "Hug me, hug me! Yes, I think it's going to happen! He's asked me!"

The two friends hugged each other, then stepped apart. Batsheva's eyes were wet. "I'm so happy for you, Liz. He's a wonderful man." She was happy she could say this sincerely, without reservation. Her anger at Elizabeth had blown away like a dark cloud, leaving no trace.

"Oh, my dear. Don't cry, Batsie. It will all work out. You'll see, you'll see," Elizabeth crooned softly, feeling her own eyes moisten. They smiled tearfully at one another, sharing the happiness and the pain, grasping each other's fingers tightly.

The table sparkled with crystal glasses, large ones for water, smaller ones for wine. Fresh roses, lilies, and chrysanthemums from the garden had been arranged by some graceful artistic hand and eye. The colors were all soft and muted. When the large candlelabra was lit, the light bounced off an overhead chandelier, breaking into a thousand prisms that danced along the wall, casting rainbows over them all. The table was set for six. So they were expecting him, she thought.

The clock ticked away. "Shall I begin serving now, sir?" a servant asked diffidently.

Lord Hope looked up irritably at the clock, as if it were somehow to blame, then at his wife. "I suppose you'd better, Gretchen. It doesn't look like he's coming." Lady Hope glanced at Batsheva and sighed. She was a plump, kind, generous woman, a romantic fond of novels and love stories. And now, after her husband's talk with the girl, she was prepared to change the plot—as her mind insisted on putting all life's events into a tidy, sequential, and familiar format—into the story of star-crossed lovers, and not, as she had originally supposed, that of a scheming, immoral married woman out to seduce an innocent, guileless novitiate. As such, she was now prepared to champion them against all odds. She actually had much in common with Elizabeth. She, too, insisted all endings be happy. She put her arm around Batsheva. "He'll turn up, my dear, never you fear. And we must not forget, we still have things to celebrate." She clasped her hands together, beaming at Elizabeth and Ian. Such a lovely girl, Elizabeth, she thought. "It will be so nice to have a house full of women, instead of just you awful boys."

"We're not so bad, Mum," Ian protested, giving his mother a fond bear hug.

"You'll absolutely crush me, you careless boy." She made a shooing motion with her plump, motherly hands, then smoothed down her disordered dress. Her face beamed.

It was all so perfect. The lovely meal, the wonderful, accepting parents, Elizabeth and Ian united happily. And there she was, again unable to eat anything, unable to drink the wine, sitting next to an empty seat. Why did I come, why? she asked herself bitterly. I am doomed to be an outsider forever, always pressing my face up against the glass, looking in at love, at friendship, at family, unable to partake. Like a ghost. Perhaps, she thought darkly, perhaps it would have been better to have finished with it that day in Tel Aviv.

"Now, Batsheva, you are not to worry, dear. Ian's brought all your special foods from a restaurant in Golder's Green. It's all—what's that word?" Lady Hope wrinkled her nose in concentration, then smiled, remembering. "Yes, it's all kosher. And yes, this is a brand-new set of dishes and silverware, so please, don't worry. You may eat whatever you like." She beamed. It was all so exotic and romantic, she thought. She just loved being in the middle of it.

"I . . . I . . . just don't know what to say, how to thank you for all your trouble." Batsheva looked shyly around the table and found such acceptance and warmth in the kind eyes of the parents, the familiar eyes of Elizabeth and Ian. They suddenly seemed like family to her. She wanted to cry.

"Now, what is this?" Lord Hope looked down at the first course. "Some kind of stuffed fish? And this red stuff . . ."

"No! Lord Hope, it's horseradish, you're supposed to take only a tiny bit, it's very hot . . ." Batsheva said anxiously as she saw him pile the hot spice on his plate like a vegetable. But it was too late, he had already put a large spoonful into his mouth.

"My Lord!" His face reddened and he reached out blindly for the water, gulping it down. They all watched him anxiously. He looked around the table. "You know, that was quite good!" The laughter rang out, loud and unrestrained so that no one heard the door open.

"David," she whispered, afraid saying it out loud would break open the dream and he would disappear. But other voices, feeling no such compunction, called out loudly and heartily, giving credence and solid reality to the vision.

"David!"

"My dear boy!"

"You've had us worried to death!"

"Sit down, sit down and taste this wonderful red stuff!"

She was almost afraid to look at him after all these weeks. Perhaps he had changed. Perhaps she would not find in his eyes the look that had haunted her and filled her nights and days with restless, inconsolable longing.

"My dear," he looked down at her and raised her chin. His touch went through her like a flame. His face was terrible and exquisite. He seemed to have aged and paled, the way people do after a long, painful illness. But the eyes that met hers, through which she seemed to glimpse his soul, were full of beatitude, a reflection of her own.

* * *

What strange creatures we humans are, David thought. If someone were to walk in now and tell me I must leave this chair in this house next to this woman, I would fight him, I would be prepared almost to kill him. And yet, in three days I will leave her, perhaps forever, of my own free will. Was it possible? How had he made such plans? He thought of Father Craven, of Father Gerhart, and he remembered the conversations long into the night, the confusion and his final capitulation. Now, sitting next to her, it seemed like a bad dream. Did she want him to go? Did she know? He glanced at her flushed face bent over her plate. He was almost afraid to look at her.

"Forgive me for coming!" he whispered.

She couldn't speak a word, her heart was so full.

"You aren't angry that I did?"

She shook her head and her eyes spilled over with hot tears of love and gratitude. How can you say it, or even think it! they said. But he saw only the heat. Passion? Anger? His heart beat faster. There was no way to rush the meal. There were toasts, and good wishes, and questions and jokes and stories. It became intolerable to him.

"Excuse us." He got up abruptly, taking Batsheva's hand. He led her away down the dark garden path where the scent of jasmine and honeysuckle mingled with that of the newly budding roses. He had meant to question her, to demand explanations, to plead. But seeing her bent head, her flushed, lovely face, he went into a kind of trance, forgetting everything. He led her to a garden bench. "Are you cold?" He didn't wait for an answer, taking off his coat and draping it over her soft, vulnerable shoulders. His fingertips lightly touched the delicate silkiness of her gray dress, which shone like liquid silver in the moonlight. Her eyes, too, seemed to glitter with the cold light of the moon, mysterious and unapproachable. What did you expect? he told himself, bitter with disappointment. And he understood again why he had said yes to Father Craven and Father Gerhart. He had made plans to leave her, to forget. "I am so sorry for coming, for making you so unhappy."

She turned to him and he saw the shock that compressed her nose and mouth and widened her eyes. "Unhappy? How can you . . . ? I am like a starving man who has been fed. He may be freezing, his clothes may be thin and torn, he may be humiliated, but he is not unhappy. He has been given food to live for one more day." She touched his face tentatively, all the longing held back. "David." She rested her cheek against his, making no demands, asking for no solutions. She felt like Noah's dove who, having flown the world over the deep floodwaters in a hopeless search for shelter, finally found its way back to the safe warmth of the Ark.

There is a strange hope that comes to people who have battled hopelessness and despair: the terminally ill, the childless, the failures. It is a hope that defies the mind and refuses to listen to rational arguments. It sprouts from barren soil and, denied all nourishment, continues foolishly to grow. It came now to David and Batsheva as they sat holding each other silently in the dark moonlight, spinning impossible plans. She would divorce Isaac and they would marry, and the identity and religion of each would be preserved. Yes, there in the moonlight, close together, it seemed so simple; why hadn't they thought of it before? It was so clear that it must be done that way, so easy. David felt the energy flow through him. If only he could settle the whole thing now! This moment!

He woke early and went into the garden to read and watch the day break, an old childish habit. He was surprised to find his father already up.

"It is all settled. We will marry."

His father looked at him, profoundly startled, but said only "ah," in a strange, noncommittal way.

But David, caught up in his wonderful vision, hardly noticed. He paced around with restless energy. "We were just not thinking straight. It is all so simple really. She will divorce and we will each keep our own faith."

"And the child?" his father asked mildly.

"Akiva? He is her child, he will be raised in her faith. Really, so many other couples have managed this arrangement, we were foolish to make such a story of it." But in his heart he began to see the obstacles rise again, like black, impenetrable monoliths.

"And what if you have other children, what of them? And what about all the holidays, the rituals, you must do together, as a family?"

"Really, Father. We can work it out, I know we can. Please!" He realized that he was directing his anger at the questioner when it was the insoluble questions that he wished to crush and destroy. What would happen if they had another child? Belief could not be shared and divided. One believed or one did not, the way one loved or one did not.

"Oh, you might pull it off for a while. But I'll tell you what will happen. You will grow apart a centimeter at a time until there is a mountain between you that you cannot cross." His eyes looked far off, remembering. "And don't think she will be allowed to raise her son if she marries you. You don't think the rabbis will allow that, any more than a priest would. They will give him back to his father to raise, probably as the price for agreeing to the divorce."

They had not considered that. It was unthinkable. He remembered her loving hands washing Akiva's small, precious body. He bent his head low in pain and felt his father's arm around him.

"I love her so, Father. What should I do?"

"I don't know. Nothing is simple. We are forced into these hard, absurd, and incomprehensible choices. But that's life, isn't it? No rhyme or reason." He studied the dark, handsome face of his eldest son. "You are so like your mother. If only she were here now, I'm so sure she could help you."

"What? Why do you say that?" They so seldom spoke of her.

"She would, perhaps, tell you . . ." He bit his lip as if preventing himself from saying any more.

"I can't live without Batsheva." He gripped his head in despair and sat quietly for a few moments, not moving. And when he finally lifted his head, his face was full of a terrible, calm light. "But I would rather do that than hurt her, or put her in a position where she would agree to hurt herself out of her love for me. I must go away," he said definitely. "I must leave, now, before it is too late."

"David, you're being rash! Give yourself time to think about it!"

"No! That's just the point, I can't think about it, because if I do I'll never have the courage to go through with it! I am nothing special. Just a weak, selfish human being and every ounce of who I am wants her, needs her! I must not allow her to even consider such a sacrifice for me. Father, say good-bye for me? To her, to Mother and Ian and Elizabeth. I will write, tell her that?"

The older man squeezed his son's broad, muscular shoulders. He was so incredibly proud of this boy. If only I could take the pain onto my own shoulders, he thought, the sharp despair on David's face cutting deep into his own flesh. He wanted so much to stop him, but knew he couldn't. "Well, Rome is not that far away. You will fly down a few times, won't you?"

He gave his father a curious look. "But I am not going to Rome, Father. I am going to the Pontifical Biblical Institute in Jerusalem."

He packed his things quickly and sat down to write a note. He read it over and tore it up and wrote out another one. It was wrong, wrong. It didn't say a hundredth of what he felt, didn't explain a thousandth of what needed to be explained. But he put it in an envelope and addressed it to her. He could not think. I must run away, was all that went through his head. I must get out of here, away from her, now while I still have courage.

He passed her door, which was slightly ajar, and heard the fall of blocks from Akiva's quiet, industrious playing and the child's untroubled laughter. How he loved that little boy, he thought. That beautiful son that he already considered his own dear child. His eyes followed a shaft of light that lit up the still-dark hall and glimpsed a ruffled bedspread and the dark wave of hair spread out upon the pillow. He laid the note down gently and then leaned against the doorframe, pressing his lips to the cold, polished wood.

Chapter twenty-four

"Cigarette?" Jean-Paul leaned toward him politely, holding out a package.

David shook his head. The man, the only other novitiate from the seminary who would be traveling with him, was vaguely familiar to him, but basically a stranger. Still, he was grateful for the company and for the real voice that stilled the insistent, strident inner voice that had been with him since he left Batsheva's bedroom door. "Call her," the voice insisted loudly. "How can you leave her? It is the mistake of your life!" it proclaimed. "Call her, call her, call her . . ." Once or twice he had actually gotten as far as the telephone, but had dropped it with trembling fingers back into the cradle before the number connected.

"I should stop," Jean-Paul sighed, taking a deep puff. "Ah, excuse me, do you mind?"

David shook his head with a faint smile that the other man returned with a slight touch of irony.

"I hope you will forgive me, brother, but you look as if

you've just come out of a confessional without absolution. Or is it just plane travel that depresses you?"

"No, just tired."

"I understand that. I haven't slept a wink for at least two days. Excitement, eh? What do you think we will find there?" He didn't wait for an answer, his question arousing his own imagination. "Shepherds and shepherdesses with long wooden staffs climbing the hillsides . . ."

David listened to the histrionic recital with disguised amusement and felt his eyelids grow heavy, until the voice survived just as a faint, slightly intrusive buzz like the impersonal noise of the airplane as it sped through the skies, putting incomprehensible distance between him and the only real connection to life he had ever known. He was so tired and defeated. He had not really slept since Friday morning. Each time he had drowsed off he suddenly became terrified of giving in to sleep, and he fought to keep control. But it was not only that. In the last month, he thought, he had gone through an incredible number of transformations. He had been at the edge of losing faith completely in his vocation. Only the long, difficult conversations with Father Craven and Father Gerhart had brought him back, and then only to the point of agreeing to put off any decision, to go away where he might look with a clear and undistracted gaze into his deepest soul.

And then had come Ian's phone call and the invitation to join Elizabeth and Batsheva at the house. He had been startled and disbelieving at first. Had she really agreed to come, she who had made him promise to go away? What must it mean then, her agreement? He had racked his brain, afraid to hope, afraid he had misunderstood, and then, finally, he had been overcome with happiness. He had readied his soul to leave the Church to embrace her, for it seemed to him that she, with her simple goodness, her living, vital beauty and warmth, held all the real answers he had been seeking. With her and with the child he had come to cherish like his own, he would begin to build a real life, not the thin shadow of a life the Church offered him. For the life of a priest, it at once seemed to him, was a thin, vicarious existence. He would be kept apart from the cares, the joys and sorrows of ordinary men and women, experiencing them coldly, once removed, the way a reporter does. Even his relationship with God would be filtered through other priests, through the pope, through hundreds of years of canon law and official dogma.

And now, sitting in the plane that would take him to Jerusalem, he felt he had come full circle. He felt vanquished, as if his return to the Church had the desperate tread of the weary, battle-scarred soldier to any home that would offer him some shelter from the dangers of living. Still, he was grateful for the Church's open arms, the way it took care of everything so that he would not have to think anymore, struggle anymore. The Church would care for him and he would be its child. It would save him. All he needed to do was to believe.

The plane dipped and righted itself as the sky around it grew dark and the clouds disappeared. Below, surrounded by endless water, the lights of unknown millions blinked questioningly, as if conversing with the dark universe that covered them like a blanket. Always this feeling of dustlike insignificance overcame him in the air. His problems, his personal happiness and griefs, seemed to dwindle until he was ashamed of them, and of himself for not recognizing their ridiculous pettiness. It is the old trick of Adam, he thought. His overweening pride, his forgetfulness. One minute one did not exist, and the next one did, and then again, one did not. An endless cycle. It was only false pride that made one man believe he was any different from or better than another. There was an equality conferred by birth and death that nothing could change.

He looked around him, studying the faces of the men and women on the plane. His eyes settled on an old, white-bearded

Hassidic man deep in study, or prayer—which, he could not tell. His mouth, hidden by the beard, moved in silent speech and he stroked his beard and swayed slightly to and fro. And what was the difference between himself and such a man? he asked himself. Were they not both flesh and blood? Would they not both feel pain when they were hit, feel hungry without food and cold without clothing and shelter? He took it a step further. And if the plane should crash and their bodies should not survive, would not their souls return to their Creator and go on living? Would a Jewish soul, because it did not believe in Christ, because it believed only in one God, a God that could have no son, no immaculate intercourse with a human woman, was that soul without salvation, lost? Was it condemned, then, despite all its fineness, its purity, its faithfulness, to eternal hellfire?

He was shocked, as if he had realized this for the first time. If the answer was yes, that meant Batsheva, too. Akiva, too. And the old man who sat piously reading and praying. He, too, was damned. I don't believe that, he thought suddenly. Really, I don't believe it at all.

The first thing that he noticed when he got off the plane was the sun. Politely aloof in England, it came alarmingly close in Israel. It was almost a companion, a living presence. It seemed lower down in the sky, and its heat, pervasive and intimately close, reached almost inside of you to warm your heart, your lungs. The old man, a few passengers ahead of him going down the stairs from the plane to the waiting bus, stepped over to the side, knelt, and, putting his face flat upon the ground, kissed the dry, ancient earth. He rose up with dignity, wiping the dark grains of soil from his lips.

"Holy Land," David thought, feeling the term infused now with a new meaning.

Jean-Paul snickered. "Wonder how it tastes. I guess after

all that kosher food they served on the plane, it must be an improvement."

David did not see his companion look at him with a face full of the expectation of comradely laughter, for he was thinking: Soon I will be there. Soon I will see Jerusalem, her Jerusalem. The thought distracted him to the extent that he was hardly civil to Father Quinn, who had come to meet them and take them back to the dormitory. He hardly felt the curious glance of the father and Jean-Paul as they questioned him and he didn't reply. He was not with them, but off somewhere, hovering, waiting for the moment that the city would come into view.

The highway from the airport was flat and smooth and newly tarred. He felt somewhat disappointed at the level ride. Where were the hills she had spoken so much about? Then, gradually, the car began to climb. It went through a forest and a mountain that had been sliced in half. He examined the white-pink layers of ancient sedimentary rock. Layer after layer, generation after generation, people after people, had cherished this place, fought over it, died for it. He could feel the car straining now, putting all its mechanical strength into the steep climb, and he felt himself straining with it, almost exhausted with the effort. And then all at once it seemed to rest. He held his breath. Was he imagining it? Or could it be? A white city, purely white, nestled between hills and valleys, shining brilliant and unreal in the white gold of the afternoon sunlight. There was no majesty here. The hills were modest and low, nothing like in Switzerland, where the very height suggested frightening power. No, this was almost villagelike in its plainness and lack of pretension. The houses seemed a mere backdrop to the magnificent breadth and height of the sky. There was more heaven in the view than earth. It was just as she had said.

For some reason this thought made him happy. It was almost as if she was with him, seeing it together with him. His mood changed and he became talkative and friendly, joking with his companions. But underneath he felt he was not the same. Something was changing; doors long closed were opening up and he was fearful and enchanted at what was behind them. But he did not yet know what it all meant, where it would all lead.

In the morning there were matins and a healthy breakfast of wonderful fruits and vegetables, the best he had ever tasted. They seemed freshly picked—the oranges still bursting with the fresh, pungent perfume of the branches that had held them such a short while before, the tomatoes swelling with ripe, juicy tartness that made them a rare delicacy. Fruits of the promised land. They really were special, he thought. Then the classes began. Some were in the Pontifical Biblical Institute, a large stone building with enormous old trees behind the King David Hotel, while others were given at Hebrew University on Mount Scopus. He found himself fidgeting through classes in theology. It seemed to him the same, tired, fantastic story apologized for and made palatable to the intellect. He could find nothing worthwhile in it.

He sought a closeness to the ineffable, and yet all their efforts were to make one believe that God could be at once both Godlike and manlike. It seemed to him a terrible reduction, a road that carried him in the opposite direction from where he felt he wanted to go. Then also, he began to question the whole concept of Original Sin. How could it be that God held the child responsible for the father's sin?

The Jews, he learned, believed the opposite. Each child was born pure, with no taint of sin. And even sinners, he learned, could do penance by recognizing their sins, renouncing them, and acting differently in identical circumstances. They needed no one as intermediary, but each had his own direct connection to God.

This idea, that we are born pure with nothing to atone for

but our own very personal sins, appealed to him deeply. He found himself looking forward to two classes: Hebrew and the Old Testament. The teacher was a Jew, a black-velvet skullcap, and he was introduced to the class by Father Quinn with affection as Reb Gershon. He had learned the Old Testament before, but always as an adjunct to the New. Now he felt he was seeing it for the first time. At first he felt surprise and curiosity, which soon grew into a profound amazement that bordered on shock. All the things he had sought most, admired most in his faith, the love for one's fellow, the need for loving-kindness and charity, for justice and for mercy, he found had their origins in the Books of Moses. It contained the whole blueprint for a human society at its most civilized. Even "Love thy neighbor as thyself," that which he had always believed the most Christian of ideas, that, too, was written plainly in the Hebrew texts given Moses. In many ways, its words seemed to bring him closer to the goodness and holiness he had always searched for than the harsh words of the New: "If anyone comes to me and does not hate his own father and mother and wife and children and brothers and sisters, yes, and even his own life, he cannot be my disciple." "Think not I have come to bring peace. I have not come to bring peace, but a sword."

Why had he not understood this before? Why had he dismissed the whole contribution of the Jews as insignificant and wrong? He had been taught, had he not, that Jesus said, "I come not to change the Law, but to strengthen and verify it." But it had never occurred to him, never seemed important to him, that Jesus himself came of Jewish parents, and the Law he spoke of was this same law of the Jews. He realized with a deep shame that although he had loved Batsheva, he had belittled her beliefs, considering them in the same light in which an indulgent parent considers the unsophisticated thoughts of a favorite child: with love and pity and hope for the future. He had, in fact, not looked at them at all so much as the opposite. He had overlooked them, as if they were a kind of defect, which in his love he was bound to accept, like a deformed hand or foot.

This in general, he thought suddenly, was the way Christians looked at the Jews. Some hated them, hated their beliefs, while others were prepared to love them in spite of their beliefs. That seemed to him totally absurd, like hating or ignoring the crust of the earth that forms the whole foundation for one's firm existence on solid ground. It is simply this, he told himself: Without the Jews, there would have been no Christians. The idea that the Christians had taken over the role of the children of Israel, had usurped the position of the Chosen People because the Jews had sinned, not only seemed to him wrong, but positively galling and ungrateful.

He felt himself exhilarated and frightened by his thoughts. He took to walking through the city for long hours, trying to calm himself, to make sense of it all. The Jews fascinated him: the blond, blue-eyed schoolgirls, the dark, almost black-complexioned young soldiers. They did not seem to be from the same people physically. In fact, it seemed like a small international community, a blending of the physical features and colorings from every nation on earth. Were they a people? Or did they just share a religion unrelated to race? How was it that they had survived all these centuries at all? He became obsessed with these questions, with a single-minded concentration that shut everything else out. He found himself spending long hours after class talking to Reb Gershon, haunting the reading rooms at the National and University Library at the Hebrew University of Jerusalem, which contains the greatest collection of Judaic manuscripts in the world. He began simply, with Cecil Roth's *History of the Jews*. He read with surprise and then with discomfort, and finally with almost an agony of shame, the matchless history that began with an intelligent, unsatisfied boy in Ur of Chaldea who questioned the blind beliefs of his parents and his time in gods of wood and stone; a boy, he thought, with a sense of revelation, not unlike himself.

It was a brutal, savage story. A history of martyrdom and suffering, of unbelievable achievement and scholarship. And throughout, there was the constant, shameful role of the Church in persecutions, in forced conversions, in inquisitions, expulsions, and massacres—a constant, unflagging determination to degrade and wholly destroy the very people and culture that had spawned it. Why, in this very city, he thought, less than nine hundred years ago, the Crusader Godfrey de Buillion had rounded up all the Jews into a synagogue and set it on fire, destroying the entire Jewish population. He saw the flames in his mind's eye, and smelled the burning flesh, and in his imagination a beautiful dark-haired woman looked out with tortured, accusing eyes, a small child cried out in anguish.

It was late when he finished reading. He closed the book with trembling hands and touched his face. It was burning with shame and humiliation. How is it that I never knew, never understood? It was as if one had found out one's own dear and loving mother had in her youth been a camp guard at Auschwitz. For the Church was his mother, he thought. He had always thought his attachment to it was a striving for something higher, something full of goodness. Then how was it possible, this terrible, incontrovertible evidence of unbridled cruelty? He thought of Batsheva. How could she love him, knowing what the Church had done, his own people had done, to her people? It was good that he had left her. He was not worthy of her.

But then all his old loyalties surfaced. My terrible thoughts about the Church are a blasphemy. He was again in an agony of split feelings, of uncertainty. He had a sudden, irrational urge to go down upon his knees and beg forgiveness. But from whom, and for what, he could not really say.

* * *

"I say, old chap, don't you think you're overdoing it a bit?" Jean-Paul sat by his bedside. David looked up at him. What did he want? He pulled the covers up over his head. Jean-Paul pulled them down again. "You haven't been to matins or to class in a week. Just what do you think you're doing?"

"It's none of your business. Please go away," David pleaded with him, too weak to argue. He had not spoken to anyone of what he had been going through. It was as if he had found something out about his own family, his parents, that filled him with incredible shame, and he wanted to hide it, to deny it.

But suddenly he felt this man was his brother. He sat up and gripped his arm. "I have been reading the history of the Jews . . ." He hesitated. What did he want to say? He was again confused.

"Sad business, that." Jean-Paul shook his head. "But what d'you want to read that for? Too depressing."

"Then you've read about it. About what the Church did."

"Of course, I'm no expert. I know that the Church has made every effort to save souls. I admit it hasn't tried hard enough with the Jews. Sad, a whole country full of people who deny their own salvation. But it's their own stubbornness. A 'stiff-necked' people, eh? Salvation is theirs, but they refuse it."

"'Has made every effort, hasn't tried hard enough . . .'" David ran his hand through his hair. I am going mad, he thought, totally furious. "If we had made any more effort, we would have wiped every last Jew off the face of the earth long before Hitler even took his shot at it."

The other man got up, stiff with offense. "I don't know what your problem is, David. I was just reaching out to you in Christian charity. You should also know Father Quinn has been asking about you. I think you're in for some trouble. Why don't you come back to class?"

David lay down again and hugged himself. I must get out

of here, he thought. Get out or go crazy. And then, in a flash of sudden inspiration, a plan formed out of the formless chaos of his troubled soul. The desert, he thought.

He bought a backpack and filled it with crackers and cans of food. He packed a flashlight and, as an afterthought, a few candles. He took canteens of water and a sleeping bag and a hat and then boarded a bus to Beersheba. Only when the vehicle actually began to move did a sense of panic hit him. He had no clear idea where he was going, or how long he would stay; no solid, mapped-out series of steps that would lead him from point A to point B. He, a man of intelligence and careful planning, who had envisioned his life piece by piece ever since his earliest childhood, now found himself adrift, rudderless on a vast, chartless sea.

He watched the landscape change, the thin foliage finally erased by the desert's merciless desolation. And yet, it provided a landscape that was without distraction, the awesome monotony of sand, cliff, sand, rolling hills, dark-gray granite, repeating itself like a visual incantation that lulled the mind of the beholder into a trancelike stillness and expectancy.

He got off the bus alone at a stop in the middle—as far as he could tell—of nowhere, somewhere outside Beersheba, although how far he could not tell. Other stops had had too many people, or boasted a small roadside stand with soft drinks that spoke of tourist buses and little clicking cameras. He looked around him at the steep cliffs of gray-white stone, bare except for random tufts of stubborn foliage harshly nurtured between the rocks. By the side of the road someone had thrown down a neatly chiseled staff. He picked it up, feeling its good weight, the friendly warmth of its sanded surface, and took it as an omen that he had come to the right place.

He made his way slowly at first, climbing and pulling himself up with the help of his staff, or sometimes with just the pressure of his strong hands on the unyielding stone, still hot from the incredible strength of the waning desert sun. The sweat, which had bathed his body in a fine mist at first, began to run, streamlike, down his arms and back in endless rivulets until his thin cotton shirt and jeans clung to him as if he had jumped headfirst into a pool of water. Imperceptibly, the light began to change, going from white-hot steel gray to buttercup yellow and finally to a burnished copper glow, like dying embers.

His body, at first welcoming the diminishing strength of the heat that had pummeled it and squeezed it dry, suddenly felt its loss as a fine shiver of cold ran down his spine. With a suddenness that was incomprehensible, the heat and light vanished without a trace as the earth became colder and darker than he had ever dreamed possible. With icy fingers, he searched for his sweater and unrolled his sleeping bag. He lifted his canteen straight up, draining its last drops, and took a few ravenous bites from his dry crackers. He was starving, he realized, his overstrained body crying out for replenishment. But he just didn't feel he could get involved in the opening of cans, in tasting and swallowing. He wanted his body to leave him alone, to be quiet and undemanding; to leave him totally free to think and feel about more important things. He took another handful of crackers and ate quickly and without pleasure, simply to be done with it.

Using his flashlight, he gathered together some stones—moving them with enormous care lest he uncover a scorpion's nest or a desert snake—to form a protective pillow around his head. A sense of the dangers surrounding him sometimes made a wave of shock run through his stomach like a sudden cramp, but his mind was curiously unalarmed. Fierce optimism? Indifferent fatalism? He wasn't sure which.

He took out a single candle, lit it, and placed it upright between the stones. Silently, he watched its tiny flickering flame struggle bravely and foolishly against the overwhelming darkness, watching it so closely that even after the wax had melted and the flame had extinguished, its brilliant glitter still danced behind his eyelids.

He crawled into the sleeping bag and tried to get warm. He looked up at the crescent moon and the stars that had never appeared to him before so close and filled with light. All of his senses seemed amplified, almost drugged. There was a new clarity in his eyes that made vivid distinctions between rocks and little desert plants bathed in the silver sheen of moonlight; a new alertness in his ears that picked up and combined the keening of small desert birds, the rustle of rare branches, the tiny grating sound of windblown gravel, turning them into a kind of music. He smelled the dry, almost chemical-like dust of the barren, phosphate-rich earth and the salty, earthy odor of his own exhausted body until the smells became one: his and the earth's. Adam, he thought, newly risen from the earth, a vessel prepared by God to hold a piece of godliness, a soul. He hugged his chest and clenched his eyes, suddenly afraid of the darkness, the wilderness alive with unknown and unseen dangers, afraid for the very body whose needs he so wanted, so tried, to forget. That was wrong, that urge to be pure spirit, he understood. To be pure soul, he realized, was to be an angel, was to be dead. To eat, to drink, to make love, were all means to an end, not to be despised, but to be cherished, to be elevated to godliness with pure intentions. His love for Batsheva was purely good, as upright and unblemished as the golden flame that illuminated the darkness. It is not good for man to be alone—God said this, he thought. He does not ask this of us. Even Moses, matchless leader and prophet, even Aaron, the highest priest in the holy temple, were married and had children. He hugged himself in an agony of confusion and fear and despair.

"They wandered in the wilderness in a desert way," he prayed softly, his teeth chattering from cold and fear. "They found no city of habitation. Hungry and thirsty, their souls fainting inside them, they cried out to the Lord in their trouble and He delivered them out of their distresses. He led them on a straight path, saving them from all harm . . . He has satisfied the longing soul, and the hungry soul He has filled with good." God, he whispered, please help me. I'm lost. I want so much to sit by Your side, to please You. But I can't seem to find You, to understand what it is You want of me, to understand who You are. And then, searching for the perfect words to sum up his plea, he said: "Unto Thee, O Lord, do I lift up my soul." Point my way, O Lord. Give me a sign . . .

His eyes began to relax, their harsh pinched lines smoothing into sleep. Wave after wave of calming darkness washed over him so that he no longer felt the hard ground, the individual pieces of unrelenting stones, pressing into his back and skull. He was conscious of nothing but his thoughts, almost free from the grip of his conscious mind, floating above him in curious objectivity. In the darkness, he saw a ladder that reached from just beside his head to heaven. He peered at it curiously as figures suddenly appeared, slowly climbing up. Then one turned and beckoned to him. He strained to see who it was. Father Gerhart. He beckoned with a lusty, insistent sweep of his vigorous arm. David felt no pull, no urge, not even guilt, as he lay watching until the figure finally shrugged and turned, continuing its solitary upward climb until it disappeared totally. And then he saw Batsheva and Gershon. They smiled down at him but did not beckon. He felt angry and rejected watching them climb away from him, leaving him so far below, but then he realized that, unlike Father Gerhart, they had left behind a trail of light for him to follow if he wished. But his body was paralyzed even as he strained to lift his feet. He felt someone had jumped on top of him and was wrestling him to the ground, pinning his hands and legs to the earth, immobilizing him. He wrestled with the dark, solid presence, his hands pressing into the heavy, muscular flesh that was suffocating him, until suddenly the pressure lifted and began hurrying away. But he grasped it by the leg and wouldn't let it go. "Bless me," he called out. "You tried to kill me and now you must bless me," he said so loudly that he awoke to find himself shouting into the pale new light of dawn.

For almost two weeks he wandered, staff in hand, through the desert, stopping at roadside stands and hotels whenever his supplies or his strength ran out. His face turned a deep, rich brown and the skin of his arms turned almost leathery. He lost weight, growing leaner and stronger each day, and felt a similar lightening taking place in his overburdened soul. And yet, although he was totally alone and went days without speaking to another human being, he began to feel a strange presence accompanying him through the almost deathlike isolation, a companionable, unnameable presence that seemed as close to him as his own skin; as invisible and yet as unmistakably real as the wind. At times it seemed to be leading him, blanketing him with comfort and protection, and at times to be following behind him, allowing him to choose freely every step of the way. It was at times awesome, and at times as comfortable and familiar as the food that nourished him, the water that slaked his burning thirst. This was what she meant, he thought. To feel God's presence when you brush your teeth, when you eat your breakfast. It was not filtered through anything else, not removed, but alive and almost palpable. He thought of the children of Israel, wandering in the wilderness for forty years until they knew Him, until the bond was forged, the marriage consummated.

But out of the desert, would all the clarity leave him, the presence depart? What did he know now that he hadn't known before? What answers would he bring back? His eyes filled with tears. Nothing. No closer really. But that, too, was simplistic. He knew he had to take the plunge and risk losing everything. He must go back.

He got off the bus in the center of Jerusalem's shopping district and walked along the Ben Yehudah pedestrian mall. And because he had often enjoyed sitting in an outdoor café watching the people go by, he walked into the Café Atara and sat down, ordering an Israeli breakfast.

He watched the people passing by, listening to the humming, friendly sound of their combined voices. After all those thousands of years, this is what is left, he thought, with strange pride. This incredibly young, vital people. He felt the hope, the bounce in their footsteps, as they passed him, going off to jobs, to look at pretty dresses. And all those children. The city rocked with them, teemed with them. Wherever you looked there were young children, babies, and pregnant women. This chapter, following the others, seemed the most incredible of all. How is it they survive, he asked himself. Where does this endless strength, this tenacity, come from?

He took his elbows off the table and leaned back as the waitress bent over him, placing steaming coffee and fresh rolls and butter in front of him. And as she did this, a glitter caught his eye. He reached out impulsively, catching her gold necklace in his hand.

"Please, sir!" The girl backed away and he saw that he had offended her and she had misread his intentions in the obvious way. But all that did not matter now, he told himself. He felt himself on the edge of some tremendous discovery that would change his entire life. "Where, what . . . where did you get that?" he asked her, first in English, and then, when he saw she did not understand, in impatient Hebrew: "May ayfo zeh?" He stood up. He simply could not sit another minute, not another second.

She backed away still farther. But he saw something had calmed her. Tourists were allowed their crazinesses, he supposed.

"I received it . . . eh, how you say?" she bit her lower lip in concentration, "got it, yes, in the store." She pointed down the street.

Like the air that rushes into a balloon and then rushes out again at the tiniest hole, his euphoria now left him. She had bought it at a jewelry store, a tourist trap, this, which he had considered a rare and priceless heirloom. But how? Why? His excitement began to swell. This at least was a trail to follow.

He rushed with long, deliberate steps to the place she had pointed to and looked into the display case. He sucked in his breath. There, displayed like common souvenirs, were hundreds of them, the little golden charms in the shape of hands, exactly like the one that had been his mother's most cherished heirloom. He took out his watch chain and held up the little golden hand that never left him—it was supposed to be a good-luck charm. But now, for the first time, he felt that it was the sign he had prayed for, the hand of fate finally pointing him in the inevitable direction his life was meant to go.

The hand, he learned from the *Encyclopedia Judaica* at the National and University Library, was an ancient Jewish amulet called a *hamsah*. Inscribed with a mysterious Kabbalistic combination of Hebrew letters defining God's name, it was used by Jews in North Africa, Morocco, and Spain to ward off evil spirits. A Jewish amulet. He closed the book, and like a drunk who has emptied one bottle, went off desperately in search of his next. His hands shaking a little, his lungs almost afraid to breathe, he took down the volume C-Dh and looked up the name Cresas:

> **CRESAS, ASHER** (d. 1419?), Spanish-Jewish philosopher, theologian, and statesman. Imprisoned in 1367 on trumped-up charges of desecrating the Host. Later released. Wrote Hebrew poetry. Member of the Catalonian Jewish community who negotiated with the king of Aragon for a

renewal and extension of Jewish privileges in 1393. With the accession of John I, Cresas became closely associated with the court of Aragon and was accorded the title "member of the royal household" (*familiaris, de casa del senyor rey*). His son, Hasdai, was murdered in the anti-Jewish riots of 1394. Other members of the family were later forced to convert to Christianity under the threat of death.

His direct descendant, Antonio Cresas, was educated by Jesuits in the famous university of Coimbra. In 1614, he was appointed Professor of Canon Law and enjoyed an unrivaled reputation as scholar and preacher. During this time, he became a member of the Marrano group at Coimbra, which consisted of a number of distinguished figures at the university, all of whom came from forcibly converted New Christians, who continued to secretly practice some form of Judaism. The group secretly held regular religious services at each other's homes in Coimbra, in which Cresas acted as rabbi. On November 23, 1619, Cresas was arrested by the Inquisition and sent to Madrid for trial. After a short interval of hesitation, he suddenly announced to the Inquisitor that he wished to be a Jew. He was kept in prison for five years while earnest endeavors were made to win his soul back for the Catholic faith. In spite of torture, he maintained complete silence, saying only the Hebrew prayer: "Listen, O Israel. The Lord is our God, the Lord is One."

On July 20, 1624, he was burned at the stake. He was survived by a wife and a son, named David.

He blinked; then, holding perfectly still, he allowed his eyes to wander farther down the page to the entry subheaded "Modern Times."

DAVID CRESAS (1894–1943), author and physician, head of the Sephardic Jewish community of Amsterdam. Cresas served as physician and underground head of the rescue network which aided thousands of Jewish refugees. In September 1943, he was deported with his family to Westerbork and from there to Auschwitz, where they perished. It is believed that he was survived by a daughter, Gracia Mendes Cresas, a professor of philosophy at the University of Heidelberg, who allegedly fled to safety, although this has never been substantiated.

He walked out into the sunlight and felt its power illuminate every dark, secret place in his body and mind. It was so bright, so incredibly, frighteningly clear. It all made sense now. The constant searching, the dissatisfaction, the endless questions that, until this moment, had had no answers. If one believed in Jung's collective unconscious, the inheritance of certain basic insights handed down as a fully furnished room from generations of unknown ancestors, then he had finally opened that secret chamber that held the deepest key to his needs as a human being. He thought of his mother—that dark, intelligent face, a face like no other woman's he had ever met until Batsheva—why, they might have been relatives, he realized for the first time. He had despaired of finding someone to fill the dark pit in his soul his mother's death had caused, and he had fled instead to the dark mothering presence of the Church. But the Church could not hold him, as it had not been able to hold his ancestors.

He wanted to shout in joy, but instead he walked blindly forward, his feet taking him where his mind still refused to go. He followed the noisy, commercial streets of the city northward, climbing, always climbing. He felt the change. A quiet came over the people, as the streets narrowed into old alleyways. He heard the riot of birds flying in enormous packs over the black, mysterious complex of the Abyssinian Church. On the opposite side of the street was a large, modern building filled with black-suited teenage boys with long *payot.* The boys were studying the Talmud, and as their voices drifted out into the streets, he followed the chanting like a hungry stranger follows the scent of fresh bread.

The streets of Meah Shearim, so narrow one cannot walk two abreast; so narrow and winding one might get lost quite easily and find one had come full circle and was back in the modern city once again. He did not want this to happen. He wanted to find his place there. He wanted to do something irrational. To dance; to laugh out loud; to run up and down the street; to kiss startled little babies in their carriages; to carry the heavy baskets of bearded old men; to hug the pretty, bashful, long-braided little girls like a father. A hot swelling, a flash of love, lit him up inside. My people, he thought.

Chapter twenty-five

Back home, surrounded by the solid comforts of the life she had built alone for herself, without the help of a father, or lover, or friend, there, in that place, Batsheva felt her feelings slowly return to her, the way a frostbitten arm or leg slowly and painfully returns from its numbness. The interview with David's father had been short. Something about "the best thing for both of you . . . and he's only thinking of you . . . he is worried they might take the child away from you if you married a Gentile . . ." all said in this very kind, very sincere, even choked-up way. Oh yes, so very kind they all were. Lord Hope, and David, and her father, and Isaac. All, so very, very kind, so very good. They thought only of her, of her happiness, wanting to spare her, to love her, to provide for her future . . . to teach her . . . She had listened to David's father wordlessly, the color draining from her face and her eyes going lifeless. There had even been a lingering smile on her face—frozen there from the wonderful dream of just hours before. And she had heard nothing really, but that he had left her of his own free will, without saying goodbye, without facing her.

She had thrown herself into work, preparing a one-woman show for a famous gallery. She had been pleased with the prospect before, but now she became obsessed with it. To make it on her own, to show them all—the arrogant bunch of them!—who she was, and that she needed no one. A few times a day she would stop working and stand perfectly still as her body trembled with rage, thinking: How dare he? How dare he! Was she this object, this plaything, this eternal child over whose body decisions must be made in which she was never to have a say? Who the hell did they think they all were, she would think in a white fury of hatred and bitterness and despair that took her captive. No one, human or Divine, she told herself, would ever control her life again. Let me be damned then. Yes, if this is what being good and obedient has brought me! And she would feel a potent poison, an evil, leap up, licking her heart like a flame, and she would become afraid. But it was beyond her control. She was in the grip of something so terrible she did not even understand its danger. The faith that she had taken for granted all her years, that she was born with as some children are born with a silver spoon waiting in a gift-wrapped package, had never yet been subject to such a test. A struggle began in her soul and she did not understand that it would be a fight to the death. She could not lose it and remain who she was. She would be reborn, a different person completely: hard, clear-eyed, needing comfort and direction from no one, trusting no one. This was what she felt she wanted now. To be totally separate and alone, to do exactly as she pleased without regard for anyone else; to use, instead of being used, for a change. And why not, she told herself, her eyes hard with a kind of animal glitter. And why the hell not?

So she worked hard at her photography, going out early and coming home late. She hired babysitters for Akiva and spent very little time with him. She did not want to feel the kind of softness he evoked in her. She needed to be hard now, to be totally ruthless, she told herself. Wherever she looked, she could find only ugliness and hatred, hypocrisy and violence, things she had seen before occasionally, but now saw exclusively, inescapable images that surrounded her like prison walls. They were good pictures technically, excellent really, like Diane Arbus photos: the cunning pleasure and horror in the faces of slum children bashing each other's faces in; the lascivious, belligerent face of an old drunk sitting on a park bench. They were fascinating in the darkest, ugliest way—like newspaper reports on child murders.

She studied the pictures she had taken and felt confusion and a nameless fright. But what can I do about it, she asked herself stubbornly. This is what the world is. I am not responsible. What I did before was a sugar-coated lie, she told herself. Only now do I see the truth. The gallery owners felt puzzled and uneasy when they saw the pictures, but agreed they were excellent. They would include them if she promised to bring her earlier works as well. Well, I don't care, as long as I get paid, she told herself. What did it mean to her? Only paper and chemicals.

She couldn't stand to be near Elizabeth and Ian. All that happiness, that joy, she thought with dark cynicism. I know what marriage is, and so will they. Just bending and bending; even the best of men, that's all they want, for you to be beneath them in all ways. All the rest is a lie. Someone to mold like putty, she told herself. Then why did David leave you? You were ready to give in, to be molded by him. But she would not listen to that kind of question; she smothered it, ignored it, made believe she hadn't heard.

"You look absolutely . . . stunning," Elizabeth said, looking her over. It was true, but there was something else there, too, that made Elizabeth uneasy. She had expected depression, sadness, after that disastrous weekend. But this was much worse. She kept trying to connect through the old lines of friendship and kept finding them cut off. The black-silk dress Batsheva wore was very low-cut in the front and back, not her style at all. It made her body look polished, like a young racehorse, but rather hard, too, as if she were mocking her own soft beauty. She gleamed with a svelte, cold loveliness one often saw in beautiful young women married to rich, dull men.

"Thank you," Batsheva answered her vaguely, shifting her eyes, not wanting to make contact with Elizabeth's. She couldn't look anyone in the eyes. And there, in the glittering, crowded room, full of acquaintances and strangers, she did not have to. She stood over to one side, drinking a tall, cool glass of vodka and orange juice, and she felt herself grow calmer and colder. She watched with only the most cursory interest the way people stood before her pictures. A year ago, she would have been beside herself with excitement, every nerve quivering with expectation, alert to the slightest positive or negative reaction in the eyes and faces of the people facing her work for the first time. But now she felt oddly removed, contemptuous—of the people and of her work. Yet, still, she felt the inescapable horror of the artist, his utter vulnerability in having his inner vision, almost his soul, hung up for the first time before so many critical eyes. Despite her detachment and the alcohol coursing through her veins, it made her suffer. She was totally helpless. It was as if she were splayed up there, naked, and everyone was free to examine the most intimate details of her being.

Most people crowded around the pictures of Jerusalem. But she couldn't bear to look at them. It was as if she were watching people look at her own dead body lying unconscious and helpless at a wake. She did not want to know what they thought of those pictures; she simply couldn't bear it. It wasn't her anymore. The girl who had taken those pictures had died. I just don't want to remember her, the little fool, the helpless child, letting everyone step all over her. She wandered over to the corner where the new pictures were displayed. She saw discomfort and cynical fascination in the eyes of the viewers, an interest that was almost obscene. And suddenly she felt someone take her arm and whisper low.

"I don't believe it. Batsheva?"

She turned and found herself face-to-face with Graham MacLeish. She smiled at him before she remembered who he was, and then her smile faded. The past.

"What . . . ?" he began.

She lifted the drink to her lips and took a long sip. "How are you?" she said lightly, as the hot alcohol sent up a new supply of courage and indifference. "You look well."

His blond head, gray now at the temples, gleamed with a slick shine. His hair was perfectly cut and parted, with just a slight curl over the broad, handsome neck. His body, aging now, looked well cared for.

"My God! What is going on? We thought you were . . . ?"

"Plainly not. Come back to life." She was growing incoherent. How much vodka was in that drink, she wondered with mild interest, taking another sip.

"Hello, Graham," Elizabeth called out to him. The two gave each other long, appraising looks. Hers said: You look old and wasted. His said: You look beautiful and happy, unfortunately.

"All that about Batsheva was just a mistake, as you can see," Elizabeth spoke quickly. "She is living here now."

Graham was looking at her arm linked through Ian's with a malicious kind of envy.

"Oh yes. My fiancé, Ian Hope."

"Ah yes, the young poet of renown who has set London on its ear," Graham said in his jeering voice.

Elizabeth's jaw twitched in anger. "Ian, this is Graham MacLeish, an old friend." She emphasized the *old*. "Graham used to be a critic."

"Ah, my dear, still am, still am. Don't write me off so

quickly yet." His eyes glittered with malevolence as her words cut into him. He turned to Batsheva and by some clever trick of manipulation, made his face look smooth and youthful. "You know, my dear, the last time we met there were so many obstacles in our way. But now we are both free. I'd like to show you the town."

"Batsheva's already seen the town, Graham, thank you," Elizabeth broke in, putting her arm protectively through Batsheva's. "Are you really free, Graham? My, my, coeds getting picky these days?"

Batsheva looked at Elizabeth carefully, surprised at the bitchy tone. She was obviously trying to get Graham away from her. Was she jealous? Was she being protective? She looked at Graham and saw something ungenerous and painful shine dully out of his tired eyes. She looked at her friend and saw alarm and—something else—desire? Hatred? But she didn't probe it too closely, because she had already decided. He was just what she needed now. She smiled at him, took her arm out of Elizabeth's, and slipped it through his. "Why don't you wait for me after the show, and drive me home," she told him.

"Batsheva," Elizabeth whispered loudly, trying to tug her away, "may I speak to you privately?"

Batsheva shook her arm free. "You know, that's the problem with everyone. They're all so bloody considerate, full of such love for me. Leave me alone, Liz! I'm a big girl now." Her eyes were dull and hard. Elizabeth stared at her speechlessly.

The rest of the evening, Graham stayed by her side like a dark shadow. People would come over to him, recognizing the face that had once been a familiar constant in the *Times Literary Supplement*, and Batsheva would hear the witty, meaningless repartee, so devoid of any real feeling, and smile inside. That was what she wanted, exactly that. Just a useful, surface relationship with people.

Inside, she would be hard and hidden so that no one would be able to touch her again, hurt her so badly again. Out of the corner of her eye, she saw Elizabeth and Ian hovering nearby, watching her, like two worried mother hens. But they could not do anything to interfere, she saw with bitter satisfaction. No, they would not interfere, but stand by and watch as what must happen, happened.

More people poured through the gallery doors, until the room was packed, until it hummed with the loud, insistent hum that voices take on when people want to be heard above a crowd. People crowded around her, introducing themselves and moving cigarettes and drinks out of their hands to shake hers. Some of the faces looked genuinely impressed, genuinely glad to meet her. They glowed with respect and recognition. She was afraid to meet those kind of faces. I don't deserve your respect, she thought. But then there were other faces, full of self-serving friendliness and feigned interest: faces that wanted something from her, that felt she was worth cultivating for her beauty, her talent, her connections. They all looked a little like Graham, she thought; those big, plastic smiles and the lifeless, grim eyes. She could fend for herself among them, she thought, feeling the way a brave but foolish and untested young animal might feel surrounded by predators. But something of the ugly, self-serving hypocrisy around her filled her with an instinctive revulsion that seemed to cut off her supply of air.

She slipped out of the door before anyone could see her and walked through the dark streets of London. She walked quickly, wanting to feel her pulse throb, her aching heart beat faster and faster. She looked into well-lit windows and heard laughter, the sound of children crying, of families—the ordinary flow of life, and it tore at her insides. She felt so alone, so tired, in the foreign city. Homesickness washed over her with its relentless, shivering coldness, homesickness for the white city with its gentle hills. She looked up into the sky. Could those be the same stars, the same moon? Like God, they followed you everywhere. She clenched her fists and raised her eyes to their brightness, patches torn out of a black curtain revealing the brilliant light beneath.

God, she prayed. Why am I here? Why am I on this earth, dreaming this earthly dream? What does it all mean—our goodness and our evil, our trials and our failures? She felt so small, a bit of dust in the dark, meaningless universe. How must God see her? A tiny speck in His vast creation? Yet, why did she never, even in her darkest moments, ever stop feeling that He cared? Perhaps we are born with a piece of God within us; that is how He knows our thoughts, our hidden desires, our petty evils. Perhaps that is what the soul is. And if we are all Godly vessels, how we have debased Him with our terrible ideals, our awful failings. Why does He allow it? Allow Himself to be attached to our humanness, our weak, unworthy, sordid lives? Perhaps, she thought, Rabbi Silverman was right after all. Perhaps there is something so powerful and stunning in the choice, the purely human choice of good over evil, that only one such choice in a million is worth all the evil that went before. Like the birth of a star, it lights up the universe so powerfully, it leaves a trail of light that can be seen millions of light years away.

When she got back to the gallery, it had already emptied out. The owners were very pleased—the sales had been excellent. She saw Elizabeth and Ian hadn't given up and were waiting patiently for her. Graham walked over to her and took her arm securely. She disengaged herself and walked around the room, looking at the photographs for the first time that evening. She was afraid, the way one is sometimes afraid to look into a mirror. But they were good, not perfect, not nearly as good as she felt they ought to be, but certainly a little worthwhile, she allowed herself. Almost against her will, she stood before her favorite, one of the pictures she had taken that afternoon so long ago on a

Jerusalem hilltop, and closed her eyes. All the feelings of love and closeness to something ineffably sacred and beautiful came flooding over her, and the dam she had constructed with such bitter finality washed away, and she felt the dark flame inside her extinguish in the baptism.

She walked over to Elizabeth and laid her head down on her shoulder and felt her friend smooth down her hair. She was crying, too. From the corner of her eye, she saw Graham watching them, motionless, with snakelike threat and the bitterness of a loser. He walked over to them: "Batsheva, shall we go?"

"I'm sorry, Graham. I can't . . ."

"Sorry to hear that, my dear." His voice became very dignified and clipped. "I suppose your parents have been to visit you since you've been here. How are they? I thought I might give them a call to let them know how well you're doing." He had guessed everything.

"Don't do it, Graham," Elizabeth said in a low, threatening tone.

She was afraid, and that pleased him and confirmed his suspicions. "Why, I thought the Hebrews were a very tight group, very clannish. Won't they be thrilled at the congratulations, at the implied monetary success of their little Jewish princess?"

Ian took a step forward and with a sudden, subtle movement gripped Graham's arm and hand in what outsiders could have easily mistaken for an enthusiastic handshake. Only Graham could feel the tremendous, unsubtle pressure of the younger man's concentrated fingers tearing into his shoulder and crushing the bones of his hand. "My dear Graham," Ian said with a slight smile. "I think it's time for you to go home and go to bed. And I don't think it such a wise idea to call anyone at so late an hour. Why, you might get a reputation for doing irrational things, like that recent review you wrote. Some of that material wasn't exactly original, now was it?"

Graham stopped struggling to get his hand free, and his face flushed darkly. "I . . . I footnoted it."

Ian didn't budge, his smile fixed. "Not exactly, dear fellow, as you well know. It was taken straight out of a student paper. I know because the student is a friend of mine. But no one would believe a lowly student, now would they? But they might believe me." He let his grip relax.

"It was just an oversight—tell that to your friend, will you? But you're right. I should be going." He looked at Batsheva and smiled his wry, bitter smile. "Give my regards to your parents the next time you see them, will you?" He took one step closer to her. "It could have been perfect, my dear. A real pity." He took her hand and kissed it, then walked out, jaunty and dignified, flashing a rugged, sophisticated smile that dazzled the young hat-check girl until she realized he had left no tip.

"It was a magnificent show. We are so proud of you!" Elizabeth hugged her tightly.

"Thank you. Thank you both." Batsheva took Elizabeth's and Ian's hands and pressed them together in her own. "I've been under some kind of evil spell, I guess. Thanks, both of you, for everything."

"Do you want to come to the house to celebrate?"

"No. I just want to go home and go to sleep. I want to see Akiva, to make sure he's okay. I've been terrible to him lately." There was also something else she wanted to do that had nothing to do with Akiva or sleep, but she was ashamed to admit it. She kissed them both goodbye and hurried home. When she walked into the dark house, the babysitter thanked her for the generous tip and left. She sat by Akiva's bedside for a while, listening to his untroubled breathing. She touched his little face. He was fine. Nothing had happened to him. When she got up, she felt that she had regained enough of her strength and equilibrium of soul to face an ordeal she had been avoiding for months.

She walked quickly and deliberately into her bedroom and opened the top drawer of her dresser and reached in underneath the soft, silky underthings and pulled out a packet of unopened letters from Jerusalem. She had not read one.

She got into bed and opened the first one and read in David's clear, generous script all that had happened to him from the moment he left her. And as she read, her heart began to beat loud enough for her to hear it. At first she read with trepidation and disbelief, and then with incredible, unfathomable joy.

On the long-distance phone line between London and Jerusalem, Batsheva and David spoke in brief, practical sentences: Yes, they agreed, she and Akiva must come to Jerusalem at once. No, they agreed, it wasn't a good idea for them to be seen together in public until the divorce proceedings were over. Of course that meant David, as much as he would like to, wouldn't come to the airport. Would she manage by herself? he asked her. With all the suitcases and Akiva? Perhaps she shouldn't pack too much so they wouldn't be too heavy to drag off the conveyer herself. And would she manage to find a cab all right? And not to forget to give Akiva Dramamine so he wouldn't get planesick . . . He talked and talked with a nervous energy, almost babbling, and then he suddenly fell silent.

"David," he heard her whisper in a small voice, but so clearly he seemed to feel the small breath of air that escaped her lips caress his ear when she said the *v*.

"My love," he whispered back, cradling the phone, his throat contracting. "When?"

"Thursday." They both fell silent, making the quiet calculation of the impossible and wretched minutes, half hours, hours, and whole days that stood between them like an implacable enemy and the dangerous bridges they had still to cross.

* * *

The light breaking through the clouds Thursday morning didn't wake David as much as they gave him license to finally take his tossing, unsleeping body out of bed.

"God!" He looked in the mirror at his unshaven, leathery brown face, his red eyes, with horror and amusement and disbelief: Could she want that? He splashed water on his face, dried it, and because he had no idea what to do next, went to look out of the window.

Black rain clouds presaging the deluge of the *yoreh*, the first rain to break the nearly seven months of seasonal drought, blocked out the light. A pang of irrational disappointment ripped at his chest when he realized it wasn't going to be a perfect day. He felt a sense of personal failure.

"Might as well get dressed," he said out loud.

"Might as well take a walk," he said, before he had even finished buttoning his shirt.

Might as well take a bus, he thought, running with all his might to catch one. He wasn't thinking as much as he was sleepwalking, acting out some irresistible dream. And even, finally, boarding the bus that would take him to Ben Gurion Airport and thereby throwing all their sensible resolutions and practical strategies out the window, he couldn't think of anything but that one little letter, that *v* that had touched his ear like a kiss. "David," she had said with all the old familiar passion he had so feared might have died or faded and been lost to him forever.

He had no idea when the plane would land, or even what airline she was using. And since there is no indoor reception area at Ben Gurion, he wound up waiting outside, along the long metal ramp where arriving passengers emerge. He was afraid to leave his place even to go inside to get a cup of coffee lest she choose just that moment to come through the door. He formed new sensible resolutions: He wouldn't go near her. He would sit in a corner, far away, and be content with just seeing her. And each time the arrival board lit up with a flight from London, he stood up and watched the steady stream of strangers pouring through the doors, his eyes devouring each one, feeling a fresh stab of despair that each one wasn't a beautiful, black-haired woman with a curly-headed little boy.

The *yoreh*, which began as a trickle, suddenly burst through all restraints, falling in enormous, stabbing sheets of wild abandon, running off his hatless head, drenching his thin shirt, making his pants drip and cling like a bathing suit. But he hardly noticed, for at that very moment, the doors opened and he caught a small flash of dark, shining hair that joined the stream of bodies like a drop of flotsam on a great river. He strained, craning his neck, taking a small step forward, the rain dripping off his bare head in steady streams, almost blinding him. A slim arm, a small hand clasped securely. A little head of bobbing curls.

He walked past the old Sephardic women, their arms outstretched to welcome dark, prodigal sons; past Arabs in business suits and Greek Orthodox priests; past cabdrivers hawking rides to Haifa and Tiberias in broken English; past hefty security guards who called after him aggressively, each step a little faster until he was running like a madman and had swept her and Akiva completely off the ground, covering their faces and hands with a hundred kisses and hugging them to him for dear life.

"Oh, Lord. What have I done!" he said, putting them down, trying to wipe away the wetness from Batsheva's face with his wet hands. He put his hand into his pocket and pulled out a wad of dripping tissues, which he held out to her foolishly, forgetting what he was doing, lost in her eyes, her face, which just kept getting wetter and wetter as tears of happiness so intense, so full of blessing, streamed down her cheeks, almost breaking his heart. She laughed and they looked at each other long and hard. He ran his fingers through his hair with quiet despair and joy, picking Akiva up and blowing on him absurdly to try to dry him off.

"I've . . . oh . . . soaked you both . . . done it all wrong, I've ruined . . . I wasn't going to, really . . . it . . . it . . ."

Batsheva reached up, placing her small, soft palm over his mouth. She traced the outline of his lips with the tips of her fingers, the way a blind woman might, her fingers wandering to his ears, losing themselves in his dark hair. For a single moment, everyone and everything blurred around them into a silent whirlpool of indistinct shapes and colors as she put her arms around him and rested her head on his chest feeling, she thought, what Anna might have felt had it been Vronsky, and not the train, that had come rushing toward her out of the fearsome unknown, to enfold her forever in the loving safety of his honest, unwavering passion.

Chapter twenty-six

"Ah, no, again," Mrs Ha-Levi said nervously as the phone rang. The calls were short and mysterious, and always at the same time of day. It had been going on for a week. She bit her fingernails and adjusted her wig, waiting for the servants to answer it. She was afraid to answer it herself, as frightened as a child. "Who was it, who was it?"

"The same, ma'am," Louise, a large black woman who had been with the family many years, said sympathetically. It was spooky, all right. A stranger, identifying herself only as a friend, asked about the health of Mr and Mrs Ha-Levi and—getting the answers she desired—refused to identify herself, refused to say anything more than she would call back later.

Mrs Ha-Levi bit her knuckle in anguish. "And what was the message this time?"

"A friend of Miss Batsheva will be calling you today at six o'clock P.M. with some very good news."

Mrs Ha-Levi opened her mouth in surprise, as if she wanted to say something, then closed it. It had been almost two years since the accident, which she insisted on calling the event that had taken her only child and grandchild from her. The shock had been so numbing, and she had been so involved with helping her husband, protecting him, that she herself had not been able to face it squarely in all its horror until recently. And then something very strange had happened, a subtle change that she could not have imagined or foreseen.

She had never questioned God, never questioned her husband before. Whatever is, is right. God was good. One must obey one's husband, as one obeyed one's father. She had tried to tell Batsheva this . . . that beautiful, willful child. At first she had been terribly ashamed, almost humiliated. She had brought this child up, and now she had gone and committed the worst sin—the taking of two lives! She had felt everyone looking at her accusingly, the neighbors, her husband. And so she had cowered and bent over in humility, as if waiting to receive further blows that must, by rights, come to her as punishment. The shame, the shame of it, to have raised such a child! To have failed in one's mission in life so utterly!

But as time wore on, and the days of mourning ended and the house emptied of strangers, she found herself remembering her days as a young mother. She remembered silly things, strange things, so vividly, as if it were a movie reel: There is Batsheva, a tiny child, barely able to talk, toddling over to her with a blow-up rattle.

"Is this the last time? The very last time?" she sees herself asking her. Her face has a little frowning smile as she bends down to the child.

The child nods emphatically. "No more!" she hears the baby affirm in her little lispy, chirping voice, her eyes wide with innocence and sincerity.

She feels herself straining, blowing up the toy. It is difficult. The air keeps escaping through the hole the moment she rests or takes another breath. Her lips hurt. Her chest aches with the effort. She gives the little girl the rattle and sees her eyes widen with delight, taking the toy and pressing it against her small red lips with both hands. She can see the small hands, the red lips and the tiny teeth working to open the plug, to squeeze out the air. And as soon as it is done, the child toddles back to her.

"More!" she demands.

"You mustn't open it! No more, no more!" She hears herself growing angry, trying to keep her voice calm. She sees the little girl grab her coffee cup. Its contents rise like a typhoon wave over the edge.

"More!" the child demands. "More!" she insists, pushing the flat rubber thing at her.

"Is this really the last time? You promise? You won't touch it?" she hears herself pleading, demanding.

The little girl nods, and the innocence in her eyes seems to melt. Her lashes sparkle with undropped tears. Again she feels herself inhaling deeply, pinching the opening this time. The flaps slip open and the air keeps escaping. Finally, she finishes. "Here. Now go away and play." And then, as clear as day, she sees the little girl grab it gleefully with two grasping fists, pressing the plug to her lips, *psssssssssssst.*

It made her want to laugh and cry. Silly story. She didn't even understand why she remembered it. Perhaps because Batsheva had grown up to be such a good, obedient child. But if they—all those inquiring eyes, the friends, the relatives, the strangers who had come to comfort and stayed to pry—would hear it, they would think it had a different meaning. They would nod knowingly and see the seeds of willfulness, stubbornness. But what did any one of them know? Had they seen her as a little girl sitting patiently on the bed, letting her mother brush her long black hair into soft bottle curls? Had they heard her light, running steps, her call: "Ima, look!" always to share some new miracle she had discovered—the glow of a firefly, the bright, jewel-like glitter of a rock?

A happy child, she told herself. A good and happy child, she repeated, her weak, dependent nature gaining strength and conviction. She could not have done the evil thing they said—her Batsheva, no. It wasn't possible. To her husband, she said nothing. He mourned silently, tearlessly. He had refused to see or talk to anyone for more than six months. She had had to remind him to eat, remind him to sleep. He spent the whole day locked away in his study, sitting in a leather chair—reading, reading. She had no idea what, or why.

"What are you trying to do, Abraham?" she had pleaded with him. But he had only looked at her and shaken his head. She had waited for it to pass, for him to come to her with words of comfort, and then she would have unburdened her heart to him, reminding him of the child they had loved so much, convincing him that everyone must be wrong about the accident. But as the months passed and he began once again to go out in the limousine to attend to his business, he never once came to her to broach the subject.

For the first time in her life, she began to feel a resentment toward him taking root in her heart. For the first time, she had felt the need to hide her feelings, to dissemble. And like most guileless, uncomplicated people, once she began to lie, she got irretrievably caught up; like a bird in a fine net, the more she struggled to get free, the more she entangled herself. She could not even be sure anymore when she said "Good morning," to him, if she really meant it.

And so, when the phone calls had begun, she had told him nothing. She looked up at the clock and smoothed back the wrinkles on her aging hands. It was noon.

* * *

The ringing of the phone sent waves of cold fear and anticipation up and down her spine. She must answer this herself. She was prepared. It rang two, three times and she couldn't bring herself to touch it; but then it might stop, she realized, and she grabbed it in a panic. The servants watched her, alarmed and curious, wondering if they could help her. They all felt so sorry for the woman. She had lost so much weight. Her matronly clothes hung from her shoulders, and her once plump face, which had been aging in a healthy, graceful way, looked ravaged and careworn.

"Batsheva," they saw her whisper softly, and they looked at each other in alarm as she pressed the phone to her ear, cradling it as tenderly as a baby. She closed her eyes and the tears streamed down the premature wrinkles of her face in unheeded rivulets. They saw her write something down, then carefully replace the phone in the cradle. And when she looked up at them, it was with a face that was transformed and made younger, as if the years of misery had been no more than bad makeup now washed away. She didn't move for a few moments and then they heard a soft, gurgling sound that frightened them until they realized it was a giggle. She jumped up and down, clapping her hands like a child. She went to each of them and hugged them.

"They are alive, alive, both of them," she babbled like a madwoman, skipping down the immaculate parquet floors of the great hall toward her husband's study.

He looked up with surprise and annoyance as the door to his sanctuary was flung open. When he saw it was his wife, his feelings changed to alarm and amazement.

"She . . . ha!" His wife pressed her hands to her lips, bent over with laughter. She grabbed his hands and pulled him out of his chair, dancing before him with the little mincing steps of a bride. "My husband. We have a child, a grandchild!" His white face, stern and impassive, turned away from her in speechless confusion and she remembered who she was, who they were. "My dear husband. I am not *meshuga*. I have just had a phone call. Batsheva is alive and in Jerusalem. She is going to get a divorce. She wants us to join her. The baby is alive! Think of it, Abraham. Both of them alive, alive!" She saw him stagger backward with one uncontrolled, drunken step and reached out in alarm to steady him.

"Come, sit down. Ach. I said it so fast." She helped him back to his chair and repeated everything. The phone calls. The inquiries. Batsheva's voice. The need to pack, to get tickets . . . His eyes, which reflected the violent changes taking place in his soul, misted with profound joy and gratitude and disbelief. And then they began to glitter with a kind of hardness. He was undergoing the metamorphosis that takes place in every parent whose missing child turns up safe and sound. First, the incredible relief and happiness. But then something else takes over, an anger, so hot, so violent, one would be ready to beat the dickens out of the child for all the needless worry and aggravation he has caused. This same series of emotions took place in Abraham Ha-Levi's heart. But they were magnified many times. Because of the depth of his grief, his joy and gratitude rose to unbelievable heights. And when his emotions turned to anger, it knew no bounds.

His wife saw the struggle taking place inside of him but misunderstood it. She shared the joy, but felt the anger toward the world that had misjudged her darling child. "We must make plans to go, now," she urged him. "I will call the travel agent."

"Put down the phone! We will go nowhere!" He got up and paced the room, a lion in a den, the arsenal of his anger, so long directed uselessly at Isaac, so long buried and repressed, opening up with the force of a bomb. "She has been alive all this time," he muttered to himself, "and yet she has caused me this suffering, caused me to reach the brink of my sanity, to question my belief?" He looked at his wife with eyes that blazed like a fire out of control, eyes that dried all tears with the heat of their anger.

"I have sat *shiva* for her. I have buried her in my heart, do you hear me? She is dead to me."

Fruma Ha-Levi, the timid butcher's daughter who had never stopped wondering at her good fortune in being a handmaiden to the illustrious Abraham Ha-Levi, pressed her fingertips deep into her face, as if she were wearing a mask she wanted to rip off. She sat down on the sofa and picked up a beautiful Waterford vase from the coffee table, and she held it with the familiar care and awe she felt toward all the things in her husband's house. She looked at its sparkle, its rainbow brilliance. He had gone to a store and chosen it without discussing it with her. He had brought it home and placed it on this table because it pleased him to do so. She had had nothing at all to do with it, she thought, as her hands tightened around it in a violent spasm of fury and grief. With a sudden, wholly unexpected strength, she smashed it against the wall.

"You stupid man!" she said with a whispered vehemence, a disgust that stunned him. "You have decided, yes, you. The way you decided on a husband for our only daughter! *Our daughter!* Not just yours. And I let you, trusted you! No. Not trust. Fear. I was afraid for myself and so I let you pick my child a husband the way I let you pick out the china and crystal. You only told me about it afterward, when it was all arranged. She was only eighteen! After all those years being away at school, and here you arranged to have her married and living at the other end of the world! So far away from me! And never once did you think of my feelings, of my grief! And then, when she called, our Batsheva, our only daughter, when she called and asked for our help, you . . . you hid it from me. You decided there was to be no help. You didn't talk to me, you didn't say a word to me. You decided. You sent her back to him when she had enough sense to run away! And I was angry at her, at my poor, unhappy little girl, for leaving that monster. I was angry because she dared to upset you, the great and holy Abraham Ha-Levi! I let her go back to him until she was ready to kill herself and her own child, my good child! Yes, rather than to make you sick, to make you angry, she was ready to jump out of the window with her child in her arms." Her voice rose hysterically.

"Silence now! You don't understand! You cannot understand that I had to do what I did."

But she would not be silenced. All the words from all the years that had been kept in check by loyalty, by fear, by religion, by love, rushed like the wind, contemptuous of all obstacles, from her brain and heart to her lips and into the space between them, constructing a barrier, so opaque and cruelly barbed that husband and wife could no longer find each other.

"I am going now. You will never separate us again."

He heard the door shut with a dull, distant finality. He groped his way back to his chair and sat there, unmoving, watching the thin light coming through the curtains grow grayer and thinner until it disappeared altogether in the darkness that crept over him with the stealthy cunning of fog. He heard the distant sounds of life filtered through the heavy oak door she had closed behind her, and he felt himself cut off from them for good. He sat motionless, deep in a mystery that belonged to the indecipherable night. And then, because he was a man of habit and could not think of anything else to do, he took out the volume that he had worn shiny and wrinkled with countless readings and rereadings and opened it to page one and began again:

"There was a man in the land of Uz, whose name was Job; and that man was whole-hearted and upright, and one that feared God, and shunned evil . . ."

Chapter twenty-seven

And this is the way the rumor started in Meah Shearim: Mrs Finkelstein, leaning out of her window at 7 A.M. to hang out wet laundry, noticed that Mrs Harshen's line, usually full, was empty. She naturally mentioned this to Mrs Glick and both women wondered if Mrs Harshen was well. Mrs Glick, at the butcher shop, met Mrs Halperin, and told her she thought Mrs Harshen wasn't well, and then the butcher, Mr Cohen, mentioned that Mrs Harshen hadn't been in yet for her Sabbath chickens, and, it being already Thursday, this was accepted by all as a very strange and alarming piece of news. The butcher, mentioning this to his wife, was told that his son—who normally studied under Isaac Harshen's tutelage at the *kollel*, had come home early, since his teacher had not arrived for three days in a row to give his usual lesson. And then, sitting down next to her husband, her hands still wet and red from the heat of the dishwater, the butcher's wife whispered that Mrs Schultz had told her a young woman (Mrs Schultz had said a beautiful young woman, but Mrs Cohen edited that out as inappropriate information for her husband, who was not supposed to be interested in such things), hatless, and wigless, had been seen entering the home of Isaac Harshen right after Sabbath prayers. Mrs Cohen's eyebrows had risen perceptibly and her voice had an indignant, hushed tone, implying a clear understanding of the impropriety of such a visit and the interpretation she was now giving it.

Mr Cohen listened alertly with a pained expression. He was upset both at the information, which implied such a serious indiscretion—an unchaperoned visit from a woman—to such a distinguished and tragic member of the male community, as well as his own inability to silence his wife and thus overcome the strength of his Evil Inclination to listen to such wonderful gossip. But once caught in the trap of listening, he wanted to know everything. When did the woman leave? Who was she? Had she gone to see him again? The first question was asked delicately and with a great deal of reluctance, for one certainly did not want to discuss such terrible implications with one's pious, unimaginative wife. There was also the terrible sin of slander and evil gossip involved, and also the need to judge each man favorably, despite appearances to the contrary. But as it turned out, Mr Cohen needn't have worried: The only answer forthcoming from his wife turned out to be nothing more than an exasperating and uninformative shrug of the shoulders.

This conversation was repeated, more or less, in dozens of houses in Meah Shearim. The answers began as an exercise in imagination by those who, unlike the butcher's wife, could not bear the vacuum of an honest lack of real information. A sister perhaps, with news about an ailing mother? But all Isaac's sisters were married matrons, not young, bare-headed girls. A young neighbor sent by Mrs Harshen to inform him of her illness? But then, certainly, in the dark, she would have chosen a young boy to go. A *shidduch* from the matchmaker, perhaps? This last one, the most unacceptable of all, was put forth by children too young to have been listening to such conversations who were quickly hushed and sent off to bed. No matchmaker would condone the scandalous visit of a girl unaccompanied by her parents and brothers. And besides, custom had it that the man came to visit the girl at her own well-inhabited and well-lit home. Besides, Isaac had not even been declared a widower, owing to the unfortunate lack of his wife's body. And although he would have been able to get a *heter*—a dispensation—to take a second wife failing the recovery of his first wife's remains, he had chosen not to.

No one, no one at all, guessed the truth until Mrs Harshen, in a paroxysm of uncontrollable aggravation, opened the door to Mrs Finkelstein, Mrs Glick, Mrs Halperin, and Mrs Cohen—who had all come to fulfill the *mitzvah* of visiting the sick—and collapsed into their arms shrieking: "She has come back, that wicked, crazy girl! My poor Isaac! *Vey, vey*, my poor son!"

And this was the way that all of Meah Shearim, and the many outlying religious enclaves in the north of Jerusalem, and in the *haredi*—literally those who trembled in their fear of sin—stronghold of Bnei Brak, learned the incredible, miraculous truth: that Batsheva Ha-Levi Harshen had not died at all but had disappeared for reasons still undecided, and now, for reasons still ferociously debated, had returned to her husband.

The rumors, like waves of a hurricane, battered the community and rocked the Hassidim faithful to the Ha-Levis to the depths of despair and to the heights of incredible rejoicing: She and the child had been kidnapped by rival Hassidic groups eager to destroy the Ha-Levis and after the payment of a huge ransom by her father, she had been returned. She had run away and gone to live with a Gentile in sin in Europe. She was following the prophecy of the old rebbe that had come from the Divine throne itself to separate herself and the little heir to the dynasty from the sinfulness of the Hassidim, who needed to undergo terrible suffering in order to be worthy of him. The stories, rumors, conjectures, and bits of real information intertwined, coiling around each other with the complicated precision and confusion of macramé until it all seemed like truth, or a fantastic fable from the books of the Hassidim.

And then a sudden, tense quiet settled on the community as it realized there would be more to come.

Isaac Meyer Harshen, dressed in an impeccable black suit, looked down at himself and picked off microscopic pieces of lint from his jacket with immaculately clean fingernails. By no look or word did he betray to any one of the students milling around him the tension that was building inside of his chest like the steam worked up by an engine that can propel a train across many barren miles. Idly, he thought to himself what the reaction of these simple, uncomplicated boys would be if he should turn to them casually and say: "My wife is not dead at all. She will be here in twenty minutes." He looked at his students in contempt. What fools they all were! How they listened to him with such awe and respect as he twisted the teachings of the Talmud to suit his own ends. Some of them had wives at home. He wondered about them, how it would feel to touch them, the new young brides, slim and frightened under their modest sheets. He had not had a woman in two years.

Oh, the matchmakers had been busy with him, but Abraham Ha-Levi had made it very clear that the moment he remarried, the power and the possessions would all revert to their original owner. He was in no rush to return to his former poverty and obscurity. Besides, he had always been good at repression. So he repressed and hid his natural feelings, his need for love, for physical passion, sublimating them into a raging, bitter self-discipline that everyone mistook for piety.

Batsheva had personally brought a letter asking for a divorce the week before, when he had, thankfully, not been home. So he had already plunged through the initial stages of shock and anger and even some relief and had now arrived at a calm plateau in which he had only two goals: to come out of it all looking good to his Hassidim, and to see her punished profoundly. This meeting, which was to take place at his insistence, had a number of purposes: to take her measure for the combat that was ahead; to intimidate her as much as possible; and to see her again, close up and alone.

He paced, looking out of the window. "Go now!" he said to the students with an abrupt, impatient gesture of his hand. They were used to the harsh manner of their brilliant teacher, his lack of manners and delicacy, and did not think it amiss. Closing their heavy Talmudical volumes, they left. He gave some thought to how he should meet her. Standing, at the door? No, too forthcoming. Well, then, seated behind his desk? Too controlled, lacking in danger. It must be in the bedroom. He must get her into the bedroom.

Like a general, he ticked off his objectives: First, he did not want a divorce. He wanted his wife and child back with him as before, the undisputed leadership of the Ha-Levi dynasty placed squarely into his hands for good. Second, he wanted it clearly established that her disappearance had had nothing to do with him, that it was all from her own weak, sinful nature, which he, in his magnanimity and piety, would be willing to overlook. He wanted everything to be exactly as it had been.

But, not being a stupid man, he understood that he must necessarily have a fallback position. If she insisted upon the divorce, she could have it then. But under no circumstances would she be able to consider having the custody of the child. For only as father and guardian of the child could he retain with some legitimacy his power as leader of the Ha-Levis. He tried to remember his baby son, but could evoke nothing more than smells: the sour odor of spoiled milk; the rank, animal odor of dirty diapers. He wrinkled his nose in distaste.

He walked over to his desk and pulled out the file prepared by the detective agency. It was the same agency parents in Meah Shearim were now using to check on prospective marriage partners for their sons and daughters. The grooms were followed to make sure they took no midnight trips to Tel Aviv's whorehouses, that they did not wander into stores selling forbidden books and lascivious magazines, that they were as diligent in their studies as the matchmaker swore. The brides were followed to see that they were dressed modestly at all times, accepted no rides from strangers, and led active lives that boded well for clean houses and well-washed children. The prospective in-laws' finances were also checked to make sure they were not holding back any money that could be demanded as dowry, or an apartment that could be handed over to the young couple as a gift to save the young scholar the worry of paying a mortgage or rent his whole life. In comparison, their work for Isaac had been easy. He had asked them to find out only one thing: if any man had accompanied Batsheva Harshen when she came into Ben Gurion Airport. He looked with satisfaction at the clean, full pages of the report on David Hope. Yes, his fallback position was a very good one indeed.

Batsheva stood before the door of the home she had come to with all the fragile, beautiful hopes of a young bride and had left full of fey knowledge. She had dreamed of this place, in dark, colorless dreams that had filled her with a sense of immobility and imprisonment. She had been sure she would never have the courage to enter it again. But here she was, about to knock, to face Isaac Meyer Harshen once more.

It was a lovely house, she reflected with some surprise. Its white stones looked like an ancient sculpture, full of cryptic meaning. In her bowels she felt a rumble of fear. It was a mistake to have agreed to meet Isaac here alone, she told herself. But then, he could hold up proceedings for months if he wished, and she so wanted to get this over with. She felt as if she were alone piloting a boat down a dark river, the banks on either side thick with trees. Who knew what dangers lurked behind them, waiting to rush out at her as she made her slow, lonely progress through them? But at the end of it was David, his arms outstretched to meet her. He had wanted to come now, too. Dear, foolish man. What the rabbinical court would make of that! She had told him not to meet her at the airport, but he had not listened. David, David! Her heart contracted thinking of him standing there so solid and handsome, his whole beautiful soul written clearly on his face as he waited there to gather her into his arms, come what may.

She pressed her lips together, calling up every ounce of courage she had ever possessed, and knocked on the door. Come what may. It was eerie, as if one had suddenly been transported back into time. Nothing had changed and yet everything had. The pictures, lovely landscapes, had all been taken down and in their place were prints of old rabbis in long beards and dour expressions. The lovely china and crystal were gone—into Isaac's mother's house no doubt, she thought wryly. And it was clean, immaculately, aggressively clean, full of the harsh, unpleasant smell of detergents, window cleaners, and polish. She could just see her mother-in-law's relentless, unmerciful housekeeping in every corner, erasing any sign of life, of habitation by normal human beings. Its cold negation of life made her shudder. And suddenly he was standing there before her.

"So," he said, his fingers making boxes that he then crushed by rubbing his hands together.

"Hello, Isaac."

"I received your letter."

Was he going to keep her standing there by the door like a stranger? She shifted uncomfortably from foot to foot. "Yes. And we need to talk about it. May I come in?"

He bent over and swept his hand into the room in a theatrical display of exaggerated courtesy. She walked past him and sat in a wing chair, gaining comfort from the way its sides protected her. She put her purse into her lap—still more protection. Something about his eyes violated her. If only she could read them better. If only she were not so afraid to look at him. She had practiced for this—she was a woman of the world now, she had told herself. She knew how to deal with all kinds of people. She thought of Nigel and his bloody nose. Just let him try . . . Her fingers tightened around her purse.

He sat down on the couch and leaned back, studying her with insolent appraisal, his brows knitted. His eyes followed the beautiful lines of her face down to her soft, exquisite neck and bosom.

"You look well, wife."

The words, so possessive, went through her like an electric shock. *Wife?* "That is what we need to talk about, Isaac. The wife part." She went on rapidly, afraid her courage would fail her. "I know, after all that has happened, whatever love you might have had for me must be gone and you will welcome this chance as I do to end this farce. I don't want anything. You can have it all—the house, the money, the furniture. I only ask that for the sake of our son, you don't drag this out. Let it be done with, quickly."

"My dear wife," he began in his soft, dangerous voice. Again a wave of fear passed through her. "You don't understand me at all. I am thrilled that you have returned." He got up and walked slowly over to her, kneeling suddenly at her feet. He pried her fingers from the bag and held them in his tightly. "I ask nothing more than for you to come back to me with our son. I will ask the court for *shalom bais*."

She pulled her hands away with revulsion. *Shalom bais*, she thought with real horror. The irony of it. Domestic peace. Harmony between husband and wife. The ideal of a Jewish marriage.

She had heard of abused women wanting to divorce their husbands and the husbands dragging it out for fifteen years with those words: *Shalom bais*, they would tell the rabbinical court, and the court would believe them and tell the couple to try once again. She knew that under Jewish law, a woman could not divorce her husband. He had the exclusive right to deny her her *get*, her writ of divorcement, without which she might never marry again in the eyes of God and the state.

In the Talmud it was written that if the rabbis decided a woman had been wronged and was entitled to a divorce, then they had the authority to beat the reluctant husband until he agreed. But that was not the practice in the modern State of Israel, which nevertheless adhered completely to the Talmud in all other matters dealing with marriage and divorce. Why, they had even jailed a husband for ten years for refusing to give his wife a divorce on the grounds of his impotence, but because he still refused to give her a divorce, she remained unable to remarry, growing old and childless and bitter in her faith. Ten years!

She saw the pleased smile that lit the corners of Isaac's mouth, and it threw a spark into the smoldering fire in her chest, illuminating her mind and her heart with the clear flame of determination. "You can say anything you like, Isaac, that is true," she said calmly. "But I promise you, all of your faithful Hassidim, the Hassidim who have accepted you because my father chose you, will hear all the sorry, intimate details of our marriage." She was satisfied to see the smile fade from the corners of his mouth.

He rose to his feet as the realization hit him that he was no longer dealing with a frightened young girl who could be bullied and tortured. He felt a grudging respect growing inside of him, and a growing need to see her grovel before him.

"I am sorry to hear that you wish it so. You know, the Talmud says God Himself weeps when a husband divorces the wife of his youth." His voice rose piously.

"I don't think He will this time, Isaac," she said dryly.

Like chess players, they were both quiet, considering their next move. Isaac gave up the hope of getting her into the bedroom. Batsheva abandoned the idea of offering him more money. Finally, she looked at him wearily and asked simply: "Isaac, I don't want to hurt you any more. Let us be reasonable and treat each other with compassion. You know I can't stand the sight of you. I will divorce you in the end. Whether or not you make me fight and hang out all our dirty laundry is up to you. What is it you want?"

"I want my son."

"You don't even like kids, Isaac. Get married to someone like your mother. You'll have ten before you know what hit you."

"Still the same dirty little slut," he said viciously. "I will not let my son, the heir to the Ha-Levis, be brought up by a whore and her Christian lover."

Her face went white. "What are you talking about?"

"Ah, so you see I can also prepare surprises. Not just you who kidnaps and fakes suicides. What right have you to ask anything from me? You, who put me through months of mourning for my child, who made me say *kaddish*, the prayer for the dead, for him. Yes, I know about David Hope, the priest. I have my ways. Nothing is hidden from me. Like God." He smiled again.

She felt herself fill with loathing and contempt and fear. She was simply afraid of him, of what he was capable of doing. And guilty, too, for the pain he had no doubt suffered because of her. Perhaps he was right, she thought. Perhaps she had no right to enjoy happiness after what she had done. Perhaps God would stand beside Isaac against her. *Mida k'neged mida*—measure for measure. She had stolen his son from him—now he would take Akiva from her.

Isaac spoke again, not looking directly at her, but over her, at her agonized brows and forehead: "I am asking you again, for the soul of our son, for the good of all the people who look to both of us for guidance and for example, will you come back to me?" He stood over her now and as she sank deeper into the chair, he seemed to tower like an immensity that cannot be overcome, that blocked out all light. The young Batsheva would have broken down in tears and run away. But she was not that pure, fragile child anymore. She was a woman whose faith had undergone terrible trials and had emerged whole. It sustained her now. She got up and faced him.

"Isaac, I am sorry for the suffering you have gone through because of me. But it is not a tenth of what you made me suffer. You are a bully, Isaac, and a faking hypocrite—I pity the poor people who come to you for help and for instruction. How you must ruin their lives." He grabbed her by the wrists and held her hard, his breath coming in hot, quick gasps that burnt her face.

She looked at him in surprise and contempt, at if seeing him for the very first time. He was tall, but not powerful. His arms were thin and unaccustomed to any real work. His face, contorted in rage, was almost laughably like that of a villain in a cartoon—mean and petty and cruel. Why would God want to stand by him? He had never repented of his cruelty, never done *teshuva* as she had, suffering for her sins, becoming a better person because of them. In a way, she almost felt sorry for him. She was filled with love—for God, for Akiva, for David. But there was no love in Isaac, perhaps not even the capacity for loving, which may have been beaten out of him when he was a small child shivering in fear behind the rusting iron bars of the yeshivah. She felt pity that he had never been able to lift his eyes and really see the exquisite white beauty of the city he had lived in all his life.

But then the crushing pressure of his hands on her wrists took away her pity, replacing it with pain and fury. "I loathe you. You make me want to throw up. I'd rather be dead than have you touch me again. But you don't frighten me anymore." She loosened a wrist from his grasp and in a cool, calculated movement of her whole body, thrust her palm up hard against his nose. He cried out in pain, dropping her other wrist, and brought both his hands up to his face to catch the streaming blood.

She grabbed her purse and as she turned to go her eyes met his. She saw them glitter above his bloodstained hands with the serious, murdering light of a true enemy.

Chapter twenty-eight

The rabbinical court of Jerusalem is housed in a small, unassuming suite of rooms in the old Ministry of Religion building near the Russian Compound, called so because of the overwhelming presence of the Russian Orthodox Church. The green-and-white church, with its onion-shaped spires, lends a mysterious foreign air to the low, ramshackle buildings around it that house government offices, the police station, and an old prison complex where the British once hanged young Jewish resistance fighters. But most of it is devoted to providing rare downtown parking spaces.

The irony of her strange and prosaic surroundings was not lost on Batsheva as she made her way toward the triumverate of *dayanim*, rabbinical judges, who would decide her fate. Here, in the shadow of this foreign church, amongst the ghosts of hanged men, surrounded by these cars, three men would decide if her life was to have any real happiness or meaning or if she would be forced to give up one of the two people she loved most for the sake of the other. Gratefully, she returned the comforting squeeze of her mother's hand.

After her disastrous meeting with Isaac, she had lain awake wondering if she should not just run away again and live with David and Akiva, without risks, without trials. And always she came back to the same irreversible conclusion: She believed in God and she was bound by His Law, the *Halacha*, as handed down from generation to generation, carefully interpreted and occasionally changed by only the most respected and learned scholars of the time. She could not run away from it because it was simply a part of her, like her heart or her lungs. One cannot cut out one's lungs and live, she told herself.

As she entered the small courtroom she breathed deeply, feeling the tangible expansion of her chest as it filled with the unseen yet lifegiving oxygen. If only her faith would expand, she thought, and fill every doubtful cavity of her mind with belief that it would all end well. Then, as she studied the faces of the three men before her for clues, she realized that it was not her faith in God or His Law that she lacked. It was her faith in man, in the men who had been delegated to carry out His Law. She knew that she could tell nothing about them from their outer appearance. They all wore the same long black suits of Meah Shearim—the same shades of black Isaac, her father, and Gershon wore. They all had beards and glasses. But she knew they were not interchangeable. It was the difference in their intelligence, in their true piety and learning, that would decide her fate. And this she could not tell by looking at them.

Isaac sat up front with his mother and two Hassidim. His mother stood up and fanned herself vigorously as she saw Batsheva enter, her face lined with the wrinkles of hate. Batsheva saw Isaac turn and look over her head, dismissing her as if she were a ghost, as if she had already ceased to exist. And then the hearing began.

Isaac spoke first: "As the distinguished *dayanim* know, my wife ran away with my son two years ago. All of us thought she was dead. I cannot tell you what anguish I have suffered. I asked

God so many times why? What did I do to deserve such a *Gehennom*? I think I must have deserved it, yes. I must have sinned greatly to have suffered so." His voice became very mild and humble. "And because I accepted this long ago as God's will, I bear no hatred toward my wife, the way Joseph bore no hatred toward his brothers for selling him into slavery in Egypt because it was all God's will. Despite the terrible injustice, the grief she has made me suffer by taking away my child, I am prepared to take them both back and rebuild our family. I ask for *shalom bais*. I love my wife."

Batsheva listened to him, stunned. In the worst scenario of her wildest imagination she could not have dreamt that Isaac would pull this kind of a performance. She had expected his righteous anger, his arrogant superiority. But this phony humility, this accepting piety, was beyond anything she imagined him capable of. With horror, she saw the two judges on either side, Rabbi Getz and Rabbi Millstein, look at each other and relax, leaning back in their chairs with approving little nods. Only the judge in the middle, his thick white brows knit together sternly, reserved judgment. Rabbi Magnes looked down at Isaac piercingly, without expression.

"And you say you feel no anger toward your wife. You are willing to accept her back in love?" Rabbi Getz asked.

"I have suffered, but I have uprooted all anger from my heart. As He is compassionate, so must I be," Isaac said piously, looking at his mother, who nodded, her lips a thin line of hatred.

"And will you be able to start a new life after two years of such a separation?" Rabbi Millstein inquired, running his fingers through his beard.

"Everything will be exactly as it was. Exactly as it must and should be," Isaac said without hesitation.

The white head of Rabbi Magnes looked up for the first time and his clear eyes, which had not grown dim but sharper with countless hours of studying the tiny print of Talmudical exegeses and commentaries, took in Isaac's hard, glittering eyes, the strained, unnatural lowering of his head. Rabbi Magnes gestured impatiently toward Batsheva to begin.

She got up shakily and for a moment the realization of the enormity of the tragedy that could befall her, the happiness that could be denied her, took away her voice. She felt her mother pat her arm encouragingly and began softly to fill the room with the story of her marriage to Isaac Meyer Harshen. She told them of the false accusation against her virginity. She told them of how he had burned her books and made her a prisoner in her own house. How, slowly, he had taken away from her all of her pleasures, denying her all of her needs until she felt she was being destroyed. Until she felt that she would rather be dead and see her son dead than to suffer so. As she spoke she looked straight ahead, her eyes never budging from Rabbi Magnes. She did not hear the door to the courtroom open and she did not see the tall, distinguished man, bent down with age and grief, enter and sit down quietly in the back.

"When I was pregnant with Akiva, my husband beat me so badly I could not stand, forcing me to turn over my money to him so that I was penniless. He explained that the Rambam said that a man is allowed to beat his wife in order to get her to obey him. But he did not tell me that the Rambam also said a woman is allowed to divorce her husband if she finds him disgusting and loathsome. This I learned through my own diligence." She glanced at Isaac's grudging acknowledgment of the point gained. "I ask the court for my divorce because I despise Isaac and will never be a wife to him in any sense. I married Isaac because I was young and ignorant and thought I would be pleasing God, my father, and mother. But I don't believe God means us to suffer. That is why His Law allows divorce. But most of all, I ask a divorce for the sake of my son. I would have been able to bear my own suffering, but I could not watch my child destroyed. It was for his sake that I was willing to betray my parents and cause them such pain." She looked down at her mother's ravaged face and her eyes filled with tears. And then very quietly and simply, she told them of how Isaac had treated his son, remembering suddenly the story of the ice cream. There was complete silence as she described the way Isaac had taken spoonful after spoonful in front of the heartbroken, crying child. And she saw in the eyes of the judges that they understood how such a small thing can break a mother's heart. "I ask the court to end my suffering and let me go free to raise my child with love for other people, for God and for His Law."

The man in the back of the room held his head in his hands and rocked back and forth. The sweat began to roll down his face, and as he took out a handkerchief to wipe his eyes and forehead, his eyes, full of horror and grief, looked up only once. They met the clear, stern gaze of Rabbi Magnes as they had once before, long ago.

Rabbi Magnes gestured to Isaac. "Is this true?"

Isaac's eyes shifted uneasily. "The woman was disgracing me. She wore the clothes of a harlot and people would tell me that she wandered alone through the hills at night taking forbidden pictures. I warned her and she would not listen to me. I had no choice but to chastise her, the way a father disciplines a child." He stopped in confusion and embarrassment as he remembered what she had just told the court about how he disciplined his child. He blushed furiously and rushed recklessly ahead. "Her books, her clothes, all brought disgrace to me. I thought I could educate her. I offered, begged her, to let me lead her, teach her. But she was stubborn and willful. I had no choice . . ." And then, because he was only human and not a machine, just for a tiny instant he forgot himself and looked at his wife with all the real venom of his heart flashing brightly incandescent on his face. And when he remembered himself and again donned the mask of his humility, he saw in the sharp, clear eyes of Rabbi Magnes that this battle was lost. So he changed tactics.

"Perhaps then, what she says is true. Perhaps she cannot be a wife to me. I will divorce her then, and gladly. I also have a life and I don't need any more grief. Then I ask the court for only one thing: Give me my son Akiva before she ruins him altogether. Before he is lost completely to the Jewish people." He pulled out a sheaf of papers and waved them like a battle flag. "I have proof that my wife is planning to marry her lover, a Christian, a man who studied for the priesthood."

A shocked, audible gasp exploded through the courtroom. Batsheva saw her mother's eyes fill with disbelief and quick tears. She saw the judges move uneasily in their seats, all compassion and understanding erased from their faces. Rabbi Magnes folded his hands before him and looked carefully at Batsheva. "Is this true?"

Her whole body went weak with fear. But then she felt new strength flowing into her from another source. Anger. "David Hope is a man I met in England more than a year after I left Isaac. He was at one time studying for the priesthood." She heard a low intake of breath once more, an ominous silence. "David came to Israel three months ago and learned that his mother was a Jew. Since then, he has been learning with Reb Gershon, who will vouch for the depth of his scholarship and understanding, the beauty of his character. I swear before God that I have not sinned in any way. But it is true that I cannot help loving him. He will make Akiva a much better father than his real one."

"So, you admit you plan to marry this man after your divorce?" Rabbi Getz said with shock and irritation.

"Yes." The simple answer took a huge amount of courage. I am lost, Batsheva told herself in despair, looking at the puzzled, quizzical faces of the judges. She could just see the lurid scenario going through their minds. Perhaps they had developed a little sympathy for her by now. Perhaps they even believed Isaac capable of cruelty, of wife beating. But nothing he had done could ever excuse a good Jewish married woman, no matter the provocation, from slinking off into the night and coming back in love with a man who had once studied to be a priest. Were they not flesh and blood, these judges? Were they not the same as all the other people in Meah Shearim who would judge her case by the surface and condemn her for it?

She looked up at them in despair, seeking out the tangled brows of Rabbi Magnes. "I will say this, *kavod harav*. I came back to Israel to arrange my *get* because I believe in the *Halacha*, God's Law, and that it will be interpreted carefully without regard to social pressures, or rumors." She stopped, her throat tightening, holding back tears of desperation. "My hope is the Law. I believe I am entitled to the divorce by Law. David is a Jew, by Law. I have not sinned, by Law. And so there is nothing to prevent me from marrying him and bringing up Akiva, by Law. I submit my happiness into your hands as interpreter of the Law and ask only for justice."

Rabbi Magnes rose. "I will ask you to bring Akiva and David Hope to court tomorrow, since they are also involved." Rabbi Getz and Rabbi Millstein looked up in surprise.

Isaac got up, furious. "To have this Christian in the same room with my son! I will not tolerate it . . ."

Rabbi Magnes turned his steady gaze upon Isaac and nodded with a cryptic smile. "A scholar should know the Law." Batsheva was pleased to see Isaac Harshen, all false humility gone, all arrogance clearly written on a face contorted with hatred and rage, sit down and shut up. Like a shadow, the tall man in the back of the room got up and walked painfully and silently out of the courtroom, attracting the attention and compassion of only one pair of clear, intelligent eyes under heavy white brows.

* * *

Information about the divorce proceedings of Isaac and Batsheva Ha-Levi Harshen spread like a chemical fire throughout Meah Shearim. Rival Hassidic groups saw in the trial validation for all the rumors and controversies of the past two years. Groups hostile to the Ha-Levis pointed out the disgraceful behavior of Batsheva and her shocking liaison with an apostate as proof of the eternal evil of the Ha-Levis, brought on by excessive indulgence in material things.

This opinion, stated openly on street corners and printed in little back-room presses on large posters that were pasted up zealously, defacing walls and mailboxes all over town, infuriated the Ha-Levi Hassidim, and brought them to blows with their detractors. They in turn printed up posters that proved that it was Isaac Harshen who was to blame—an interloper who had no right to lead the Ha-Levis now that there was a true heir. The posters brought down as proof his disgraceful treatment of Batsheva as well as the decisions he had made that had cost several people their lives. Other dark doings—heatings of young yeshivah boys, bus-stop burnings—were also alluded to. Things reached such a pitch that the police, who were usually avoided by all groups as part of the collective secular, Zionist enemy, were actually called upon to restore order by both groups after their leaders received death threats and one actually had a grenade thrown at him, which, miraculously, did not explode.

Batsheva knew nothing of all this. David put Akiva on his shoulders and began cutting a path for her through the crowd, which quieted ominously as they passed. Then one by one the jeers and the blessings began pouring forth:

"God Bless you!"

"Filthy goy!"

"May God watch over you!"

And then as they reached the safe portals of the Ministry

of Religion, someone shouted out: "Dirty whore, adulteress!"

David turned, his face flashing with fury, held back only by Batsheva's soft, restraining whisper. But soon he realized that whoever had uttered those words was now screaming in pain as a flock of Hassidim, like avenging angels, descended upon him.

The same small, dark room she had feared the day before seemed like a sanctuary to Batsheva now as she entered it with David and Akiva and her mother. Gershon and Gita were already there. Gita took Batsheva in her arms in a warm, wordless embrace full of comfort and support. They all rose as the judges walked in. But Isaac was not there. The judges glanced at each other and at the clock, concerned, then busied themselves with looking over written evidence. Batsheva, thinking of the angry crowd, wondered if he would be able to get through. After almost fifteen minutes the door burst open and Isaac walked in.

The change in him was dramatic and almost pitiful. The mask of calm humility that he had worn much of the day before was gone. Even the arrogance and anger of his real face was no longer visible. Instead, he looked white and shaken, the way a bully looks who has at long last encountered someone meaner and stronger than himself. The walk through the angry crowd had destroyed any illusion he still harbored of coming out of this trial untouched, even enhanced among his Hassidim. How quickly they had turned upon him! He was in a state of shock.

"We shall not waste any more time," Rabbi Magnes said curtly. He waved to Reb Gershon. "Do you know David Hope?"

"Yes, *kavod harav*," Gershon answered. "I was his teacher when he was in the novitiate program. He was very interested in learning about our religion and I set him up a course of independent study in Jewish law and history. Then, about two months later he came to my house very moved and excited and said he believed his mother was a Jew, which, as we all know according to Jewish law, makes him a Jew. Naturally, I found it hard to believe, and so I checked it out with the highest authorities both here and in Amsterdam and London. They confirmed that his mother was a Jew from a very distinguished family. And then I called his father." Gershon stopped, looking at David. "He told me that he had always known that your mother was a Jew. But she had made him swear on her deathbed that he would never tell you and that he would raise you as a pure Christian. She had been there, in Germany, during the Holocaust, in the middle of all that hatred. She was terrified. She thought she was protecting you. But when I told your father you already knew, he confirmed it." Reb Gershon turned back to the judges. "David told me he wanted to return to Judaism and asked me to teach him."

"And what have you taught him?" Rabbi Getz asked suspiciously.

"I began teaching him the Shulchan Aruch and then we went on to the Talmud, Mesecas Gittin."

A gleam of humor flashed in Rabbi Magnes's eyes. "Humph. *The Tractate on Divorce*. Appropriate. And did you find him an able student?"

"Not only able, *kavod harav*, but absolutely a genius of rare intelligence, more than anyone else I have ever met. As it says in the *Ethics of the Fathers*: He is like a sponge that loses not a drop. Most important, his learning is of the highest form. He learns in order to do. For all the time I have known him, he has been sincere and exacting in keeping all the Commandments."

"But can this not be just a show?" Rabbi Millstein pointed out. "First he wears a cross and now he is a Talmudical scholar. It seems extremely convenient to me." He shook his head cynically.

Rabbi Magnes turned to his colleague and said very softly, so that no one not sitting next to him could hear. "And so you question his sincerity? And how is this relevant to the case before us?"

"*Kavod harav*. If this man is to be a father to Akiva Ha-Levi

Harshen, must we not examine his qualifications carefully? Is not his sincerity in returning to his religion an issue in those qualifications?" Rabbi Millstein whispered back.

"I see. And what of the sincerity of Isaac Harshen, the father? Do you not question that?"

"Well, I . . ." Rabbi Millstein began, then stopped, his surprise turning him momentarily speechless.

"But, *kavod harav*, we all saw Isaac Harshen grow up. We know his parents and his grandparents. We know his reputation as a scholar and a *yera shamayim*, a God-fearing Jew." Rabbi Getz broke in with a furious whisper of indignation.

"Ah, so you know all about Isaac Harshen. I see. So you were not surprised to learn that he brought a false accusation against his virgin bride, a crime mentioned specifically in the Torah? You were not surprised to learn that he beat her when she was with child and took all of her money from her—things he admits?" Rabbi Magnes said very quietly, with extreme irritation.

Everyone watched the active, inaudible debate, surprised at the thoughtful silence and embarrassment that descended upon the two rabbis as they thoughtfully stroked their beards, considering.

"I suggest we must talk to the child and to David Hope privately," Rabbi Magnes said quietly. "Do you agree?" The two men nodded and got up, walking with Rabbi Magnes into the room adjoining the courtroom.

"Please send Akiva in. Alone."

Batsheva sat tensely, her ears straining. She heard some laughter and then soft voices. About fifteen minutes later, Akiva walked out and ran to David, hugging him.

"David Hope." David kissed Akiva and released himself from the child's tight embrace. He walked slowly toward the back room, as one walks in a dream to meet one's fate. His eyes met Batsheva's and a moment of fear and longing and love passed between them that warmed his heart and terrified him. He felt a pat on his arm.

"Don't be afraid, David." Gershon nodded encouragingly and winked. "They won't eat you."

The minutes passed, and the people seated in the courtroom began to fidget. A half hour passed, and they began to get up from their seats to stretch their legs. When an hour had gone by, the tension in the room seemed to crackle with the dangerous power of an electric cable torn loose by a storm. Finally, an hour and a half after he had gone in, David opened the door and came into the courtroom. His face was pale and drawn, Batsheva noted with panic, but when his eyes met hers they shone with a radiant light. Twenty minutes later, the *dayanim* filed slowly back into the courtroom.

Rabbi Magnes looked at Rabbi Millstein and Rabbi Getz. "My distinguished colleagues, may I speak also in your names?" The two men nodded with dignity, in complete agreement. "According to *Halacha*, a woman is allowed to demand a divorce on two grounds: a physical defect in her husband, or his conduct toward her. In this case it is the husband's conduct—conduct that is so unworthy that she cannot any longer be expected to continue living with him as his wife. As it is written in the Talmud, *Ketubot* 61: 'A wife is given in order that she should live and not suffer in pain.' The grounds established here are based on Isaac Harshen's continued breach of his duties as laid down for conjugal life. As it is written in *Yad, Ishut*, 15:19 based on *Yevamot* 62b: 'Let a man honor his wife more than he honors himself, love her as he loves himself, and if he has assets, seek to add to her benefits, and not unduly impose fear on her, and speak to her gently and not be given to melancholy or anger.' Also, as it is written: 'If a husband habitually assaults and insults her, or is the cause of unceasing quarrels so that she has no choice but to leave the common household, she is granted a divorce.' Because you have treated your wife this way, it was her right to leave you and you must give her a *get* so that she is permitted to marry any man she chooses."

"Even this man, her lover!" Mrs Harshen got to her feet and pointed in hysteria at David.

"Silence! How dare you address the court! But since an accusation has been made, we will deal with it. In order to prove adultery, there must be two witnesses who swear such is the case. Do you have such witnesses?" Mrs Harshen collapsed into her seat. "Moreover, since Isaac is a scholar, he knows that if he had suspected his wife of committing adultery he would have been obligated to divorce her immediately, but instead he asked for *shalom bais*, which means he does not even accuse her of such a terrible thing." Isaac slumped in his chair, defeated. "As for the custody of the child—"

Batsheva moved to the edge of her seat and held her mother's hand tightly.

"It is the usual practice of the court to grant the custody of a small child to his mother. Here, of course, there have been mitigating circumstances." He paused uncomfortably and glanced at his colleagues. "Although we have examined David Hope and have found him to be a sincere and learned *baal teshuva*, a penitent," Rabbi Magnes leaned forward, "actually, we were amazed by the depth and clarity of his intelligence and learning and do not doubt his sincerity. However . . ." Batsheva's heart seemed to stop. "However," Rabbi Magnes went on with quiet deliberation, "the court cannot ignore the fact that Batsheva Harshen, in an act of unfathomable recklessness, kidnapped her son and almost took his life." Batsheva saw Isaac straighten his back and look at her with a little smile.

This was the moment of her darkest fear, the moment she knew had had to come. It was the moment of reckoning, the meting out of justice. God was compassionate and merciful, but

He was also a God of strict justice. That moment, when she had held Akiva's life in her hands and had willfully, selfishly, thought to extinguish it because of her own unhappiness, her own inability to bear seeing him be beaten down into his father's dark image—that moment must be paid for. She bent her neck lower with a calm hopelessness, the way a queen might facing the guillotine, wanting it to be over quickly, hoping to keep some shred of dignity. Isaac must not see her cry, she had made that promise so many years ago. How, she thought with brief horror, how will I live knowing my son is once again in Isaac Harshen's hands, under his control? The time for running away was past. She had taken her only escape hatch and with her own hands sealed it up forever. They all knew she was alive. Wherever she went they would find her and bring her son back. She glanced at David and she saw the terrible light of understanding in his eyes.

"Given all her grounds for divorce, the court cannot understand why Batsheva Harshen simply did not come forth years ago and ask for a divorce and custody. Therefore, because of her erratic behavior, the Court has decided that Isaac Harshen shall be . . ."

"Please, *kavod harav*," a voice gruff and low came suddenly from the back of the courtroom, and Abraham Ha-Levi, his face bright with the appalling, radiant glow of suffering that puts a man close to death, came slowly and painfully down the aisle. "I would like to tell *kavod harav* why my daughter did not ask for a divorce years ago." His voice grew phlegmy and choked, almost inaudible. He stopped and cleared it, and as he did so, he raised his head and for the first time met his daughter's eyes.

"Years ago, only months after Batsheva married Isaac, she called me and told me of her suffering. But I was a righteous man, you see. I knew everything about duty and piety. It was not that I was a harsh man, no. I was full of pity and compassion, you see. But it was all for myself and the vow I had been forced to make. So there was no pity left for my only daughter or her tears. And then she ran away. I came to Jerusalem. Not because I feared for her. Not because I wanted to help her. But because she would not play the part, you see. I came to threaten her. But then, foolishly, I collapsed. But I am a clever man, clever, and I am always, because of my cleverness, I am always successful. I used my weakness more effectively than I could ever have used my strength. She sat by my side and I saw the pity in her eyes, the love, the regret, and I thought: Now I will have her for good. Now I will make her swear a solemn vow on the life of her parents, on the memory of her grandparents and all the Ha-Levis that had ever perished to sanctify the Holy Name, that she would stay with Isaac and fulfill the *mitzvah* of providing the Ha-Levis with an heir. I told her of the sacred vow I had made to her grandmother on the train to Auschwitz. I told her it was now her responsibility to keep that vow." He wiped his forehead as the sweat poured down his face. "I must have done a very good job because she never once afterward complained to me. She never told me that her husband beat her. Never once did she try to seek a divorce after that. I did it so cleverly, you see. I took her love for me, for God, for her heritage, and made the most beautiful steel trap out of it, so that there was only one way out. Thank God, she had the courage not to take it. She did the only other thing she could. She went away pretending to have died. Like Jephte's daughter, who went off into the hills to live alone, to sacrifice her life because her father was a fool who made a foolish vow."

"No, Aba, not a fool," Batsheva said softly.

He lifted her head, lowered in pain and humiliation for the suffering she had caused him, lowered because she had once hated him and had felt she could never forgive him. He wiped the glistening tears from her eyes and she felt the unconditional love and forgiveness flow from his large, familiar hands, the hands that had once, long ago, reached deep into pockets filled with toys and candies for his beloved child. All the long-forgotten love of that child came flooding back to her. She put her arms around his waist and leaned her head on his shoulder and whispered: "Forgive me."

Gently, he stroked her soft, shining hair and felt the living warmth of her head. He had thought her lost to him forever. He felt the warmth of life, like a long robe, fall over his shoulders and take away the cold isolation and death that had clung to him since reading her letter. He reached out and took his grandchild's firm, active little hand in his. Alive, both of them. A miracle. He closed his eyes. He lost his balance for a moment and felt his wife's comforting arm suddenly thread through his. He leaned on her gratefully, knowing now he had come full circle. Thank you, dear all-merciful God. He looked up at Rabbi Magnes and the two men's eyes met in perfect understanding.

"No, Batsheva. You must forgive me. It was my vow. I am the continuation of the Ha-Levis. I cannot, for my lifetime, push that burden off on anyone else."

Rabbi Magnes's thick brows knitted together and his finger threaded thoughtfully through his snow-white beard. He glanced at his colleagues, who nodded in agreement. "This is important information. We will now retire to discuss it and then will give our final decision."

The three rabbis rose and disappeared behind the closed door of their chambers. The agonizing minutes passed like hours. Then, finally, the door opened and the judges filed out with solemn, unhurried dignity. There was no sound in the courtroom except the brush of their clothes against their chairs, and the soft tick of the clock. Even the noise in the street seemed to fall mysteriously silent in anticipation.

Rabbi Magnes cleared his throat. "Taking a life, even one's own, is an inexcusable act that cannot be forgiven. Even a failed attempt at such an act cannot be excused under any circumstances."

So, I am lost, Batsheva thought.

"However, in light of the new evidence before us, the court recognizes that perhaps no such act was ever seriously contemplated. Given the extraordinary state of mind of Batsheva and her desire to spare her father's feelings, the court feels that there were mitigating one-time circumstances that are not likely to occur again in her lifetime. In this light, the court has decided that Batsheva Harshen is to have conditional custody of the child under certain strict guidelines. First, he must be brought up in Jerusalem and may not be taken out of the country without specific permission of the court. Second, his father is to retain full visiting rights. If these terms are not met, we will reconvene and reconsider our decision. Is that clear?"

Batsheva, leaning on her father, nodded gratefully, full of incredulous joy, unable to believe that it was really over. It was like that blessed moment right after giving birth when all the hellish pain is finally behind you and you hold the new baby, safe and perfect, saved from the million illnesses and deformities and mishaps that faced you both every step of the way for nine months. Unable to speak, she mouthed the words *thank you.* And for a moment it seemed as if a rare gleam, a softening, took place in Rabbi Magnes's fierce, old eyes.

The scribe wrote out the bill of divorce, which was then read out loud: ". . . Thus do I set free, release thee, and put thee aside in order that thou may have the permission and the authority over thyself to go and marry any man thou may desire. No person may hinder thee from this day onward, and thou art permitted to every man. This shall be for thee from me a bill of dismissal, a letter of release and a document of freedom, in accordance with the laws of Moses and Israel."

The rabbis witnessed the document with their signatures and then it was rolled up and handed to Isaac. He grasped it, and as is the custom, threw it to Batsheva; then he turned on his heel and walked furiously out of the courtroom. She caught the precious scroll, pressing it to her heart, and in so doing showed her acceptance of this freedom, officially ending her marriage to Isaac Harshen. Cries of "*Mazel tov*" rang out around the room. She embraced her father and mother and then sought David's eyes and trembled, filling with the wondrous benediction she saw reflected in his shining face.

Abraham Ha-Levi walked slowly out into the street and faced his Hassidim, his head bent low with humility and final acceptance of a role he had so long fled. He raised his arms and the crowd grew tensely quiet. "According to the Law, a *talmid chacham* is not only a brilliant scholar. He is also a student of the wise, following the good and pious life of his teachers." He raised his eyes, and the crowd saw a terrible anger contort his features. "Isaac Harshen has proven himself no *talmid chacham!*"

He shouted with all of the pent-up rage that exploded like an atom bomb hurled from its secret silo. "I renounce him! I throw him out of any authority!" The crowd broke into loud shouts of joy and of furious disbelief. Abraham Ha-Levi raised his hands once again and waited patiently for the quiet to reassert itself. When the crowd stopped, all anger drained from him. "I am the heir to the Ha-Levis. Take me if you wish or reject me. But do not put the burden of your belief on anyone else."

At this the crowd seemed to divide. Those who hated the Ha-Levis called out to each other to follow Isaac Harshen, having found a new hero. As for the rest—a noise, like the roar of the seas dividing before Moses' outstretched arm, rose in exaltation and bounced off the white church and the long, low prison walls, and the pavement reverberated with the thunderous, joyous pounding of thousands of dancing feet.

Chapter twenty-nine

David Hope and Batsheva Ha-Levi were married, according to the Law of Moses and Israel, after the prescribed three-month period between a divorce and remarriage. It was a simple wedding, as different from her marriage to Isaac Harshen as white is from black.

Batsheva rose early and looked out her window, all her plans dependent upon the blessing of good weather. As if by a miracle, it was one of those wonderful rare days that sometime happen in Israel in the middle of January: a day as warm and fragrant and bright as spring. A day where the sky, so cloudless and blue, proclaims there never was such a thing as a storm, there never will be such a thing as a storm.

She put on a simple white dress of a beautiful soft silk moiré and attached her veil to a few fresh roses that she pinned into her shining black hair. When she looked into the mirror, she saw a woman she had known once long ago, in the first spring of her eighteenth year. Her life had been sadder and sweeter than even that spoiled, vibrant, carelessly happy young child/woman had ever dreamt possible as she leapt recklessly headlong into the adventure of life. She trembled a little, remembering how naïve she had been, how unprepared for reality. Could one really start over, erase all the bitterness of the past from one's heart and mind? Was there really such a thing as a clean slate, a purifying rite of repentance? I don't know, she thought, afraid.

She wanted so much to come to David as a new bride, without knowledge, without memories, simple and pure and good. He deserved that. She wanted to give him herself as one bestows the gift of the first fruits picked from new trees that have blossomed and yielded for the first time. She looked at the white dress that shimmered with radiant purity in the morning light. If only I could be like that inside, she mourned. Was it possible? Or would she carry the touch and smell of Isaac Harshen on her body and in her nostrils until the end of time, allowing his memory to come between her and David?

And so the bride, exquisite and tremulous, said a silent prayer. I ask you, dear Lord, for only one thing—to wash me clean of the past.

David Hope also noticed the beauty of the day and took it for an omen, a benediction. He put on a clean white shirt and a dark-blue suit. As he shaved, he rubbed his palm anxiously over his face, feeling for any stubble. It must be absolutely soft and smooth. He looked at himself and smiled foolishly, a little embarrassed by the unbridled, unbelievable, and (no doubt, he told himself) immature and unmanly but nevertheless wonderful state of absolute bliss that filled every corner, every ounce, of his entire body and soul. To have her near him always—her and the boy whom he already loved like his own son! To wake up in the morning and just reach out and find her lovely face so close to his he would feel her soft, fragrant breath on his eyes and mouth! To be able to reach out and hold her without guilt, with the full love of God within him! Could it be possible, such happiness?

He had never imagined it. Always before he had felt weighted down with the sense of darkness and sin that they had convinced him was Adam's legacy to mankind. Becoming a Jew, he was released from that. It was wrong. Sin could not be given as an inheritance. Each of us was born Adam on the first day of creation, born pure with the ability to choose good over evil. Our connection to God was direct. We needed no one to plead for us. Our prayers, silent, only thoughts perhaps, went to Him directly.

How else could one explain this wonderful, perfect day, the first day of the rest of his life as Batsheva Ha-Levi's husband and lover, father to their children?

The ceremony took place on the hill called the Tomb of Samuel the Prophet. Abraham Ha-Levi, Lord Hope, Ian, and Rabbi Gershon each held one corner of a prayer shawl above the heads of the couple as Rabbi Magnes recited the blessings of marriage. And as the ceremony began, Batsheva looked behind her and saw the dear faces of her mother and Elizabeth, Gita and Lady Hope, look at her full of deep happiness. She turned her face forward and looked out at the hills of Judea and the white stones of the houses nestled in their sides and into the immense, almost white illumination that was the sky.

And all at once she understood what the artist Chesterton had meant when he wrote that white is a color—not just a lack of color. It was a shining and affirmative thing—as rich as red, as intense as black. And goodness, too, was not just an absence of sin, an avoidance of the wrong moral choices. It didn't mean just not being cruel or sparing people revenge and punishment. Goodness was a vivid and separate thing, like a gift or a strong embrace. It was as real and tangible and positive a thing as the sun that had risen that morning to give them this brand-new day in which to begin again.

Reading Group Discussion Questions

1. The Biblical story of Jephte and his daughter can be found in the Book of Judges. Why do you think the author called her book by this title? Are there any parallels between the life of Batsheva Ha-Levi and the biblical figure of Jephthe's daughter? If yes, what are they?
2. In the opening quote, the author uses the words of Aliosha from *The Brothers Karamazov*: "Dear children, do not be afraid of life. How good is life once you have done something good, once you have been true to the truth within you." Why do you think the author chose this quote? To what characters, and to what incidents might it refer?
3. Many of the characters in *Jephte's Daughter* are motivated by the need to fulfill obligations—religious, social, family—that are larger than their personal need for happiness and fulfillment. In what way does their attempt to be true to their obligations set them free, and in what way does it entrap them?
4. The concept of "women's role in life" is very rigid in the haredi world Batsheva finds herself. How would you describe that role and in what way do the women characters fulfill it—Batsheva, her mother, Mrs Harshen. In what ways do they defy it?
5. How would you describe the character of Elizabeth. What is her motivation? Although she has a completely different

background and culture, in many ways, she and Batsheva undergo similar experiences. Describe them.

6. At the beginning of the book, Elizabeth and Batsheva discuss the idea of the continuum, or the rainbow; the idea of the great chain of being. When does this idea reappear in the book? Is it significant?
7. The men in *Jephte's Daughter* are vastly different in background, but have many similarities. Can you talk about how Abraham Ha-Levi, Isaac Harshen, and Graham MacLeish relate to women, to themselves, to their studies?
8. What did Batsheva expect from marriage? What did she receive? Do you think her expectations were realistic, or unrealistic?
9. *Jephte's Daughter* was based on a real story; the tragic death of a young haredi woman how leaped to her death with her small child in her arms, killing them both. Do you think the author should have followed the original story. Why? Why not?
10. In the book, the characters discuss whether art is removed from life, or whether the artist has a responsibility for the moral consequences of his art. Look up this passage (pages 313–4) and join the discussion.

About the Author

Naomi Ragen

Naomi Ragen is the author of four international bestsellers: *Jephte's Daughter*, *Sotah*, *The Sacrifice of Tamar*, and *The Ghost of Hannah Mendes*. Born in New York, she attended Brooklyn College and received an MA in English from the Hebrew University of Jerusalem. For the last thirty years, she has made her home in Jerusalem. The translation of her books into Hebrew in 1995 has made her one of Israel's best-loved authors. An outspoken advocate for gender equality and human rights, she is a columnist for *The Jerusalem Post*. Ragen's first play, *Women's Quorum*, was commissioned by Habima, Israel's National Theater.

The fonts used in this book are from the Garamond and Gill families.

Other works by Naomi Ragen are published by The Toby Press

Sotah

The Sacrifice of Tamar

Chains Around the Grass